WHITE SPACE

BOOK I OF THE DARK PASSAGES

WHITE SPACE

BOOK I OF THE DARK PASSAGES

ILSA J. BICK

EGMONT
USA
NEW YORK

EGMONT
We bring stories to life

First published by Egmont USA, 2014
443 Park Avenue South, Suite 806
New York, NY 10016

1 3 5 7 9 8 6 4 2

www.egmontusa.com
www.ilsajbick.com

Typography by Torborg Davern

Library of Congress Cataloging-in-Publication Data

Bick, Ilsa J.
White space / Ilsa J. Bick.
pages cm. — (Dark Passages ; book 1)
Summary: A seventeen-year-old girl jumps between the lines of books and
into the white space where realities are created and destroyed—but who
may herself be nothing more than a character written into being from an
alternative universe.
ISBN 978-1-60684-419-9 (hardback) — ISBN 978-1-60684-420-5 (e-book)
[1. Mystery and detective stories. 2. Horror stories. 3. Science
fiction.] I. Title.
PZ7.B47234Wh 2014
[Fic]—dc23
2013033060

For Sarah:
This time, you live.

Father, this thick air is murderous.
—SYLVIA PLATH

PART ONE

COME
AND
PLAY

LIZZIE
Uh-Oh

AT FIRST, MOM thinks there are mice because of that *scritch-scritch-scritching* in the walls. This is very weird. Marmalade, the orange tom, is such a good mouser. But then Mom spies a dirty footprint high up on the wall of her walk-in closet.

A footprint. On the *wall*.

That's when Mom feels someone watching, too. So she turns her head real slow, her gaze inching up to the ceiling vent—and there they are: two glittery violet eyes pressed against the grate like an animal's at the zoo.

A crazy lady is in the attic. The *attic*.

The sheriff thinks she's been hiding since fall and sneaking out for food at night: *She coulda slipped in when the contractors were here. It happens.*

Well yeah, okay, that might happen to normal people who live in towns and cities and don't know how to reach through to the Dark Passages and pull things onto White Space, or travel between *Nows*. But Lizzie knows better. The crazy lady is something out of a bad dream: a rat's nest of greasy hair; skin all smeary like she's taken a bath in oozy old blood. Her hands, sooty and man-sized, are hard with callus, the cracked nails rimed with grime. She smells really bad, too, like someone raised by mole rats or bears. When the sheriff tries asking questions, the crazy lady only stares and stares. She doesn't utter one single, solitary peep.

Because she can't. She has no tongue. No teeth. Not a thing, except this gluey, gucky, purple maw, as if the crazy lady spends all her time slurping blood jelly.

So, really, she's just about what Lizzie expects. Which is kind of bad, considering.

Like . . . *uh-oh.*

2

DAD SWEARS UP and down that he didn't have anything to do with it: *I told you, Meredith. After what happened in London, I'm done.*

Mom isn't having any of that. *Really?* Pulling out her pan-ops, she extends the temple arms, flips out the two extra side lenses, and then hooks the spectacles behind her ears. *Show me your hands, Frank.*

Oh, for God's . . . Sighing, Dad lets Mom get a good look, front and back. *See? Not a scratch.*

I see, but that doesn't prove anything. You've brought back hangers-on from the Dark Passages before and not realized it. Taking a step back, Mom peers at Dad through purple lenses. *Turn around, Frank.*

Waste of time, I'm telling you. Holding out his arms, Dad

does a slow turn like the tiny pink ballerina in Lizzie's music box. (There's nothing special about getting into *her* head; she's only plastic and a little boring. No book-world, nowhere to go, no roommate, no hot shop, no mocha Frappuccinos, not even homework. That silly thing's got nothing to do but twirl and twirl, although Lizzie loves the little brass nib that trips a hidden compartment. Just think of the secrets she could hide, the way Dad does with some of his characters.) *Nothing hanging on, is there?*

No. Pulling off the panops and flipping the extra side lenses shut, Mom chews her lower lip for a second. *What about the Peculiars? If one's cracked . . .*

Dad shakes his head. *Already checked. No dings, no nicks, not even a hairline fracture. There's no way anything leaked out. Come on, honey, you're the science whiz. You've done the calculations. Once you seal a Peculiar, nothing can get in or out, right?* When Mom nods, Dad throws out his hands, like a magician going *ta-da. See? I've kept my end of the bargain. I haven't reached into the Mirror to invite or bind it since London.*

Unless you don't remember. You've lost time before. There are six entire months from London you don't recall at all.

Oh, believe me, Meredith. Dad's face grows still and as frozen as the expression of one of Lizzie's special dolls—except for his dark blue eyes. Usually so bright, they dim the way a fire does as it dies. *I remember more than you think.*

Mom doesn't seem to hear. *Or maybe . . .* She presses a hand to her lips, like she might catch the words before they pop out of the dark and become real. *Or maybe it's stronger and you're healing faster. This is what the key warned us about. Every time you take it in, it leaves a little bit of itself behind, and vice versa.*

The manuscript doesn't say exactly that. *The key says* stain, *like an old watermark. You could say that about any experience, Meredith.*

Yes, but some *stains have a way of not coming out.* Mom's jaw sets in a *don't try to talk your way outta this one, buster* jut Lizzie knows. She saw it just last week, when Mom set out an apple pie to cool and then didn't buy Lizzie's explanation when she said the cat must've done it. (Sometimes, Lizzie thinks they really ought to get a dog; they'll eat anything.) *Maybe it can* make *you activate the Mirror without you being aware or having any memory of doing it.*

Now, Meredith . . . Dad says her name as if Mom is five, like Lizzie, and bawling her head off over a scraped knee. *You're getting hysterical over nothing. You saw my hands. Besides, I can't go through the Dark Passages to any other* Now *because you have the Sign of Sure, remember? Without it, I've got no way of getting back to this* Now, *and I would never risk that. Sweetheart, please believe me. That woman in the attic? She's just some weird, demented vagrant.*

Maybe she is. Mom's mouth goes as thin as one of the seams on Lizzie's memory quilt: scraps of every bit of clothing Lizzie's ever worn sewn into special patterns and decorated with Mom's thought-magic glass, including the twinkly Sign of Sure, which Mom didn't make but is like the panops and Dickens Mirror—very old and from some other *Now. Then let's talk about you, all right? I know you, Frank. It's been years since London, and it's all wearing off, isn't it? You're having trouble with this new book. So you're tempted, aren't you?* When he doesn't answer, Mom grabs his arm. *Talk to me.*

I . . . All of a sudden, Dad can't look Mom in the eye. *It's just a little writer's block.*

I knew it. Mom's face crinkles, like she's as sick as Lizzie after all that apple pie. *God, I knew we should've found a way to destroy that thing, because it's never* little *with you, Frank. When the book just isn't coming, you get desperate. That's* exactly *how you were in London, and look what happened.*

No. Dad's jaw is working, like there's a bad taste, or a ton of words piled up on his tongue that he knows he oughtn't let slip between his teeth; enough words for a whole other and much scarier story, the kind he writes best: books guaranteed to melt your eyeballs. *That wasn't* exactly *how I felt in London. There were . . . other things going on.*

Like what? When Dad doesn't answer, Mom crosses her arms over her chest. *Like* what, *Frank?*

Things you obviously can't or don't want to remember, Meredith.

And just what does that *mean?*

Only that things happened. Dad looks away. *When you . . . when we weren't together. That's when things were—*Dad licks his lips—*bad.*

Yes, as in desperate. Do you even remember *what you said?*

Yes. Dad's lips must be very stiff, because he's having a hard time getting his mouth to move. *I said I felt . . . crowded.*

You said it felt like your skin was too tight, like there was something growing in your chest. You even worried you might have cancer, remember? Mom shakes her head. *I just never connected the dots or understood how much you craved the rush. I should've known you'd lose control.*

Me? Lose control? Dad gives a tired little laugh. *Oh, Meredith, you have no idea. You really don't. Do you . . . can you even remember what we were like* before *the Mirror?*

Remember? For a second, Mom looks confused. Her eyelids

flutter as if there's been a sudden strong breeze, or Dad's thrown her off with a trick question. *I'm not sure what you . . .* Mom's eyebrows pull together. *What else is there to remember? I mean, it was so long ago.*

But I remember you in the beginning, Meredith. Dad's face changes a little, like something inside hurts. *Every detail. Each moment. Where we met. Your hair. Your smell. Everything.*

What are we . . . ? Now Mom looks a little scared, as if she's being asked to play a silly little piano piece that she never practiced because she thought it was so easy and only now realizes this was a *big* mistake. *What are we talking about? The beginning of what? Do you mean when you couldn't sell anything? Is that it? When the publisher canceled your contract for the second book because the first one didn't do well? Or . . . or . . .* Mom's eyes drop as if the answer's fallen out of her brain and gone *boinka-boinka-boinka* onto the floor. *Or when we lived in that miserable little trailer and you taught grade school English and we had to live on food stamps . . .*

No, Meredith. Dad captures her hands in his. *That's all stuff in any article or bio or on the back of a book jacket, for God's sake. I mean . . . do you remember what I was back then? Do you remember how much I loved you? How I would do anything to keep you from . . .* Turning Mom's hands, Dad kisses each palm and both wrists—and the long, stripy scars from where Mom hurt herself way before Lizzie. *Oh, Meredith . . . Love, that man is still here. I'm right in front of you.*

Of course. Mom's eyes are shiny and wet. *Of course I know that. But that . . .* Taking back her hands, she blows out, getting rid of the bad. *That's not what we're talking about. Don't try to change the subject, Frank. We're talking about you, not me. Don't you realize we almost lost you in London? Do you know how hard it was to put that thing back into the Dark Passages because you didn't want to let go?*

Yes. At that, Dad's face crumples, caving in on itself as a sand castle collapses beneath waves that just won't stop. *But that wasn't the only reason.*

Because it's an addiction, Frank. Mom grips Dad's arm so hard her fingers star to a claw. *You let it trick you into believing you were in control; that what you wrote was* your *idea. That what's on the page stays on the page.* Dad mumbles something Lizzie can't catch, and Mom says, *Excuse me?*

I said, you should know.

What does that mean? Don't try to put London on me. That was not my fault. The skin around Mom's mouth is as white as the special skin-scrolls onto which Dad pulls his stories. *You were the one who put together that letter by Collins and then his story about Dee's Black Mirror with what Mary Dickens wrote about her father. It was you who realized all the mirrors Dickens installed in the chalet weren't even listed when Gad's Hill went up for auction.*

Yes, all right, fine. But you were obsessed with the possibility that the Mirror might be real; who insisted we prowl London for that damned key. You wouldn't leave until we figured out which island and tracked down the panops, the Sign of Sure, and that Mirror. (Only Dad says another, very bad word along with *that Mirror,* so Lizzie knows they've totally forgotten she's there.) Dad aims a finger at Mom. *You didn't mind using the Mirror when you needed it. But I suppose that's okay, right? Because you're just so good at knowing when to stop. You've got so much self-control.* Dad's laugh is crackly as a crow's. *Take a look at your arms, Meredith, and then tell me you know how and when to stop.*

*That's not fair. That was different. I was different then. I was
. . .* Mom's mouth quivers, and her eyes have that confused
look again, as if she's been telling a fib and lost the thread of
the lie. *I was*—her mouth twists as she works to knot words
together—*we were . . . that is, I had to . . . I was trying to . . .*

*What, Meredith? What did you have to do? What are you
remembering?* Now Dad looks a little excited, like he wants
to grab Mom's arms again but doesn't dare because he might
break some spell. *Tell me, Meredith; tell me fast. Don't hold back.*

Hold back? I . . . Mom hugs her middle the way Lizzie does
when she has a tummy-ache. *I don't understand. Why are you
badgering me like this? I don't know what you want me to say.*

*What's there, Sweetheart; say what's right on the tip of your
tongue.*

There's nothing! Mom is gasping now, her voice all tight
and little-girl shrill. *Nothing, Frank, nothing's there, there's nothing to say! You're confusing me. I'm not that woman anymore.*

Oh God. Dad lets out a laugh that is only air, no real sound
to it at all, the way a dog laughs. *God, don't I know.*

*Then, if you love me, Frank, you'll stop this! Just . . . just stop,
stop!*

All right, all right. Dad's hands are up, patting the air as if
Mom has turned into some scared little animal backed into
a corner and, he's afraid, might bite. *Okay. Calm down. I just
thought—*

What? The word comes out broken. *What did you think?
This isn't about me! This isn't my fault!*

No, Sweetheart, of course it isn't. I'm sorry. I just . . . Dad forks
hair from his eyes with one hand. *I don't understand. So* close

. . . *but there's some spark, an essence I can't quite wrap my hands around and put where it belongs* . . . Shaking his head, he bites down on the rest and sighs. His shoulders slump like he's suddenly so tired he can barely stand. *I'm sorry. You're right. You're not the woman you were then. We were talking about me.*

That's right. And then Mom says it again, as if repeating the words makes them that much truer. She is calm now, as perfect and beautiful as a Lovely, one of the little people Mom creates whenever she flameworks a world. To everyone else, the worlds are only metal and swirly colors and tiny people and animals and flowers and other, stranger creatures captured in glass. The really dangerous ones, the Peculiars that live in her dad's loft—nobody outside the family ever sees those. Even Mom has to wear her special purple panops to make doubly sure she catches enough thought-magic. *We're talking about you and the Mirror.*

Yes. That's right.

We're talking about you, in this Now. *We're not talking about then.* Mom has pulled herself as straight and tall as one of the long metal blowpipes she uses to collect glass gathers from her furnaces. *We're not talking about another* Now.

No, we're not, and I swear to God, Meredith: what happened in London won't happen again. You'll have to trust me that far.

Trust? You want my trust, Frank? Then show me the new book.

No. Dad says it without thinking, the word popping out like a hiccup.

Why not?

Because. Dad swallows. *I can't.*

You mean you won't.

I mean, I can't, *Meredith. Not yet. It's not done. You know*

I don't like anyone, even you, seeing work in progress. Would you want me looking over your shoulder when you're in the studio?

London didn't happen to me.

I'm aware of that. Meredith, please, if I show you the new book . . .

Frank, an insane woman, with no tongue, was in our attic. Mom says each word really slow, like Dad is deaf or very, very stupid. *And you're worried about falling a little out of love with your book?*

They go round and round, but Dad finally gives in. He goes out to his barn, which is his special private place, and returns to unroll his new book right there on the kitchen table. And yup, there she is, penned with spidery words in Dad's special ink: the crazy lady with her nightmare eyes, buried between words on page five—forever.

Page fifty-eight. The age Dickens was when he died, as he was working on Drood . . . All the color dribbles from Mom's face, until her skin is so clear Lizzie can see the squiggle of teeny-tiny blue veins around her eyes. *Oh God. Frank, it's taunting you. That can't be a coincidence. It's telling you it came out of the Mirror. Don't you see?*

Meredith, I . . . Poor Dad is completely confused. *But I didn't do it. She doesn't belong there. There's no character like her in the story at all.*

But she's there, Frank. You must've pulled her out and put her there.

If . . . if I did, I . . . I don't remember. Dad looks really spooked for the very first time. *Meredith, I honestly don't. But if that's true . . .* Dad stares at his hands, turning them over and over, front to back, like he's never seen them before and has no idea what hands are or what they can do or who they belong to. *Why am I not cut?*

At the look on Dad's face, Lizzie's stomach cramps, like the time last winter when she got the flu and spent a lot of time hanging over the toilet. (Which scared Dad like crazy; he's a real worrywart when it comes to her. *Every* little scrape and sniffle . . . Mom always says Lizzie won't break, but the way Dad refuses to leave her room at night when she's sick, and keeps real close, makes Lizzie wonder just what her dad is afraid of. As if once, so long ago Lizzie can't remember, she was really, really sick. Maybe even sick enough to die.)

You should tell about the crazy lady, Lizzie thinks. Her skin is prickly and hot. *This isn't Dad's fault.* But, oh boy, she is going to be in so much trouble.

Then she thinks about something else: that page number, that five-forever the crazy lady got herself to. How come *that* happened? Had she even thought about a specific page? No. Heck, she isn't all that good with numbers yet anyway. Yeah, she can *count* and stuff. She's five; she's not just a dumb little kid. She knows what she calls "forever" is really an eight instead of the symbol for infinity standing up instead of lying down; that twenty is more than ten; and two plus two is, well, *duh.* But clocks and telling time? Forget it. Same with years. She just sent the crazy lady where she thought the woman ought to go, is all.

So what if . . . Lizzie's insides go as icy as Mom says a Peculiar is, because you need the cold to slow down all that thought-magic. *What if it's a little bit in me, too, only I just don't know it? Like Dad? Like how the monster-doll sometimes makes me feel?*

What if London happens to her?

Meredith. Dad's face scrunches, like he might cry. *Honey, I honestly don't remember writing her.*

Mom's shaking fingers keep trying to knot and hold themselves still. *Then how do you explain that . . . that* thing *in our attic? She popped out of the Dark Passages on her own?* She and Dad stare at each other, and then Mom whispers, *Oh, Frank, is that even possible? Can they . . . could* it *do that? Act independently? If it got too much of you, could it have absorbed your ability to—*

I don't know. That's not the way it's supposed to— Then a new thought seems to bubble into Dad's mind, because he glances at Lizzie, his eyebrows knitting to a frown.

And Lizzie thinks, *Oh boy.* She wonders if Dad remembers what he once said: that even though she's only five, Lizzie is *precocious,* which is adult-speak for *crap, she's smarter than us.*

Burn it. Mom quick grabs the book and runs to the woodstove and stuffs all that skin into the fire. The scroll, the special White Space Dad makes himself and onto which he pulls his stories, catches with a *whump.* Lizzie bets the words tried to fly away, but Mom's trapped those suckers good, slamming the cast iron with a big *clang.* The pages scream bloody murder as all the White Space turns to ash.

That's not going to do any good. Thick crayon-black lines of new worry are drawn around Dad's eyes and along his nose. His voice is all shaky and yet very tired and heavy, which Mom once said is how doom sounds. Like when you know that, oh boy, your car's about to crash and you can scream yourself silly all you want, but too bad.

Or when you're Dad, and you finally wake up and understand that not only have you been gone for six solid months you don't remember, but something very, very bad has slipped from the Dark Passages—and it's your fault. That all the terrible, awful things happening in that London are because of you, and there's no thought-magic in that *Now* to fix it. When you realize that you have to save yourself and especially Mom and get out, fast, and use the Sign of Sure to swoosh from that London to a different Wisconsin.

The book's in my blood, Dad says in his heavy doom-voice. *The energy's in my brain. I can't unthink it, Meredith.*

You can choose not to dwell on it. You can choose not to write it. Think about something else. Dream up anything *else.*

But what about this book? I've gone too far. The characters are already in motion. If I just stop, I don't know what will happen.

So what?

Meredith, think. Even without the Mirror, I've still had enough juice to pull the characters onto White Space for years. Maybe you're right, and it's finally wearing off, but sweetheart, I feel them. The characters will find their way out, somehow. Either they'll bleed into other stories or each other's, or worse, but if I don't reach the end and their stories aren't resolved . . . if they really can *make the jump on their own—*

I don't care, Frank. Mom shivers as if she just can't get rid of the really bad dream clinging to her brain, but keeps seeing it happen again and again, no matter where she looks. *Do what you have to, but kill them. Kill the book.*

What do you think you just did, Meredith? You can destroy the manuscript or my notes, but it's still here. Dad presses a fist to his chest. *The book's inside. You'd have to kill* me.

Then use them in another story. Take the characters, change their names, and—

It doesn't work that way, and you know it. They're all infected. Their original stories would break any new book-world wide open. That's why I send all my notes and ideas for new work away to London for safekeeping in the first place. Hell—Dad lets out a weird, high laugh that sounds a lot like the way the crazy lady looks— *you might as well seal me into a Peculiar, if you really want to be sure.*

What about the Mirror?

You mean, destroy it? Meredith, you were the one who said it would take a tremendous amount of energy. Simply breaking it wouldn't work, right?

Yes, that's right. A glassy red bead of blood swells and trembles on Mom's lower lip, followed by another and then another. *Maybe we should take it back to the island, where the barrier's thinnest. Let the island swallow it up.*

Meredith, no. Think. Honey . . . it's a tool. *You can't go back, and I won't lose you ag—* Dad stops a second. *I won't let us lose each other and what we have, how much we've accomplished. If the Mirror and panops and Peculiars exist, there has to be something, somewhere, that will help us use them more safely. We just haven't found it yet. Maybe that's what we need to concentrate on.*

That could take years, Frank.

So what? What's time to us?

Plenty, if we end up dead in another . . .

No one is going to die, Meredith. I won't let that happen.

Then what if . . . Mom's nibbled her poor lip so bad her chin is smeary with blood. *What if you stopped writing? I don't mean forever. Just for now. Like with the Mirror. Take a break. You feel all that accumulated energy from them now, right? Your . . . your juice? So let the characters fade. Maybe they'll die on their own. People have abandoned ideas and stories before.*

It wouldn't work. Every book is like a virus. Eventually, the stories find a way out, no matter what. Dad cups Mom's face in his hands. *Meredith, they live in my* blood. *They are as real to me as you and Lizzie. I've got to write. I can't stop. I'll go crazy.*

Oh, Frank. Big, scared tears roll down Mom's cheeks. She hooks her hands over Dad's wrists like she might fall if she doesn't. *I know it's hard, that it hurts, but you've got to try. We've got Lizzie to think about now. After so long, so many times that I . . . that we l-lost . . . Frank, she's just a little girl. What about her? What if one of those things—*

I'll be okay. Lizzie can tell they've forgotten her, because they jump as if she's suddenly popped into this *Now* right out of the Dark Passages. *I bet I can help.*

No. Now it's her dad who shakes his head. *No, Lizzie, you don't know what you're saying. This is not for you. It's too dangerous.*

Frank. Mom's face is wet. *Did you just hear yourself? Don't you understand that you* are *risking us by risking yourself?*

Meredith. Sweetheart. Dad's eyes are watery and red. *I know you're afraid, but I'm still here, and I would sell my soul for you, I would die for you, I would take your place and never think twice, but please,* please, *don't ask me to stop. You don't understand what could happen. I swear, Love, I've still got it under control—*

Control? Mom screams. She pulls away from Dad, leaving him with nothing but air. *You've got it under* control? *Then what the hell was that woman doing in our attic?*

3

SO, IN THE end, Dad promises to stop working on the new book, not to try writing it again or even make notes to squirrel away in London. Not one word. He swears to let this story fade away. Cross his heart.

Hope to die.

4

TWO MONTHS LATER, Mom sends Lizzie to call her father for supper.

This is the first time since the crazy lady that Lizzie's gone to Dad's barn, which broods on a hill. Mom's told her to stay away: *Your father needs space and time to mourn.* Like the book inside, Dad has to rot.

Lizzie's missed the loft. Before, Dad let her play as he worked, and she made up tons of adventures for her dolls with all her special Lizzie-symbols: squiggles, triangles, spirals, curlicues, arrows, ziggies, zaggies, diddlyhumps, swoozels, and more things with special Lizzie-names. Just a different way of making book-worlds for her dolls, that's all. Not that either parent knows what she can do. If her mom found out? Oh boy, watch out. So she doesn't tell. No big deal. No one's ever gotten hurt.

Well . . . not counting the monster-doll, which started out life as a daddy-doll but got left in her mom's Kugelrohr oven too long on accident because Mom let her set the timer and Lizzie messed up. The heat was so bad the monster-doll's glass head melted, his eyes slumping into this giant, creepy, violet third eye. Afterward, the monster-doll was really cranked, like, *Hello, what were you thinking, you stupid little kid?* She tried explaining it wasn't on purpose, but oh boy, the monster-doll wasn't having any of *that.* Mom said he was ruined and tossed the monster-doll into the discards bucket, but Lizzie felt guilty because the whole thing really *was* her fault. So, quiet as a mouse, she snuck back into Mom's workshop and fished the monster-doll's head from the bucket.

Problem is . . . her stomach gets a squiggly feeling whenever they play. The inside of the monster-doll's head is all gluey-ooky, the thoughts sticky as spiderwebs. Every time she pulls out, she worries there's a tiny bit of her left all tangled with him. Sometimes, she even wonders if she oughtn't to swoosh the monster-doll to a special *Now* where he can't hurt anyone. She hasn't, though.

Because, really? Some monster-doll thoughts are . . . kind of exciting. He shows her how to do stuff in other *Nows*, too, most of which isn't that scary. Well, except for that humongous storm this past July. Wow, it took her three whole days to figure out how to turn that thing off. But she's got it under control.

Like Dad.

5

LIZZIE SLIPS FROM the house with Marmalade on her heels. The night is deep and dark and very cold. The stars glitter like the distant *Nows* of the Dark Passages. Icy gravel pops and crunches beneath her shoes.

At the barn door, though, Marmalade suddenly balks. "Oh, come on, don't be such an old scaredy-cat." When the orange tom only shows his needle-teeth, she says what Mom always does when Lizzie misbehaves: "My goodness, what's gotten into *you*?" (Really, it's the other way around; Mom doesn't know the half of it.)

But then Marmalade lets go of a sudden, rumbling growl and spits and swats. Gasping, Lizzie snatches her hand back. Wow, what was that about? She watches the cat sprint into the night. She's never heard Marmalade growl. She didn't know cats *could*. She thinks about going after the tom, but Dad always says, *De cat came back de very next day.*

Sliding into the still, dark barn is like drifting on the breath of a dream into a black void. Ahead, a vertical shaft of thin light spills from the loft. Voices float down, too: her dad—

And someone else.

Lizzie stops dead. Holds her breath. Listens.

That other voice is bad and gargly, like screams bubbling up from deep water. This voice is wrong. Just *wrong.*

Uh-oh. Her skin goes creepy-crawly. If Dad's doom-voice could be a feeling, that's what drapes itself over her now, like when she gets a high fever and the blankets are too hot and heavy. Only she can't kick this off. She remembers how Marmalade didn't want to come inside. How Marmalade sometimes stares, not at birds or bright coins of sunlight but the space *between*, while his tail goes *twitch-swish*. The cat *sees* something Lizzie doesn't. So maybe Marmalade knows something now, too.

Lizzie chews the side of her thumb. She has a couple choices here. She can pretend nothing's happened. She can run right back to her nice, safe house where her mother waits and there is hot chocolate and supper, warm on the table. Or she can lie and say Dad wasn't hungry. Or she could sing, *La-la-la, hello, it's Lizzie, Daddy; I'm coming up now!* Yeah, she likes that one. Make a noise; give Dad a chance to pull himself together so he can keep his promise to Mom, and it will be their pinky-swear secret.

But wait, Lizzie. The whisper-voice—she knows it's not her—is teeny-tiny but drippy and gooey somehow, like mist blown from a straw filled with India ink. *Don't you want to see how he really uses the Mirror? He's never let you watch. Go out and play, he says. That's what adults always say when what they mean is, Get lost, you stupid little kid.*

This, she considers, is true.

Oh, come onnn, Lizzieee, the voice coaxes. *Thisss is your big chance for something really gooood.*

The tug of that voice is the set of a fishhook in her brain. It is, she thinks, a little bit like the monster-doll's voice. But so what? She's played with the monster-doll in lots of times and *Nows*, and no big deal. Besides, wouldn't she like to know about the mirror?

You bet I do. Her tongue goes puckery, and her heart gives a little jump of excitement. So she decides, *Just a peek.*

Lizzie creeps up the ladder, oh-so-carefully, quietly. Three more steps . . . two . . . Then, she hesitates. Lizzie might be just a kid, but she's no dummy. The gargly voice reminds her of when she's stayed too long in her monster-doll's head: a feeling that is sticky and gucky and thick.

Oh, go on, you old scaredy-cat, the whisper-voice says. *You've come this far.*

So Lizzie watches her fingers wrap themselves around the last rung, and then she's easing herself up on tiptoe—

6

THE LOFT IS one big space. Floor-to-ceiling bookshelves line the north and west walls. Feeble light fans from table lamps. The

only picture, a copy of *Dickens' Dream*, hangs on one wall.
Dad says what makes *Dickens' Dream* so interesting is that the
painter died before he could finish, and *that* guy had taken
over for another artist who blew his brains out after working
on a couple of Dickens' books. (Which kind of makes you
think, *Whoa, who got inside* his *head?*)

On a low table just beneath the painting, Mom's purple-
black Peculiars gleam. Lizzie knows each by sight: there is
Whispers, and there are *Echo Rats* and *Shadows, In the Dark*.
Purpling Mad. *Now Done Darkness*, where the poor mom gets
eaten up from the inside out, that monster-cancer chewing her up, *munch-munch-munch*. And a whole bunch more.
Whenever Dad finishes a scary book—one so frightening
that Mom would absolutely and positively have a stroke if she
knew Dad's read a single word to Lizzie or, worse yet, that
Lizzie's *visited*—Mom slips on her special panops, which help
her see all the thought-magic of the book-world: the energy
of real life mixed with make-believe. Like when her dad
says, *Oh sure, honey, let's give that brave, smart girl your eyes*. Or,
*Hmm, how about we take a couple letters from your name and put
them riiight here?* If you know how to look, there's her whole
life, all these Lizzie bits and pieces, tucked in her dad's books:
the orange tom here, the squiggle-monsters there, Dad's big
red barn.

Mom draws out a bit of all that thought-magic to seal in
a Peculiar, because it's already way too easy to slip into one
of her dad's books. It's why Dad's famous, a *bestseller*. People
are always *dying* for him to hurry up and write the next book
already. They love that feeling of being lost somewhere and
somewhen else. Sometimes Lizzie doesn't want to pull herself

out of a book-world at all, just like kids who pretend to be superheroes and run around in costumes.

As her eyes slide from the Peculiars to Dad's desk, Lizzie's throat suddenly squeezes down to a straw. She'd hoped that Dad would be there, looking at the night through a big picture window facing the high heifer pasture. Lots of times he'll just sit there, and Lizzie swears he's watching something play itself out, as if on a big television tuned to a secret channel. Mom says Dad *flashes back*, kind of like visiting a very special, private *Now*. Not for real; he doesn't go anywhere or slip through any other Dark Passages than the black basement of his brain, where there are whispers from *waaay* back, when he was a boy and lived in this creepy old farmhouse at the very bottom of a deep, cold valley surrounded by high, snowy mountains in a very bad Wyoming.

But right this second, Dad's not flashing back to that valley. He's not at his desk, and Lizzie feels that awful, heavy blanket weigh her down just a little bit more. She thinks, *No, Dad, no. You* promised. *You crossed your heart.* But he must've been dying inside, the story in his blood hotter than the highest fever, burning him up.

Dad has been a busy, busy bee. A new skin-scroll is unfurled over his desk. What he's already pulled onto the scroll's White Space with special ink is a bright red spidery splash: letters and words and whole paragraphs. A heavy scent, one that is like a crushed tin can left out in a storm, fogs the air.

Dad stands at the Dickens Mirror, which is not an oval but a slit, like the pupil of a lizard's or cat's eye, with all sorts of squiggle-monsters and arguses and typhons and spider-swoozels and winged cobcraas squirming through its wood frame. The glass isn't normal either but smoky-black, like old char left from a great big bonfire.

And Dad . . . he's not acting like Dad. What he's doing doesn't even seem human. Because Dad is *growling*, like something's waking up in his chest, raking curved claws over his insides, trying to break his bones and bust from his skin, just like the mom's cancer in *Now Done Darkness*, or the million creepy, furry spithres that tremble like spiky petals from that girl's mouth in *Whispers*. Dad's face is all twisted and crooked, as if his head got ruined in Mom's Kugelrohr oven.

In his right hand is his wicked-sharp lunellum. Normally, Dad only uses the knife, which is decorated with special symbols, when he makes his White Space skin-paper. Not tonight, though, and Lizzie knows doom when she feels it. The person in front of that Mirror is in the middle of becoming a thing she's never seen before.

So make a sound! A tiny panic-mouse claws her brain. *Sing a song! Do something to save him! Do something, Lizzie, do* anything, *before it's TOO LATE!*

But then *too late* happens.

The blade kisses her dad's left palm, quick as a snake, and Dad goes, *AARRGGHHH!* His head whips back as another roar boils and bubbles: *AAAHHHH!*

On the ladder, Lizzie jumps. *Dad!* the panic-mouse in her brain squeaks. *Dad, Daddy!* All the hairs on her neck and arms go spiky as a porcupine's quills. She watches in mute horror as a bloody rill oozes down her father's wrist to weep ruby tears.

The knife flashes again. The skin of Dad's right hand splits in a red shriek. The lunellum *thunks* to the floor as her father slams his bleeding hands, really, really hard, against the Mirror. The stand wobbles; there is a squeaking, wet sound as her father's blood squelches and smears the glass; and Lizzie hears a very distinct, metallic *click* like the snap of a light switch.

And then the lizard-eye of that Dickens Mirror . . . changes. It starts to shimmer. The surface wobbles and ripples in undulating black waves, like a river of oil spilling across ice. Her father's blood pulses, hot and red and *alive*; his blood writhes over the Mirror, and where his blood touches, the smoky glass steams. Long, milky fingers of mist curl around her father's wrists and begin to pulse and suck—and all of a sudden, they are not white as milk or heavy mist but first pink and then a deep, dark bloodred.

The Mirror is drinking her father. The Mirror's greedy fingers spiral up and up and up in a tangle of rust-red vines to web his neck and face, as if her dad is a piece of blank parchment onto which something new is being written in blood.

"Blood of My Blood," her father says, but what comes out of his mouth is a voice of one and many: overlapping echoes and whispers from down deep and very far away. "I feed you, Blood of My Blood, Breath of My Breath. I feed you and I invite you. I release you and I bind you and I draw you. Together, we are one, and there are the Dark Passages and all of space and time to bridge."

The mist twines around her father in a shimmering vermillion spiderweb. The blood-web tightens and squeezes, hugging her father right up to the churning, rippling glass. The black glass gives, the inky mouth of that Mirror gapes, and then her father's hands slip through, *sinking* into the glass, as he reaches down its throat and into the Dark Passages.

Run! the panic-mouse screeches. *Run, Lizzie, run! Get Mom!* But she doesn't. Her heart *bumpity-bumpity-bumps* in her chest, and she has never been so scared. In all the Lizzie-worlds she's made and the *Nows* she's visited and the hours she's spent here with her father, she has never seen anything quite as terrible as this—and she simply can't move.

The glass fills with something white and sparkly and thick and formless as fog that swirls and ripples—and knits together to form a face. But not Dad's face, oh no. Whatever lies beyond the glass is still becoming: oozy and indefinite, there and then not, as if the face is pulling together the way hot glass slumps and folds and becomes something else. Even as she watches, the face solidifies into a nightmare of raw meat, bristly teeth, a snaky black tongue—

And eyes. *Eyes.* Two are black. They are a crow's eyes, a cobra's eyes—dead eyes with no pupils and no eyelids either.

But the third is different. Instead of the blue-black cyclops eye that is her monster-doll's, this third eye is a silver storm, both mirror and ocean—and her father is there, his reflection pulling together from the swirling, smoky whirlpool to eel like a serpent, and oh, his face, her dad's *real* face!

Maybe she makes a sound. Or maybe, like a snake, the whisper-man tastes her with his tongue, because all three eyes cut sideways and then—

He sees me. Her hand catches the ball of a shriek. *He sees me, he sees me, he sees me!*

And then.

Her father.

Turns—

EMMA
Blink

1

"EMMA. EMMA?"

"What?" Emma snapped back, awareness flooding her mind in an icy gush, an arrow of sudden bright pain stabbing right between her eyes. Blinking past tears, her gaze sharpened on a pair of windshield wipers thumping back and forth, pushing rills of thick snow.

Driving. I'm in a car. Her hands fisted the steering wheel. *But where am I going? How did I get here?*

"Emma, are you okay? You look kind of out of it."

"I-I'm fine. Sorry, Li . . . Lily." She stumbled over the name, but *Lily* felt right in her mouth and Emma *did* recognize her, sort of: leggy, blonde, a touch of the valley girl.

"Have you figured out where we are yet?" Lily asked.

Oh man. They were *lost*? Jesus, how long had she been gone this time? "Not yet, but I bet we'll be up . . . up . . ."

"Emma?"

"Jasper's," she blurted, the word catapulting from her

mouth like a rock from a slingshot. "I bet we'll be up at Jasper's in no time."

"Are you—" Lily let out a shriek as a fork of lightning stuttered. "Is that *normal*?"

"For Wisconsin," Emma said as thunder bellowed and the lumbering Dodge Caravan—*a rental; yes, I remember complaining about the bad shocks, the mushy steering*—jumped. "Happens all the time, Lily." She tried to keep it light, but her voice didn't feel as if it belonged to her at all. God, leave it to her to vacate at the worst possible time. The *blink* had been so different, too: not just a blackout or snapshot flash but a whole *sequence*, fading fast. What had she seen? A little girl and a . . . a cat? Yes, but what was its name? Something to eat . . . Jelly? No, no, that wasn't right.

Come on, Emma, you can do this. Just relax and let it come.

But she couldn't relax. Her head killed. Her vision fuzzed and then blistered as her headache pillowed and swelled. The space before her eyes opened in a spiky, purple-black maw, violent as a bruise. The doctors had always dismissed it as a variant of a scintillating scotoma, a visual symptom of a migraine. But hers wasn't anything like a normal person's, which figured. No bright firefly flashes for her, no shimmering arc or fuzzy spiral. Hers began as a rip in thin air, like a hole being munched right out of the backside of this world. The doctors made reassuring noises about petit mal seizures and an Alice in Wonderland syndrome, but all their talk boiled down to the same thing: *Honey, so sucks to be you.*

Can't afford to blink *away again, not while I'm driving.* Although she'd clearly been away already, hadn't she? But why now? *Come on.* Emma put a finger to her forehead, right above her nose, pressing the hard circle of a lacy titanium skull plate beneath muscle and skin. *Think.* When had she taken her last dose? This morning? Last night? Two days before? She couldn't remember. The docs were always on her about that, too: *Emma, you need to be more compliant.* Easy for them to say. It wasn't like she was *trying* to be a pain in the ass, but let them choke back pills for a week or two, see how much they liked it. The anti-spaz meds completely messed with her mind. The headaches might evaporate, but reality also misted to a blur until she felt as flat and lifeless as fading words on a tattered page. She didn't know what was worse: no headaches, seizures, and *blinks,* or wandering around all hollow and zombied-out, like an extra from *The Walking Dead.*

Well, just muscle through it. Gripping the wheel harder, she squinted through tears. The world beyond the windshield was shimmery and nearly colorless, that relentless curtain of snow going to gray, about to fade to black as the day died. But what she saw around the edges of that purple maw was wrong: craggy mountains on the right, the drop-off of a valley on the left.

What? Her eyebrows pulled into a frown. That wasn't right. Sure, Wisconsin has plenty of valleys, but the mountains were pimples. They were zits. *Nice* zits but still zits.

God, where are we? Her eyes slid to her driver's side window, frosted with a rime of thin ice. And right then she had the strangest, weirdest impulse: to press her hand to the glass, feel the burn as the ice bled. *One push, where the barrier's thinnest. That's all it would take.* Push hard enough and the glass would open to swallow her up and then she would fall . . .

Another crash of lightning broke the spell, made her heart flop in her chest. Beside her, Lily let out a yelp and clutched the dash. "How can it *do* that in snow? Come on, Emma, you're the science brain. Is it supposed to do that?"

"Sure, if cold air passes over warm water," she said, relieved her voice didn't shake. Temples throbbing, she forced her eyes forward again. The metal plate above her nose seemed to be burning its way through the bony vault of her skull. What had *that* been about? Bleeding *ice*? Pushing through melting glass, a thinning barrier, to some other world? *You nut, who do you think you are—Neo? Stop this. Come on, get a grip.* "It just means we've got to be close to Lake Superior. That's why the thunder's so loud. If we were further away . . ." She bit off the rest. Lily probably didn't need a lecture on acoustic suppression and the reflective properties of ice crystals—and she *did* know Lily, right? Sure, they were both juniors at Holten Prep; Lily was in her . . . her . . . What class was it? English? History? Basket-weaving for the mentally deranged?

What's wrong with me? Her tongue skimmed her lips, tasting fear and salt. Coming back from the *blink* this time was much worse than ever before, her mind pulling itself together like molten chewing gum pried from the underside of an old shoe. But why? Usually, it was *blink-blink* and, whoa, when had she decided to take up skydiving? All right, the fugues— pockets of time for which she had no memory—weren't quite as bad as that, but if she ever needed a go-to for why eighteen pairs of shoes suddenly appeared in her closet, she was set.

Don't freak. That just makes everything worse. Come on, you know who you are. You're Emma Lindsay and she's Lily . . . Lily

. . . She swallowed around a sudden knot of panic. *Lily who?*

"Maybe we should turn back," Lily said.

No, I don't think we can. I don't think the storm will let us. But those were crazy thoughts. A storm couldn't think. Ice didn't bleed. You couldn't tumble through glass to fall into forever and all times like some kind of crazy Alice. Of course, a purple mouth shouldn't make Swiss cheese of the world, but that didn't stop her addled brain from conjuring one out of thin air. Understanding why didn't make what she saw any less scary.

Then a real memory—what a weird way to think about it—floated from the fog of her thoughts. "If we go back, won't your parents make you do that dogsled thing for wannabe warrior-women?" Emma asked.

"Yeah, but compared to this?" Lily grunted. "Dog shit looks pretty good."

2

WHEN EMMA WOKE up yesterday morning, life had still been pretty normal. Well, as normal as it got for a kid with a head full of metal, killer headaches, visions that appeared more or less at random, chunks of lost time, and nowhere to go over Christmas break.

Heading north hadn't been the plan. The stroke over a year ago turned Jasper into a zucchini—on June 9, to be exact: her birthday, and Jasper's, too. They always had two cakes: ginger cake with buttercream frosting for him, dark chocolate with velvety chocolate ganache for her. She'd been jamming candles into Jasper's cake—try fitting fifty-eight candles so you didn't get a bonfire—when, all of a sudden, something right over her head *banged* so hard the cottage's windows rattled. Racing upstairs, she'd found Jasper, out cold, sprawled in a loose-limbed jumble like a broken, discarded doll. These days, Jasper languished in a dark room, his head turned to a white sliver of window hemmed by coal-black shutters. He wore diapers. He was mute. The entire left side of his face looked artificial, like a waxen mask melting under too much heat. His left lower eyelid drooped, the eye itself the color of milky glass, and his mouth hung so wide she could see the ruin of his teeth and the bloated dead worm of his tongue. The last time Emma ventured in to read aloud—she and Jasper used to make a game of trying to finish *Edwin Drood*—Sal, the lizard-eyed, pipe-puffing live-in, shooed her away. When Jasper had been boss, Sal behaved. Now, with the old bat out of the attic, Emma felt about as welcome as a case of head lice.

Best to stay in Madison. The Holten folks had paired Emma, on full scholarship (which translated to *smart and weird but poor*), with Mariane, a Jewish exchange student from London who was big into decorative art. Seeing as how Emma worked glass, that was all good. So she and Mariane would eat Chinese and see a movie, which, apparently, Jewish people all over the world did on Christmas. Maybe chill with a couple Beta boys at the university, drink beer, eat Christmas brats. Binge on *X-Files* and *Lost* and watch the Badgers get slaughtered in the Rose Bowl. All-American, Wisconsin stuff like that.

She could use the time to throttle back, too. Head over to the hot shop and work a pendant design she'd mulled over for months: a galaxy sculpted in miniature from glass, encased in glass, yet small and light enough to wear around her neck.

When she mentioned her idea, the gaffer cracked, *Maybe we'll start calling you Orion, like that cat.* She'd laughed along with him and the other glassblowers, but *Men in Black* and that cat's amulet *had* given her the idea in the first place. Not everything had to stay make-believe.

So that was the plan, anyway—until that asshole Kramer called her to his office, shut the door, and said, *"Ms. Lindsay, we need to*

3

HAVE A LITTLE chat about that last assignment."

"Okay," Emma says. She watches Kramer withdraw a mug of steaming Mighty Leaf green tea from his microwave. A little alarm is *ding-ding-dinging* in her head. He hasn't offered her any. Not that she minds: green tea tastes like old gym socks, and the Mighty Mouse brand, no matter how swank, probably does, too. For him not to offer, though, she must be in *deep* doo-doo. "Is something wrong, Professor Kramer?"

"Is . . . something . . . *wrong?*" Kramer gives his tea bag a vicious squish between his fingers. He sets, he chucks; Mighty Mouse goes *ker-splat* against the far wall. On a corner of Kramer's desk, a radio mutters about *the continuing investigation into a young girl's gruesome discovery of eight . . .*

"'*Orrible* murders and ghastly crimes," Kramer grates in an angry, exaggerated cockney, and stabs the radio to silence. "These screaming twenty-four-hour news cycles are as bad as Victorian tabloids." He fires a glare through prissy Lennon specs. "Well, yes, you might say there's something *wrong*, Ms.

Lindsay. I'm trying to decide if I should merely flunk you out of this course, or get you booted out of Holten, despite your circumstances. Just what kind of game do you think you're playing?"

She's so flabbergasted her jaw unhinges. "P-Professor Kramer, wh-what did I *do*?"

In answer, Kramer jerks open his desk drawer hard enough to make the pens chatter and yanks out a sheaf of paper-clipped pages, which he tosses onto his desk. "You might have gotten away with this . . . this *rubbish* if I was any other instructor, but I'm writing a *book* on the man, for God's sake. No one except researchers is allowed access to this material. What, did you think I'd simply ignore this? Time to wake up, Ms. Lindsay. I'm not the headmaster, I don't care about your sad little history, and I'm sure as hell not your bloody psychiatrist. Now I want to know where you got it."

She has no idea what he's talking about. Her eyes fall to the first page:

WHITE SPACE

A Short Story

by

Emma Lindsay

Lit. Seminar 058

"Got it?" She swallows. "I *wrote* it."

Kramer's ears flare Coke-can red. "You've got balls, I'll give you that. Where did you get this? Did you download it from a pirate site?"

She's getting a very bad feeling about this. *Oh boy, is that possible? No, don't be silly. The guy's dead.* "I-I don't know what you're t-talking about, sir."

"You want to play it that way? Fine." Kramer tweezes out a single sheet. "Take a good, hard look at *this* and then convince me why you shouldn't be expelled."

This is not happening; this is a nightmare. Tears threaten. *Shit, don't cry.* She does what Kramer wants—and as her burning eyes trip over the watery letters and spaces of one word, then jump over white space to the next word and the next and the next, it's as if an invisible fist has wrapped around her throat and begun to squeeze.

> *So how long would it take? There had to be a way to figure it. Maybe he should've stripped the clothes, but then what? Couldn't bury them. The ground was frozen solid, and some things wouldn't burn: snaps, buttons, zippers. And didn't nylon melt? He thought it did, and there'd be the stink.*
>
> *And didn't how long really depend on how bad you wanted something? How much you were willing to risk? Sure. So, clothes or no clothes, if you were a wolf or coyote and starving because Wyoming winters were hard and game, scarce . . . and there was dinner lying right there? All that easy meat?*
>
> *A wolf would strip that body to bones in no time.*

A wave of unreality washes over Emma. A sudden headache spikes right where it always does, under that lacy cranial plate the doctors screwed into place between her eyes so her brain wouldn't bubble out. (When the doctors had first shown her the plate, she'd thought, *Great, the perfect accessory for every occasion.*) The pain is blinding, and she shuts her eyes against the sudden tilt as the world seems to slump and run like superheated glass.

"Right. Wasn't that interesting, Emma? I thought it was. And now let's listen to *yours*, shall we? You've no objection if I read while you follow along?" Kramer asks, but it's one of those rhetorical questions a person knows better than to answer. As Kramer drones, she stares at words and sentences that, up to five seconds ago, she thought were hers alone.

> *There had to be a way of calculating how long it would take. There must be rules, like physics or math; there were variables to take into account. Temperature, of course, but also the clothes. Maybe he should've stripped the clothes, but then what? He couldn't bury them. The ground was frozen solid, and burning wouldn't work because zippers, snaps, buttons didn't burn and Gore-Tex melted.*
>
> *Didn't how long depend on how hungry you were? How badly you wanted something, and how much you were willing to risk? So if you were a coyote and starving to death because the snow was deep and the Wisconsin winter, hard—and then you stumbled on something that couldn't fight back? Meat that was free and for the taking?*
>
> *God help him, but he knew: a coyote would strip that body in no time.*

"Other than your substitution of Wisconsin for Wyoming?" Kramer drills her with a look. "You see my problem."

Emma just shakes her head. She is so mortified she wants to melt into the linoleum. God, maybe she really should be better about taking those damn pills. Better to be a zombie than feel this.

"I said, *write* in the style of Frank McDermott," Kramer seethes. "I didn't say *steal.*"

4

THE SEMINAR WAS a mistake.

She'd had an open slot for a junior-year elective. Any class coy enough to be called "Out of Their Minds: Madness and the Creative Process" made her nervous. Her adviser was more direct: *Are you sure about this?* The admin people at Holten Prep knew her . . . ah . . . shall we say, *unusual* circumstances. But since the only other alternative was animal husbandry, which was a Wisconsin thing and included a unit on neutering piglets, it was kind of a no-brainer.

What she hadn't realized was that Kramer meant for them to write the occasional story in the style of *fill-in-the-blank.* This was a problem. Creative writing already weirded her out, and now she had to crawl around the heads of these guys, too? Seriously? Most of these writers ended up killing themselves. But there was no way she was getting sucked into making little Wilbur squeal.

The Bell Jar had been on this past summer's reading list, and she'd decided to get a jump on it, starting right after finals and a couple days before her seventeenth birthday. Well . . . *big* mistake. The book completely freaked her out. Somehow she got . . . she became *lost*, slipping into the story the way she might slide into a tight pair of skinny jeans, and then into Esther's head. Started looking at the world differently, too, as if staring through a bizarre set of lenses that showed her phantoms no one else could see. And once or twice, swear to God, she heard someone call her name, only to turn and find no one there.

Yet that feeling was . . . *familiar*, somehow. Like, *I know this. This once happened. At some point, I was really and truly nuts.* As if by reading all about Esther Greenwood, Plath's stand-in for herself, she was remembering what it was like to go slowly insane; to be trussed in a straitjacket and forced to gag back too-sweet medicines and then locked away beneath a bell jar to rave. Which was crazy.

The Bell Jar was bad: an infection, a fever raging through her body, burning her up. It got so awful she spent a couple hours studying a wickedly jagged razor of clear glass, filched from the discards bucket at the hot shop, and thinking, *What if? Go on, do it, you coward. You know you want to; you know this is the best way, the only way to pass through into . . .*

Through? Into *what*? What she'd found down in Jasper's cellar years ago? (And nope, no way she was thinking about *that*, nosirreebob.) And go where? Who the hell knew?

She hadn't sliced and diced—obviously—but the temptation to cut, to filet herself, really hack those arteries and watch the blood bubble, still occasionally slithered into her mind like the black tangle of a nightmare she just couldn't shake.

Honestly, after that whole *Bell Jar* mess, the prospect of studying the work of insane writers, slipping into their skins, made lopping off Wilbur's balls almost attractive. But she was stuck.

5

THE CLASS HAD started with science fiction, which was okay, although Kramer was in love with the sound of his I'm-from-Cambridge-and-you're-not voice: *To paraphrase the incomparable though deeply disturbed Philip K. Dick, whoever manipulates words manipulates the existential texture of reality, as we blahdiddy-blahdiddy-blah-blah.* But when Kramer began bloviating about quantum foam and Schrödinger's cat and dark matter and more *blahdiddy-blahdiddy-blah-blah*, and everyone else was *oh, awesome, that's like, dude, so* Star Trek . . . she just couldn't help herself. Dark matter could only be inferred. In the case of Schrödinger's kitty, collapsing probabilities through observation had *nothing* to do with massless particles popping out of quantum foam. And quantum effects *could* be observed on the macroscopic level at near absolute zero within the energy sink of a Bose-Einstein condensate, which therefore proved Hardy's Paradox regarding the interaction of quantum and anti-quantum particles that might actually coexist in related timelines and alternative universes . . .

A single death glare from Kramer, though, and she clammed up. Fine. Be ignorant. Mangle science. See what she cared.

After that, the class drifted to horror, specifically Wisconsin's Most Famous Crazy Dead Writer, Frank McDermott, who was originally from somewhere in Wyoming and lived in England a good long time, but who was keeping score? Besides writing a bazillion mega-bestsellers, McDermott's claim to fame was getting blown to smithereens by his equally wacko nutjob of a wife. (Ed Gein, Jeffrey Dahmer, Frank Lloyd Wright and the Taliesin murders, McDermott—Wisconsin was full of 'em. Had to be something in the water.) With his *new! important! biography!* Kramer hoped to solve the BIG MYSTERY: where was Waldo . . . er, Frank? Because, after the explosion, not one scrap of McDermott remained, not even his teeth. Which was a little strange.

Originally a quantum physics star—lotsa theories about multiverses and timelines and blah, blah—Meredith McDermott was fruitier than a nutcake. Years in institutions, suicide attempts—the whole nine yards. Maybe she turned to glass art the way a patient might take up painting, but what she made was unreal; museums and collectors fell all over themselves snapping up pieces.

Turned out the lady was also a complete pyro. She would've had plenty on hand in her studio, too: propane tanks, cylinders of oxygen, acetylene, MAPP. To that she'd thrown in gasoline and kerosene and, as a kind of exclamation point, a bag of fertilizer.

The fireball was immense. The explosion chunked a blast crater seventy feet long and fifteen feet deep. Emma bet Old Frank was tip-typing away in writer heaven before he knew he was dead.

Even so, there ought to have been plenty of Frank McDermott shrapnel: bits and pieces zipping hither and thither at high speeds to get hung up on branches or blast divots into tree trunks. Science was science. No matter what the movies said, for a person to completely vaporize, you needed either an atomic bomb or about a ton of dynamite. So why couldn't the police find a single, solitary bone? A watch? *Something?*

All that was recovered at the scene were the barn's iron bolts, sliders, and hinges—and a coagulated lake of slumped, amorphous glass.

And only the barn burned. The house hadn't. Neither had Meredith's workshop or the woods or even the fields, despite the fact that the local fire department was twenty miles away and no response team arrived until hours after the explosion. Just plain weird.

And where was Meredith? What happened to the McDermotts' little kid? All the police ever found was the family car, miles away after it lost an argument with a very big oak. No bodies, though. Just a dead car.

And a whole lotta blood.

6

THE UNFINISHED MANUSCRIPTS were also weird.

Three—and there might be more—were quietly decomposing under house arrest in some vault in England. No one was allowed to see or handle them, period. All scholars like Kramer got were a few choice bits copied from the originals: not enough to make much sense of the stories but just enough to whet their appetites.

This tallied, though. McDermott was a squirrel. Not even his editors were allowed to hang on to his original manuscripts, which were penned on homemade parchment scrolls—no one was quite sure whether these were vellum or the hide of some more exotic animal—with a special ink McDermott also formulated himself. Since the guy made more money than God, the editors put up with it. They also mentioned how the longer they handled those scrolls, the more the ink changed color *to a shade as vibrant as freshly clotted blood*, as one editor put it. Even this wasn't necessarily news. From the description, Emma thought McDermott's brew must be chemically related to iron gall ink, which oxidized with exposure to air. In other words, the ink rusted, and the stuff literally ate through parchment. All the academics made this sound so *spooky*, but honestly, it was just chemistry. Mozart and Rembrandt and Bach used the same ink. So did Dickens. BFD. All McDermott had done was tweak the original recipe so his work had a built-in termination date: a nice way of sticking it to people like Kramer. Give McDermott an *A* for effort; Emma almost admired the guy.

Probably would have, if she hadn't been so freaked about her story.

1

WHAT KRAMER HANDED her was a fragment—a note, really—from a book she'd never read, because McDermott never got around to writing it. All that scholars like Kramer knew about this novel, *Satan's Skin*, came from this and a few other jotted entries. The plot involved a demon-grimoire stitching itself back together, only the pages had been reused in other books and so the characters kept jumping off the page while debating the nature of quantum realities. Some loopy *Matrix* meets *Inkheart*-with-a-vengeance crap like that.

Her story was about these eight kids stranded in a spooky house during a snowstorm who begin to disappear one by one. Okay, it wasn't *all* original; she'd taken a cue from this awesome John Cusack movie. (Sure, the film was completely freaky. All the characters turn out to be alters: different personalities hallucinated by this completely insane, wacko killer. But the idea that people who *thought* they were real *weren't*— well, it was just so cool.) Her first draft had written itself, pretty much. Considering how writing creeped her out, this should've tripped some alarms.

As it happened, her story was a subplot of *Satan's Skin*. There were differences. In McDermott's version, the kids— and yeah, there were eight—were nameless. The oldest, a complete psychopath, murdered his nasty drunk of a dad, who deserved it, the abusive SOB. (All McDermott's dads and quite a few moms were the same, too. Guy had some serious parental unit issues.) In her version, the characters had names, but her hero—this sweet, sensitive, gorgeous, hunky, completely *yes-please* guy—had killed his nasty dad in self-defense and was haunted by what he'd done.

Both her draft and McDermott's fragment shared something else: neither ended. Kramer said McDermott's note stopped in midsentence, a little like *Edwin Drood*, although Dickens had the decency to put in a period before up and dying. Hers was like McDermott's. Not only had she written herself into a corner; she couldn't figure a way to tie up all those loose ends. The last sentence just sort of floated all by its lonesome. Since her assignment was only a first draft, she had the go-to of needing feedback from the Great Bloviator . . . er, Kramer.

But, to be honest? Imagining a final period or *the end* set up a sick fluttering in her stomach. She just couldn't do it. She'd never admit this to a soul, but . . . well . . . her hero was the perfect guy and she . . . she really *liked* him. In *that* way. Okay, okay, fine, she even *daydreamed* about him, and how lame was that? Mariane had this stalker thing for Taylor Lautner—seriously, the girl was obsessed with those pecs and that six-pack—but at least she drooled over a real guy. Emma's perfect boyfriend was an idea that lived in her head, but he was also so *real*, the most well-rounded of her characters. The others were just one-dimensional placeholders. This guy she actually thought of as a complete person. Wrapping up his story would be so *final*, a lowering of that damn bell jar. Once done, her guy was finished, no way out of the box—not unless she decided to chuck science and write herself into *The Continuing Adventures of Emma Lindsay, Loser and Social Misfit.* Maybe that was why writers did sequels; they just couldn't let the story really die.

Anyway. Her draft and McDermott's fragment were virtually identical.

"Other than the madwoman in the attic, which is so utterly Brontë but perhaps understandable considering Meredith McDermott's long history of mental illness, that subplot is baffling," Kramer said. "It's as if these teens in *Satan's Skin* are . . . stand-ins? Alters? Different possible versions and aspects of McDermott himself? Because, clearly, the man's reworking his abusive past. That miserable childhood in Wyoming always haunted him, and of course, the snow and deadening cold are symbolic of slow soul murder. Very Joycean, wouldn't you agree? He does much the same with the mother in *Whispers*—absolutely brilliant; we'll be reading that after break . . . and of course, madness as a slow cancer, a rot eating away at the very fabric of reality, is rendered with stunning effect in this very bizarre little Victorian pastiche that exists only in fragments itself and yet is thoroughly *blahdiddy-blahdiddy-blah-blah.*"

Numb, Emma grayed out. Who gave a wet fart what McDermott had in mind? How had she copied a manuscript she hadn't known existed?

Hating Kramer would've been easy; he was *such* an asshole. But she couldn't, not really. From his perspective, she was a cheater, a plagiarist, the academic scum of the earth. But he just didn't know the whole sordid story.

No one did.

8

EVERYTHING SHE KNEW about her bio parents fit the back of a stamp, with room to spare. Dear Old Drug-Addled Dad tried a two-point set to see if Baby really bounced against a backboard. (Uh, that would be no.) Mommy Dearest boogied before Dad tested whether *she* might be less sucky on a layup. Later, Daddy hung himself in lockup because—*oops*—someone forgot to confiscate the shoelaces of his All Stars. Big whoopsie-daisy there.

Cue ten years of Child Protective Services and a parade of foster parents, group homes, doctors, staring shrinks, clucking social workers. Her headaches got worse, thanks to Dear Old Dad. All that head trauma started off a chain reaction of growing fractures. She got older and uglier as her skull grew lumpier and bumpier.

Then Jasper, a crusty old sea dog with a fondness for bourbon, Big Band, and paint, showed up. Why he wanted to foster a kid, especially one with her history and looks, she never could figure. (Before her surgeries, she could have been a stunt double for those bubble-heads playing the Mos Eisley Cantina.) Jasper got her surgerized so her brain wouldn't go *ker-splat* all over the floor. Fixed up her face, too. Then he whisked her away from all the do-gooders to an ancient stone cottage *waaay* up north overlooking Devil's Cauldron, a dark blue inlet of rust-red sandstone layered over ancient volcanic rock on the northern tip of Madeline Island in Lake Superior.

By day, Jasper piloted charters and wandered around in a ratty cardigan and muttered to himself. Nights, he tossed back a couple belts, cranked up a wheezy old cassette recorder, and slathered canvasses with eerie, surreal landscapes choked with bizarre creatures, as Frank Sinatra or Dean Martin burbled, or *Bleak House* or *The Old Curiosity Shop* or a dozen other Dickens novels and stories spun themselves out on the air. Some of the creatures Jasper painted, she recognized: woolly mammoths, dinosaurs, prehistoric benthic creatures, weird insects with three-foot wingspans. Others—the ones with stalk-eyes and tentacles and screaming needle-toothed navels—were so Lovecraft, they looked like they'd slithered from the deep wells of inky nightmares.

What Emma never did understand was that when he finished, Jasper pulled a Jackson Pollock, slopping thick white paint onto each and every canvas. When she complained there was nothing left to see—and what was the *point?*—Jasper would toss back another shot and explain that the creatures, which existed in the Dark Passages between all the *Nows*, were too powerful to let out: *Every time you pull them onto White Space, you risk breaking that* Now. (And oh well, when he put it *that* way, it all became so *clear*. So much for a straight answer.)

With a story as Harry Potter as this, Jasper ought to have been a wizard. She should have had strange powers. But no, Jasper was just odd; a small army of surgeons stenciled a road map of skillfully hidden scars onto her scalp and gave her a normal, if titanium-enriched, skull; and she loved Jasper so much that seeing him as he was now hurt like nails hammered into her heart.

9

AND NOTHING BAD happened once she was with Jasper. Summers, she biked around Madeline or kayaked over to Devils Island with Jasper, slipping in and out of sandstone sea caves or wandering the forested sandstone while her guardian sketched. Jasper said the island got its name from the old Ojibwe legend that Matchi-Manitou, some honking huge evil spirit, was imprisoned in a giant underground cave at the entrance to the spirit worlds, and only the bravest warriors could pass through the black well at the center of the island to fight the thing, *blah, blah*. Some vision quest crap like that. The only well she knew on that island was near an old lighthouse and keeper's cottage. Still, whenever there was a really big blow, the roar and boom of the sea caves—of big, bad Matchi-Manitou—carried clear to Jasper's cottage.

Still, nothing horrible happened. Okay, she was lonely. No friends. Maybe it was crusty, tipsy, bizarre Jasper, who would scare a sane kid, but no matter how hard she tried . . . she was a dweeb. Smart, but still inept and weird.

Whatever. Really, everything was good.

Well . . . until the year she turned twelve and went down-stairs into the cellar to look for a book and where . . . where . . .

Well, where something happened down cellar that she'd really decided not to think about, or remember.

Really.

10

THE BLACKOUTS—THE *BLINKS*—STARTED a week after the inci-dent down cellar. Each began the same way: a swarming tin-gle like the scurry of ants over her skin; the boil of an inky dread in her chest. The world thinned; her brain superheated. Then that purple-edged maw opened before her eyes and she would swoon into an airless darkness, tripping into the space between one breath and the next.

And then—*blink-blink*—she was back.

Often, she retained glimpses: the ooze of fog over slick cobblestones; a string of gaslights marching over a faraway bridge and a huge clock face that she *almost* recognized. A long hallway and rough carpet against her feet. A white night-gown that whispered around her legs. A huge red barn. A deep valley ringed by craggy, snow-covered mountains.

Sometimes—the worst times—she remembered *things*: bulbous monsters with tentacles and a patchwork of eyes; creatures that lived someplace dark, far away, and very, very cold. Or, come to think of it, that lurked behind the white paint of Jasper's canvases.

Mostly, though, there was nothing. She would simply *blink*

awake with a sizzling headache arcing from the plate between her eyes to another at the very base of her skull, as if a switch had been thrown and a circuit completed: *zzzttt!* The *blinks* lasted anywhere from a few seconds or minutes to a good long while, but she apparently functioned: got to class, turned in papers, took tests, worked glass, drank Starbucks. Clearly, even in a blackout, she was a girl with priorities.

The doctors said her migraines were to blame for these pesky little episodes. Her symptoms even had a name: the Alice in Wonderland syndrome. Of course the darned thing *would* be rare as hen's teeth, but they assured her that she would outgrow it: *don't you worry your pretty little head about it.*

She told none of the doctors the full story, how long she was gone, or what she saw. The meds she already took were bad enough. With her history—the jigsaw puzzle that was her skull, her headaches, that spiky purple mouth—they'd think her wires had gotten totally crossed and drug her so thoroughly she'd never find her way out of the fog.

She read scads about the syndrome and other, stranger cases of people *almost* like her: the lawyer who suddenly disappeared and turned up six months later; the schoolteacher picked up on the streets with no memory of who she was. Problem was, Emma didn't wander or end up as a bum. Well, so far as she could remember. But she definitely went places, that inner third eye channel-surfing through movies she never followed to a conclusion. Maybe that was lucky. What would happen if the tether on her life snapped? Would she die? Float around in limbo? Remain stuck forever on the other side of the looking glass?

Well, yeah. She thought she might.

11

NOW, THE DAY was gone, the storm had them, and she and Lily were lost, no question. After her little sit-me-down with Kramer, she'd snagged Lily, rented the van, and skedaddled. No one would even know to start looking for them for a week, easy.

"Try the radio," she said to Lily. "Maybe we can pick up a station." She didn't really believe they'd get anything; it was just a way to keep Lily from freaking out completely and give *her* some space to think about what to do next. She listened as Lily patiently feathered the knob. FM was nothing but fizzles and pops, which figured. AM wasn't much better, just static from which only a few broken words surfaced: *police . . . brutal . . . killings . . .*

"God, I can't turn on the radio without hearing about that poor little girl. Can you imagine what it was like to find all those bodies? In the basement of her own house?" Lily said.

Murders? Emma had no idea what Lily was talking about. "Anything?"

"No." Sighing, Lily threw up her hands. "Any other suggestions?"

"Try the weather bands," Emma said. "Different bands are assigned to different regions. Might give us an idea of where we are."

There was nothing between channels one to five, but as Lily clicked to channel six, the radio cleared its throat with a loud *pffssstt.* "There, right there, hold it," Emma said. She listened as the steel wool of a voice fuzzed: . . . *extremely dangerous storm. Once again, the National Weather Service has issued a severe weather advisory for the following counties: Bayfield, Ashland . . .*

Okay, that was good. Those counties were northwest, which meant—

Taylor, the radio voice said. *And peekaboo, I see you, Emma. I've got you . . .*

What? Emma gasped. Her heart turned over in her chest. *What?*

"Emma?" asked Lily.

Emma couldn't answer. The radio kept jabbering: *I've got you, so let's play, Emma. Come down and plaaay, Blood of My Blood, Breath of My Breath, come and plaaay . . .*

The hairs on her neck prickled. Oh my God, that almost sounded like . . . like *Kramer?* Yes, she would know that tight-ass Brit's voice anywhere. But how could that be? And he sounded close, too: not just a sputter seeping from the dashboard radio but coming from directly *behind* her.

Like the voice is whispering into my right ear. But that's nuts. There's no speaker in the ceiling or the headrest. She flicked a glance at her rearview. *You're losing it, kid; you've lost it, you're as crazy as they say you—*

Her heart slammed into her throat.

Because, in the mirror, there were . . .

LIZZIE
Save Dad

HER FATHER *TURNS*. . . .

"Ah!" Lizzie flinches, and then her left foot isn't on the rung anymore. Gasping, she lunges forward, wrapping her arms around the ladder. Her heart *thump-thump-thumps* so hard she feels it in her throat. She wants to wait, not try getting down until the shakes go away—but she mustn't, she mustn't, she mustn't!

Oh Dad, Dad, Daddy!

Somehow she gets down, half tripping, half slithering, and then she is pelting out of the barn and over the slippery gravel drive. The rock snatches her shoes, and she falls, ripping the knees from her jeans. The pain is strangely good, quick and bright as a firecracker and much better than the acid fear on her tongue. She claws her way up, shivering so hard her teeth go *clickity-clickity-clickity-click*. But now there is the kitchen and a square of warm yellow light and her mother, framed like an angel in a painting. Lizzie bursts through the kitchen door, the door going *bam* so the windowpanes complain and the glasses chatter in the cabinets. "Mom, *Mom!*"

"Lizzie?" Her mother's eyes probe Lizzie's face and then she gasps at whatever she's read. "Stay here, Lizzie, stay right here!" Quick as a whip, Mom is out the door and sprinting for the barn. She doesn't even bother with a coat.

A stiletto of terror pierces her heart, and Lizzie thinks, *Oh, Momma, Momma, be careful, be careful, be careful!* Face pressed to the glass, she waits and waits and waits, scrubbing away breath-fog so she can see the moment her parents emerge from the barn, the very second her mother rescues her father.

Hurry, Mom, hurry. The windowpane is going all wobbly, as if her house is starting to melt. Lizzie's eyes burn, the tears chasing each other down her cheeks so fast they *drip-drip-drip* from her jaw. "Hurry, Mom," Lizzie whispers, her voice thinning to a watery squeak. "Save Dad. Pull him out before the whisper-man slides all the way inside and fills him up. Hurry, hurry, hurry."

But Lizzie, you saw. This is not the monster-doll, but a voice that is calm and reasonable and centered in a clear patch of the storm in her mind. The voice is, in fact, a little like Mom's that last time Lizzie raised a fuss about lima beans on a Try-It Tuesday: *Just try one little no-thank-you bite.*

Now, Lizzie, this calm little voice says, *you saw, honey, how far he reached? And when he turned?*

"No, you're *wrong!* I'm not *listening* to you." Lizzie presses her hands over her ears. "La-la-la, I can't hear you. Mom is strong and smart, you'll see. Mom will beat him, Mom will—"

All of a sudden, across the yard, the barn door crashes open with so much force, the muted smash of wood and metal seeps through the window and into the kitchen. "Yes!" Lizzie's heart, full to bursting with fear and worry, seems to rocket out of her chest. She is dancing on tiptoe, bouncing up and down. "Yes, Mom, yes, you got him, you . . ."

But then Lizzie's voice dies on her tongue, because all she sees

EMMA

Eyes, and Nothing Else

ALL EMMA SAW in the rearview mirror were eyes, and nothing else. The eyes weren't hers, which were a deep, rich cobalt: an unearthly, glittering blue that almost didn't look real. Her right eye, with its tiny golden flaw in the iris, was especially strange. A birthmark, the doctors said, but get a few drinks into Jasper and he'd say it was her third eye, which made about as much sense as all his wild talk of *Nows* and Dark Passages.

These things in the mirror . . . she'd never seen anything like them. Two were black as stones and smooth as glass, with no whites, no pupils. The third eye was a mercury swirl floating in midair, suspended in a milky cloud. No face, at all, stared back.

No, Emma's mind gabbled. *No, no, no, no!* This was worse than a *blink.* This was like the barrier between her life and someone else's was breaking down, some freaky parallel universe leaking into hers. *I should do what the doctors want. I should take the pills.* Dimly, she was aware that the radio was still sputtering about a manhunt: . . . *so far authorities believe at least eight children may have met—*

She watched, paralyzed, as that milky cloud in the mirror gathered itself, folded—and then the silvered glass *moved.*

"Ah!" Emma flinched, her hands jerked the wheel, and then the van shimmied, first right and then left. Emma fought the impulse to slam on the brakes. The snow was deep and very wet, with a thick layer of compressed ice beneath. The van wallowed, the heavier rear trying to swing past and outrun the front. *Oh no no no, God, God, don't lose it!*

"Emma!" Lily screeched. "Look out, look out, *look out!*"

Emma's eyes snapped to the road just in time to see a flash, dead ahead: a sudden bright pop like the death of a light bulb after a blown fuse.

"Shit!" Emma jinked right, much too sharply. Already skidding on a knife's edge of control, the van's wheels locked, the rear slewed, and Emma felt the van begin to spin at the same moment she realized that this was not lightning dead ahead but a *light*: a single bald eye, bouncing and bright and very large—and *growing.*

"NO!" Lily screamed.

ERIC
Poof

1

SNOW BLASTED HIS helmet. The west wind screeched like a cat. Eric wrestled the Skandic Ski-Doo back on course, leaning and carving through deep snow as the sky flared with a flash of lightning. The storm's fingers pried and tugged at the loose folds of his jacket, slipping in through minute gaps in the zipper, chilling him to the bone. He couldn't feel his face and, worse, the shakes had him now: one part cold, three parts shock. Fear kept slithering up his throat, trying to suffocate him.

What have I done? What am I going to do now?

A crisp *click* in his helmet and then a voice sizzled through the tiny speaker: "Eric?"

"Yeah, Case." His voice came out strained, a little breathless. *Come on, get a grip. You'll just freak him out more than he is already.* "What's up?"

"Do you know where we are?"

"Sure, we're—" He stopped. They were on a road.

A road?

Whoa, wait, that wasn't right. When had they left the trail? His eyes flicked left, then right. The sled's sole headlight was good but not great, and it was like trying to look beyond the limits of a silver fishbowl. He made out a forested hill on the left: a black-on-white expanse that rose beyond the limits of his headlight, the snow-shrouded trees slipping away as he passed. The hill felt large, too high, a little unreal.

Mountains. There were *mountains*? Actual high peaks? In Wisconsin? Swallowed by dark and snow, he couldn't see to the very tops, but he just had this feeling that it was true. To his right was a black chasm of a valley, its drop-off outlined in the intermittent wink of green reflectors along a guardrail.

What was going on? His eyes fell to the Skandic's odometer, his brows knotting to a frown. The gauge said they'd already gone sixty miles. That far? In the storm, their speed hovered around fifteen. Do the math, and they'd been on their sleds for *four hours*.

That had to be wrong. They ought to be home by now. He tried to recall if they'd passed a single town. There were three on the way to the cabin, seen from the trails as glittering strings laced through the trees like Christmas decorations, but he didn't remember having seen any towns or lights at all, and now they were on a road curling around a mountain that shouldn't exist, not in Wisconsin. When had they left the snowmobile trail?

He said, "Case, how long have we been on this road?"

"I don't . . ." Whatever Casey said next was garbled by static.

"Say again, Case."

More static. "I . . . ember. It . . ."

Interference from the storm, he guessed, which made some sense. Their system was old and hardwired into each sled's battery, with headsets plugged into jacks. Eric did a quick peek and tapped the side of his helmet to signal Case to say again. A second later, there was more fuzz, and then Casey's voice stuttered through the hash: ". . . said I don't remember. I've been following you and . . . peekaboo, I see you. You can't run, you can't hide, and it's time, boy, time to come down and play, come and *plaaay*, come . . ."

Jesus. "Case?" Eric twisted to look back at his brother. "What are you—"

Whatever had his throat cinched down tight.

Because Big Earl was there, right behind him, slouched in the rumble seat.

Big Earl, who was . . .

2

"IS HE DEAD?" Casey's cheeks are streaked with tears; a slick of snot smears his upper lip. His jeans puddle around his ankles. The whippy wood switch has slashed right through Casey's flannel shirt, scoring the boy's skin with angry red wheals and splashes of blood. "He's dead, isn't he?"

"I don't know." But that's a lie. In the space of eight months, the Marines have turned him from a gawky eighteen-year-old kid into a very fine killing machine. So he knows. His right hand cramps, and he forces his fingers to relax. The empty bottle of Miller Lite—*Great Taste! Less Filling!*—thuds to the cabin's rough floorboards. Eric watches the bottle roll a half-turn, then another, and butt his father's left leg.

Big Earl doesn't flinch, and is beyond telling Eric just how badly he's going to hurt him. Instead, Eric's father stares up at the bare rafters, his muddy brown eyes at half-mast, his liverish lips sagging in a slack O. There is something off about Big Earl's head. That dent in his left temple, mainly. A thick red tongue leaks from the split in his father's scalp. More blood dribbles from his left ear to soak into a tired braid rug.

A blast of wind buffets the cabin. The windows rattle in their frames with a sound like bones. That breaks the spell. Blinking away from the body, Eric looks up. The afternoon is nearly gone, dark only a couple hours away.

They have to get out. They can't stay here. He has to think. He can't think. What's wrong with him? The world has gone a little soft around the edges, a bit out of focus. The cabin's hot, the air sullen with the stink of rancid beer and fresh blood. Maybe call the police? No, no, they'll throw him in jail, and he doesn't deserve that. This isn't his fault. Big Earl pulled his gun; Big Earl squeezed the trigger.

They have to get out.

Sidestepping the body and a litter of empties scattered around a puke-green Barcalounger, Eric goes to his brother. "Come on, Case," he says, gently. "Let's get you cleaned up."

"Oh-okay." Casey's flop of blond hair is damp with sweat. His eyes, an indefinite storm-cloud gray and now watery and red-rimmed, slide to Big Earl. Casey makes a strangled sound. "I'm going to be sick, I'm going to . . ."

They get to the kitchen sink just in time. Afterward, Eric turns on the cold water full blast. The cabin has a septic system and no garbage disposal. They'll probably stop up the pipes. Big Earl always yelled when they clogged the johns:

Who the hell used the whole roll on his ass?

"Hang on." Eric snatches an old dishrag from a towel bar, soaks the cloth in cold water, and wipes his brother's mouth. "Better?"

"Yeah." Tears leak over Casey's cheeks. "I'm sorry."

"Not your fault." Eric pitches the soiled rag into the garbage can under the sink. "It was an accident."

Actually, it was self-defense. The sight of Big Earl standing over Casey with that switch of whippy ash; the whickering sound that damn thing made as it cut the air . . . Something in Eric just broke. Eighteen years of pain and empty promises: God, enough was enough. Two long strides, and then he was wrestling away the switch, snapping it over his knee. Big Earl had turned with a drunken bellow—and that's when Eric saw the Glock in his father's fist, the bore larger than the world. Eric ducked as the gun roared. A bullet zinged by his ear, but then the bottle was in Eric's hand and he swung.

And like that, Eric's future went *poof!* Up in smoke.

3

HE WON'T LET Case come along, but tells his brother to find something to replace his ruined clothes—even one of Big Earl's shirts, if it comes down to it—and be ready to go just as soon as he gets back. *Where* they would go, how far they ought to run . . . Eric hopes that works itself out.

The drifts are high. Big Earl is 250 pounds of dead meat, so the ride out on the sled takes time. Four miles from the cabin, Eric squeezes the brake and cuts the engine. He sits a moment, listening to the howl of the wind, the rasp of ice crystals spinning over snow, the dull *whump* of heavy snow sliding off a drooping evergreen. A hard winter. A lot of animals starving, he bets.

He has to peel out of his gloves to untie Big Earl. His fingers shake and he can't make them work right, but he finally gets the job done. Then he stands a moment, staring down at the body slumped in the Skandic's rumble seat. Except for the blood and that dent, Big Earl looks almost normal. Well, for a drunk sleeping it off.

Parents are supposed to take care of their kids. A kid shouldn't have to join the Marines and risk ending up as roadkill or minus a couple body parts, all so he can scrape together enough money for college and not get the crap beaten out of him by his own dad.

Planting a booted foot, he gives the body a shove. For a long moment, nothing happens. Then his father's body shifts and slews sideways in a languid swoon, settling to the snow like a sack of dirty laundry.

"I'm not sorry you're dead," Eric says as he throttles up the Skandic. He pulls away without a backward glance. "I don't care."

Yet when he reaches the cabin and puts a hand to his face, he feels tears there: frozen to his cheeks, hard as diamonds.

4

NOW, BIG EARL was back. Big Earl was right there; had hitched a ride on this lost road to nowhere. His father's head was lopsided, caved in where the bottle had crushed bone and brain. His wifebeater was a bib of gore, and Big Earl's brains slopped in a grotesque tangle of moist pink worms.

"NO!" Eric shrieked. His hands clamped down hard on the Skandic's handlebars, sending him into a sharp turn he didn't want. The Skandic canted in a scream of snow, first right and then a grinding left as he carved deep, trying to compensate. Casey was yelling something, but Eric didn't answer, couldn't. Was that thing still on the sled? No, no, the weight wasn't right; the weight had *never* been right; it was never there to begin with. *Get control, get control!* He felt the sled hit something—a chunk of ice, maybe; a rock; it didn't matter. The Skandic bounced, and then the runners stuttered as the sled spun.

"Eric!" Casey's voice now, spiking through Eric's helmet speaker: "Eric, look out look out *look out!*"

A sudden wash of silver-blue swept around the curve fifty feet ahead, and then twin shafts of light pinned him like a bug. Above the roar of the storm, he heard the churn of the car's engine coming on way too fast.

Frantic, Eric jerked the sled hard left. The sled skated, skipped, drifted sideways, the runners skittering, and he felt the machine buck and jump between his thighs. At the same moment, he realized that the car—no, it was a van, big and blocky and still coming—was shrieking into a drunken skid, out of control, grinding right for him.

For one long, nightmarish second, the world slowed down. Eric saw the right rear fender swinging in a wide arc, heard Casey screaming in his helmet, felt the stutter of the Skandic's engine in his legs, even saw the white blur of a face—a girl— swimming behind frosted glass.

He was going to die. This was what Big Earl wanted;

this was his revenge. The van would kill Eric when it hit, or the Skandic would rocket off the road and smash into the guardrail. The snowmobile would stop, but he would not. He would keep going, catapulted like a stone into the black void of the valley, and he would fall a long, long way down to where Big Earl waited.

Only one chance.

He took it.

ERIC

A Gasp in Time

1

ERIC JUMPED—A WILD, desperate leap—hurtling left as the van slewed right. For a second, it felt as if he simply hung there, suspended in midair, like Keanu Reeves dodging a bullet. Through the spume of snow splattered on his faceplate, he saw the massive bulk of the van growing larger and larger, darker than the night. The red eye of the van's taillight, hot and angry, loomed and became the world, and he thought, *I'm dead.*

The van sliced by, shaving air less than six inches away: so close he felt the suck as it swept through space. He thudded face-first into the snow, the stiff plastic of his breakaway faceplate jamming hard enough to flip up and click free of its tabs. A bright white pain shot through as his teeth sank into his tongue, and then he was choking, his mouth filling with blood.

Above the roar in his ears came a high shriek of metal—and then, for just an instant, the world seemed to skip: a gasp in time and space, as if the storm had taken a deep breath and held it.

Someone started to scream.

Eric pushed up on trembling arms. His head was swimmy with pain. Panting, he hung on hands and knees like a dog, his brain swirling, coppery blood drizzling from his mouth. Then he dragged his head around, and his breath died somewhere deep.

Oh my God.

2

THE VAN HAD jumped the barrier. It should've kept going, tumbling over the lip of the road to crash into the valley below. Instead, the van hung on a ruin of crumpled metal, like the badly balanced plank of a kid's teeter-totter. The van's lights were still on, and the engine was running, but just barely, coughing and knocking in hard death rattles bad enough to make the chassis shudder. The air smelled of acrid smoke and hot oil.

In the van, someone was screaming in a long, continuous lash of sound. Eric saw the van bounce and begin to rock up and down, up and—

No, no! "Stop moving, don't move, *don't move!*" Ripping off his helmet, Eric swarmed to his feet and began to run, bawling over his shoulder, "Casey! Get your headlight on the van!"

As light flooded over the vehicle, the driver—the girl he'd seen spin by—leapt into being, framed in a rectangle of iced glass, frozen in an instant out of time. In the glare of the headlight, her hair was dark, and her skin, a cold bone-white. For a bizarre moment, Eric thought she looked dead already.

"Listen!" he bellowed over the wind. "The van's jumped the barrier. The front end's left the road. Do you understand?" When she nodded, he said, "Okay, unlock the doors, but don't do anything else. Don't move!"

There came the *thunk* of locks being disengaged, and then all the windows buzzed down, and he thought, okay, that was pretty smart. Lowering the windows would allow the wind to flow *through* the van instead of push against it. She'd already popped her shoulder harness, too, but wasn't moving otherwise. Very smart.

"Hi." Her voice was shaky, but she wasn't going to pieces on him either. Smart, cool in a crisis—and she seemed familiar somehow. "I'm sorry," she said. "Are you okay?"

"Yeah, I'm fine. What's your name?" His drill sergeant said if you called the wounded by name, they wouldn't die. Probably Marine voodoo, but it couldn't hurt.

"Emma."

"I'm Eric." He saw something flit through her face—surprise?—but then he was arming snow from his face and eyeing the back door on her side. The handle was within reach and tempting, but his angle was off, and he was afraid of unbalancing the van. "Who else is in there?"

"Just Lily." Emma opened her mouth to say something else, but then a sudden shock of wind grabbed the Dodge, and her eyes went wide.

"Easy." His heart was jammed into the back of his throat. "It'll be okay. Take it easy."

"I'm . . . I'm trying," she said in a breathless wheeze. The van creaked, and then it began to rock: up, then down, then up.

"Eric," Casey said from somewhere behind. His voice rose: "Eric, Eric, the van; the van's going to . . ."

There came a scream, short and sharp as a stiletto, and then the other girl was turning around, trying to scramble over the front seat: "What are you waiting for? Get us out, get us out, get us *out!*"

"Lily!" Emma shouted, and Eric could see from that tight grimace that it took all her self-control not to look around. "Don't move, Lily, don't—" There was a loud squall, and Lily screamed again as the van dipped and slipped another inch and then two.

Eric didn't even think about it. His right hand pistoned out to wrap around the handle on the driver's side back door. As the van tipped in a drunken sway, Eric backpedaled, but the vehicle outweighed him by nearly two tons, and his heels only scoured troughs from the snow.

"Eric!" Casey shouted. "Eric, let go, let *go!*"

The van lurched. There came a long grind of metal, a high screech as something tore, and then Eric was choking against the stink of gasoline blooming from the ruptured fuel line. The van's headlights swung down, the arc lengthening with a rending, gnashing clash of metal against metal.

Inside, Lily was shrieking: "Do something do something do something!"

All of a sudden, the back tipped, and Eric's feet left the ground. *No, no, no!* For one dizzying, horrifying instant, Eric saw himself hurtling over the barrier, his arms and legs pinwheeling through the dark all the way down. Then Eric's knees banged into the ruined guardrail; a jagged edge ripped through his jeans to slice meat, and he grunted with sudden pain.

"Emma, come on!" Stretching his left hand, Eric leaned so far forward that there was nothing but air beneath his chest, and *still* he couldn't bridge the gap. Emma's hand was maybe four inches away, but those inches might as well have been miles. "Give me your hand, Emma," he pleaded, desperately. "Give me your *hand!*"

She tried. He felt her fingers brush his, and he grabbed, fumbled to hang on—and for an instant, he had her, *he had her* . . .

Then the van tilted. The front fender chopped air . . . and Eric slipped. Blame the snow; blame that he was off-balance or the sudden list of the van. Whatever. He just couldn't hold on. His hand slid away and he thudded to the snow in a heap.

No, no, no, don't you screw this up! Rolling, he got his boots planted, swarmed back to his feet. *Save her, save her, save—*

3.

THE VAN BELLOWED, loud and long, in a tired, grinding groan. Held up by nothing more than twisted metal hooked under the rear axle, the overbalanced undercarriage hitched, skipping out another sudden, violent half-foot before the rear axle finally snapped.

The van slid away: there one moment and then not. It plunged into the dark, and Emma vanished.

But he heard Lily—all the way down.

RIMA

So Never Digging Around a Goodwill Ghost-Bin

1

IN THE HOUR before dark, the storm came on fast. They spotted just one other vehicle: a truck, judging by those taillights. The truck was perhaps an eighth of a mile ahead, visible only as an intermittent flicker of red, although every now and again, Rima spotted a faint drift of black. Truck was burning oil, probably.

"Man," Tony said, "I hope this guy knows where he's going. Otherwise, we are completely screwed."

"Why?" Rima asked.

"Well, we ought've gotten to Merit by now." Tony said Merit was a dinky little town, which had to be right, because she couldn't find it, not even in the road atlas. "But the valley's wrong. This part of Wisconsin's pretty flat. And those mountains we saw just before dark? They're not right either."

Oh, perfect. Rima didn't want to say, *You got us lost?* All the umpteen trillion counselors she and Anita had seen said that negative statements weren't helpful. The problem was the only positive things Rima could think of were along the lines of, *Wow, Anita, you only sucked down three pipes instead of four? You go, girl!* So she said, "Have we passed any place you recognize?"

"No," Tony said, after a long moment. "Can't say we have."

So they *were* lost. The thought made her hug herself tighter—and oh boy, *big* mistake. A jag of bright, splintery pain radiated to her right jaw, and then her cheek exploded: *ker-POW!* Grimacing, Rima trapped the moan behind her teeth, thought to the kid's whisper: *Calm down, honey, it'll be okay.* In a few seconds, the pain's grip loosened and she could breathe again.

Idiot. The parka was her fault, a Goodwill refugee with duct tape slapped here and there to mend the holes. The parka's previous owner had been a little girl, barely twelve, named Taylor. You wouldn't think that would be a problem, except Taylor's final moments were a jumble of glassy pain and a single clear thought: *Daddy, don't hurt me; I'll be good, I promise!* The asshole killed her anyway, pitching the kid over a fourth-floor balcony to break on the sidewalk like a raw egg.

To be honest, Rima had nearly tossed the parka back with the other whispers: drug addicts, an old lady murdered by her son, a guy with high blood pressure whose last, very bad decision was to mow the grass on a hundred-degree day. Leaving behind poor little Taylor felt wrong, though; no one but a screwed-up parent could so completely mess with your head. So she took the poor kid.

Swear to God, though, when she grew up and actually had some money? Rima was *so* never digging around a Goodwill ghost-bin. Like, *ever*.

2

FATHER PRESTON, THE headmaster at All Souls, called it a gift. Her drug-fogged mother thought she was possessed. Rima just called them *whispers*, the bloodstains of the dead. Once Rima touched something for long enough—soothing, drawing—the whispers eventually dissipated, like morning mist under a hot sun. Whispers such as Taylor's, whose death had been violent, took longest and were acid in her veins.

Of course, Rima was to blame for her mother's drug habit because, oh, the *strain* of living with a possessed kid. There had been spiritualists, psychics, and so much incense you needed a gas mask. A hatchet-faced voodoo priestess was the worst, graduating from a raw egg squirreled under Rima's bed to catch the departing demon—Rima's room stank like an old fart for a week—to a noxious stew of ammonia, vinegar, and olive oil Rima was supposed to toss back with a smile. Uh . . . *wrong.* That voodoo chick was always trying to *spill* Rima's blood, too. The crazy bitch never said *cut;* she always said *spill,* like Rima was this big glass and whoopsie-daisy, look at that mess. Not a lot of blood, Anita explained: *Just a half-cup to feed the spirits.*

Oh, well, when you put it like *that* . . . If Anita wasn't so dead serious loopy, the whole thing might've been funny. Eventually, the voodoo also went bye-bye, either because Anita got tired of Rima being just so *ungrateful,* or the priestess thought she was a lost cause. Whatever.

The damage was done, though. Last week, dead of night, her mother got her supplier to pick the lock of Rima's bedroom. Before Rima knew what was happening, the supplier had pinned her wrists while Anita pressed a very long, wickedly sharp boning knife to Rima's throat. No spilling, not for Anita, nosirreebob: she was going all the way.

The only reason Rima survived was the supplier got cold feet and booked. After another tense half hour, Anita drifted off from all that meth she'd smoked to work up the nerve and then all the downers she popped to take the edge off. It took Rima what felt like a century to ease out from under, and even then the knife won, the keen edge scoring her flesh with a hot spider's bite.

That was just too darned close. Stick around, and one morning she'd wake up shish kebab. Forget Child Protective Services; they'd only shuffle her from foster home to foster home for the next two years until she turned eighteen. Then it was a handshake and *YOYO, baby.*

Why wait?

3

CALIFORNIA OR CANADA, she figured. California had the movies; maybe she could learn makeup or something. Canada . . . well, everyone in Minnesota who wanted out went to Canada, but only because it was closer than Mexico.

Her thumb got her to Grand Rapids. After a night shivering in the thin light of the visitor's center doorway, she was contemplating the merits of a bus to Milwaukee when Tony's vintage Camry, a drafty four-door hatchback from the early Pleistocene, rattled into the lot, trailing a single crow that bobbed along like a black balloon on an invisible string.

Okay, crows were bad. But there was only the one. So

maybe this wouldn't be so much of a problem. She decided to chance it.

They got to talking. He was a preacher's kid, not a born-again, and a nice guy. Same age, same grade, and from his stories, the public high school bullshit factor sounded about the same as Catholic school's, minus the uniforms and grim-faced nuns, some of whom could definitely use a shave.

When he offered a lift, she said yes, despite the crow. Settling into the front passenger seat, she cringed as the whisper sighed and cupped her body.

"You okay?" Tony asked. "I know the seat's a little shot, but I got the car for a song."

Yeah, no shit. No one would want a car whose last passenger had, literally, lost her head when the impact catapulted her right out that busted windshield like a cannonball.

"I'm fine," she said, and this was true. The woman had been dead-drunk when she died. A fuzzy moment of awareness, a spike of fear, and then *blam*! No white light, no meet-up with old friends and family, no floating around for final good-byes or if-I-stays. Just *hello, darkness, my old friend*, which meant the dead woman's whisper was easily soothed. After an hour, Rima couldn't finish a sentence without punctuating with a yawn. Dropping her seat, she blacked out, only coming to when

4

THERE'S A THUNK of a lock and a squeal of hinges as Tony drops into the driver's seat, wreathed in the aroma of fried eggs, salty grease, and coffee.

"Here." He thrusts a large brown paper sack into her hands. "I didn't know if you liked ham or sausage, so I got one of each. There's coffee, too, and some sugar and milk. Or they've got that artificial stuff, in case you like that, or orange juice."

"No, this is great. Thanks." The paper sack warms her hands, and the aroma is so good her stomach moans. She hasn't eaten in almost two days. "You didn't have to do this."

"I know. It's just I would've felt guilty eating in front of you."

He doesn't lie well. He could easily have wolfed something inside and she'd never have known. "I don't have a lot of money," she says, which is the truth. Her nest egg's a whopping $81.27, all that was left after her mother found her stash. Again. All that coke, it's a miracle Anita still has a *nose*, much less a sense of smell. Dirty socks Anita'll let go until they sprout hair and teeth and start moving up the evolutionary ladder, but squirrel away a wad of cash? Then the woman morphs into a frigging bloodhound.

A blush stains Tony's jaw. "Hey, don't worry about that. You're doing me the favor. Otherwise, I'd have nothing to do but listen to the radio, and all they talk about are those murders. Can you imagine that poor kid finding—"

"How about we eat inside?" The last thing she wants to dwell on is death, especially murder. "It'll be warmer and we won't mess up your car."

"Too late," Tony says, throwing a rueful glance. The Camry's backseat is strewn with clothing, crumpled fast-food bags, three shoeboxes of cassettes—mostly Lloyd Webber musicals (if Rima hears "I Dreamed a Dream" one more time, she might be forced to hurt someone), a wheezy old cassette recorder, vintage comics like *Tales from the Crypt* and *Vault of Horror*, and a couple Lovecrafts with nightmare covers of gruesome monsters boiling with tentacles.

She laughs. "How about we don't mess it up more than it is already? Those comic books must've cost a fortune."

"Um, no, I paid regular price, but it'd be nicer inside, yeah." Tony's grin is hesitant, but when it comes, his whole face lights up. With his mop of brown curls and light blue eyes, he's really pretty handsome.

"Great," she says, and reaches for the door handle.

"Hang on." He depresses the master lock on his door. "The power locks are all screwed up so you can only open them from my side. I keep meaning to get them fixed."

Crossing the lot, she spots the birds: five very large, glossy black crows ranged round a rust-red truck slotted beneath a gnarly, naked maple. Four crows brood on a trio of low-hanging branches, their inky talons clamped tight. A fifth teeters above the grinning grill like a bizarre ornament.

She knows, instantly. Death—very recent, very strong—has touched that truck. Like the crow floating above Tony's Camry, the birds are a dead giveaway, no pun intended. The more there are, the closer they come to a house or car or place, the more violent the death. One bird, she can handle. Times when whole flocks blanket the roof at the Goodwill, she takes a pass. And forget cemeteries.

"You okay?" Tony tosses a look at the truck. "What?"

"Nothing." He doesn't see the crows. No one normal ever does. Still, as she hurries inside the rest stop, she holds her breath. She doesn't actually believe that old saw about breathing in dead spirits, but there's always a first time for everything and she has enough problems.

Just as she's about to turn into the ladies' room, a hard-faced kid in baggy, olive-green fatigues cuts a sharp dogleg. "Hey," she says, pulling up short. "Watch it."

"Say what?" He whirls, incredibly fast, his fists coming up. The kid's pupils are huge, black holes rimmed with a sliver of sky blue. Then he spazzes, blinking away from whatever horror show he's watching. "Oh. Hey," he says. "I'm sorry. I thought you were—"

"Hey, Bode!" Another kid, also in olive drab, stands at a table in the fast-food joint. Even at this distance, she spots the angry sore pitting the left corner of his mouth, and the kid's so meth-head jittery he could scramble a couple eggs.

"Hey, Chad," Bode says. And then to Rima: "I got to go." Before she can shrink back, he puts a hand on her arm. "You sure you're okay?"

His touch is volcanic, atomic, so hot she can feel the death cooking into her flesh. "Oh, yeah," she says, faintly. "I'm good."

As soon as he lets her go, she bolts into the bathroom, making it to a stall just in time. Later, as the taste of vomit sours her mouth, she hangs over the bowl—lucky for her, no one died on that seat—and thinks about Bode. The guy's touch was mercifully brief and fragmentary, but she'd seen enough. Ten to one, he's that truck with the death-crows. The real question is who, exactly, is dead?

Because when Bode touched her, he *changed*. Just for an instant, but enough so she saw Bode's head—

5

"OH, HECK," SAID Tony.

Rima blinked back to the here and now. "What?"

"The truck's gone," Tony returned grimly.

"Maybe there's a turnoff." Something sparkled then, and she squinted through the snow frothing the windshield. Way off to the right, there was a sharp glint—glass?—and something very black and formless floating over the snow. "Is that . . . ?" She almost said *smoke*, but the word died halfway to her teeth.

Not smoke.

Crows.

And, in a crush of splintered trees, an overturned van.

PART TWO

THE
VALLEY

LIZZIE
Whisper-Man Black

ONLY MOM POPS out of the barn, and she is screaming: "Get in the car, get in the car, just get in the car!" Mom hauls Lizzie down the porch steps, practically throws Lizzie into the front seat. She thrusts the memory quilt into Lizzie's lap: "Hang on to that; don't let go, no matter what!" Mom's hand shakes so bad the ignition key stutters against metal, and she's sobbing: "Oh please, oh please, oh please, come on, come on, come on goddamnit, come on!" She lets out a little cry as the key socks into place and the engine roars.

Then they are moving, moving, moving, going very fast, racing after their headlights, her mother hammering the accelerator. The force slams Lizzie back against the seat; her teeth come together—*ka-chunk*—and her tongue screams as the taste of dirty pennies floods her mouth. But Lizzie is too scared to cry; she is absolutely silent, quiet as a mouse, as the car fishtails, kicking up gravel rooster tails.

We're never coming back. She clutches her memory quilt in both hands. The glass might be magic, and those stitches as strong as her mother, but Lizzie's life is unraveling. *I'll never see my house again. I'll never find Marmalade.*

She cranes over her shoulder. Peering through the rear window is like seeing a movie through the wrong end of a telescope. She watches as their farmhouse, Wisconsin-sturdy and built to last until the end of time, recedes. To the left and across the drive, the big prairie barn hulks in the gloom, and that is when her sharp eyes pick out the pulse of a weird orange glow that is very, very wrong.

"Mom!" she says, urgently. "Mom, the barn's on fire!"

"I know," her mother says. "I set it."

"Mom!" A blast of horror rips through her body. "We've got to go back! We've got to get Marmalade! We've got to find Daddy; we have to *save* him!"

"We can't save your dad."

"But Mom!" Lizzie's frantic. Why doesn't her mother understand? "Daddy *needs* us!"

"No, he needs *it*, Lizzie. He hangs on, takes it inside, and the horrible, awful things it asks in return . . ." Her mother's voice falters, then firms. "Lizzie, why do you think we came here after London? Why do you think we live so far away from other people?"

So no one gets hurt. She thinks of the terrible things in her father's books: squiggle-monsters and spider-things growing in people's chests and crawly things in tunnels and parents eating their kids. What Mom says is true.

Because when her father turned from that mirror . . . his face was gone. No eyes, no nose, no mouth. Nothing but a shuddering, churning blank.

Then this thing with no face raised her dad's hands like a

policeman stopping traffic. The cuts were gone. Her father's palms were smooth—until the skin split and lids peeled back and there were eyes, one on each palm. They were not her father's eyes, because they were not hers. Like father, like daughter, their eyes are identical: a deep indigo with a tiny fleck of gold on one iris. Lizzie's birthmark floats in her right eye and is the mirror image to her father's on his left.

But the eyes that stared from her father's palms were whisper-man black. The whisper-man was in there, and her dad was the glove, just as Mom said he'd been, years back and before Lizzie, in the other London.

But what if I can make the whisper-man want me *instead?* This is a new thought, and so stunning Lizzie's chest empties of air. *If I can get it to leave Dad and slip into me—*

There is a sudden, massive flash. The light is so bright the inside of the car fires the color of hot gold. A split second later, Lizzie hears the rolling thunder of an explosion.

"Oh God," Mom says. In that molten glow, Lizzie sees the shine of her mother's tears. "Oh God, forgive me."

"No, Momma, no!" She could've *fixed* it; she could've made it *better.* "Why did you do that?"

"You don't understand." He mother drags a hand across her eyes like a weary child. "It was the only thing left."

"No, it wasn't! I could've fixed things, I could've *helped*—"

From the backseat comes a flat, mechanical beep. Her mother gasps. The sound is so jarring and out of place it seems to come from the deep, dark valley of a dream.

"It's your phone," Lizzie says.

"I know that," Mom says.

Beep.

"Should I answer?" Lizzie asks.

Beep.

"No," her mother says.

"But what if . . ." Like a birthday wish, Lizzie's afraid to say it out loud. "Mom, what if it's Dad?"

Beep.

"It might be his voice, but it wouldn't be him, Lizzie. Your father's gone."

Beep.

"But what *if*—"

"I said no!" her mother snapped. "Sit down and—"

No, Lizzie thinks, furiously. Against her palms, she feels the sudden tingling surge as the Sign of Sure, sewn on her memory quilt, feeds on her thoughts: all that energy stored up in her brain that wants to whisk her through the Dark Passages, that must find a way out. *No, Momma's wrong; I can fix this. I'll make it want me. I'll build a forever-Now and swoosh the whisper-man there with the Sign of Sure.*

She unbuckles her belt.

"What are you doing?" her mother raps. "Sit down, young lady."

"I don't have to listen to *you*," Lizzie spits, and then she is scrambling up, twisting around in her seat, reaching for her mother's purse. Through the rear window, she can see the forest's black walls squeezing the road, as if her past is a book whose covers are slowly, inexorably closing. Then, in the sky, she sees something else, and for a second, her heart forgets how to beat.

"M-Mom?" The word comes out in a rusty whisper. Her throat clenches as tight as a fist. "M-Mom, the s-sky . . . i-it's . . ."

"Oh no." Her mother's eyes flick to the rearview, and then she cups a hand to her mouth as if she might be sick. "Oh my God, what have I done?"

"Mom?" Lizzie can't look away. "Mom, what *is* that?"

"The Peculiars . . . all that stored energy, I'd hoped it would be enough to take out the Mirror, but I didn't stop to think that your father had already opened the gateway; he'd *bound* that thing and . . . My God, I've only given it more *fuel*." Mom sounds as broken as the Peculiars and the Mirror. "What did I *do*?"

Behind them, the sky is moving. High above the trees, something steams across the night: a boiling wall of white so dense that the stars are winking out, one by one.

Something has bled into this world, all right. Something is storming after them. Something is running them down.

Not an aurora.

Not clouds.

What is coming for them is the fog.

EMMA

Not the Way I'm Made

"EMMA." PAUSE. "EMMA."

A voice, very distant, as tinny as a radio. For a horrible second, her ears heard that weird hiss—*peekaboo, I see you*—and she thought, *Kramer?*

"Emma?"

She didn't answer. Wouldn't. Couldn't. God, she was freezing. She hurt. The cold was intense, the snow burning across her skin like a blowtorch. When she pulled in a breath, she heard a jerky little cry jump out of her mouth as something with claws grabbed her ribs and ripped her chest.

"Emma?" The voice was closer now, on her right, and it wasn't the radio or Kramer at all. Why would she even think that? "Emma, come on, wake up."

A . . . a boy? Where? Emma tried moving her head. There was a liquid sound, and then a thick, choking chemical funk.

"Emma, can you hear me?"

Her neck screamed. So did her back. Her forehead

throbbed, a lancet of pain stabbing right between her eyes, not only from the *blink* but . . .

We crashed. I'm still in the van, but I saw that little girl again, too, and someone or something was . . . chasing her? But what? She couldn't remember. The threads of the vision were fraying, unraveling. Didn't matter. She dragged a hand to her aching forehead. She felt the familiar nubbins and that bigger circle of her skull plate just beneath her skin, but also something wet and sticky that was not gasoline.

Blood. Cut. How deep? Her fingers slid over torn flesh but not metal. She must've hit pretty hard. Her head was swimmy and she was already dizzy from gas fumes. Her stomach did a long, slow roll. *No, please, I don't want to puke.*

"Emma, can you hear me?"

"Yeah," she breathed. She tried prying her lids open. They felt sewn shut, and she had to work to make her muscles obey. Then the darkness peeled away, and she winced against a stab of silver-blue light. "Bright."

"Sorry." The featureless blot of the boy's head and shoulders moved between her and the snowmobile's headlight. "Better?"

"Uh," she said, and swallowed, waiting for her stomach to slither back down where it belonged. It was only then that she realized he was on his hands and knees, peering through a window. The van had flipped. She was lying on the roof. Or was it the ceiling? She couldn't think. What was the last thing she remembered from *this* world? The sensation of whizzing through space, a free fall, and then the *bang* as the van plowed into something nose-first. Her back had slammed the windshield, and she'd rebounded, flying past the steering wheel, her shoulder clipping the driver's side headrest as she shot for the rear window, as Lily screamed and *screamed*.

"Lily?" Her voice came out in a weak little wheeze. "Lil?"

"Hey." The boy squirmed in, sloshing through gasoline until his face was right up to hers: so close she could feel his warm breath on her cheek. "Hey, look at me, stay with me. Here," he said, lacing his fingers around her left hand. "Feel that? Remember me? Eric?"

"Yes, I . . . I do. I remember." It took a lot of work and concentration to swallow. "But where's Lil?"

"We need to get her out of there." Another boy, a voice she didn't recognize. "That gas isn't stopping. I've never seen so much gasoline. How much you think this thing *holds*?"

"Yeah, yeah, I know." Eric tossed the words over his shoulder, while his eyes never left hers. "You guys got a blanket or maybe a first aid kit? She's bleeding pretty bad."

"First aid kit in the trunk," the boy said again. "Hang on."

A girl's voice: "I'll come with you." The boy and girl moved off, their voices dissipating like smoke.

"You're going to be okay." Eric's grip on her hand tightened. "I've got you now, Emma. You just keep looking at me. Don't worry about anything else, all right? Can you tell me what hurts?"

Everything? "My head. Chest. Hurts to breathe. I think I hit the steering wheel."

"Might be nothing more than a bruise. What about your neck?"

"Eric." She swallowed back against another tidal surge of nausea. "Where's Lily?" When he hesitated, she thought, *Oh God.* "Lily . . . she . . . she's dead, isn't she? I got her killed, didn't I? Where is she? Is she"—ignoring the knifing pain in her neck and shoulders, Emma tried to turn her head—"was she thrown or is she still . . ."

"Emma, does it really matter? Seeing won't change anything."

No. She used her eyes the way she might her fingers, tracing the shape of his nose, that line of jaw, tangling in hair that was wavy, black, and thick. Even in the gloom, she could see the deep blue of his eyes. *You don't understand, Eric. Seeing is believing. Seeing changes everything.* Aloud, she said, "Thank you for not leaving us."

"Not the way I'm made." He cupped her cheek. "Come on," he said, gently. "Let's get you out of here."

CASEY
Dead Man's Shirt

"OH BOY." TONY was kneeling in deep snow by the Camry's rear tire. "This is not good."

"No shit, Sherlock," said Casey, smearing ice from his cheeks. He grimaced as snowmelt trickled down his neck to soak the collar of Big Earl's shirt. Casey hadn't wanted the thing, but his was shredded, cut to ribbons by Big Earl's switch, and blood-soaked to boot. At first, shrugging into Big Earl's oversize flannel had been like slipping on the slack, discarded husk of a gigantic python, and just about as pleasant. The thing was a little better now, but that wasn't saying much, all things considered. The shirt felt . . . *squirmy.* Not alive, exactly, but every now and again, he thought he could feel it actually moving in tiny creeps, as if trying to worm into and wrap itself around the muscles and bones of his much smaller, slighter frame. Which, of course, was crazy; the thing was just a dead man's shirt. Still . . . he could feel his skin flinch and cringe, withdrawing the way cats slithered low to the ground when they just didn't want to be touched. He shrugged, wincing as old flannel raked raw flesh and clotted blood. "Man, that tire's flatter than a pancake."

"Wh-what happened?" said Rima, doing the freezing person two-step. "I thought you were being c-careful."

"I was, but . . ." Tony sighed, his breath huffing in white steam the wind grabbed and tore apart. "If I had to guess, I'd say one of these downed spruces. Branches are sharp as spears. Probably drove over one buried under the snow."

"Do you have a spare?" asked Emma, shivering. Gasoline didn't freeze, and she and Eric were drenched, the stink hanging over them in a noxious cloud. Tony had dredged up a space blanket for her, but it didn't seem to be doing much—not that this broke Casey's heart or anything. "Or maybe a pump you could run off the battery?"

"The car's buried," Casey said, impatiently. Idiot. She looked like hell, too. In the flashlights, the shock-hollows beneath her eyes were purple smudges. Wouldn't let Eric touch the gash on her forehead, but had bandaged it herself. Not such a hot job either. She also seemed kind of out of it: like she zoned every so often.

She's probably high. Big Earl's voice misted over his mind. *Or drunk. Probably why she crashed.*

Now, he'd had Big Earl in his head about as many times as he'd slid into the old fart's clothes. Like *never.* The fact that he did hear Big Earl now should've freaked him out, but Casey was surprised to find that he was more . . . interested.

"Look," Casey said to Emma, "you can change the tire five times, if that'll make you happy. Even if you manage to get the tire to reinflate, take a look around. Snow's way too deep. There's no way this car's going anywhere."

"Wow," Rima said. "N-n-negative often?"

"*No.*" He wanted to smack her, and this was also a new impulse. Big Earl had been the one to hit first and never ask questions later. "I'm just saying."

"But if he's got a spare or a pump, it's worth a try," Eric said. "We can't be any worse off than we are now."

Oh, wanna bet? Casey wasn't sure if that was his voice or his dad's—not that it mattered, because he agreed. But he kept his mouth shut. None of these people had a clue, but he knew: *This valley is wrong. It doesn't belong.* The valley was a big black mouth and that road was its throat, and they were at the bottom, in the dark and the cold and the snow that just kept coming, like dirt filling a grave.

Which they could use, come to think of it. Casey's eyes slid to the van. Through the window, he could make out a fur-trimmed parka that had once been white but was now oozy with blood and lumpy-bumpy from the body underneath.

"Well . . ." Tony looked uncomfortable. "I think we're already worse off. I don't have a pump, and my spare's leaning against the wall of our garage. I did lawns this summer, so I took it out to make room for the mower. Just never got around to putting it back."

"So what do we do?" Emma asked.

"We get you someplace warm," Eric said.

"You know, we're all kind of cold," Casey said. He saw the sharp look Rima threw his way. *Yeah, yeah, bite me.*

"Ease up, Case," Eric said.

"Ease up?" It figured. Eric got to play G.I. Joe; poor widdle Emma was saved; and still, here they were, oh-so-screwed.

"In case you haven't noticed, no one's going anywhere warm. We're *stuck*."

"Yes, but we still have the sleds."

"Which won't fit everybody."

"Case, I know," Eric said, "but getting upset won't—"

"You know, I'll feel whatever I want." Casey's fists bunched. He took a step toward his brother and enjoyed the surprise in Eric's eyes. "Quit bossing me around."

"Casey," Emma said. "He didn't mean anything by it."

"Am I talking to you?" Casey rounded. "Do you see me talking to you?"

"*Casey,*" Eric said, shocked. "What's gotten into you?"

"Guys," Rima said. "*Stop.*"

"Yeah, yeah, whoa," Tony said, putting his hands up. "Everyone, calm down. This isn't getting us anywhere."

"Well, that's good, because we're not *going* anywhere," Casey spat.

"But Eric's right. You've got sleds," Tony said. "Can't we use them?"

"Are you deaf? I just said: there's not *room* for everyone. My sled is a one-man. It doesn't have enough power to make it back up that grade; it's too steep. I'd sink, or just get stuck, or roll. Eric's got the only two-seater, and it hasn't got enough zip to get back up either. We're both stuck down here with you." Casey leveled a look at Eric. "Right?"

Eric's eyes narrowed as if Casey was some bug he'd never seen before. "Yes," Eric said after a long pause. His gaze slid away, but not before Casey registered the hurt. "He's right."

For a split second, Casey felt a sharp prick of shame. What

was wrong with him? This was *Eric.* His brother had nearly gotten killed saving him.

Bull, Big Earl whispered. *He was saving himself. You aren't doing anything you shouldn't have done a long time ago. He's afraid you'll get strong, stronger than him. Strong as me.*

Right. Yeah. Eric *should* be afraid. Served him right for boogying off to boot camp and leaving Casey with Big Earl in the first place.

"Even if by some miracle we did manage to load everyone on the sleds and get back up? I don't know this road. I've never seen this valley, to tell you the truth. I have no idea where we are in relationship to anything, and the way the snow is coming down"—planting his hands on his hips, Eric gave the snow an angry scuff—"visibility would be pretty bad. We'd have to go slow, and I think . . ." He looked back up at them. "I think we'd probably run out of gas. I don't have a tent or shelter in the Ski-Doo."

"So you're saying we'd freeze to death," Emma said.

"I'm saying I really don't want to find out."

"So then what?" Rima clamped her hands under her armpits. "Stay in the c-c-car? Won't we just freeze to d-d-death here?"

For the first time, Casey noticed how small she was, like a doll. The snow was up past her knees, and the wind grabbed her wild, shoulder-length curls. That duct-taped parka was so ratty, Casey bet you could see daylight through it. If *he* was cold, that girl must be freezing. She seemed, actually, kind of nice, and pretty, too, with intense, violet eyes. He slid a gloved hand into his parka and felt the bunched wool of a spare watch cap. Didn't people lose most of their heat through their heads? Maybe he ought to give her his—

Not your problem, boy. Big Earl's voice seemed to steam like breath, wreathing Casey in the fruity reek of old beer. *Every man for himself.*

Casey hesitated. He actually thought back to his father, *Yeah, but she's cold.*

So what? Casey heard the sneer in Big Earl's voice. *You look out for numero uno, boy. None of this do-gooder crap Eric's always spouting out his piehole. You're better than that.*

Right. Casey crushed the cap back into his pocket. Not his problem.

"I'm saying you guys have a better chance of riding out the storm in the car than with everyone piled onto the sleds." Eric nodded at the faint dimple of the road snaking away from the car. "But a sled could still make it fine down there. This road has to go somewhere."

"Well, we were following a truck," Tony said. "That's how we ended up down here to begin with. We lost him about a quarter of a mile back. I'll bet there's a turnoff or something you could find with the sled."

"Worth checking out." Eric shrugged. "Okay, I'll go."

"I'll come with you," Tony said. "I got some flares we can set up, and I think my dad stowed a couple walkie-talkies in the trunk that he uses when he goes hunting. I don't know the range, but they're worth taking along. That way, we can find the car again *and* maybe keep in touch."

"No way," Casey said. "If Eric's going, then I am out of here, too—and on my own sled, thanks."

"But Casey, if you take your sled, that l-leaves us with

n-nothing." Rima's face was going so white with cold, her eyes stared like sockets. "What if s-something happens to you g-guys?"

"Yeah," Casey snapped. "So . . . what, *I* should freeze my ass off to keep *you* company?"

"Casey!" Eric snatched at his arm. "Calm down. Stop it!"

"What?" Batting his brother's hand away, Casey squared off and set his feet. "You want to fight, Eric, huh? Well, bring it on, bro; let's go."

"Guys, please, this isn't helping. Don't argue," Emma said.

Casey rounded on her. "You know, Emma, just shut the hell up. If you hadn't almost gotten us killed, we wouldn't be stuck down here in the first—"

"*Casey!*" Eric rapped, though Casey noticed that his brother was careful not to touch him again. "What is *wrong* with you? Leave it! What's done is done."

Casey bristled. "Yeah, what's done is done, all right. *You* did a real nice job with Da—" He bit down on the rest.

No one said anything for a long moment. The wind whistled and fluted through warped metal. Finally, Eric said, much more quietly, "Someone has to check this out, Case. I can't force you to stay, but I think you should, just in case."

"In case what? In case things get *worse*?"

"In case I don't make it. You're my brother. I don't want you to get hurt, and right now, it'll be risky sledding. But come morning, when the storm dies, you might find a better way out, and for that, you'll need a sled."

"*If* it dies," Casey said. "You ever think that it might not? No, of course you didn't. So, instead of us getting somewhere safe, now we're down here . . . Oh, but I forgot." He did a mock head-slap. "What's done is done."

No one took the bait on that. After another moment, Tony said, "Eric, man, you really shouldn't be alone. What happens if you get stuck? A sled that big, I'll bet it takes more than one person to get it out of a drift."

"Tony's right," Emma said. "You've got a two-seater. Leave the other sled, but I'll come with you."

"No way," Eric said. "You're hurt."

"All the m-more reason she should g-go with you," Rima said. She threw a defiant look at Casey, as if daring him to disagree. "Like you s-said, she needs to get someplace w-warm. L-last time I ch-checked, that's not h-here. If you f-find a place, she c-can stay while you c-come back for us."

Hands still on hips, Eric looked from Rima to Emma, then sighed. "All right. I don't have any other warmer clothes for you, Emma, but there's a spare helmet in the Skandic, so you won't totally freeze."

"I'll be okay," Emma said. "You'll be my windbreak."

Oh, ha-ha. An itch of annoyance dug at Casey's neck as he saw Eric crack a grin. *I see what you're doing, bitch, but he's* my *brother. I knew him first. He belongs to me.* When Eric turned to him, that stupid shit-eating grin slipped, which was just fine with him.

"Case?" Eric said. "Please, I'm asking you to stay."

"Fine," he said. "Be a hero. Be a Boy Scout. It's what you've always wanted, right? Here's your big chance to impress us."

"Jesus," Tony said. "You just don't quit."

"Case," Eric said, patiently, "it's not *that*—"

"You know," he said, "I don't care, Eric. Whatever. You and Emma, I hope you're really happy together."

The others ignored him, which was par for the course, the idiots. But come morning, if Eric wasn't back? He was gone and *good riddance to bad rubbish*, as Big Earl would've said. Strange, how comfortable all those ideas felt now. For that matter, he couldn't tell if that was his voice in his head anymore or Big Earl's.

And stranger still: only an hour before, Big Earl's shirt had been way too big. A Boy Scout troop could have pitched it, gathered round, and sung "Kumbaya." But now?

Now, the damn thing actually fit Casey like a second skin.

LIZZIE
I Want to Tell You a Story

"LIZZIE, IT'S LIVED in your dad's skin. It may have your father's voice, but it won't *be* him, don't you understand?" Mom gulps back a sob as the cell in Lizzie's hand chirps again. "Please, honey, don't answer. I know you want to, but you can't save him. Your father is gone. Now sit down, turn around, and put on your seat belt."

"No," she says. "I won't." Parents don't have all the answers, and Mom has already failed, hasn't she? Heart thumping, she hangs over the front seat to stare out the car's rear window. Behind them, the fog is a greedy mouth swallowing up this reality, gaining fast. Mom just said that all the energy from the Peculiars is there, all tangled up with her dad and the whisper-man—and Mom should know: energy's never gone. So her dad isn't either. The whisper-man only *thinks* he's got her dad.

But I'll fix you. Just you wait and see. She punches up the cell. "Daddy? Daddy, are you there?"

"No, Lizzie." Sparing her a sidelong glance, her mother

makes a grab, but Lizzie cringes away and out of reach. "Please, hang *up*."

Lizzie doesn't answer. The glass on Lizzie's memory quilt ticks and rattles, and she can feel it starting to heat. Gripping a tongue of fabric in her right hand, she uses her index finger to trace a special Lizzie-symbol: two sweeping arcs, piled like twin smiles, stabbed through with a *zagdorn*, capped with a bristle of four horns.

"Lizzie." Mom risks a peek, but without her panops, Lizzie knows that her mother can't see these symbols and wouldn't know what they were even if she could. "What are you doing?"

"Dad?" Lizzie grips the cell in her left hand, tight. The *barndil* hovers in midair. *Make a* luxl *next; yes, that's the right sign.* "Dad, are you there? You have to talk to me. I *want* you to talk to me."

Are you sure? The reply is immediate, as if the voice has been standing at the door, waiting for Lizzie to throw open the lock and invite it in. *This is what you want?*

"Yes," Lizzie says. "I'm sure. I want this. Let me talk to my dad."

"No, Lizzie, *don't!*" her mother says, sharply. "Don't want it. Don't *invite* it! Listen to me!"

No. The voice in Lizzie's head is a sigh, a susurration, and the words are black slush, freezing her veins. *Listen to me, Little Lizzie. Are you willing? Are you sure?*

"You bet." Her finger's moving faster now, the glass of the memory quilt crackling as the symbols fly so fast and furiously she can barely keep track of all the weird shapes, how they're knitting and weaving together: *swhiri, molumdode, czitl. Teoxit.*

"Yes. I'm here. Talk to me, Daddy," she says at the same time she's drawing and thinking hard, *I want this; I've got the Sign of Sure and I want this. Want me, use me, take me instead of* . . .

"L-L-Lizzie?" Dad says, only hesitantly, as if he's never had a voice and just decided to give this a try for the very first time. "H-honey?"

"Dad!" Lizzie's heart leaps because it's her dad, it is. *Cau-lat!* her finger screams. *Stim syob duxe!* "Daddy, it's me!"

"No, Lizzie," her mother says, "it's not—"

"L-Liz . . . Lizzie?" Dad's voice wobbles. "Lizzie, is that y-you?"

"Yes." Her lips are quivering, and her eyes burn, but she can't cry, she mustn't cry now; she has to focus and be sure; she has to be quick. *Frit. Yaanag.* "Daddy, listen, I want to tell you a story. Are you listening?"

"Yes, I'm . . . I'm listening, honey. I'm . . . yes, I'm here," her daddy says, but she can tell he's not really, not all the way. He's still down deep. Well, she's going to fix that. Oh boy, just you wait and see.

"Once upon a time, there was a little girl named Lizzie," she says. *Ptir. Zisotin.* "And she loved her daddy very, very much. Her daddy wrote books—scary, scary books—but she didn't care, because no matter what he did, he was still her daddy." *Smin trevismin.* "Lizzie thought he was very, very brave to reach into the Dark Passages where the monsters live—and she wanted to be just like him. So she tried really hard to make new *Nows*."

"What?" her mother says. *"What?"*

Riwr. "She drew adventures and she gave her dolls names and she grabbed them from her daddy's book-worlds, and they all went away to other *Nows* together." *Pripper.*

"My God," her mother whispers, "you used the dolls? You *switched*? Lizzie, how did you *do* that?"

"But th-then . . ." Lizzie falters, the *zared* only halfway to being. "Then . . ."

"Go on," her dad says, like a little kid. He's much closer now. "What happens next?"

She swallows. *Come on, come on, don't stop now.* She watches her hand move—down, up, cross, *swizzuloo*—and complete the *zared*. "Then, one summer, it was really hot and dry and the plants were thirsty and she wanted to help. So she did something she'd never tried before. She made a storm, a big storm, a monster storm from a different *Now*, and she brought it back."

"Oh God," her mother says.

"*You* did that?" Dad whispers—and is he crying? She hopes so, but she's not sure. "Honey, it rained for three days straight. There were kayaks on Main Street."

"Oh boy, I know." She has stopped drawing. Her arm is tired, but her finger is fire and strange electric tingles ripple over her skin, stroking the hair on her arms and along her neck. Her brain is as white-hot as the sun. "I was really dumb. And the crazy lady in the attic: I did her, too. I made her move the block to a different story."

"What?" her mother says.

"How?" Her dad sounds way interested now.

"You said there was a writer's block," Lizzie said, "and I thought, okay, I'll just get her to suck the block out of your story and cough it up way high in the attic where you can't see. That's why she was all inky and dirty. She kept slurping down your block whenever it started to get bad again."

"Oh my God," her mother says, a touch of wonder in her voice now. "A house has *stories*. You took it literally. The attic is a different *story*."

That's it; that's exactly it. Lizzie clutches the phone. "So don't you see, Daddy? You don't need the whisper-man anymore. You have *me*. I'm all the Sign of Sure you need. *I'll* help you." Her eyes brush the symbols, pulsing and swarming through the air. They are good and well-formed, and now she can see that they are beginning to go purpling mad. Good. Purpling mad is rare; purpling mad is the color of energy and power and thought-magic. "We can make book-worlds and go to other *Nows* together."

"No," her mother says.

"You will?" Dad laughs, like, *Wow, there goes a butterfly!* "Oh, that's exactly what I need. Are you sure? You have to want this, sweetie. You have to be sure."

"I'm sure." Hot tears splash her cheeks. "I want you, Daddy. I love you. I'm so, so sorry I got you in trouble."

"That's okay, sweetie, I've got you," he says. "Now, come home, honey. Concentrate and come to Daddy, and we'll build great worlds."

"I will, Daddy, I will, but you have to make the whisper-man go away. Send him back. Put his fog where it belongs and Momma will bring us home."

"Oh, well now," her dad says, "I can't do that."

She knew it. She had this really bad feeling: this story was too good to be true. *Jumgit.* "Why not?" she asks, not that she really wants to know. She's got to keep her dad interested just a little while longer . . .

"Because I like him," Dad says, simply, the way he says, *Oh look, there's a bug.* "He's my friend."

"No, Daddy." She's running out of time. The fog is almost on them. The shapes flying from her finger are the right ones; they have to be. "No, no, Daddy, it can only be *us.*"

"Oh, don't be silly, there's plenty of room. He's my friend and you're my daughter and so he's yours and you're mine, Lizzie; you're mine, and I see you." His voice is changing again, crooning and thinning to a whisper: "Peekaboo, I see you, Lizzie. I see you."

"I see you, too, Daddy," Lizzie says, picking up the cadence, chanting the mantra. *Sk'lm.* "I see you—"

"I see you, so come and play, Lizzie. Come play . . ."

"Come . . ." She falters, the symbol she's sketching only halfway to being. What was she supposed to do next? "Come play . . ."

"*Yesss*, Blood of My Blood, Breath of My Breath, come play, *Lizzieee*; come, let's *plaaay* a game; come and—"

"Play." What was she thinking? She gives her finger a long, stupid stare. What was she doing? "Come play," she says, slowly. "Come—"

"Lizzie!" Her mother's hand lashes out and smacks the phone from Lizzie's hand. The cell flies against the dash, then tumbles to the foot well, but the voice still seeps from the speaker: *"Come plaaay, Blood of My Bloood, come plaaay . . ."*

"That's enough. Shut that thing up," her mother grates. When Lizzie doesn't move, her mother's palm flicks, quick as a whip. The slap is crisp and loud as the snap of an icicle. "Damn it, Lizzie, do what I say! Hang up *now* while there's still

RIMA

Soother of the Dead

"TIME," TONY SAID.

"Already?" Rima was practically worshipping the heater. The air dribbling from the vents wasn't exactly toasty, but better than nothing.

"Sorry. That was fifteen minutes." Tony turned off the Camry's engine, and the fan cut out. "I'll crank her up again in an hour."

"Something to live for." Rima tucked her hands under her arms again as another stutter-flash of lightning burst high above. She jumped, but the crow prancing on the hood didn't flinch. That thing was seriously creeping her out, and she didn't understand either. Yeah, there was the woman who'd died in Tony's Camry, but her whisper was very weak and nearly gone. Lily's body was in the van. Could it be Taylor's death-whisper in her parka? That would be a first. Once Rima wore something—started soothing that death-whisper—the crows eventually went away.

She gasped as a cannon-roll of thunder boomed loud enough to make the car shimmy. Taylor's death-whisper reacted, squirming over Rima's arms. *Easy, honey,* Rima thought. *Easy, we're all scared.* "What keeps *doing* that?" she asked.

Casey's voice drifted up from the backseat: "Thunder-snow." He'd been so quiet back there, Rima had almost forgotten about him. A relief, actually: Casey was one nasty kid. "It's just a thunderstorm with snow instead of rain."

"Oh." She watched as Casey went back to reading one of Tony's old comics by flashlight. On the lurid cover, two kids ran from some guy wearing these severed heads strung together like an ammunition belt. Rima looked away with a shudder. Read something like that and you'd guarantee nightmares for a week.

"Cold?" Tony made a move to peel out of his parka. "You can take my sweater."

"No, don't be crazy. I'm okay." A lie, but she wasn't going to take his clothes. Besides, who knew if he was the original owner? She eyed the crow. Was that because of something Tony had? Or Casey? Both?

"At least take the gloves. They're spares." Tony tugged a pair of brown woolen mittens from his pocket. When she still hesitated, he said, "I just bought them new a couple weeks ago."

They were probably fine, then. She tugged on the mittens, waited a second, felt nothing except wool, and then slid her hands beneath her thighs with a sigh of relief. They could be stuck in that car for a very long time—and that made her think of something. She didn't want to suggest it, but they had to be practical. "You know, if they don't find anything, or we have to stay here awhile, we should check out the van. There might be food."

"Are you volunteering?" Casey asked.

She didn't want to go. "Sure. My idea, after all."

"You'll freeze before you make it five feet," Tony said, and sighed. "It's okay. I'll go. I should, anyway. I've got a shovel in the trunk, and we need to keep the tailpipe clear."

"You shouldn't be out there alone."

"Oh gee, I wonder who should go with him," Casey put in.

"No one's asking you," Tony said.

"Yeah, right." Casey gave him the hairy eyeball. "Whatever. Give me a chance to clear the snowmobile. You want to unlock the doors?"

"Sure, sorry." Tony stabbed at the control, and the locks *thunked*. Bullying open the door, Casey pushed his way out of the car on a raft of bitter wind and without a backward glance.

Tony looked over at Rima. "Is it my imagination, or is Casey getting even meaner?"

"It's not your imagination," she said, turtling into hunched shoulders. The outside air hacked at her face like switchblades.

"Rima, jeez," Tony said, and then he was tugging off his scarf to twine around her neck. "Take this. My mom made it. I've got a hat and . . . Hey." He gave her an odd look. "Rima, are you all right?"

"Yes." Her voice sounded very tiny in her ears. The death-whisper in that scarf was very strong, swelling in her chest and boiling over in a red tide. She blurted, "I'm sorry about your mom."

Shock flooded his face. "What?" he said. *"What?"*

"She knew you were scared." A sudden tingle ran through her fingers, and before she knew what she was doing, she'd peeled off a mitten and laced her fingers around Tony's wrist. At her touch, she heard him suck in a quick, astonished breath; felt the sting of his surprise and the keener, glassy edge of his grief. "But it didn't matter. She loved you, Tony."

"My . . . my mom . . ." His face was whiter than bone. "How do you . . . ?"

"It's kind of a long story," she said, surprised that Tony was someone she wouldn't mind telling. "How about we talk when we're someplace safe?"

She would remember this moment later. By then, it would be abundantly clear that no place in this valley was truly safe. Unfortunately, she wasn't a mind reader, only a soother of the dead.

"That better be a promise," Tony said.

"It is. Be careful." She released him, but she felt their connection draw itself in an invisible strand, like a spider spinning silk. "I mean it."

"I know. You stay warm," he said, and then he backed out of the car and was swallowed by the storm.

TONY

Maybe God's Just a Kid

1

THEY WORKED BY flashlight, having set three flameless flares Eric had found in the Ski-Doo's cargo bin at equally spaced intervals along the road. The flares had a weird kind of bulb Tony had never heard of—LED?—but gave off a lot of light, maybe even more than flares you lit with strikers. A good thing Eric was prepared, too. Of the two measly flares Tony had dug out of the Camry's trunk, one was useless, the paper corroded and the powder inside dribbling out, which Eric said was probably magnesium and explosive when exposed to water. That had spooked him so bad, Tony didn't dare strike the second flare and, instead, just tucked it in a coat pocket. Probably just as well; with all that spilled gas from the van— and how much had that thing held, anyway?—strike a match or light a flare, and they might end up barbecued.

After three minutes of shoveling, he was puffing; by ten, his muscles screamed. He kept hoping the work would dull him out, but Tony's mind just wouldn't quit. How had Rima known about his mother? How *could* she?

Almost a year gone by and his mother's death still felt like a slow nightmare, the kind where you're running in place from a monster with a million eyes, spiky teeth, and a zillion tentacles. Tony got so he hated mornings, because that meant one more day watching his mother get eaten up alive. Lung cancer gutted her, chewed her up inside, until she was nothing more than a papery husk of skin stitched over brittle bone. She reeked: an eye-watering fog of rot and shit and sour vomit. Whenever she coughed, he kept expecting bloody hunks of gnawed lung or liver or intestine to come flying out of her mouth. She always wanted a kiss, too. He couldn't say no; he wasn't a monster; he loved her. Yet no matter how much he washed his teeth afterward, her taste stayed with him. Got so bad he wanted to rip off his lips, tear out his tongue. Forget food.

Come to think of it, wasn't that when he'd started in with the horror comics, the Lovecraft? Yeah, had to be, because that's when he'd brought home the *Twisted Tales* Casey had been thumbing through, and Tony knew *that* because of what happened when his preacher-dad got on him to *make time for God.* The second story in the comic was about a platoon fighting off this giant rat, only the soldiers turned out to be toys. So when his dad started in, Tony showed him the story: *Dad, you ever stop to think that maybe God's just a kid and we're the dolls?* That shut his dad up good.

His mom finally, *finally* died a week before Christmas. As soon as the principal showed up in his chem class, Tony knew. He'd driven home, taking it as slowly as he could. There would be people at the house: the deacon and pastor, probably a gaggle of church auxiliary ladies trying to find room in the freezer for the ten trillion casseroles sure to turn up. Would his mother still be there? Or would they have taken her to the funeral home already? He hoped they had. He didn't need to say good-bye. Her dying had been the longest good-bye of his life.

On the way, he passed a burger place, and he was suddenly, inexplicably *starved*. So he pulled in. Ten o'clock in the morning, and he couldn't cram in the onion rings fast enough.

Three blocks from home, he pulled over just in time to vomit everything into the gutter. He vomited so hard, and for so long, that he thought his stomach would fly out of his mouth and land with a squishy splat. When he finally lurched into the house, which reeked of Kraft macaroni and cheese, his father was too deep into his own grief to ask Tony where he'd been, and Tony saw no reason to volunteer.

For the next two weeks, he endured meaningful looks, mournful sighs, and a steady stream of people who were just *so sorry*. The church ladies brought over so much tuna fish casserole he kept expecting his shit to squirm with cheesy noodles.

But his mother was gone. No viewing, no open casket. He never saw her again, and he was so frigging relieved, he knew God would hate him forever.

Now, here was proof. There was a dead girl out there. His car was useless. They were stuck in the snow, far away from anyone who might help them.

And now Rima had touched him and stroked the nightmare to life.

2

NEARLY AN HOUR later, they were done. Tony was drenched in sweat, but now that he'd stopped moving, he could feel his clothes stiffening as his sweat began to freeze. "Let's go back and crank on some heat. Then we can deal with the sled."

"Fine with me." Steam rose from Casey's watch cap in curls, which the wind shredded. "What about the van?"

Tony tossed a glance over his shoulder toward the general direction of the spruce grove. Maybe fifty, sixty yards, and nothing to see, not even the suggestion of trees. Slogging through the deep snow would be a complete hassle, and he was tired, scared, and not exactly thrilled with the idea of rooting around a dead girl. Yet he *had* promised, and it wasn't as if Rima didn't have a good point about food. Tony turned the flashlight back to study the trail they'd broken through the snow and all around the Camry. Their tracks were already filling, an inch of new snow dusted the hood, and the wind had thrown two or three more inches onto the trunk. If this kept up, they might be at this all night. Wait too long and digging out the van could take hours.

"I'll check it out. Take me fifteen minutes," he said. "You get warm."

With the balaclava, Casey's face held about as much expression as Jason's, only Jason's hockey mask was white. "If we can't see the van, you won't be able to see us."

"I'll look every couple yards and make sure I still can, okay? If I lose you, I won't go any further."

"Whatever," Casey said, already turning away. "Your funeral."

ERIC
Devil Dog

1

SHE'D LOST HER gloves somewhere along the way, so Eric had taken Emma's icy hands and thrust them beneath his parka. *Body heat,* he'd explained; *keep them out of the wind.* Her hands were still there, but warm now, her long fingers laced over his stomach. Her chest spooned his back. Eric liked how that felt—as if her touch was a kind of promise.

Emma's voice fizzed through his headset, "What are you thinking?"

About how good you feel. How I like that we kind of fit together. How I think we could talk about things. "I'm thinking it's weird," he said, swiping a thin rime of fresh snow from his plastic visor. Thank God, he'd found the faceplate before he and Casey ventured into the valley. With this wind and cold, driving the sled without one would've been impossible. At bare minimum, his nose would have fallen off, and he'd be looking at some serious frostbite.

"Yeah, me too," she said. "Something's . . . *off.* You know?"

She was right. The turnoff Tony and Rima described was

a half mile back of the wreck. There'd been tire tracks, but the storm reduced their speed to a crawl, and eventually, the tracks were no more than suggestions. They'd been about to turn back when Emma spied a slight silver smudge in the distance that grew brighter and more distinct as they approached, still using the truck's tracks as a guide. Fifteen miles from the turnoff, those furrows took a sharp dogleg left at a mailbox nailed to a post and so lathered with snow they couldn't make out the name. Eric didn't care. A mailbox meant a house, and that meant people.

The driveway was long. Two miles and change, according to Eric's odometer, which was . . . a little odd, but people did like to spread out in the country. Then the silver smudge suddenly resolved to an actual light—and became a farm.

But there's something really strange about this setup. Through a slant of driving snow, Eric eyed the truck, which had been pulled right up to the house's front stoop. The truck was 1970s-ancient: a burnt-red Dodge D200 two-door pickup with a crew cab. Someone—two guys, judging from the size of the prints—had driven up, swung out, and taken the steps, and not all that long ago. The footprints were filling in, but Eric still made out the treads. Only a thin white mantle of snow glazed the Dodge's windows and hood.

"Wyoming plates," Emma said. "I can tell from the bucking bronco on the left. Read it in a book somewhere."

"Yeah?" At her tone, he craned his head over his shoulder. They were close enough that their helmets bumped. "You say that as if it means something."

Instead of replying, she swung off the Skandic and waded against the driving snow and through thigh-high drifts to the Dodge. The wind snatched Tony's space blanket, pulling it out behind her like a flag made of aluminum foil. "What are you doing?" he called. Dismounting, he slogged against the suck and grab of the snow at his calves. He watched as she crouched to swipe the Dodge's front plate, which was a brighter red than the car, with raised white reflective letters and numbers.

"Sixty-seven," she said, tracing with an index finger. "See? Stamped in the upper right-hand corner."

Hunkering down beside her, he studied the plate a second, then shrugged. "Okay. So?"

"So . . . does that mean the year the plate was issued? Because that would be weird, wouldn't it?" She looked at him, the legs of a furry blood-tarantula staining her bandage as it bunched with her frown. "We always get a renewal sticker every year, not a new plate."

"Do you guys have a vintage car?" When she shook her head, he said, "Well, that explains it, then. They're probably vintage plates, like the truck."

"Maybe, but don't vintage cars have special plates? Like blue or something, and a different numbering system? This looks like a regular license."

"Well, maybe it's different in Wyoming than Wisconsin." He waited a beat. "You want to tell me what's eating you?"

"What's *eating* me?" Grunting a humorless laugh that was mainly air, she pushed to a stand. "You mean, more than everything else tonight?" She shivered and pulled Tony's space blanket tighter around her shoulders. "I don't know . . . it's just"—she turned a look from the truck to the house—"this feels . . . *off.* I know I keep saying that, but it's not right, Eric. I just can't put my finger on what it is, though."

He stood, wincing a little as his knees complained.

"Everything looks weird at night. Plus, we're in a storm, and you're hurt." The urge to comfort her, pull her into a hug, was very strong, and he throttled it back. "A lot's happened, Emma. You crashed. You lost a friend. I don't know about you, but when my day started, I sure didn't see myself ending up here." If anything, his day had started out even worse. As spooked and worried as he was . . . *I actually feel better here.* A crazy thought. He looked down at her face, so ghostly white and pinched with cold. *I feel better here, with her, than I have with anyone anywhere else in as long as I can remember.*

"Yeah, you can say that again." Her eyes shimmered, and she looked askance. Even with that thick screen of snow, he saw her jaw clench. "I know all that," she said, meeting his eyes again. She pulled herself straighter. "But that's not what I mean. Look at the truck, Eric. It's barely covered. All this snow, but it's like it just got here."

"Well . . ." He threw the Dodge an uncertain look. "Maybe it did. Those guys' tracks are only just now filling up."

"But Eric, we've been on the sled for a long time, at least an hour, don't you think? Long enough for the tracks on the road to almost disappear. And the crash . . ." She swallowed. "Eric, that happened a couple hours ago, right? The sled's odometer says we've come a little more than fifteen miles. But the turnoff wasn't that far back from the van where Tony said he and Rima lost the truck."

"A half mile, yeah." He saw what she was driving at. Even if it also took whoever drove it here an hour, that meant these guys should've been here for quite a while. The truck's tracks hadn't deviated. The driver hadn't stopped or turned off somewhere else along the way. The way the snow was coming down, not only should the truck's tire tracks up this long driveway have filled in, but that Dodge ought to be nearly invisible.

So how come we still see tracks? Why isn't there more snow on this truck? On an impulse, he tugged off a glove and put his hand on the truck's hood.

"Is it warm?" Emma asked.

"No," he said, taking his hand back. The metal had leeched all the feeling, and he *haahed* a breath and shook his hand to push the blood into his fingers to warm them. *Man, that was cold. Burned like a blowtorch.* "But with barely any snow on it at all, it ought to be."

"Right. That's what I mean by *off.* Sounds crazy, but . . . it's almost like the storm wanted to make *sure* we saw the tracks, this truck." Emma inclined her head at the Skandic. "I mean, look at the sled. It's already filling up."

"Yeah," he said, taking in the thickening layer of white on the sled's seats and foot wells. Screwing his hand back into his glove, he studied the house, a two-story with a large wrap-around porch, which reared up from a field of solid white. A glider, laden with snow, hung from chains to the right of the front door. More snow pillowed in hanging baskets suspended from hooks on either side of the porch steps. The porch light illuminated the front door in a spray of thin yellow light. The door was black, hemmed by sidelights of glowing pebbled glass. To the left, a large bay window fired a warmer, buttery yellow, and further back, a feeble glow spilled through a side window. Kitchen, maybe. The second story was completely dark.

"Somebody's home for sure," he said, wondering why that didn't necessarily make him feel any better. His nerves were starting to hum with anxiety, and a creep of uneasiness slithered up his neck. "Must be the guys with the truck."

"If they live here, then why do they have Wyoming plates?"

"Maybe they're just visiting."

"Then where are the other cars? Or trucks? This is a farm. Where *is* everything? Where are all the other machines?"

"Well, they wouldn't leave them out in the snow. Maybe they store everything," he said, turning from the house to look at the barn, which stood off to the right, maybe a good seventy, eighty yards away. A large spotlight, with the kind of shallow metal shade that looked a little like a flying saucer, surmounted a very tall pole in the very center of a wide-open space; fence posts marched to either side. The top rungs of a large corral were visible, but no animals had been out for some time. The snow was unbroken and very deep, and that barn, huge and hulking, felt deserted: an enormous hollow shell and nothing more.

"No equipment sheds," Emma said, coming to stand beside him. "No silos. If you've got animals, you usually have a silo for grain. There aren't any water troughs in that corral that I can see, and no equipment sheds. So maybe there are tractors or something in there, but I'll bet there aren't. Eric, this feels like someone's *idea* of a farm, like a movie set."

"Maybe it's a hobby farm," he said, and wasn't sure he even convinced himself. Turning from the barn, he stared back at the house for a long moment, listening to the dull slap of snow on his helmet. "Whatever it is, we can't stay out here."

"I know." Huffing out a breath, she shook snow from Tony's space blanket. "I guess we knock."

He didn't want to, though he didn't see a choice. "Stick close, okay? People in Wisconsin can be pretty strange."

"Ed Gein," she said.

"Lived on a farm," he said.

"Jeffrey Dahmer didn't."

"But he should've." He felt his mouth quirk into a lopsided grin. "Gein, Dahmer, Taliesin . . . it must be the water."

"Yeah." She gave him a strange look. "Must be."

"Are you all right?"

"Just a headache." Closing her eyes, she pinched the bridge of her nose. "Bad."

"You hit your head pretty hard."

She shook her head. "I've had headaches for a long time. I'm supposed to take medicine, but . . ." Her voice dribbled away.

The tug of his attraction—that insane urge to hold her—was so strong it hurt. He imagined removing that helmet, cupping her face in his hands, and then . . . "We need to get you inside. Hold up a sec." Wading back to the Skandic, he lifted the seat, dug around in the storage box, and came up with Big Earl's Glock. He felt her stare as he jammed the muzzle into the waistband of his jeans at the small of his back. "When we go up there . . ."

"I know. Stay close."

"I'm not kidding around. I mean it," he said, almost angrily. "I don't want you getting hurt worse than you already are."

"Too late for that," she said.

2

NO STORM DOOR, which was weird. No peephole and no doorbell either, just an old-fashioned brass knocker. Eric gave a couple quick raps. Waited a few seconds. Hammered the door with his fist. "Hello?"

"That did something," Emma said, nodding toward the door.

Eric saw a swarm of darkening shadows in the pebbled sidelights as someone approached. A moment later, the knob rattled and the door swung open on a balloon of warm air scented with the unmistakable aroma of macaroni and cheese.

"Yeah?" The guy was maybe just a year or two older than Eric: not tall but compact, wiry, and lean as a whippet. Like the truck, his clothes were vintage, olive drab BDUs, although it looked like the kid had taken pretty good care of them. BODE was embroidered in dark blue letters on a subdued ribbon over his left breast pocket. Over the right was another ribbon: U.S. ARMY. From the SSI on the left shoulder, whoever had owned them back in the day had been Airborne, and 7th Cav. He recognized the subdued badge: that distinctive shield with its black diagonal stripe and silhouette of a horse's head. The kid's gaze flicked from Eric to linger on Emma. "What happened to you?"

"My friend and I were in a wreck," Emma said, and then her voice wobbled a little. "Eric and his brother and two other people stopped to help, only their car's stuck, so we followed your tracks and—"

"Whoa, you guys crashed?"

"Yeah." Eric studied the guy another long second. Those BDUs were way out of regs. Pockets were a little strange, too. Slanted and a little big. The whole getup was like something a guy might wear in a chop shop, but the way the kid carried himself was . . . military. On the other hand, *he* was a newly minted Marine; what did he know? Maybe they did things differently in the Army, or the uniform belonged to a relative. "You Army?"

"What, the uniform give it away?"

He pushed past the sarcasm. "Seventh Cav?"

"C Company, Second Battalion, yeah." The kid's sky blue eyes narrowed. "So? You got a brother over there or something?"

"No. Just me . . . I mean, soon." Eric stuck out his hand. "I'm Eric. Just finished basic at Parris."

"Yeah? A devil dog? Hey, that's cool." Something in the guy's face unknotted, and he grabbed Eric's hand. "Bode. You got orders?"

Since killing my father? Well, not so much. He forced a grin. "Lejeune. I hear we're going to ship out to Marja."

"Where's that?"

"Um . . . Helmand Province, I think." At the kid's puzzled expression, Eric said, "You know, Afghanistan."

"Afghanistan." Bode still looked mystified.

"Bode?" Another voice, drifting up from behind. "Who is it?"

"Got us a devil dog," Bode said, and now Eric saw another kid, also military and in the same olive drab, about five feet back. A paper napkin was tucked at his neck. Bode said, "That's Chad. We're on leave. Chad, this is Eric and that's—"

"Emma," she said.

"Hey," Chad said around macaroni and cheese. His face was narrow, his nose no more than a blade, and he was pretty twitchy, kind of wired. To Eric, he looked a bit like a small and very anxious rat. Chad swallowed, said, "So what's going on? You guys broke down?" His nose wrinkled. "Man, what'd you guys do, take a bath in gas or something?" To Emma:

"What are you wearing? You look like a baked potato."

"Space blanket," she said.

"What?" Bode and Chad tossed a glance, and then Bode said to Emma, "You mean, like one of those souvenir Apollo things? From Cape Kennedy?"

"What?" she asked. "You mean, Canaveral?"

"Naw," Chad said. "They changed it. That's the old name."

"Say, can we come in?" Eric interrupted. "It's really cold."

"Ah sure, yeah, jeez." Then Bode glanced past Eric's shoulder. "Hey, look at that. It stopped snowing."

"What?" Five seconds before, the blowing snow had been thick and driving. Now, no snow fell at all, not even the occasional solitary flake. *Like someone turned it off.* Eric stuck his hand beyond the porch railing. *No snow. What—*

A static burst, followed by a staccato buzz, sounded from his left-hand pocket, and he jumped. The walkie-talkie; Eric had forgotten about it.

"It can't be them," Emma said. "We're too far away."

"Those your friends?" Bode asked.

"Might be, but she's right. They're fifteen miles back," Eric said.

"Radios sometimes travel better at night," Bode said.

"Yeah." The handset's oversize antennae caught on the inside fabric of his pocket, and Eric fought to work it free. A hash of static and broken words crackled from the unit's mechanical throat: *mur . . . danger . . . bodies . . .*

"Hey," Bode said. "Sounds like you snagged the same police channel we—"

He broke off as Eric got the handset out just in time for them all to hear the scream.

TONY

It's a Mirror

TONY LOST THE Camry after ten yards, although Casey's flashlight and the brighter crimson penumbras from the three flares were still visible. After five more yards, the snow swallowed the third and farthest flare; at twenty-five, more or less, the second disappeared. Casey's flashlight dimmed, but Tony could still pick it out. As an experiment, he waved his flashlight over his head in a big arc. A few moments later, Casey's light bobbed a reply. So far, so good.

He walked for what seemed like a very long time and until his face ached with cold. Clots of snow had gathered on his chest and shoulders, and his eyelashes dripped iced tears. Wow, had the van been this far? He didn't think so. He turned to look back. Casey's flashlight was gone, but the flare nearest the Camry still flickered, the pinprick of light as fuzzy as a red cotton ball.

Okay, relax. So long as you see the flare, you're still okay. But where was that stupid van? Fifteen more steps and he would call it—

His boot came down with a splash. Gasping, he jumped back as the smell came rolling up. *Gas.* Was that right? He aimed his flashlight, and frowned. Gas pooled over the snow. He lifted a careful heel, eyeing how the gas slopped and rippled around his boots. *Deep. This can't be right; no car holds this much gasoline. You'd need a tanker truck for it to have leaked this much.*

Even so, that the gas was still liquid was wrong, too. Shouldn't the gas have seeped into the snow, or . . .

Wait a minute. He shuffled, felt his boots skate and slide as the ripples expanded in ever-wider circles. That wasn't snow under the gas. It was *ice*, as smooth and featureless as silvered glass. Beneath his feet, his face wavered and swam, his reflection so perfect that he could see the swirl of snow haloing his head. *It's a mirror.*

"That is too weird," he said, just to hear himself. His heart was suddenly thumping. "This has to be an optical illusion or something. You can't make a mirror out of ice. It's just . . . I don't know . . . compacted snow and gasoline and . . ." He stopped. Never a whiz at chemistry or science, even he knew that made no sense.

Yeah, but then what is this? Flexing his knees, he pushed off on his toes with a little hop. His boots *splished*, the gasoline sloshed, but the mirror-ice didn't give or crack. He'd stirred something up, though. As he watched, a gelid veil smoked from the pool in thick, white tongues. Mystified, he swept a hand through the mist, watched as his palm cleaved the suddenly nacreous air. Where his hand touched, there was a slight give, a webby stickiness that reminded him of pushing through musty cobwebs down cellar.

This wasn't right. A creeping uneasiness slithered up his

spine. The curtain of fog was rising, not lifting from the ice so much as growing. He aimed the spear of his flashlight straight up. The light didn't penetrate more than a few feet before the smoking mist swallowed it whole. The beam's color was off, too: not blue-white but a ruddy orange, like old blood. Yet he saw enough.

The fog was moving: not dissipating or being swept away by the wind but weaving and knitting itself together over his head. The fog was walling him in.

Oh boy. His mouth went desert-dry. He should . . . yeah, he should really get out of here. The fumes were thickening, dragging over his face in cloying fingers that worked into his nose and down to his throat to worm into his lungs.

Which way? He turned a wild circle, but the fog gobbled up his light. The air was getting worse, too. He tried pulling in thin sips, but the tickle at the back of his throat became an itch, then a scratch, and then he was coughing and couldn't stop. He felt his throat closing even as his mouth filled with spit. Something squirmed in his throat, like maybe there was an animal with furry legs and sharp claws crawling around in there.

Crazy, that's cra—

Something ripped behind his ribs, as if the blade of a hot knife had suddenly sliced through muscle and bone. Grunting, he clutched at his chest, felt the boil of something clenching, bunching. God, there *was* something inside him! This was like his mother, the way she clawed at her chest.

Can't . . . can't breathe. His fingers raked his throat, scored his flesh. *No air . . . can't . . . got to get out, get out, get—*

A hand slid onto his shoulder.

CASEY

This *Is* Creepy

"CASEY, IT WAS fifteen minutes a half hour ago," Rima said.

"Tell you what," Casey said. "You're so worried, you go."

"We should *both* go."

"Why? So we can *all* get lost and freeze to death? Tony might have gone around to the other side of the van. That would block the flashlight. He could be turned around, facing the other way. We wouldn't see the flashlight then either."

"But he signaled us every couple of minutes before you lost him."

"I didn't lose him."

"God, would you *stop*? I'm not blaming you. All I'm saying is there's been nothing for a long time. We should see him coming back at least."

This was probably true. Maybe too much glare? Casey thumbed off his flashlight, then pressed his face against the icy slab of window glass. Nothing to see. He chewed on his lower lip. Maybe they *should* go. "Do you remember if Tony had a rope or extension cord or, I don't know, something we can tie off to the car?"

"He wouldn't have anything long enough to reach the van."

"I know that," Casey said, impatiently. "But if we can extend our reach, get away from the car a good fifty feet or so, then one of us can keep going with the flashlight, right? The other one hangs back and yells."

"Oh, right," she said. "Sorry. That's a good idea, Casey."

He knew that. "So was there anything?"

"I don't remember. Maybe we should check your sled?"

He should've thought of that. He was pretty sure he had chains and a couple bungee cords. Popping his door, he flicked on his flashlight, almost climbed out, but then remembered those stupid locks. Reaching over the front seat, he yanked the keys, pocketed them—and frowned. Ducking out of the car again, he sniffed. "You smell that?"

"Yeah." She was looking at him across the Camry's snow-silted roof. "That's—"

"Gas." He faced the direction where the van lay. "I didn't smell it before."

"Maybe the wind changed direction?"

"No, I—" And that's when it hit him. "It's stopped snow-ing. There's no wind."

Rima turned her face to the black, featureless bowl of night sky. "Can that happen? I mean, all of a sudden like that?"

How should he know? Did he look like he worked for The Weather Channel? *But she's right; this is creepy.* No wind, no snow. Like someone hit a switch or turned off the spigot. If anything, the air was much colder now, and heavier somehow. "Come on," he said, then stopped as his boot came down with a small *splish*. "Hey, what . . ."

Whatever else he would've said died right then and there. Because from the darkness came a scream.

TONY

She Has to Be Here

TONY WHIRLED, THE flashlight tumbling from his hand to fly into the fog. The night came slamming down as he back-pedaled, his feet slipping, his balance finally going. He went down like a rock. The impact was like wiping out on an ice rink: a solid, bone-rattling blow that drove the air from his lungs. Gasoline sheeted over his body; cold fuel slapped his face. His throat closed on a mouthful of gasoline, and then he was choking, his vision starting to speckle with black filaments. Ropy drool poured from his open mouth. His thoughts swirled in a swoon: *Passing . . . out . . .*

At the last possible second, the knotted muscles of his throat relaxed, and he pulled in a great, wrenching gasp. His chest throbbed; something inside there seemed to *push*. There was still gas in his mouth, too, and the fumes got him coughing again.

Someone out here. On the ice. *With* him. "Whooo?" The word rode on a breathy shriek. "Who's . . . who's th-there?"

No answer.

"C-C-Casey?"

No answer.

Oh God, oh God, I'm in so much trouble. With his flashlight gone, the night was inky and close. He couldn't seem to pull in enough air. The fog's webby fingers threaded up his nose and steamed into his brain, and then he was gasping as the fog squirmed into the space behind his eyes. His head went swimmy. The thinking part of his mind knew he was hyperventilating and only making things much worse, but he couldn't help it. If he didn't get out of this, if he couldn't find his way back, he was going to faint, or freeze, or both.

He pushed to his feet and stood a moment, swaying, his pulse rabbiting through his veins. The fog was thick, but the flares showed through the storm, right? So, it stood to reason that if he could just get a little closer to his car, he ought to pick one out. From there, it was a cakewalk. All he had to do was get himself pointed the right way. Put the van at his back, and he was set.

He shuffled forward, pushing through the fog, the gasoline slopping and gurgling around his boots. After twenty steps, he still hadn't found the van and panic started to bleed into his chest again. *Where could it—*

Bam! A bomb went off in his face, right between his eyes, and he screamed with pain. Blood flooded his mouth, then spurted from his broken nose in a great spume, and he simply dropped in a sodden heap. He couldn't get up. Everything hurt, even his hair. Blindly, he put out a gloved hand, felt an upside-down door handle. In his terror, he'd run right into the van. Which side? He slid his hand down a bit then felt his glove sink into something soft and flaccid. *"Ahhh,"* he said, the sound coming out as a thick half-moan, half-scream. He must be at the passenger's side window and that dead girl. Then his brain caught up to what his hands, even through gloves, had already registered.

There was the coat, yes. But . . .

No. He thought back to that slithering touch, and a swell of terror flooded his chest. *No, no, she has to be here; she's dead, she's dead, she—*

Over the thunder of his heart, Tony heard something new.

A single . . .

    lonely . . .

        splash.

TONY
Get Up, or You're Dead

TONY FROZE.

Behind him. Someone there. Not Casey or Rima; he knew that. They would've called out. Even with the fog, he ought to see a little light, but—

Splash.

God, what was that? He felt the scream boiling on his tongue. That wasn't an animal. No animal in its right mind would be out here, in the cold and dark, just hanging around, waiting for a dumb, stupid kid to bumble—

Splash.

Get up. Every hair on his head stood on end. *Get up, or you're dead. Get up, or it will find you. Get up, run, do something, get up!*

But he did not get up. He couldn't. Instead, Tony shrank, shivering, against the van, his nose still dripping blood, which was beginning to freeze to his chin.

Splash. Pause. *Slosh.*

The handset. He had the walkie-talkie. He could call for help. Call *someone*.

Slosh.

Eric can't help. He's probably too far away. I'm all alone out here and— Another *splish*, and now the lake of gasoline rippled and broke against his legs. *Getting closer, coming right for me.* He had to do something, do *something*.

Slosh. Splish.

He eased the handset from his pocket.

Splash. Pause. *Splash-splash.*

He brought the handset to his mouth.

Sploosh.

"Help." His voice was so low, so small, there was almost no sound at all. "Help, help me."

Splash-splash . . .

"Help," he said, louder now. "Help me. Somebody, help!"

SPLASH-SLOSH-SPLASH . . .

"No!" Tony shouted. He stared in horror as the blackness gathered and folded and formed shadows in the dark: something monstrous and denser than the night, and it was right there, it was *right there, it was right—*

"HELP ME!" Tony shrieked. *"HELP ME, SOMEBODY HELP—"*

CASEY

Full Fathom Five

"CASEY!" RIMA GASPED. "That was Tony!"

"I know." The words felt thin in his mouth, like flat letters on white paper. "I can't see . . ."

"HELLLP!" Tony's shriek tore through the night. *"PLEASE HELP ME!"*

"Tony!" Rima floundered around the hood, and that was when Casey heard not the *shush* of snow but a *splash*.

Water? He sniffed, and then his eyes widened. "Hey, do you *smell* that?"

"What are you . . ." She stopped moving and looked down, then shuffled her feet. Casey heard the slap and gurgle of liquid against the Camry's metal chassis. "Gasoline?" she said. "But where did it come from? The van? How? The van couldn't possibly hold that much."

"I don't know," he said. Even if you factored in a rupture in the Camry's tank, that wouldn't explain this. "Look, I think we need to take a second here and . . ."

Another shriek from Tony, agonized and shrill, and then

Rima was sloshing away from the car: "Tony! Tony, we're—"

"No!" Casey's arm pistoned out; his fist closed around her arm. "Don't! Wait!" He heard her gasp and felt her go rigid. "What?" he said.

"Let me go!" And then she was shrieking, batting at him, like she'd completely lost it: "Let me go, let me *go*!" Flailing wildly, she tried twisting away. "Don't *touch* me!"

"Rima!" Jesus, what was *wrong* with her? The girl was still screaming, and from across the ice, in the dark, Tony shrieked again: a drill bit of sound that cored into the meat of his brain, and *God*, all Casey wanted was for Tony to stop screaming and for this nutcase to stop hitting him. "Rima, stop, *be quiet*! You want whatever's out there to find us, too?"

"Let go, let *go*!" In the light from his flashlight, he could see the cords standing in her neck and the glitter of an animal fear in her eyes. "Take your hands *off*!"

"Fine! Okay! There, you stupid . . ." As soon as he released her, she staggered, her feet tangling and slip-sliding. Without thinking, he reached for her again—to steady her, give her a hand; he was just trying to *help*, for God's sake—but she aimed a kick, a goddamned *kick*.

"Don't touch me!" she shrieked. "I told you not to touch me!"

"All right! Fine! Fall on your ass; I don't give a shit!" Another blood-curdling scream from Tony set his teeth. "Just get back in the goddamned car!"

"What?" Rima was wild-eyed, her face drained of color. "No! Are you crazy? We have to *help* him!"

Was *he* crazy? "We *can't*! What's already happened has happened! We have to get inside, get off the snow!" Casey was already splashing back to the car. The gasoline fumes were starting to get to him; he could feel the burn in his throat. Breathing was hard, and his head ached. Lurching for the back door, he felt his boot suddenly skate, and he thought, *Ice? Wait, what happened to the snow?*

Another scream boiled from the darkness, but the sound was now much different: formless and queerly garbled, a drowning kid's gurgle, and as liquid as this improbable lake of gasoline.

I don't want to know, I don't want to see this. Desperate now: "Rima, we can't help him. We can't even *see* him!"

She still wasn't moving, the idiot. "But we can't just *leave* him."

"Yes, we can, and I'm going," Casey said, and then he was grabbing the handle of the back door before he remembered: *locked.* Damn stupid . . . He was shaking so bad he couldn't sock the key into the lock, had to hold it with both hands. *Come on, come on.* He felt the key ram home, and then he was twisting the key, hauling back on the handle. The door opened with a shriek, the hinges crying out. He practically dove into the car. Craning round, he saw that Rima hadn't moved.

Well, screw this shit, and screw her. He dragged the door closed with a hard *thunk.* The locks socked home, and only then did he allow himself a relieved sigh. *Safe.* Or as safe as he could be in this nightmare. Of course, if whatever was out there came for them, he wasn't so sure about that either. Car windows broke, didn't they? You'd have to be one strong mother to do it, but a rock, a hammer, a stout piece of pipe, and then he was screwed. Man, what he wouldn't give for a weapon.

Outside, Rima was a murky silhouette, still as a statue.

Fine, let her die out here; he wasn't risking his ass for a guy he'd just met. What was he supposed to do, anyway? Throw snowballs? *Spit?* God, his head was killing him from all those fumes. The metal box of the car muted Tony's screams, so they were only bad and not bone-chilling, as if he were listening to a horror movie leaking from a distant television—but that was still plenty horrible enough.

Shut up, Tony. Casey squeezed his eyes tight. The taste of gasoline furred his tongue. Swallowing made him gag. Saliva pooled, and he spat, trying to rid himself of the taste. *Shut up, Tony. Shut up, and die already if you're going to, but shut the f*— He let out a startled yelp at a sharp *bap* on the window behind his head. Turning, he saw Rima at the door. *"What?"* he shouted. "What do you want now?"

"Open up!" Rima's fist hammered the window again. Even in the gloom, her eyes were bright and raw with terror. "Casey, please, open the door! Something's coming! Quick, open the *door!*"

Oh, so *now* she wanted in. Fine, fine, crazy stupid bitch . . . Still fuming, he reached for the lock, no real thought behind it at all, only reflex, and then Big Earl, who'd been so quiet, boomed, *What the* hell *you doing, boy?*

"What?" He hesitated, his fingers hovering in midair, twitching a little like the legs of a spider. "I'm . . . I'm letting her in." Thinking, *I'm talking to a dead man. I'm having an argument with a ghost.*

What the hell for? You lost what little sense you had? It wasn't just that Big Earl was huge in his head. Casey felt the big man's phantom arms crush his ribs, drive the breath from his chest. *She made her bed. She had her chance.*

"Casey!" Rima slammed both palms against the window, hard enough that he felt the jolt in his legs. "*Please!* Don't leave me out here!"

"I . . . Dad, no . . . I have to h-help . . ." His hand wouldn't obey. What was wrong with him? It was as if he were a robot whose circuits had frozen. "Can't l-leave her to d-die out there. What if there really is s-something . . . ?"

This is your problem. You think Eric thought about anything other than getting rid of me? You think he didn't mean *it?* Big Earl oozed contempt. *He might have killed me, but at least he had the guts to do what needed doing.*

"S-stop comparing me to him." A lick of anger, but his skin was suddenly pebbly with gooseflesh as a dark chill rippled through his veins. *What's wrong with my hand?* Then, another and much stranger thought: *Is it mine?* "I'm my own p-person. I can handle m-myself."

"Casey!" Rima pounded again. "Open the door!"

Then be a man.

This was the problem with being Big Earl's son: you hopskipped right over being a kid. True, he didn't particularly like Rima; he wasn't going to put himself on the line for her. But opening the door was so simple. *And it is* the right thing to do. *A man makes his own decisions, too.* So why did his hand refuse to move? "Dad, she just n-needs to—"

You giving me lip? You saying no to me?

"N-no, sir . . . I m-mean . . ."

Spit it out, boy.

"You're . . . you're *d-dead*," Casey stammered. Whatever held him in place, was wrapped around his body, tightened its grip, like the muscular arms of a gigantic octopus. His ribs felt brittle as crackle-ice. His chest didn't want to move. "Why . . . h-how can I still be h-hearing you? P-please, I h-have to open the d-door, just l-let me . . ."

You have to listen to me, boy.

"Casey!" Rima pleaded. "Please, listen, Casey, *please*!"

"I . . ." He couldn't make his lungs work. "Dad, n-no, I n-need . . ."

I'll show you what you need. His father's voice sizzled in his blood. *Take you down a peg.*

"N-no, Dad," he gasped, thinking to his hand: *Move,* move*! Hurry, unlock the door, unlock the door!* "S-stop. Just l-let me . . ."

And that was when he saw his hand . . . *glimmer.*

"Ah!" he screamed as the skin rippled and wavered as if underwater. Everything around him—the sense of the car seat beneath him, Rima's terrified shouts, even the numbing cold—suddenly dropped out, as if the soundtrack to this movie had hit a glitch. There was only his hand, which was trying to deform and shift, growing larger, rougher, thicker, and cracked with calluses. Tufts of hair sprouted over the knuckles. It was as if his hand had slid into Big Earl's skin. Or maybe Big Earl was only turning him inside out the way you shucked a messy glove and what he now saw was what lay beneath.

Or he's in my blood, eating his way out. This couldn't be real. Dizzy with horror, he watched as Big Earl's hand jerked away from the lock.

"N-no." A sudden cold sweat slimed his neck and upper lip. "Puh-please, d-don't. Stop, *s-stop*!" He could hear his breath hissing from between clenched teeth, feel the shudder in his biceps as he tried fighting back, to make Big Earl's hand obey, to stop moving, to *stop* . . .

Casey slapped himself, very hard: a stunning blow, an open-palm *crack* as sharp as a gunshot. A cry jumped off his tongue. There was a wink of pain as his teeth cut his cheek. Very faintly, above the thunder of his blood, he heard Rima shout: "No, Casey, *stop*! Don't let him—"

"H-help," he panted, his mouth filling with salt and rust. His voice sounded so small, almost not there at all. "E-Eric, help, someone, please . . ." And then his hand—his *father's* hand—was a fist, and Casey couldn't fight it. He could feel his will draining away, the numb acceptance of a beaten dog, which he knew too well because he'd been here so many times before: kneeling, watching Big Earl advance with that switch, his fist, a belt, and knowing that running only made things a hundred times worse.

He hit himself again and again and again, and all those books had it totally wrong: there was no numbing, no going away, no mental *click* so he could float above and let this happen to that boy-shaped punching bag. He felt this, each and every blow, right into his teeth, his bones. With every punch, he heard his breath come in a grunt—*ugh, ugh, ugh*—as his head whipped to the side, snapping on the stalk of his neck. He could feel the skin tear over his cheek, and there was now blood on his chin, down his throat, and then his vision was blacking as he kept beating himself, Big Earl bellowing with every blow: *You want help, you want* help, *you want—*

"Listen to me! You're *Casey*!" Rima was right up against the glass, even as Big Earl was still raging, but—impossibly—it was the arrow of her voice, sharp and true, that pierced his terror. "You are Eric's *brother*; you are *yourself*; you are Casey, and *Casey* would open the door! Do it, Casey! Please, don't let me die out here. Open the door, Casey; *fight* him and do it now, do it now, do it—"

I'm Casey. He grabbed desperately at the thought. *I'm Eric's brother—*

No, you are mine, *boy.* Big Earl was huge in his head. *You are* my *blood, you are—*

"Casey, fight this!" Rima shouted through glass. "You are your own person!"

Mine, boy! You're mine and I'll make a man of you—

"No one *makes* me! I'm *Casey!*" Roaring, he drove his fist forward, hard and fast, throwing all his weight into a blow he aimed not for his face but the window. Through a haze of pain and tears, he saw Rima start back, and then he screamed as a bomb of white-hot pain erupted at the moment of impact, streaming through his bones to ball in his shoulder. He felt the skin over his knuckles tear, and now there was blood smeared on the window, and more dripping from his hand—but, he saw, it was *his* hand once more, *his*.

And Rima knew . . . Somehow she knew, but how? No time to wonder. In a few moments, he thought he might not care, because he could feel that one weird rocket of strength ebbing and Big Earl still there, this hulking presence at the edge of his mind, withdrawing, yes, but only as a grudging wave does from the shore: so far, and no further, because the ocean is remorseless and eternal—and it would be easy, so easy to stop fighting, to let Earl swamp him, drown him. It was only a matter of time anyway, wasn't it? Big Earl was strong—he always had been—and Casey was nothing but a kid, a runt, another mouth to feed, a miserable excuse for a son who would never amount to—

Do it, Casey. Already, he could feel the silver sliver of himself, a Casey that he recognized, going dark, starting to slide away, being pulled under full fathom five. *Do it, Casey! Do it now, open the door, save her while you still can and before he comes back, before . . .*

"Do it." The words were clumsy in his torn mouth. Swallowing back blood, he pawed at the locks, his bloody fingers awkward, but the pain kept him focused a few seconds more. There was a *thunk* as the locks disengaged. In the next second, Rima was scrambling inside on a wash of frigid air, another scream from Tony, and the stink of gasoline.

"Something's coming." Her voice was thin and tight. She wrestled with the handle, her hands in their wool gloves slipping over bare metal as she muscled the door shut. "Something's out there!"

"What? How close?" Still panting, Casey brought his good fist down on the master lock, then felt around for the flashlight. Thumbing it on, he worked his aching jaw, grimacing at a lancet of pain. His cheek was already swelling, going to be a hell of a bruise, and someone tell him just *why* had he risked his neck for this girl; why had he been *hitting* himself? *You're going as crazy as she is.* Sucking blood from his torn knuckles, he spat out copper and a gasoline fug. "Did you get a look at it?"

"No. But I heard it. It's . . . *big*, and Tony . . ." Her back was rigid, and she seemed to be quite careful to keep some distance between them. She flicked him a quick glance, her eyes raking his face, lingering on his jaw. "Listen, Casey, what just happened to you, I—"

Out of the corner of his eye, he caught sudden movement, and then something flew into the car, smacking the metal shell with a meaty thud. Startled, Casey jerked his flashlight to the window—and screamed.

"Tony!" Rima shrieked. *"Tony!"*

ERIC

A Night Coming On Fast

ON THE PORCH, as that horrible scream went on and on, they all stared at the handset he held in a death grip. Before the shriek had even fully died, Eric was shouting into the unit: "What's happening, *what's happening*? Tony? Casey? *Casey?*"

"Jesus," said Bode.

All the reply he got was the scream again, louder and so full of terror, Eric felt the sound working its way inside to ice his blood. Beside him, he heard Emma gasp.

"Eric," she said. "Oh my God, that sounds like Tony."

"Yeah, I know." Heart pounding, he clicked off the handset's volume and jammed the unit back into his parka. Whirling on his heel, he plunged down the porch steps. *God, Casey, Casey!* "Stay here, Emma, just stay *here*!"

"No! No, Eric, wait, *wait*!" Emma stumbled, the deep snow on the porch snagging her boots and dragging at Tony's space blanket. Staggering, she clutched the railing before she could take a header. "Eric, you can't go alone!"

"Emma." He snatched up his helmet. "They're in trouble,

and I'm not staying here. My *brother* is out there!"

"And no one is saying you shouldn't go." Flinging off Tony's space blanket, she floundered down the steps and grabbed his arm. "Of course you should. They need help, but so do you. It's crazy for you to go alone. Let me come with you."

"No way, Emma." Tightening his helmet's chin strap, he drilled her with a ferocious glare. "You're already hurt."

"But I can help. I'm *fine*. It's just a hit to the head. Please, let me come with you."

And here was the hell of it: he didn't want to leave her. *How can this be? We just met.* Eric could feel the tug-of-war in his chest, the need to go a claw, the desire to stay a knife ripping at his heart. *"Emma,"* he said, exasperated. He grabbed his hand back before he could touch her, afraid that he'd give in to this new and raw emotion because what he wanted . . . what he *needed* . . . Swallowing around a sudden lump, he pushed back on the impulse to hold her close, crush his mouth to hers. *What is this? Why do I feel this? What is this?* It was the sort of thing you read in bad teen novels; he didn't believe in this crap. The only person he'd loved in this world—ever—was Casey. But now there was this strange girl that he could imagine knowing better, wanted to *be* with . . . and he had no more time to wonder about this.

"Please," he ground out, "please stay here. I need to know that you're safe, and you won't be if you come. I can't help my brother if I have to worry about you, too."

"I'm not a *doll*," she said. "It's not like I'm going to break."

"But you're not real fit to fight either." It was the big kid in the olive drab BDUs, Bode. "It's not a girlie thing. You look ready to chew nails, but you're already kind of banged up."

Eric saw her jaw set. "So you going with him?" Emma fired back. "Or are you just hassling me and going to let him walk into this on his own?"

"Emma, no," Eric said, although he thought Bode was one kid he'd like to have with him in a fight. "It's one thing to ask for help with a stuck car. Whatever's going on out there, it's not their fault, or their problem."

"Yeah, what he said." It was the twitchy, narrow-nosed guy, Chad, on the steps. "We don't know what we'd be walking into."

"And that's a reason to do *nothing*?" Emma flung back. "You guys are soldiers, for God's sake!"

"Gee, thanks for that intel. I was kind of wondering where I got these funky clothes. Now tell me something I don't know," Chad said. "Anyway, I'm on leave."

"Yeah, but"—a swift sparrow of uncertainty flitted through the sky blue of Bode's eyes—"come on, Chad. You really going to let this guy walk into God knows what by himself?"

"You know, guys, I don't have time for this. I'm going," Eric said, stabbing the sled's ignition. He looked up as Emma stepped to block his way. "Emma!" he shouted over the engine's throaty roar. He cranked the throttle, blasting out a loud *vroom-vroom*, but she wouldn't budge. "Get out of the way. *Move!*"

"Not unless you take me with you!" she said.

Don't you think I want to? Please listen to me; please let me protect you from whatever is out there. "You can't help!"

"I know you're trying to protect me," she said, her words

an eerie echo of his own. She covered his hand with hers. Her eyes were intent and so strange, with that one tiny golden flaw in her right eye and the rest such an alien cobalt blue it was as if he were staring into a night coming on fast. If you didn't know better, you might think eyes like that existed only in dreams. "But I don't want anything to happen to you either," she said. "You shouldn't go alone."

. "Man, she's right." Bode had come to stand next to her. "Never go into the field without someone to watch your back. Me and Chad will come."

"You don't have to do that," Eric said, but with less force. Honestly, he didn't *want* to walk into this alone; he only wanted Emma safe.

"Aw, Bode," Chad said. "I don't know."

"Shut up, Chad, we're going." Bode dragged on a watch cap, then tugged a pair of gloves from his jacket. "Leave the sled, Devil Dog. We got chains for the Dodge, and we're less exposed that way—more protection. You got a weapon?"

It was on the tip of his tongue to say no, but then he remembered. Eric cut the engine. As the sled died with a grumble, he reached under his parka to tug Big Earl's pistol from the small of his back. "Just this."

"Whoa." Bode's forehead crinkled. "Nice gun, but . . . they issuing Glocks these days?"

"No." He saw that Emma was very still, but her eyes were wide, the question on her face practically a shout. He dodged his gaze back to Bode. "It was my dad's," he said.

"How many rounds?"

One less than it started the day with. Back at the cabin, everything had happened so fast, he hadn't bothered to check.

Knowing Big Earl, the clip would be full. Shucking the round in the chamber, he popped out the magazine. "Been fired once today already," he said, wanting to kick himself for mentioning that and not looking at Emma at all but busying himself with thumbing in the bullet he'd shucked from the chamber into the clip. Butting the magazine back into place, he jacked the slide. "So, fourteen plus one."

"Holy shit." Chad's eyebrows shot for his hairline. "That many?"

"Whoa." This seemed to be Bode's go-to. "That legal, Devil Dog?"

"Um . . . sure, my dad had . . ." He caught himself. "He bought it at some gun show."

"That's a lot of bullets," Chad said.

Puzzled, Eric felt his eyebrows draw together. "It's a Glock nineteen, standard fifteen-round mag. You can buy them all over. I've even seen them with that huge thirty-three-round clip."

"Thirty-three?" Bode said.

"That's it, man," Chad said. "I got to get me one of those. Hell with that measly eight-shot Colt."

"Huh." Bode shook his head. "Well, nice as that is, best you leave that here with her. It's only good close in anyway. More distance between us and the bad guys, the better."

"Wait a minute." Emma put her hands up in a warding-off gesture. "Get that thing away from me."

"No, he's right, Emma. You'll be all alone here." He proffered the weapon. "Come on, take the gun."

"But I don't know anything about guns. I mean, yeah, I've read about them . . ."

"What's to know?" Bode said. "Only pick it up if you're gonna use it. Glocks don't got a safety, so just point and squeeze the trigger. Oh, and make sure you don't shoot one of us."

"Ha-ha," Emma said. "No one's shooting anybody."

"Not yet," Chad said, sourly.

"Some gook comes busting in," Bode said, "you'll have to."

"What?" She shot Eric a mystified look. "What are you talking about?"

"The enemy, of course," Chad said.

"Listen, if I'm leaving this behind, do you guys have weapons?" Eric said.

"In the house." Bode hooked a thumb over his shoulder. "Bolt-action rifle, shotgun. I think there's something we can dig up for you, too. Give us two minutes to get our shit together, Devil Dog." Wading back up the steps, Bode jerked his head at Chad. "Let's go."

Chad opened his mouth to say something, changed his mind, shrugged. "You're the boss."

When they were gone, Emma said, "Why can't we all stay together?"

"I'm not having this discussion. Please, Emma, take the gun. If you don't want to do it for yourself, do it for me. You don't want anything to happen to me?" He extended the weapon, grip first. "Feeling's mutual."

Some emotion flashed through her pinched, anxious features. She nodded. "All right," she said, although she looked as if she'd be happier to accept a python instead. "What do I do?"

"Keep the muzzle pointed at the ground. Don't aim that thing at anyone unless you're going to shoot. Other than that, there's not much to it. There's a round in the chamber. Like Bode said, there's no safety, so be careful. You probably shouldn't keep it in your pocket either. If you need it in a hurry, you don't want it to hang up or snag. I'd carry it behind, tucked in your jeans around back, the way I did, all right?"

"Okay," she said, awkwardly stiff-arming the weapon down and out to one side. "Just point and shoot, right?"

"That's the size of it. But you got to loosen up. Here." Stepping around, he fitted her back into his chest and reached down her arms to cup her hands and seat the gun. "Come on, ease up, you got a death grip on this thing. It's not going to go off by itself."

"Right. Sorry." Working out her shoulders, she blew out in annoyance. "Like this?"

He felt the tension leak from her stance as she relaxed into him. "Yeah, good. But always keep your trigger finger outside the guard until you're ready to shoot. Bend your knees a little, too, like this." She wasn't a small girl, but at six-two, he thought he had a good five inches on her. Stooping a little, he butted the points of his knees into the back of hers. "Bend . . . that's good. And spread your feet . . . Excellent. See? Just like the movies."

She exhaled a shaky laugh, then half-turned until he felt her cheek on his chin. "Wonder which one we're in."

Not one with a happily ever after, he thought, grimly. *Not for me.* When this was over, he'd have to turn himself in. It had been crazy to run, a panicked and brainless move, and that was no kind of life for Casey. But before that, he could save his brother, and keep Emma safe. Of course, when everything came out about Big Earl, she wouldn't want to have anything to do with him. *But I can do a few things right before then.*

"This is important," he said. If she turned her head just a little more . . . *Idiot; stay sharp.* He forced himself to pull his head back a little. "In the movies, they pump out those bullets really fast because they're firing blanks. No kick, no climb; they never have to draw down again. But you'll have to, okay? So aim for center mass. You have a much better chance of actually hitting someone that way. But that means you'll have to wait until whoever's coming is close. I know that's scary, but . . ." His eyes scoured her face, and he knew that he really *should* let her go; she seemed to have figured out how to hold the weapon. *But this moment may never come again.* "You'll have to bide your time, Emma, pick your shot. Okay?"

"I can do that." She paused. "This is going to sound stupid, like one of those bad movies? But Eric . . . please be careful."

"Yeah." The voice came from the porch, and Eric looked up to see Chad, shotgun in hand, scuffing down the steps, with Bode just behind. "*We* will," Chad said. "Thanks for your concern."

In the wash of light spilling from the house, Eric saw Emma's cheeks color as she stepped out of his arms and turned. "Eric, I mean it—"

There came a rolling *boom*, distant but unmistakable, and Eric knew: that was not thunder. He looked over at Bode and Chad. "We have to go, *now*."

"Got that right." Bode shot the bolt of his rifle. "Playing our song, man."

Emma looked at Eric. "What *was* that?"

But it was Chad who answered. "Nothing real good."

CASEY
Where's His Tongue?

"TONY!" **RIMA CRIED.** "Oh my God!"

Jesus. Casey felt all the air wick out of his throat. Tony was pressed against the glass, palms flat, fingers splayed, like a little kid peering into a toy store window. Tony's face— what was left of it—was a macerated, staring mask of blood and skin, bone and muscle, grinning teeth with no lips and bulging eyes with very little flesh. When the boy opened his savaged mouth, more blood gushed, slick and steaming, to splash the glass.

No tongue, Casey thought, crazily. *He hasn't got a tongue. Where's his tongue?*

"EHHH EEE NNNN!" Tony gurgled. His smeary hands swarmed over the glass. *"OHHHENNN UHHH, EHHH EEE NNN!"*

"Tony! Let him in, Casey!" Rima tried reaching past to jab open the locks. "Hurry! Open up, and let him in, hurry!"

"NO! Don't open it, *don't open it!*" Before he knew what he was doing—no, no, that was a lie; he knew what he was doing, all right—Casey gave her a good one, a stinging back-handed swat. He pulled the slap at the last second; he didn't want to knock her out, just stop her. The blow caught Rima on the forehead just above her left eye. He heard her gasp, and then she went sprawling, the back of her head thudding against the passenger's side door. "Rima, damn it! Stop! We can't help him!"

"What is *wrong* with you?" Tears were leaking from her eyes, and a thin trickle of blood inched down her jaw from where she'd bitten her lip. She put a trembling hand to her forehead, like a little girl who couldn't believe that the parent she thought was so wonderful just five minutes ago could turn on a dime. "We would help *you.*"

"Then you're stupid," Casey said, flatly. "You've got a death wish. Getting ourselves killed won't save him."

"My God, what *are* you?" Her mouth worked like she wanted to spit. "How can you *do* this? Why are you letting *him* do this?"

"Him? What the hell are you—" He broke off at a sudden, wet, squeaking sound that reminded Casey of running his finger over the condensation of a bathroom mirror. He looked back to see Tony's hands scrabbling over the glass like wet spiders, his bloody fingers trying to dig in but finding nothing to grab. At the sight, Casey's stomach turned over.

Every man for himself, boy, Big Earl whispered. *You're doing the right thing. Don't listen to her. Stay strong. Be a man.*

No. But it was such a tiny thought, no more substantial than a soap bubble, and he could feel the crush of Big Earl's enormous hand over his mind. *This . . . Dad, it's not right, it's not—*

He heard himself suck in a quick breath as the night beyond Tony, that awful black jam of shadows . . . *moved.*

"What is that?" Rima's voice was a thin shriek. "Oh my God, what *is* that?"

I don't know. He didn't want to see this. Casey tried jerking his eyes away, but it was as if the same force that had controlled his hand was unfurling in the hollow of his skull, reaching fingers to grasp at his head and hold him fast so he *couldn't* look anywhere else. It was exactly like the time Big Earl came home from the pound with a mutt. Casey had been . . . he couldn't remember how old. A little kid. Ten? Twelve? He just didn't know. But the dog, he remembered: a Heinz 57, tan with a white ruff and a delirious, stubby little tail that went wild as the dog jumped up to flick its wet pink tongue at Casey's chin and try to lick his giggles.

Cut out that baby crap, Big Earl had snarled. Giving the rope knotted around the dog's neck a hard yank, Big Earl had marched the animal into the woods behind their cabin. Reluctant now, the dread growing, Casey had trailed, wishing he were anywhere else.

It's not a damn pet. I'm trying to teach you something here. Take this—his father thrust that wicked Glock into Casey's hands—*and kill that thing . . . NO.* Clamping a hand over Casey's head, Big Earl turned him back, the way you'd crank a hot water tap, when he tried backing up and looking away. *Do it, you little pissant. Grow a couple, and be a man for once.*

If he had been the man his father wanted, Casey should've shot the bastard dead, right then and there, and saved Eric and him all this trouble, these years of grief. But he was just a kid, and what Casey remembered was how everything inside just . . . stopped, the way that dog's stubby tail suddenly stilled. The small animal had looked up at Big Earl and then to Casey, and then its dark eyes, so bright before, dulled—like it knew what would happen next.

Unlike the dog, though, Casey couldn't look away from Tony and this horror show now. Because it was only human to stare at what should stay buried in nightmares; to gawk as a wolf brought down a deer and began to eat it alive. To play shoot-'em-up video games. Or was it that Big Earl simply wouldn't let him turn away? Casey was no longer sure, and maybe that wasn't important anymore.

Now, Casey couldn't help but watch—horrified but, yes, breathless, *excited*—as a long muscular rope slithered from the blackness beyond to coil around Tony's waist.

"No," Rima said, broken. She pressed her knuckles to her mouth. *"Tony."*

"OOOHHH!" Tony shrieked. His eyes were headlamps, white and round with terror. *"OOOHHH!"*

TONY

A Thing with Eyes

THEY WERE THERE, they were right there. *Open the door, open the—*

"OOORRR!" Tony slapped at the window with fingers that were more bone than meat. With no tongue now, everything came out as mush, but they must see, they must know he needed help. *Help me, help me, don't let me die! Open the door, open the door, the* door*! "ORRR!"*

Blood poured down his throat, and Tony choked, hacking out a brackish spray that tasted of salty copper mixed with the thick gag of gasoline. He could feel his life pumping from shredded arteries and veins, and a creeping cold spreading from his limbs toward his chest, rising for his head. He was dying; he was going to *die* out here.

Rima, help, help, don't leave me, don't leave me, don't leave—

From somewhere close behind, the thing bellowed. His heart turned over. What was it, what *was* it? He could not see it; he had never had the chance, because there was only the dark, that strange fog that had contracted on itself, and then the cold slash of the night, and this thing's claws and jaws and steaming, stinking breath that smelled of rot and bloat.

Then, through the blood-smeared window, he saw Rima's face swim toward him, and he felt a bright flame of sudden hope. *Yes, yes, open the door, let me in, please!* But then he saw Casey push Rima away and . . . had Casey *hit* her?

Oh God, oh God . . . A suffocating drape of despair closed around his chest and stoppered his breath. Casey was going to leave him out here, let him die . . . *Please.* He slapped at the window again, hearing the high squeaky drag of thick blood over cold glass. *Please let me in, please save me.*

Then he felt it—the night, the fog, the monster; it was one and the same—gathering itself out there, closing in, *moving.* "Uhhh," he moaned, "uhhh, eeesss . . ."

A thick, strong rope—*no, an arm, a tentacle; what is this thing?*—wormed around his middle.

No no no! "*OHHH!*" The scream bubbled from his mouth on a choking gout of fresh blood. He felt the rope tighten and bunch, the muscles tensing. "*OHHH!*"

With one savage jerk, it yanked him from the glass. Wailing, Tony hurtled backward, rocketing through the night like a yo-yo recalled by its owner at the twitch of a finger. The rope flicked, releasing him, and Tony let out another scream as he flew in a plunging arc. He crashed to the gas-slicked ice, like a large stone dropped into a still pond. A wide corona of gasoline shot up, then splashed back down to mingle with his blood.

Got to get away. He rolled to his stomach, his parka bunching around his middle. *Oh God, I don't want to die, please.* He began a desperate, flopping wriggle, and he thought about worms trapped on the sidewalk after a hard rain. He had no idea where he was going, or how far he'd get, but if he could just get *away*, if it would stop *hurting* him . . .

Then, around the iron fist of his fear, he registered something hard digging into his belly—and remembered. There *was* something he could do. It would also be the very last thing he ever did.

No. For a second, everything stilled: the wild rampaging of his heart, the thrum of his blood, the breaths that hacked his throat. *No, I can't. God, don't ask me to.*

From not very far away, the thing let out a high, rusty shriek. He rolled onto his back, eyes bulging from their ruined sockets, straining to see, to make sense. My God, he didn't even *know* what was out there, but it would unzip his skin with a single swipe of a claw. His guts would slosh onto the ice, and then it would hunker over him and feed. He might even be still alive when it did; he would die feeling it rip him to pieces. And there was nowhere to run, no place he could find to hide.

The thing screamed again, and he felt the dig at his middle and thought, *Well, why the hell not? I'm going to die anyway.* And God, was that too weird or what? A laugh boiled in his throat to tangle with a bloody sob. A year left before graduation, and he'd never even kissed a girl. How pathetic was that? But he remembered the moment he and Rima touched. Not love at first sight so much as a connection and, perhaps, a promise. Or maybe it was nothing more complicated than hope and a single kindness. Whatever it was, he knew: despite his fear, he could do it for her.

Groaning, he forced his shredded hand into his pocket,

then willed his nerveless fingers to close. He had to move his whole shoulder to tug his hand free. He was starting to shake now, too—shock and pain and the cold and black terror so complete it was a wonder he was still alive. It took nearly all his strength just to twist off the cap. Once done, he leaned back on his elbows, panting, swallowing back blood, listening to the splash and slither as the thing crept closer . . .

Wait . . . He could hear his breath shuddering from his throat. *Not yet* . . .

And closer . . .

Please, God—he stifled a scream as ripples of gasoline broke against his legs—*if you're real, if you're there, please help me, keep me alive just a little longer* . . .

And now so close he *heard* the moist, fleshy *smack-smack* of its jaws . . .

Hang on, Tony. He could feel his mind trying to fall away in a final swoon, like a heavy boulder plunging from a cliff so high the drop was bottomless . . .

The *slap-splash* of its body heaving over the ice . . .

Focus. His heart was racing, frantically trying to pump what was no longer there. The shuddering was out of his control now, and he was cold, so cold . . . *Stay with it.* His ears sharpened on the soft *plik-plik-plik* of the last of his blood as it dripped into the larger lake of gasoline in which he lay. *Don't die yet, Tony. Stay alive a few more seconds.*

And now he smelled it: more potent than the cloying reek of gasoline, this was a stink as dank and putrid as the moist carcass of a long-dead animal, so rotten that a single touch would rupture the thin membrane of papery skin to release a runny spume of green goo, yellow pus, a liquefied heart. The smell was, he realized, the reek steaming from his mother at the very end. It was the stink of the fog itself—his personal nightmare—and it was close now, right on top of him.

Now. He put everything he had into it, all that was left. With one shaky snap of his hands, he scraped the striker against the end of the flare. The flare bloomed to life in a sputtering, bright flame. The darkness peeled back in a black shriek; the fog parted, drawing aside like curtains; and what leapt from the night . . . what he *saw* . . .

Oh my God. His mind tilted, and he nearly lost his already failing grip on the flare. *No, this can't be happening. I* read *you, but you're not real, you can't be . . .*

Then, a single, last memory: as he cringed on the strange mirror-ice, he remembered the feel of the fog's fingers worming into his lungs, snagging his blood, walking his brain . . .

To find *this*? Because this was a monster he recognized. It was something he knew, and well, because he had thought it into being, this cancer that burrowed through his mother's guts, on a dark stage in his mind.

It was a *thing* with eyes—with an insane sweep of a million myriad black and glittery eyes, a boil of writhing tentacles, a bristle of teeth, a swooning horror that even Lovecraft could never have survived *thinking*, much less writing—but it was here, it was here, it was on top on him, it was—

Tony didn't have time for more than that. No time to think how such a nightmare could be, or how it had been plucked from his mind. No time for much of anything, in fact.

With the last of his strength, Tony thrust the sputtering flame into the thing's bloody, gasoline-soaked maw and then

RIMA

Don't Look Back

IN THE CAMRY, with no screen of wind-driven snow to block her view, Rima saw it all: a quick, bright spark blooming in the dark, and then, for the briefest of instants, the brooding mass of something huge and monstrous.

What is *that?* She could feel her lungs forget how to work. *Are those . . . are those* arms? And then she put something else together: Tony had lit a flare. *Oh my God . . .* "Casey," she said, urgently, "the—"

"The gas," he finished for her. "Oh sh—"

The darkness broke apart in a fireball, a geyser of orange-yellow flame that shot toward the sky. The light was bright, worse than staring into the full round heat of the sun, and blistered her eyes. With a cry, she threw up her hands as the light seemed to sear its way into her brain—

And Tony was gone. Just like that. She knew it. She had his scarf, after all. One moment Tony was there, cupping her flesh in the most fleeting of whispers—and then not. Poof.

Wait, she thought, suddenly. *That's not how it usually hap—*

There was another huge *boom* as the van exploded. This second fireball was eye-wateringly bright, and she saw the wreck's mangled metal skeleton actually *lift* from the snow. Pieces rocketed into the air and then streamed down in blazing arcs just like those big firecrackers on the Fourth of July, the kind that blossomed in a thousand different directions. A flaming tire whizzed past the car; twisted bits of scorched metal rained in a hot shower.

"Oh shit, *shit!*" Scrambling over the front seat, Casey landed half on, half off the rear bench, then flung himself at the passenger's side door. He gave the handle a ferocious yank, then cursed. "Rima, pop the locks! We got to get out! Come on, get out, *get out of the car!*"

She saw them coming now, too: flaming streamers of burning gasoline slithering toward them over the snow. No, not snow now: *ice*, odd and milky—but why wasn't it melting? She watched in a kind of horrified paralysis as the greedy flames gobbled up distance and raced through the dark, heading right—

"Pop the locks!" Casey bawled. *"Rima, pop the goddamned locks!"*

With a gasp, Rima stretched, tripped the control, heard the *ka-thunk* of the locks, and then threw herself against the door. This time, the door flew open and she tumbled out. Casey was already there, scrambling to his feet.

"Come on," he shouted, making a grab for her arm. "Come on, Rima! Run, *run!*"

Her flesh shrank from his touch, and she had to swallow back the scream that tried crawling past her teeth. But she knew what to expect now: that she would feel the ghost of Big

Earl's hard, meaty, callused hands instead of Casey's because his father's death-whisper, clinging to the flannel shirt, was that strong.

"Come on!" Casey cried, hauling her to her feet, and then he was churning through that lake of gasoline, dragging her along as they slipped and scrambled away from the car: two steps, four, six, ten . . .

Don't look back. Rima dug in, willing herself to stay upright, feeling the treacherous ice trying to upend her. *Don't look back; run, run, ru—*

The Camry blew.

The explosion was a fist between her shoulders, and Rima was suddenly airborne, flying over the snow on a gust of superheated air. The concussive force tossed her a good forty feet, and she had time to remember that weird, rock-hard ice and what something as solid as stone might do to a person smacking into it with such force. She had time to think, *I'm dead.*

Then she crashed—but not against the ice. Hurtling like a spent meteor, she bulleted into thick snow. She was not a big girl, or heavy, but the blast jammed her deep. Snow pillowed into her mouth and plugged her nostrils. Spluttering, she flailed, trying to fight her way back to the surface, but she was socked in tight.

In her parka, Taylor's death-whisper shrieked with the terror that Rima felt explode in her chest. Her lungs were already burning from lack of air. A red haze blurred the margins of her vision. Out, out, she had to get out! But which way was up? How much air did she really have? Her heart galloped in her chest. She was cocooned so thoroughly, her parka bound her as tightly as a mummy's wrappings. With Taylor twisting and squirming, the feeling was like being trapped in a gunnysack with a nest of snakes.

Completely disoriented, she swept her arms to either side, trying to scour out an air pocket. The snow in front of her face gave, and then there was space: not a lot, but more than before.

Okay, that's good, come on, you can do this; you have *to.* Rima kept sweeping, doing the breaststroke over and over again. She felt the hollow grow from the size of a baseball to that of a basketball. There was also a little more air than before, because the snow wasn't solid ice; there were air pockets and even slivers of space between flakes. She pulled in a thin breath and then another. The air was close, but she could breathe. Although her chest and arms and face were cold, heat palmed her calves. *Must be fire from the explosion.* So now she knew which way was up. *Not good, not good . . .* A sharp nail of panic scraped the back of her neck. If she felt heat on her leg, that meant . . .

My God, I'm upside down. My feet are above my head. I'm like a cork in a wine bottle.

But wait a minute, wait . . . *I feel heat.* That meant part of her—her legs, her boots—*must* be visible. Yeah, but someone had to be looking for her. Casey might be dead or in just as much trouble. If he wasn't dead, well, she didn't think that Big Earl would let Casey stick around.

She thought of that touch, the death-whisper that was Big Earl. Casey must be wearing something of his father's. The parka? No, she thought it must be the shirt, that red-checked flannel she'd spied dragging over his knuckles earlier but that had seemed to retreat as the hours went by: a shirt that was first too big and now just right. Casey wouldn't save her, because Big Earl wouldn't give a damn. Any second now, those flames would die, and then, if Casey was still alive, she'd catch the muted cough of that snowmobile.

Wait! What was that? Had she heard something? She strained, her ears tingling. *There was something there, I heard . . .*

Something above her, beyond this prison of deadening snow . . . shuffled.

Her heart surged. Casey? Or maybe Eric and Emma had come back with help. She opened her mouth to shout—then clamped back, her throat closing down, as something else occurred to her.

The thing that killed Tony is gone. But what if there's another? A shiver rippled down her spine. *Oh God.* Her chest was a sudden scream of pain, as if Taylor's terrified death-whisper were trying to gnaw a hole through her skin and burrow itself deep inside to hide. But Rima could only wait, quivering, in a darkness that was growing thicker and more airless by the second—and it was a choice now, wasn't it? Say nothing, do nothing, and she would suffocate. *But something is there, it's getting closer, it's right on top of*—

Something slithered around her ankle, and closed.

PART THREE

THE

FOG

LIZZIE
Wear Me

AS HER MOTHER muscles the stick and they race away from what's left of their home, the fog—all that remains of her father tangled with the Peculiars' energy and that of the whisper-man—is both a fist, closing down over Lizzie's past, and a ravening monster with a mouth, gobbling up the road and this world, and still coming on strong. Seeping from the cell's speaker, the whisper-man's voice is a faint, mournful sough: *Come down, Blood of My Blood; come plaaay, come down, come . . .*

Lizzie fishes up her mother's phone. Crackling with the energy of Lizzie's thought-magic, the magic-glass of her memory quilt is a shimmering dazzle. The special Sign of Sure, the tool her dad has used to get himself back and forth from *Nows* through the Dark Passages, is as iridescent as the Milky Way. But she thinks the fog has to be much closer. Maybe she has to let it *inside*, allow it to slip into and wear her the way she does the book-people and her dolls. The way her father has invited whatever's in the Dark Passages.

But he's done it with blood, by cutting himself, so will this work? Can I grab it hard enough?

She just doesn't know. Yet this she does understand: everyone wants what they can't have, same as when Lizzie whines for a second scoop of chocolate ice cream. They *especially* want what's hard to get.

So make the whisper-man mad. Make it really work hard, get so greedy-pissed it flies for her like a moth to the hottest flame, so it doesn't get what Lizzie's doing until way too late.

I'll show you. Come on, you big show-off. Let's play my *game.* She thumbs the phone to silence. The cell rings again at once. This time, she turns off the power, which she already knows won't make a dent, and it doesn't. When the phone begins to chirp again, she pitches the machine into the black mouth of the foot well because there is no way, no *way* she's answering again. Let that whisper-man stew. That'll show him.

"Good girl," Mom says, misunderstanding. As Lizzie scrambles to buckle in, her mother chokes back another sob. "I'm so sorry, Lizzie."

"It's okay, Mom." She knuckles away tears. "It's going to catch us, isn't it?"

"If it really wants us, yes. I don't think there's much I can do about that, but it'll have to work to do it." Her mother's foot drops and the car surges with a roar. "Listen to me, Lizzie, this is important. If it wants something . . . if it needs to bind someone, it can take me. I won't let it hurt you, honey, but you have to promise me to run, run as far away as you can, and don't look back, all right? I'll be . . ." Her voice wavers, then firms. "I'll be able to hold it. But you run, promise?"

"I promise," Lizzie says, already knowing that this is a

pinky-swear she will break. Run, and as bad as this is, she thinks things could get to be a hundred million zillion times worse, because there is so much power here, enough to break this *Now* wide open. So what happens next won't be up to her mother.

Come on, come and get me. As the woods spin by beyond the car, Lizzie hunkers down into her memory quilt. Behind her, hanging in the air, the symbols for Lizzie's new *Now* hum and purple with a weird, mad energy drawn from ideas deep down cellar and from the dark where the strongest—the worst—imaginings live. Just a few more seconds and one more symbol . . .

Come on, come get me, Lizzie thinks. *Get mad and want me, wear me, want me.*

EMMA

A Choice Between Red and Blue

1

FROM HER PLACE on the snow-covered farmhouse porch, Emma watched the red wink of taillights disappear into a mouth of darkness that finally closed, swallowing up that creaky old Dodge. God, she didn't want to let Eric out of her sight. What would happen to him if she weren't around?

Well, I'm sure to find out. She pressed a finger to an aching temple. Her head *killed*, probably a combination of concussion and all those *blinks*, a lot of them. Too many. Ever since waking up in this valley, she'd been zoning out, losing chunks of time. She didn't think the others had noticed, although Casey—that nasty kid, someone she'd never have imagined related to Eric—kept throwing her speculative looks.

I see the same girl, too, over and over again, in every blink. *Kid even has a name, and that's a first.* "Lizzie," she said, trying it out in her mouth. Saying the little girl's name made all those *blinks* feel much more real, not like dreams at all but as if she was a stunt double slotting into a film of Lizzie's life. Not completely in the kid's head but close. *And everything I see is happening to her right now, at this moment.* This last time, the kid had been . . . running from something? *Afraid of her dad; something happened to her father.* She thought that was right. Emma just couldn't quite grab hold of what it was about Lizzie's dad that was freaking the kid out, although she retained a wisp of an image: Dad doing something really, really scary in front of a very odd mirror.

Coming back from these *blinks* was so different, too, like surfacing with the tangles of nightmares clinging to her like sticky seaweed. *They feel like memories, something I've always known.* She had this odd notion that if her brain was a hallway lined with doors, all she had to do was open the right one to walk into Lizzie's life.

Or pull her into mine. A weird thought. And this last *blink* . . . "Want me, wear me," she whispered, hugging herself against the cold. Tony's space blanket let out a tired crinkle like soggy cellophane. "What does that mean, Lizzie?" Made about as much sense as Jasper going on about . . . "Dark Passages," she said, slowly, to the still, cold night. "Lizzie knows about them—and different *Nows*? Like Jasper? But Jasper was *drunk* half the time."

Was Jasper talking about something that exists? The fingers of another shiver skipped up the rungs of her spine. No matter how many times she'd asked, her guardian never had explained. In the end, she'd chalked it up to the fact that he was pretty permanently pickled. *But what if the Dark Passages and the* Nows *are why he drank? Not just to forget or because he was so freaked. What if Jasper drank so it—they?—couldn't find him?* This idea had an itchy, tip-of-the-tongue feeling, something that felt true. *As if I once knew this but . . . forgot?*

Another, more bizarre thought: *Or is this something I was made to forget?*

"Oh, don't be stupid, you nut." A flare of impatience. "Jasper was soaked, and the *blinks* are seizures. They're hallucinations, like dreams. Of course, you're going to slot in stuff you know about. That's the way dreams and hallucinations are." Yeah, but she didn't *know* a Lizzie.

"Emma, stop, you're not going to solve this right now." She really ought to go inside. Yet the idea made a twist of fear coil in her gut. Why? It was stupid. There was light inside the house, and it was warm. There was *food*. She could still smell the faint, rich aroma of cheddar from a mac and cheese casserole. Bode and Chad seemed fine, if a little odd.

But this farmhouse . . . *I have seen you before, over and over again.* In the *blinks*? Yes, and no: she thought she'd actually seen a picture of the house somewhere. She ran her eyes over the porch railing, the bay window, that snow-covered swing on its chains. Come spring, she'd bet money a froth of red geraniums would replace the mounds of white humped in those hanging planters.

If spring ever comes to a place like this. Swaddled in the space blanket and her parka, still damp with gasoline, she shivered as much from cold as a sudden premonition that, maybe, it was always night here, and cold. *And that's got something to do with Wyoming. Those license plates are important. But I've never been to Wyoming.*

"Oh, don't be a nut just because you can," she said, watching her breath bunch in a gelid knot. Her eye drifted from the porch and past Eric's snowmobile to that huge, outsize barn soaring up from the snow. Wisconsin was lousy with red gable-roofed barns with stone foundations and sliders and haymows and cupolas to draw in air and dry out the hay. But this thing was *ginormous*, much too big—and wrong, too. Why? Her gaze brushed over the exterior walls, then roamed over the gabled roof.

"No cupola," she said after a moment. "No sliders, not even a ramp." There was a door but no windows of any kind. The walls were blank. It was as she'd said to Eric: the skeleton of a movie set, someone's *idea* of what a farm—a barn—should be.

"Or maybe it's all the barn you need." Then she thought, *What? Enough barn for whom?*

"Hey, Emma, you nut . . . what if *this* is a *blink*? You ever think about that? Or maybe you're dreaming." Hadn't there been some movie about this? "*Inception*," she said, and then more loudly: "So, okay, go ahead, kick me. I'd like to wake up now."

Of course, nothing happened. "Right," she snorted, watching how her breath smoked in the icy air. "It's not like Morpheus is going to show up and give you a choice between red and blue. Get a grip."

Scooping snow from the porch railing, she cupped it in her bare hands, grimacing at the burn. "So that's real." She held the snow to her nose and sniffed. Frowned. "But funky." Snow had an odor, something that she associated with frigid, frosty, old-fashioned trays of ice cubes. *This* particular scent was thicker and metallic, but not aluminum. Copper? The image of Jasper's heap of a pickup flashed in the middle of her mind. Yeah, same smell: wet, cold rust. Still, this was *real* snow.

And my head hurts. Brushing powder from her hands, she gingerly probed her bandaged forehead with a forefinger. Beneath the gauze and her skin, she could feel the circle of her titanium skull plate. So *that,* or rather *she,* was—

2

BLINK.

"Oh boy." She was inside, with no memory of having opened the door. She threw a glance at the braided mat upon which she stood. Her shoes were bone-dry: no melting snow, no puddles. To her surprise, the house was a little chilly; she pressed the back of one hand to the tip of her nose. *Cold as a brass button. Bet it's red as Rudolph's, too.*

"*Okay,*" she breathed, and felt the house fold down a bit, crouch closer—which was . . . pretty crazy. *Exactly like when I read* The Bell Jar *this past summer; felt that damn thing coming down, trapping me like a lightning bug under a jelly glass.* Yet she heard nothing in the house. Not a creak. Not a crack or pop, none of the tiny settling sounds any normal house made. No *hoosh* of a furnace either. She threw a glance at the ceiling and then down at the floor. *Whoa, no vents. No registers or radiators. So how are they heating this thing?*

Except for the gleaming hardwood floor, which held this single colorful braided rug, the foyer was a white-walled cube. No pictures. No paintings. Ahead and to the left, she saw a circular flight of stairs that twisted around and around, seemingly forever. Like the barn, the too-large stairs belonged in a little kid's fairy-tale version of a mansion or castle, and was all wrong. Another hall—black as a tomb and lined with closed doors—ran to the left of the stairs and went on a long way.

Just walls and a front door with sidelights. A hall with a lot of doors. Outside, there's a porch, a swing, hanging planters, but no storm door. No doorbell or peephole. She threw a look back at the door. *Not even a lock.* Her eyes zeroed in on the smooth brass knob.

"No keyhole," she said. "It's just a knob. Everything's been stripped down to the bare minimum, like the barn. Because this is all the house you need?" *All the house who needs?* "Maybe I'm not thinking about this the right way. Maybe"— she cocked her head at the ceiling—"maybe this is all the *house* needs."

To her left, something cleared its throat with a faint sputter.

"Huh!" Clapping a hand to her mouth, she held back a scream. She could feel her eyes trying to bug out of their sockets. What *was* that? Coming from that gloomy corridor . . . Her breath was coming too hard and fast to hear over, and she raked her upper lip with her teeth, focusing on the pain. *Calm down, you nut. Just . . . music?* No. Concentrating, she worked to reel in the sound and caught a static crackle, a gabble of nonsense syllables, a sizzle and hiss.

"Radio." The word floated on a sigh of relief. *Freak yourself out, why don't you?* Or maybe a TV Bode and Chad had left on. Had there been a satellite dish on the roof? She didn't remember one, and this house was way the hell and gone. No way it got cable. So this was more than likely a radio.

I should look for it. Eventually, they'll give the call sign, or if I really luck out and there's a weather band . . . She pushed away a sudden woozy sense of déjà vu. Hadn't this been exactly what she'd said to Lily only a few hours ago? *Well, so what if this is a weather band?* This was a farm, *duh*; farmers cared about weather just like ships' pilots and fishermen. *If I can find the radio, I'll know where we are.*

"Hah," she muttered, "easy for you to say." Carefully inching from the mat, she let herself ease a foot away but still close enough to the door to bolt if she needed to. *If the house lets me out.* "Stop it, Emma," she said. Shutting her eyes, she cocked her head like a dog trying to decipher a command, and listened. *Where* was this coming from?

Well, you could go look, you coward. But she couldn't make herself move any further than she already had. A spider of new fear scurried up her neck and stroked another deep shudder. "What are you waiting for, Emma?" she murmured. "An engraved invitation?"

And was she talking *only* to herself?

No. She ran her eyes over the blank walls, the improbable staircase, the smooth ceiling. *I'm talking to you, House*—and then she sucked in a quick breath as she realized something that neither she nor Eric had seen before, that just hadn't clicked.

There was *light* in this house, glaring and bright. But there were no fixtures. No bulbs, no lamps, nothing—only that single pole lamp in front of the barn.

Because you wanted to make sure we saw that barn, didn't you, House? Just in case we happened to miss the fact that it's as big as a mountain?

"You," she said to herself, "are creeping yourself out." With good reason, though: this valley, the house, the stillness, this sudden radio gibberish, if that's what it even was . . . none of this belonged.

"You don't belong either, House." Her voice came out flat. "It's like you're alive. I feel you watching me, waiting for me to make a move . . ."

3

SHE *BLINKED* BACK.

She stood at a bathroom sink, over which a wall-mounted, mirrored medicine chest hung. The glass was fogged with condensation. Her hair was damp, and the air was steamy and smelled of floral shampoo. A fluffy white towel was hung neatly over a steel shower curtain rod. The curtain itself was gauzy white and decorated with the black silhouette of a cat at the lower left staring up at a tiny mouse at the right.

Cat-and-mouse is right. Looking down at herself, she saw that she now wore fresh jeans and a turquoise turtleneck that brought out the deep sapphire of her eyes. *Must've raided a closet or something.* Even *blinked* out, she always *could* color-coordinate.

And now I'm in front of a mirror, and there was a mirror in that blink *about Lizzie's dad.* "But this is a bathroom." Plucking a white washcloth from a towel bar next to the sink, she scrubbed the mirror free of steam. Her face swam to the surface of the glass and firmed. She saw that she'd removed her bandage. Her forehead was a mess. "Just a plain-old vanilla bathroom in a creepy little house, not some huge, weird mirror in a big ba—"

Oh, shit. "In a big barn." Her mouth was so dry she had no spit. *Be calm.* She carefully smoothed the washcloth, then folded it in half and draped it over the towel bar. *Think this through.*

"Right. Okay, so there's a barn," she said to her reflection. "So what? What does this prove? That you're still in that weird Lizzie-*blink*? Or only dreaming?"

Yet Lily was dead. That was no dream. And her forehead hurt. Squinting at her reflection, she gingerly finger-walked the wound. The ragged edges were raw, and a purplish lump bulged like a unicorn's horn. Touching it sent off a sparkle of pain.

"So this is real." At the wave of relief, she gave a tremulous laugh. "Of course it is. I've been scared in dreams, but I've never gotten all banged up or cut, and if I have, I don't remember, and I've never felt pain." *Lucky I didn't crack my skull either. Can that happen if you've already got plates*—

She never finished that thought. She felt the words curl in on themselves as tightly as snails withdrawing into their shells.

Because that was when her brain finally caught up to what was going on with that mirror—and, more to the point, what was happening *in* it.

"Oh, holy shit," she said.

4

LOOK IN A mirror, any mirror, even the goofy ones at the county fair. Raise your right hand. From your reflection's perspective, you're raising your *left* hand, so your reflection raises *its* left. Equal but opposite. Put your right hand on the glass and your reflection's left hand floats to meet you.

But when Emma raised her right hand, her reflection lifted *its* right. Equal . . . but *not* opposite.

"What?" Startled, she took a step back—

And watched her reflection take a step *forward*.

"Oh God." A sudden cold sweat started on her upper lip. *That can't be happening. I hit my head. That's what this is. I've been* blinking *a lot. I'm seeing things.* "It's all head trauma," she said, and let her right hand drift up again. "This is nothing but—"

The rest wouldn't come, because, this time, her reflection did nothing. Not a thing. Didn't move its hand. Didn't step back either.

"Stop that," she said to her reflection. "What's—" *Ohhh, God.* She heard her breath gush from her mouth. She was talking. Her mouth had moved.

But her reflection's hadn't. That thing with her face hadn't matched her words at all but only stared, mute and waxen as a doll, as soulless as a mannequin.

Get out. Her knees were beginning to shake. In another second, if she didn't get moving, her legs would give out and she'd fall, maybe faint. *Get out of this house while you still can. Run, ru—*

Her reflection moved toward her.

"Oh shit." Emma breathed. Rooted to the spot, she watched as her reflection took a step and then another and another until it was plastered against the glass, its features flattening like those of a kid peering into the darkened front of a candy store. *Run, you nut, run.* But she couldn't make herself move. It was as if she'd turned to stone.

Something tugged her wrist.

"What?" She stared at her right hand, which was starting to jitter. Her fingers twitched. "Stop that," she said to her hand. "Cut that out. *Stop!*"

Her hand . . . *moved*. On its own. Without her telling it to.

No. Stop, she thought to her hand. *Stop what you're doing.* "Don't, Emma," she said, hoarsely, as her fingers floated for the mirror. "Don't, *don't!*"

Her hand didn't care. She watched herself reach for the glass and thought back to earlier that day: that strange compulsion to push *through* her driver's side window—*where the barrier's thinnest*—and bleed to some other time and place.

"Bleed," she said, and felt her heart give a tremendous lurch. *In my* blink, *Lizzie's dad cut himself. When his blood touched that weird mirror, the glass began to change.*

"Don't touch it," she quavered. All the tiny hairs on her neck and arms bristled. This wasn't the same mirror; she hadn't cut herself. But then why wasn't her hand obeying? Whoever heard of a reflection that acted more like a double trapped on the other side of the glass? *Alice in Wonderland syndrome is right.* "Emma, don't do this."

But her hand just wouldn't listen. As her fingers met the bathroom mirror's silvered glass, a startled cry tore from her lips. The icy mirror burned; her fingers instantly numbed, and yet she was still reaching, pressing, *pushing* . . .

This is like when I was twelve and wandered down into Jasper's cellar to find a book, she thought with stupefied horror. *I couldn't stop myself back then either.* This was a nightmare, like Neo at the mirror, after he'd swallowed the red pill. *Stop, I want the blue pill,* she thought, crazily, as she kept *pushing.* "Help," she panted, "somebody, help, he—"

Now, the glass dimpled. It *rippled* and *swam.* It opened itself like a mouth.

"No!" Her heart smashed against her ribs. Wrapping her free hand around her forearm, she braced her feet and tried pulling her hand free, but her arm only kept going as first her fingers and then her hand *sank* into the glass . . .

And met the flesh of her reflection.

"God . . . House, *stop!*" she shouted. In the mirror, her reflection was still rigid and unmoving. The space on its side of the mirror was icy cold and felt . . . *Dead. It feels dead, like a corpse, like Lily.* It was as if her hand didn't belong to her anymore, or that the lines between her brain and her hand had been cut. Instead, she could only watch as her fingers spidered over her reflection: its cheeks, its nose, its jaw. *Dark—this is what* dark *feels like.*

"I don't even know what that means," she said, her voice breaking with terror. And *dark* . . . in her *blinks*, Lizzie knew about the Dark Passages. Was *this* what she was talking about? Had this been what Jasper meant?

But this is just a bathroom. Jasper was a lush. It's the wrong mirror. It's not the mirror I saw in a blink*; it's not even close to the Dickens Mirror—*

"Dickens Mirror?" *Where did* that *come from?* She watched her thumb skim her reflection's lower lip. "House, what the hell is the Dickens Mi—" She shrieked as a phantom finger ghosted over her lower lip. What she was doing to that reflection, *she* felt: *her* touch over *her* skin, on *her* side of the glass.

"Ahhh . . . *God,*" she moaned. She couldn't even turn her head away. Her whole body crawled as if she'd thrust her arms up to the elbows in a vat of decaying flesh and slick, gooey pus. If she could've unzipped and shrugged out of her skin, she would've. *I am crazy.* "Please, House," she gasped, "please,

God, let this be a dream! I promise, I'll take my meds. I don't care if I walk around in a fog for the rest of my life; I don't want to see this or be here! I only want to wake—"

Quick as a snake, her reflection seized her hand, still buried on its side of the mirror, by the wrist.

"AH!" Emma tried shrinking back but couldn't break her reflection's grip. It pulled, yanking Emma in a stumbling lurch toward the glass. She was aware, but only vaguely, that there was now no sink in her way. There seemed, in fact—and for the briefest of moments—to be no bathroom at all: the walls, the floor, the ceiling wrinkling to nothing, evaporating in a glimmer.

"NOOO!" Wailing, Emma fell into the glass, or maybe it was the mirror that rushed for her fast, and then faster. . . .

LIZZIE
Mom Makes Her Mistake

THE FOG—HER DAD, the whisper-man, the energy of the Peculiars all tangled together—rushes for them, fast and then faster and faster, swallowing trees, gobbling up the sky. The fog is not a wall but a roiling mass like the relentless churn of a tornado, and very fast, much faster than they are. Lizzie knows they'll lose this race. In fact, she's counting on it.

But Mom doesn't understand and would never agree if she did. So she tries. Her mother will not give up. She is brave, so brave, and screaming now, not at that fog but their car: "Come on, you piece of shit, *come on!*" Teeth bared, the cords standing in her neck, her mother is defiant, determined, enraged, and she has never been more beautiful. Through her terror, through whatever else is to come, Lizzie's heart swells with pride and love, and she grabs hold of this one clear thought: she will always remember the moment when her mother tried to save them.

I have to be brave; be as brave as Mom, as the kids in Dad's books. As brave as Dad.

Their car leaps forward, and then they are vaulting, storming down the road, the woods whizzing to a blur. They are traveling much too quickly for this road, which twists and turns and climbs and drops—and still the fog is remorseless, a ravening white monster.

Come on, Lizzie thinks, urging it on. *Hurry up, come on, come on, want me, want me!* Her whole body burns, *screams* with the need to finish the *Now,* finish the *Now,* finish it. Behind her, the symbols for her special forever-*Now* purple the air; they are so strong they snap and crackle as if the world were electric. Her hand is on fire. The best symbol, the most powerful and the one she must draw if the forever-*Now* is to work, begs to come into being. The Sign of Sure is so strong, the path it will blaze through the Dark Passages so brilliant, that Lizzie's head is a hot bright ball, like a sun a second away from exploding into a supernova.

Wait. She grits her teeth as tears of pain and grief squeeze from the corners of her eyes. *Wait, wait until it's got us, wait until I feel it, until the very last—*

They rocket over a rise. Her stomach drops away as the car leaves the road and then smashes to earth with a sudden, loud *bam.* The front tires explode. Something—the fender—catches. Sparks swarm past Lizzie's window like fireflies. The car fishtails wildly, the rear skidding left . . .

And this is when Mom makes her mistake. Without slowing, Mom stiff-arms the wheel and wrenches it too far.

"No, no, *no!*" her mother shouts as the car fishtails. She

fights the wheel, but this time, the centrifugal force is too great and they spin out of control.

Lizzie's forehead slams against her window. The pain is immense and erupts like a bomb. Her vision sheets first red and then glare-white. Something breaks in her head and tears, and then her hair is wet and warm. The car swerves left, and her head jerks right, snapping on the stalk of her neck. Another sharp *crack* as her head connects with glass again, and then the window has imploded in a shower of pebbly safety glass. They are spinning, whirling like a top, the world beyond dissolving into a crazy blur, going faster than any carousel. Even with her shoulder harness, Lizzie is pinned against the car door, momentum jamming her in place, crushing her like a bug. Through a red haze, she sees the trees racing for them, the trunks growing huge in the windshield.

Screaming, Lizzie throws up her arms and

EMMA

Between the Lines

1

BLINK.

I'm still in the house. Pulse thundering, Emma inched her head left, saw a procession of doors, and then looked to her right. Through a bright rectangle of yellow light, she made out the front door, the braided rug, gleaming hardwood. Blank white walls. *Downstairs again. I'm in that hall I saw from the foyer.*

The air in this hall was brain-freeze cold, bad enough to set her teeth and steam her breath, but her right hand was on fire. Steeling herself, she turned her hand palm up and inspected her skin in the gloom. No burns, no blisters, no marks, not even a scratch. She flexed her fingers, curled them into a fist. Everything seemed to work.

What had she just seen in that last *blink*? "A crash," she said. "Lizzie was in a car with her mother, and she crashed."

She dragged her eyes up to look straight ahead at a very strange door. It was not made of any kind of wood she recognized. It wasn't even a proper door. This door was a long slit, just wide enough to allow a single person to pass through, and as glare-white as the snow, as the sky around the sun at high noon on a hot summer's day. As one of Jasper's canvases, come to think of it.

She realized something else. *I've seen this before, too.* The color was dead wrong, but the shape was right. That smoky-black mirror that Lizzie's father had in his barn was a slit, too.

"The Dickens Mirror," she murmured, and frowned. What was *that* about? Dickens was . . . you know . . . überfamous. And so? They'd read *Great Expectations* in tenth grade—not a bad book; Havisham was a trip, like Dickens read Brontë and decided to bring the crazy lady out of the attic—and *A Tale of Two Cities* (total snooze). For a while there, before she was sent away to school, she had Dickens coming out of her eyeballs because of Jasper and all those tapes. They might have listened to a biography or two. No, make that a definite. Jasper had the old Dickens bio by Forster, and maybe another, more recent. *And hadn't there been something about mirrors in that one?* That was right. Dickens had scads of mirrors, all through his house, in his study, everywhere. She even remembered why: when he was a kid and his dad had gone to debtor's prison, Dickens had been forced to work in a gloomy, dank blacking factory. As an adult and even though he walked the nights away through the warren of London's alleys and the sewers coursing through the city's underbelly, Dickens hated darkness. He'd filled the rooms of his many homes with mirrors to bring in and magnify the light. So had there been a very special, very peculiar mirror? She just didn't know, and she couldn't remember a single Dickens story that revolved around a mirror.

So it's probably not something Dickens made up. Could he have had a mirror made, or just found it somewhere? The guy went a gajillion places, climbed mountains, nearly killed himself getting to the top of Vesuvius, walked everywhere, wandered around the worst of London's slums with some inspector. Ten to one, there were places Dickens visited where he'd have had tons of mirrors to choose from—or had he ever gone looking for one very *particular* mirror? *And then Lizzie's dad ends up with it?* Her memory for *blinks* was always a little hazy, but what she did recall was an argument between Lizzie's parents. *They stole it?* That felt right. They'd tracked down the mirror and stolen other things, too. But what, and why?

She gave it up. If it was important, the information would bubble up again, eventually. Maybe. *Or I'll find it in my own time, when I'm ready*—and then she wondered where *that* had come from. *My own time, as in . . . my time, a place where I really belong?*

"Don't be a nut," she said, but it was more of a tic, no force behind it. She eyed that slit-door. No knob. No hinges. No way in that she could see. *So are you part of the test, a way of seeing if I'm ready?* Ready for what?

All of a sudden, her ears pricked to a trickle of static. *Radio.* Much louder now, yammering to itself and coming from behind this slit-door. She actually made out a few words: *at large . . . murder . . . bodies.*

An eerie dark sweep of déjà vu gusted through her brain. *That's what we heard in the van. Lily said the murders were all over the news.* So, if this was such a big story, why hadn't *she* heard about some little girl who'd found bodies in some . . . "Cellar," she said, and then wished she could call that back. *Some little girl found bodies down cellar.*

"But I didn't find bodies," she said out loud. "I don't know *what* I found in Jasper's cellar." Yet that was a flat-out lie, or at least half of one. "Come on, Emma, you thought that thing down cellar was a door." She studied not the slit itself but the color. That shade of white was right, maybe identical. *And I heard whispers seeping out of the dark, just like now. When I pushed, when I finally got my hand through, I felt . . .* She shoved away from the rest. God, for something she was determined to forget and hadn't thought of for years, she could feel the memories piling up to bulge against some mental membrane—

(where the barrier's thinnest)

as if what had happened down cellar was related to what was going on now.

"What do you want, House?" And then she answered her own question: "Of course, you nut, it wants you to open the door." She thought back to earlier: her sense that if she found the correct door in her mind, she might walk into Lizzie's life. "That's right, isn't it, House?"

The house didn't answer. But the radio crackled on: *horrible . . . gruesome discovery of—*

"I'm not listening to this, House." Shuddering, she hugged herself tight. She felt sick. Her stomach coiled as if a snake had decided that her guts were a nice, dark, moist place to hang out. "I don't hear it. I don't care." She let out a high, strained laugh through a throat that didn't want to cooperate. "It's not like I can go in, anyway. There's no knob."

Which hadn't stopped her when she was twelve. Then, she'd had the same thought: no knob, no way in. A second later, she'd spotted that small, Emma-sized pull-ring, just right for a twelve-year-old. Had it been there all along? She'd

always had the queer sense that the door down cellar had *made*
the pull-ring for—

In front of her eyes, the slit-door suddenly undulated, like
thick white oil.

"Shit!" Staggering, she stumbled back on her heels and
nearly set herself on her ass. Holding herself up against the far
wall, she gaped, stunned, as the slit-door wavered and rippled.
A moment later, a knob—brassy and impossibly bright—blistered into being like a weird mushroom pushing its way out
of bone-white loam.

Just like down cellar. Closing her eyes, she counted to ten,
made it to five. The knob was still there, and now, something more, something that *hadn't* happened all those years
ago, down cellar.

In that milky slit, a tangle of creatures swarmed to the
surface in a clutch of sinuous arms and legs and bodies. Some
had what passed for a face: vertical gashes for mouths, a bristle
of teeth, serpentine stalks where there should be eyes and ears.
But the details were incomplete, running into one another,
the features oozing and dripping together, as if all that white
space was thick paint. The creatures were bizarre, a little like
those Hindu gods and goddesses, the ones with animal heads
and spidery frills for arms and legs and all-seeing eyes.

Whoa, I know these. I've seen these, and not in a blink *either.*
Despite her fear, she found that she was also as curious now as
she'd been when she was twelve. Easing from the wall, she slid
a few slow steps closer. *Jasper* painted *these, then covered them up.*

"With white paint." Like the door down cellar. She put
a trembling hand to her lips. "White slit, white door, white
space." *That means something, too.* What had Jasper said? *Every*

time you pull them onto White Space, you risk breaking that Now.

"Okay, House, time-out," she said. "I get it, I do. I'm supposed to walk through this door and into that room. I'll bet that even if I leave—go outside and wait by the snowmobile—eventually, I'll end up here again after another *blink*, because this is what you want." *This is a . . . test? Part of a process? What I've been brought here to learn and do?* That all felt right. So, really, the only choice was whether she turned the knob this time around, or on the hundredth repetition.

Just do it already, you coward.

The brass knob was icy. Heart thumping, she tried giving it a twist, but it wouldn't turn and nothing happened when she pulled.

Push, the way Lizzie's dad did with the Mirror.

That did something. She felt the shift under her hand, almost a . . . a mechanical click? *Same thing when I touched that . . . that membrane down cellar, when I was twelve. As if I've activated something.* She instinctively backed up a step as the slit-door glimmered, not opening so much as dissolving. *Melting, like a phase shift, the way ice changes to water.* And then she thought, *What the hell?*

The slit-door vanished. A faint coppery aroma, like the rust-scent of that snow, seeped on a breath of frigid air. Inside, there was no light at all. From deep within, however, she could hear the buzz and sputter of that radio. Otherwise, it was pitch-black.

No, that's not quite right. She realized the reason the door opened out. *My God*—she stared at the smooth, glassy, jet-black barrier—*it's solid.*

It was, she thought, like the mirror in her *blinks. And*

what I found in Jasper's cellar. A week after she had, the *blinks* had begun. *And I've got the feeling there's something else I'm not remembering; was* made *to forget.* But what? *And why would anyone* make *me forget anything? Who could even do something like that? How?*

At her touch, the black shuddered. Her hand instantly iced, then fired to a shriek, but she could stand this; and although her heart was still hammering, she wasn't as frightened. *It's like what happened upstairs, in the bathroom.* As if that had been a demonstration designed to show her what to do.

Beneath her fingers, the darkness *gave* and *rippled*, that weird sense of something transitioning from one state of matter to another, and then she was moving, pushing, feeling the suck of that oily black, stepping through

2

INTO SUMMER.

She is on East Washington in Madison. She knows this because the capitol's white dome is just up the hill. To her left is the bus stop on Blair that will take her back to Holten Prep. The air is warm, a little humid from Lake Mendota, where sailboats scud like clouds over lapis-blue water. Her left hand is cold. She looks, expecting to see that her hand isn't there but still wrist-deep in blackness. Instead, she holds a mocha Frappuccino topped with a pillow of whipped cream, fresh from the Starbucks down the block. In her right hand is a book.

This is a memory. She cranes a look over her shoulder. There is no room, no slit-door. The street presses at her back.

A steady stream of cars hums past. Distant tunes and radio voices tangle and swell, then fade, trailing after the vehicles like pennants. Light splashes her shoulders because it's summer. A light-aqua sundress that brings out the indigo of her eyes floats around her thighs. *This is from six months ago.*

"That's really cool."

"What?" Disoriented, she turns back to discover that she stands before a table heavy with boxes of half-priced books. Her eyes crawl to the storefront window. There is a sign advertising the sale, and the bookstore's name emblazoned in black-edged gold: BETWEEN THE LINES.

I remember this. I was here in June, after exams, a week before my birthday.

"I said your necklace is so *cool.*" The voice belongs to a guy about her age. In one hand, he cups a perfect glass sphere on a dark ribbon the color of a blood clot that she's wearing around her neck. The pendant is elegantly crafted: a miniature universe, sugared with stars, that swims with a tangle of twisting bodies and strange creatures. She knows this necklace, too. It's her galaxy pendant, the one she hasn't flameworked yet and which exists only as an idea.

"Did you make it?" the boy asks.

"Uh . . ." Well, the answer is she didn't, and hasn't the skill. She might still try—assuming, of course, that she doesn't crash, get her friend killed, and wind up going slowly insane. "Yeah."

"I really like how it changes depending on how you look at it," the boy says. "It could be this dark planet with a ton of lights, like Earth from outer space. Or it could be an explosion, like the black's about to break apart and what you're seeing is white light through the cracks, and *that* lights up all the things that live in outer space that we wouldn't normally see, you know? Like dark matter? Or what space would look like if you could somehow get outside our universe and then look back."

It's as if he's read her mind. All of that's *exactly* what she's after but doesn't quite know how to do just yet.

"Well, I—" Then she gets a really good look at this boy, and whatever she was about to say fizzles on her tongue.

Because the boy is Eric.

EMMA

As He Will Be

ERIC IS ALMOST exactly as he will be, right down to those smoldering, impossibly blue eyes fringed with long black lashes. His face is strong and lean, and his lips are full, his mouth perfectly shaped. The only difference is that he's not as muscular, and his dark hair curls over the tips of his ears. He wears denim shorts and a black tee. His hands are slender, the fingers long. He is insanely handsome, something manufactured by a dream, and that queer sighing flutter in her chest that she feels *now* she will recognize as longing *then*.

"You're—" she begins and stops. She has almost said, *You're not real. You don't belong here. You* weren't *here*. "You're not the regular girl. Who works here, I mean."

"Oh. Well, no. Just subbing for the extra cash." His eyebrows knit in concern. Releasing the galaxy pendant, he straightens. "Are you okay? Do you want to sit down or something?"

"No, I'm good." Her throat is so dry she hears the click as she swallows. "You're Eric," she says, then remembers to make it a question. "Right?"

"Yeah." His frown deepens. "Have we met?"

Not yet. "No. I, uh, I guess I must've seen you around."

"I don't think so," he says, and then his expression changes: as if *she's* glass and his gaze pierces to her hidden heart. "I would've remembered meeting you."

Her pulse throbs in her neck. It's as if he's pulled her into a private, breathless space, somewhere warm and safe to which he has the only key. If he wants to hold her there forever . . .

"Emma!" The voice comes from behind. "Where've you been?"

No. Her stomach drops, and she turns to watch the girl striding toward her. *No, no, you're—*

"I should've known. As if we don't have enough reading to do. Only *you* would buy more books. I mean, making us read *The Bell Jar? Seriously?* That thing is *so* depressing." Lily executes an exaggerated eye-roll, then plucks the book from Emma's nerveless fingers. "So what else did you find?"

"Wh-what are you doing here?" Emma croaks.

"Hello, done with finals, not ready to face Sylvia Plath? Into some serious retail therapy?" Lily's sculpted eyebrows crinkle in a frown. "Emma, are you okay? You don't look so hot."

Oh no, I lose my mind on a regular basis. "I'm fine," Emma says, but she is definitely *not.* This is all wrong. She had not come with Lily; she didn't *know* Lily back then, did she? Where had they met? On this street? In a class? She can't remember, but she does recall that she went shopping with her roommate, Mariane, and they had lost one another when Emma wandered off toward the bookstore down East Washington, thinking now would be a great time to get a jump on all that summer reading.

Wait a second. What if this *time is the* first *time?* A strange relief floods her veins. Maybe that's it. *This* is reality. All the rest—the snow, the crash, Lily's death—is the dream, or *blink*, or hallucination. The street is what's real. The taste of too-sweet coffee and chocolate still sits on her tongue. Chilly beads of condensation wet her fingers. In a few days, she will be seventeen. Lily is alive and Eric is *here*; he's real.

But he shouldn't be. He's like the pendant I haven't made yet: something I've only—

"Ugh, how can you read this stuff?" With an exaggerated shudder, Lily hands back the book Emma's chosen. "You and your horror novels . . . I'd have nightmares for a year."

Me and my . . . She doesn't like horror; with her past, her life has been gruesome enough, thanks. "Well, I—" Emma begins, and then her eyes click to the book's cover and Emma feels the blood drain from her face as her ears begin to buzz.

The jacket is smoky. In the center, there is a long dark slit edged in a fiery corona of red and yellow and orange. The slit could be a cat's eye, or a lizard's, or a split in the earth—or the mouth she sees whenever she gets a migraine, because there are shadowy figures and a writhing tangle of weird monsters struggling to climb out. Look at it a certain way, and you could almost believe they were about to leap off the cover and out of the book.

And the cover reads:

Franklin J. McDermott

THE DICKENS MIRROR
Book II of THE DARK PASSAGES

EMMA
What the Cat Already Sees

IN THIS JUNE of memory, Emma's blood turns to slush.

Another book by McDermott, in a series she's never heard of. One that she's pretty sure doesn't really exist. *Was this in the bibliography Kramer gave us?* She doesn't think so. But McDermott *knew* the Dickens Mirror; he *wrote* about it.

Wait a second. Just because he knew doesn't mean it's a real thing. Writers make stuff up all the time. The Mirror could be imaginary and something that only exists in a book.

But if that was true, and even if it wasn't, then what— *who*—was the *first* book about?

Oh, holy shit. An icy flood sweeps through her chest. *I am so stupid.* The jigsaw bits and pieces of her Lizzie-*blinks* suddenly begin snapping into place. There are still a lot of gaps; these are *blinks* after all, and her memory of them, the fine print and little details, isn't perfect, but she recalls enough: that barn, an explosion, a car crash, a dad who's a writer, and Lizzie's mom makes glass. *Emma, you nut, Kramer said that— or he will say . . . Oh, what the hell difference does it make?* She is shaking so badly, it's as if she's back in the snow, in that awful valley. What she remembered was what Kramer said about Meredith McDermott: a physicist turned glass artist, who blew her husband to smithereens.

Jesus Christ, Jesus Christ, all this—the crash, the valley, House—all this is about Frank McDermott? First I write a story that's straight out of notes for a book he never finished, and now I'm channeling his kid? This is like the moment to come, one she hasn't lived yet, when Kramer accuses her of plagiarism, and all she can and will think is, *Don't be crazy. The guy's dead.*

But no, it's even worse than that; she's dropping into the last reel because she knows what comes next. Lizzie's already in the car; that kid's about five seconds away from *dying.*

"Emma?" Lily touches her arm, but the feel is muted, as if reaching her through a layer of cotton. "Are you all right?"

"I'm . . . I'm fine." She flips the book over to study the jacket photo. The image is black and white, and the caption reads in tiny white block letters: THE WRITER AND HIS FAMILY AT THEIR HOME IN RURAL WISCONSIN.

They're all there, ranged on the porch steps: McDermott, his head cocked as if something's caught his eye, stands on the right. His wife—*so you're Mom; you're Meredith,* Emma thinks—is on the left.

Her eyes zero in on a little girl with blonde pigtails and an armful of cat, between Frank and Meredith. *Bet that's an orange tabby, too.* The cat's gaze is focused on something that must be in a tree off-camera.

Lizzie and Marmalade and . . . oh my God. Despite the day's warmth, her skin prickles with gooseflesh as she picks out the porch railing, a bay window on the left, a door with a wrought-iron knocker and pebbled sidelights, the glider on chains, hanging flower baskets spilling over with geraniums that she'd lay money on are red. *That's House.*

That is also when she realizes: McDermott is not looking *around*. The photographer captured McDermott as he was looking *up*. From the angle, she understands that McDermott is about to spot—or *knows* exactly—what the cat already sees. Her eyes inch up the picture, and then her breath hitches in a small gasp.

"Emma?" Eric says. "Are you okay? What is it?"

"I . . . It's . . ." But her mouth won't work, and she can't get the words off her tongue.

In that photograph, draped over the sill of a second-story window, is a hand.

But the fingers are not fingers. They are claws.

And then . . . they move.

RIMA
That's No Cloud

THE CAMRY WAS gone. Tony was dead, and maybe Casey, too. Rima had scrubbed as much of a pocket out of the snow as she could manage, but she was jammed in tight, headfirst and up to her thighs. Her air was going fast, the snow melting from the warmth of her breath and body heat—and now, just when she thought things couldn't get any worse, she heard something.

Coming right for me. A deep trembling seized her. She could feel Taylor's death-whisper, still clinging to her parka, cringe. *It's going to get me . . .* She felt something move and then close around her right ankle. *No!* Her heart bolted up her throat to lodge behind her teeth. *No, no!*

"Rima?" Casey, snow-muffled and distant. "Rima, are you okay?"

Oh, thank you, God. Nearly limp with relief, she wiggled her foot. *Get me out of here.*

"Good." He sounded relieved. "Okay, hang on. It'll only take a couple minutes to get you out."

Actually, it took more like ten, and she felt every single second crawl by as her air pocket got stuffier and her chest started to hurt. *Hurry, Casey, hurry.* Her head ached, the pain like nails behind her eyeballs. Then, all of a sudden, cold licked her hips and waist, and she could move her legs. Pawing through snow, Casey grabbed fistfuls of her parka and yanked. Popping free like a cork from the tight neck of a narrow bottle, she tumbled out, and they collapsed together into the snow.

"Oh!" she gasped. They'd gotten turned around somehow so she was on top. They were nose to nose, her palms flat on his chest, his hands clamped around her biceps. "Sorry."

"It's okay," he said. Deep, bloody scratches scored his forehead and cheeks. The fist-sized bruises on his jaw were purple and puffy. His parka was ripped, the arms nearly in shreds. "Are you all right?"

"Yeah. Thanks." Her voice suddenly broke, and she knew she would start to cry if she wasn't careful. She drew in a shuddery breath. "Thanks for getting me out, for not leaving me, Casey."

"I wouldn't do something like that." Casey gave her arms a squeeze. "Are you *sure* you're okay?"

She nodded. "What about you? What happened to your face?"

"Landed in a tree across the road. Got blown right out of my fath—" He stopped, licked his lips. "Out of some of my clothes. I guess the wind or something got under and tore my shirt off. My parka was all tangled up, like a noose. Took forever to work the zipper from the inside and then climb down. That's why it took me so long to find you. I'm sorry."

"No, it's fine." Her eyes traced the course of a red welt beneath his battered jaw and over the hump of his throat. She thought it was pretty lucky he hadn't strangled. "I'm glad you're okay."

"Me too." In the dwindling orange glow of the fire, his expression was unreadable. "I mean, I'm glad you're okay."

She was suddenly conscious of the feel of his body beneath hers, how close they were. How she could tolerate his touch. Taylor's whisper didn't seem to mind either. This was a very different Casey, not the mean kid from before. Even his voice was different: not rough or sneering, but normal and kind of nice.

Of course. She pulled in a small, quick breath. His father's shirt was gone, and with it, all that poison. There was no whisper of Big Earl now, anywhere on—or *in*—Casey. Did he know? Somehow she didn't think Casey had a clue—and what was it, exactly, that he could do, anyway?

Maybe he's like me, able to sense death-whispers, but my opposite. I take away the whispers; I free them. But maybe he draws them in, gives them a place to live. Or they take him. Can whispers even do that? She didn't know. In her experience, death-whispers like Taylor's were helpless; they needed her to soothe and then free them. But Big Earl was gone, so whatever was going on with Casey was either reversible, or a whisper needed more time to weave itself into Casey's skin. How long would Casey have to be exposed before that became permanent? All interesting thoughts, and something she'd never considered before. Too much to think about right now, though. Later, if there was time, they really ought to talk.

"We need to get out of here," she said. "There might be more of those things."

"Or something worse." He slid her to one side and pushed up on his elbows. "We sh—"

When he didn't go on, she looked over. "Casey?" She searched his face, saw something like amazement quickly shading to alarm—and then she realized: *Wait a second, I can really see* him. There was orange light from the dying car fire, but Casey's face was bathed in a silver-blue glow, the kind of light thrown by a full moon. "What is it?"

"Rima, turn around," he said, thickly, and lifted his chin. "Look at the sky."

She did, and her stomach bottomed out.

They lay together on the snow, staring into the black night above and at something new: very dense, milky, and shimmering as if studded with silver glitter—or stars. It boiled out of the darkness in a great pillowing mass, gathering and gobbling the night.

"Oh my God." She couldn't seem to get enough air. "Is that . . . is that a *cloud*?"

"That's no cloud," he said.

BODE

A Real Long Way from Jasper

1

"WHAT IS THAT?" Chad peered through the Dodge's windscreen. "Is that smoke? Like, from the explosions?"

"It wouldn't be white, unless they were using phosphorus," Eric said. He was in the backseat but leaned forward now, draping his hands over the front, his walkie-talkie dangling by its wrist strap. "That's more like fog."

"Or just real thick clouds," Bode said. Fog or clouds, he didn't like the look of all that open sky. Drop him into a tunnel—what he and his fellow rats called a *black echo*—any day. Not that a tunnel was a cakewalk. There was the enemy hunkering down there, waiting for a quiet kill, and booby traps: snakes, wicked-sharp punji stakes smeared with God knows what kind of poison or human shit. But scorpions were the worst. Those suckers nested everywhere: on the walls, the ceiling. Get stung, and you were gone.

Other guys called him lucky. Maybe he was. If he'd popped out of that tunnel ten seconds earlier, that mortar would've taken his head off. Instead, Sergeant Battle took the hit: one minute there, his hand reaching for Bode's, and the next—

Which is why you need to think, be careful, watch your step. The voice in Bode's mind was more hiss than whisper. *Not like I can take one for you this time around, son.*

Bode's eyes flicked to the rearview. Battle's head floated next to Eric, who was back to fiddling with his walkie-talkie. Eric wouldn't have seen Battle anyway, probably a good thing. Battle's head was a ruin. Most of the meat on the sergeant's face had flash-fried, leaving blackened bone and shriveled tendon. Battle's right eye was a crater, no white at all. His left hung on his cheek, tethered to its socket by a leathery stalk of cooked nerve. A fist-sized chunk of Battle's skull was gone, leaving behind daylight and a charred curl that had been his left ear. A goopy pink sludge of Battle's brains slopped over his neck.

"I know that, Sarge," Bode said, thinking it was lucky no one could hear *him* talking to the ghost of a dead guy no one else could see. "But you know we had to help. I couldn't send the devil dog off on his own, no backup. Wouldn't be right."

Right's got nothing to do with it. Battle's mouth was a tight rictus grin of fat maggots squirming over shattered teeth. *After all, it isn't like you don't already got enough problems.*

2

CHAD HAD NOT wanted to go.

"Man, this is a really bad idea," Chad said. They'd retreated to the kitchen to retrieve their weapons: a Remington pump, which was already minus two shells, and a four-shot bolt-action Winchester .270, as well as Chad's Colt. Bode's own service weapon was lying in scrub somewhere way back in Jasper. The desert was good for swallowing all kinds of stuff a guy didn't want found. Guns. Money. Drugs.

Bodies.

"I mean it." Chad gnawed at his sore. "Don't we got enough problems?"

"You're gonna give yourself a scar, man." Bode hip-butted a drawer of silverware shut. The cupboards above the sink weren't exactly bare, but whoever lived here had a thing for Kraft macaroni and cheese; the cupboards next to the fridge were stacked full, top to bottom. Man, they must have a lot of little kids. Who else plowed through that many Blue Boxes? Not that he minded: he'd choked down so many beans and franks in the bush, he hoped he never saw another hot dog.

Bode squatted, opened the cupboard beneath the kitchen sink, and pawed past cleaning supplies, lighter fluid, trash bags. No real weapons, though, not even a butcher knife. He felt under the sink to be sure—maybe something taped there—but there was nothing.

Weird. Farmers were always shooting shit: groundhogs, sick horses, crap like that. He stood, thought about that, staring at the black rectangle of window over the sink. So where would they stash a weapon? The barn? Maybe down cellar?

Framed in the window, Battle peered back. *There aren't going to be any other weapons here, son. This isn't any kind of* here *you've ever been.*

"A scar." Chad let out a giddy bray. "Like that's the worst thing I got to worry about."

"You don't have to worry about anything," Bode said,

flatly. To Battle: "What do you mean, this isn't a *here*? I'm standing here."

Yes. Battle's ruined face glimmered from the window's murky well. *But* where *are you?*

"I'm in a kitchen, Sarge."

And where is this kitchen?

"Look, Sarge, you got something to say, say it."

Think, son. Use your head. Does this house look like any farmhouse you've ever seen? Does it feel *right?*

"Sure," Bode said. "I mean, you know, it's a house."

It's got the right shape. It's got furniture and there are rooms. There's food and light. But there are no pictures on the walls, no photographs. Who lives *here?*

"I don't know. I haven't really looked, Sarge, but there have to be bills or something lying around. There's probably a name on the mailbox."

Are there? Was there?

"I didn't notice. It was, you know, *snowing.*"

"Man, we got to get out of here." Chad hugged himself. "This place just don't feel right."

"You need to calm down," Bode said. Chad was not the sharpest knife in the drawer. Good on patrol; definitely watched your back, and the guy could de-ass a chopper like greased lightning. But he wasn't any kind of rocket scientist. On the other hand, Chad wasn't as crazy as Bode, who *knew* he was nuts. Given Bode's day job, though, crazy is as crazy does. Battle's ghost hitching a ride in his head was just so much icing on that proverbial cake. "Let's just focus on one thing at a time, okay? First light tomorrow, we figure a way out of the valley."

"A way out?" Chad said. "We don't even know how we

made our way in. Do *you* remember how we got down here? I sure don't."

Bode didn't either. On the other hand, he'd gotten into some serious smack, so maybe that was understandable. The high had tailed off, though, and while Bode knew from experience that his memory never quite recovered a hundred percent, he really didn't recall more than jagged fragments and sensations: the stink of piss from the men's room, a thick sweat-fog hanging over the dance floor.

The moment he squeezed the trigger.

"Bode, I'm telling you, man: the cops catch us, they turn us over to the MPs and it's Leavenworth. They give you the firing squad for stuff like this." Chad hugged himself a little tighter. "I told you to let it roll, but no. You had to go and follow the LT out of the bar."

Bode was tempted to point out that the military's preferred method for execution these days was hanging, but no use making Chad more anxious than he was already. "Relax. No one saw us."

"Bode, anyone finds your gun, the cops or the MPs'll trace it right back to you."

"Yeah, but we ship out in a week. No way they'll pull us out of that."

"How you figure?"

"Man, they're hurting for guys to fight. No one'll come looking. Come morning, we get our bearings and drive on out of here. Until then, don't sweat it. Everything'll be copacetic."

"What if the owners here show up?"

Battle: *They won't.*

"They won't," Bode echoed. "Not tonight anyway."

"Man, I hope not." Chad shivered. "House gives me the creeps. Know what bothers me? The food."

Bode laughed. "Macaroni and cheese makes you nervous?"

Don't laugh, Battle said. *He's right.*

"Bode, that food was ready and waiting," said Chad. "That's just wrong. No one goes off during a blizzard and leaves his oven on."

It was a good point. "If there was an emergency, they might," Bode said, but he couldn't convince even himself.

"If there was an emergency," Chad said, "then it was a long time ago. There were no tracks and the road wasn't plowed. That casserole ought've burnt. But it didn't. I'm telling you: that's not right."

"Well, we're not going to solve that little mystery now." Turning away from the window and Battle, Bode scooped up the Winchester and the Remington pump. "Come on."

Chad's mouth set in an unhappy line, but he followed because that's what Chad did best. Yet he—or maybe Battle—had planted a seed, because Bode realized something as they drove away and the house and barn dwindled to bright islands.

There was light. The house had electricity. But there were no power lines. This far out in the country, there would have to be.

So where was the light—the power—coming from?

3

"MAYBE IT'S LIKE gas," Chad said now. He dug at his sore with a dirty thumbnail. "You know, like some kind of nerve gas or that Agent Orange."

"Agent Orange?" Eric said. There was another sharp blat of static as he switched channels on his handset. "They don't use that stuff anymore."

"Yeah, man, there's laws," Bode said. "Besides, you need a bird for that. No way anyone's flying a chopper tonight."

Chad's left foot jiggled as he *pick-pick-picked*. "Hey, Eric, you know how far it is to the nearest town?"

Sighing, Eric clicked off his walkie-talkie and shoved it into his parka. "No. I've never been down here before."

"You know where we are?"

In the mirror, Bode saw Eric's reflection hesitate. "No," Eric said. "I don't. Where were you coming from?"

"Outside Jasper," Bode said. He ignored Chad's sharp, reproving look. "Stopped off at this little cowboy honky-tonk around eight, nine o'clock."

"Jasper? Never heard of it. What's it near?"

"Uh . . ." For a moment, Bode's mind simply blanked to a white dazzle. Then a word slid onto his tongue. "Casper."

There was a small silence. Then Eric said, "Where?"

"You know . . . Casper." For a weird moment, Bode thought that this was like when you tried to explain to the hootchgirl that you didn't want any starch for your shirts, only she didn't speak but two words of English and you kept shouting, *No starchee, no starchee!* Like that would get her to understand what you wanted, which she never did. *"Casper."*

"Where's that? Is that near Poplar or something?"

"No, it's . . ." Bode licked his lips, then blurted, "Cheyenne!" He felt like he'd just passed a really tough exam he'd forgotten to study for. "Yeah, north of Cheyenne."

"Cheyenne," Eric repeated.

"Yeah, *Cheyenne*." Chad cranked his head around. "You got some kind of hearing problem? The man said Cheyenne."

"No, no. It's just . . . where do you guys think you are? What state?"

"What *state*?" Chad repeated. "Wyoming, man. Where else?"

4

ERIC WAS QUIET for so long Bode's jaw locked. He had to really dig deep to push the word out. "What?"

"Wyoming plates," Eric said, but he might as well have said *aha*. "That's why you have Wyoming plates."

"Well, *yeah*," Chad said. "So?"

"You guys," Eric said, slowly, "you guys are a real long way from Jasper, Wyoming."

"Oh hell. Are we in Kansas? We're in Kansas, aren't we?" Chad turned to Bode. "I *told* you we took a wrong turn out-side Laramie."

"You guys aren't in Kansas," Eric said.

"Then where the hell are we?" asked Chad.

"You're . . . Oh man." Eric blew out. "You're in Wiscon-sin."

A beat. Then two. Chad broke the silence with a laugh. "That's crazy."

"No."

"What are you talking about, *no*?" Chad sniggered again and shook his head. "*No*, he says. How many spiffs you smoke tonight?"

"What?" Eric waved that away. "Never mind. Look, I

started out in Wisconsin this afternoon. I know I didn't take a snowmobile into the storm and end up blown clear to Wyoming. So we're either still in Wisconsin, or somehow we've all ended up in Wyoming."

"Mountains are right," Bode said. "Valley's right for Wyoming."

"That's true. But I honestly don't think that's where we are."

"So we're in *Wisconsin*?" Chad asked. "Like *where* in Wisconsin?"

"I'm not sure of that either, but if we are . . . then we're north," Eric said. "I . . . I don't know exactly where."

"No, of course you don't," Chad said.

Battle's head still floated in the mirror, but Bode focused on Eric's reflection. "What if . . ." His tongue gnarled. Bode licked his lips and tried again. "What if we're not *anywhere*?"

"What?" Chad said.

Eric returned Bode's look. "I don't know where we'd be, then."

"What are you guys talking about?" Chad asked. "We're right *here*."

"Yeah, but where *is* that, exactly?" Eric said.

Or when. The thought was suddenly there in Bode's mind, like the rip of a fart you just couldn't ignore. "Maybe we're in between, like limbo."

Eric's dark brows drew together. "Wouldn't we be dead then?"

"Dead? You guys are nuts." Chad bounced an anxious glance from Eric to Bode, then out the passenger's side window. "Nuts," he repeated, jiggling his leg, picking furiously at his sore. "I'm not no Catholic, man."

Bode said to Eric, "Where you shipping out to, again?"

"Marja, I think," Eric said. "Probably."

"Well, I never heard of that." Chad's voice was tight with fear and anger. "Is that, like, north or south?"

"South . . . actually, southwest."

"So, like, close to Phuoc Vinh? Or Dau Tieng?"

"Dau . . . ?" Eric paused, and Bode saw that the other boy couldn't ignore that awful stink either. "You guys," Eric said, evenly, carefully, "what war are you fighting?"

Bode's mouth was dry as dust. He couldn't speak. A fist of dread had his throat.

"What *war*?" said Chad, and gave a sour laugh. "Why . . . 'Nam, of course."

ERIC

One Step Away From Dead

OH, OF COURSE. A balloon of sudden fear swelled in his chest. *Vietnam, of* course.

Yet it made a certain loopy sense. Factor in the vintage uniforms, the old Dodge, the way these guys talked—not only their slang but what they didn't know. Bode and Chad were from the past. Or Eric was in it. Or, maybe, Bode was right and the valley was some crazy kind of limbo.

But it's also real. How could that be? His right hand closed around Tony's handset. *That's real. The others are real, and so is Emma. This* has *to be real.* Or he was going crazy. The fear was an acid burn, eating its way up his throat, and Eric thought he might actually scream if he wasn't careful. Oily sweat lathered his back and neck and face, and he pressed the back of one shaking hand to his forehead, the way he used to do when Casey had been little and got sick. *Don't, don't do it.* His lungs were working like a bellows. *Come on, calm down.* Sipping air, he breathed in, held it, let go . . . in with the good, out with the bad . . . *Just hold it together.*

What if . . . what if this *was* limbo? Maybe he was being punished. Could that be it? God sent him here because of Big Earl? What kind of justice was that? Big Earl was the adult; he hurt people. Big Earl *shot* at him; he would've killed Eric if he had the chance. The beatings had gone on for as long as Eric could remember. Yes, but how long was that, *exactly*? A day, a minute, five years, *ten*?

He. Did not. Remember.

No. Eric's heart knocked in his throat. *No, no, no, how can I not know?* He remembered how careful he'd been in high school changing for gym, always slipping into a stall or coming in with just enough time to spare so that the locker room had already emptied out. *I have scars on my back, my stomach. Every beating's written in my skin. Why don't I remember?* How could his memory be scrubbed clean like that, as white as all that snow?

Because . . . because . . . because it never happened?

Before he could talk himself out of it, he bit the inside of his left cheek, very hard, wincing as his teeth sank into his flesh. *There, that hurt.* A moment later, there was the warm, salty taste of blood on his tongue, and that was good, and so was the pain. Swallowing a ball of blood, he savored the ache, grabbed the feeling, held it close. *See, Ma, I'm real. I feel pain, so I must be real.*

Unless the pain was just for show. Or—and this was a truly strange thought—he *was* real . . . but only here and nowhere else.

That's crazy. What are you, nuts? His shirt, sticky with sweat, clung like a second skin. *There's got to be an explanation that makes sense. This has to be a dream, or I'm sick and I've got a really high fever and I'm delirious or something.*

Or maybe . . . *oh Jesus, oh God* . . . maybe Big Earl hadn't missed. Maybe that bullet blasted into Eric's skull and drilled into his brain, and now he was lying in a hospital somewhere, his ruined head in bandages, a tube down his throat, IVs in his veins: hooked up to machines that were breathing for him, keeping him alive—and it was only a matter of time before someone pulled the plug.

Maybe I'm only one step away from dead.

"Oh *man*." Chad's sharp gasp cut through the maelstrom of his thoughts. "Man, you *see* that?" Chad said. "Off to the right?"

"What is it?" Eric asked, hoarsely. Really, he was grateful to have something else to worry about.

To his right, the night wasn't exactly there anymore. Instead, an anvil of thick white fog extended from the ground and rose all the way up and across the dome of the sky.

"Oh my God," Eric said, and felt the sudden kick of his heart in his teeth. "It's getting closer. Jesus, it . . . it's *moving.*"

"Bode? *Bode?*" Chad said, his voice rising. "Bode, we got to turn around, man. We got to turn around right *now!*"

"I hear that." There was a sudden lurch as Bode jammed the brake, then muscled the stick into reverse. "Hang on."

"What? No, wait, Bode. Stop!" Eric clamped a hand on the other boy's shoulder. As frightened as he was of this thing gathering itself in the sky—and freaked out by what might be wrong with him—he loved his brother more. "We can't turn back now. What about the others?"

"Devil Dog, I'm sorry, but we are bugging out PDQ."

"But my brother's still out there!" *If this isn't a fever, a hallucination, a last gasp* . . . But even if it was. *Because Casey is here, with me, in this, and that's on me.* "We can't just *leave* him."

"Yeah? You wanna watch us? We get ourselves killed, won't do him no good anyway," Chad said, as Bode swung the truck around. "Go, man, *go!*"

"I'm going." Bode mashed the accelerator. The truck's wheels spun in the snow, caught, and then they were churning back the way they'd come, the Dodge's snow chains chattering over packed snow: *chucka-chucka-chucka-chucka-chuck!*

"Bode, wait, *think*," Eric said. "You're a soldier. You don't leave your people behind. Please, don't do this."

"Screw that. Just *go!*" Chad shouted, his voice riding a crescendo of panic: "It's getting closer! *Go*, Bode, go, go!"

"I'm going, I'm going!" Bode hammered the accelerator, and the Dodge surged, the engine chugging like an eggbeater. They flew over the snow, going so fast the outside world blurred into a silvery smear. "C'mon, c'mon, c'mon, you hunk of junk! Move, move move *move!*"

Not going to make it. Eric knew that. They would never outrun that white cloud or fog or whatever it was. They would spin out, or Bode would lose control and they would die out here, because, despite everything, Eric was convinced that death, like pain, was real here . . . wherever that was.

"Bode, you're not going to make it," Eric said. "Slow down, slow—"

"Shut up." Bode pushed their speed. "Shut up, shut up!"

"But Bode—"

"Shut *up!*" Bode stomped the accelerator so hard Eric heard the hollow thud of Bode's boot. The Dodge rocketed over the snow, slewing right and then left, the wheels spinning, seeking traction, any kind of traction at all. "Marine, get it through your head: we are *leaving*!"

Chad was still chanting: "Go, Bode, go. Go, Bode, go, go go go!"

"Bode, slow down, you can't outrun it! You're going to lose it, dude, you're going to lose it!" Eric hooked his fingers into the front seat as Bode jinked the wheel, doglegging to the right. The Dodge's rear swayed. "Bode, you lose it out here, we're *dead*."

"I'm not going to lose it!" Bode shouted.

"You're going to get us kill—"

"Man, you don't shut up, Marine or no Marine, I'm tossing you out of this truck, right now!" Bode roared. "You got that? Now shut *up*!"

"I only—"

"Did you not *hear* the man? Ain't you *listening*?" In the next instant, there was a pistol in Chad's hand. He jammed the muzzle into Eric's cheek. "You want me to end this right now?"

"Hey, hey," Eric said, raising his hands in surrender. "Easy, Chad, easy, it's cool, we're cool."

"We are *not* . . . COOL!" Spit foamed at the corners of Chad's mouth, and he rammed the gun into Eric's flesh so hard the front sight clawed his skin. "We will be *cool* if you shut up, if you shut up, if you just shut *up*!"

So Eric shut up. There was nothing else he could do. This was out of his control. He shut up, and after a long second, Chad jerked the gun away.

This is a nightmare, but I'm living it. Eric felt blood welling from the fresh wound on his cheek. *I'm real; I'm bleeding; you can't bleed if you're not real.* He watched that fog, all that brilliant empty white, storming after them, filling the world. *You can't be scared to death if you're already dead.*

The truck swayed, slewing into a turn, the world beyond tilting, and Eric's blood iced, every hair on his neck prickling with a kind of stupid shock, because he suddenly understood.

The snowstorm had been a warm-up. The storm had only been a way of bringing them all together. It was the *fog* that mattered, the fog that would run them down and swallow them whole.

What then? Where—and when—will we be then?

"Oh JESUS!" Chad screamed. "It's right on top of us, Bode, it's right on *top*—"

RIMA
No Time

"RUN!" CASEY SCREAMED, and then he was dragging her over the snow. Rima staggered, nearly fell, but Casey gave her a mighty jerk, hard enough that a shout of pain balled in her shoulder.

"Casey," she gasped as they floundered, their legs digging post-holes through deep snow, "the sled, where's the sled?"

"Blast blew her off the road!" Casey's grip on her hand was iron. "Saw it from the tree, to the left, in a ditch! *No!*" He tugged her harder. "Don't look back!"

But she did—and all the strength drained from her body to seep into the snow.

The fog was a gigantic thunderhead stretching so far overhead there was no limit to it. The fog was a pillar of nacreous, roiling white that built on itself, piling higher and higher. Unlike a cloud, the fog also spread from side to side, and everything it touched, it swallowed. Rima knew the night sky was still there, that above this deadening veil were true clouds and the stars beyond, but the fog was lowering itself, filling the bowl of the valley, obliterating the sky. The fog surged, an avalanche of white steamrolling right for them.

"Come on," Casey urged. "Come on!"

Something bullet-shaped gleamed a dull silver and black from a deep wallow to her left. "There!" Rima cried. As soon as she stepped off the road, Rima sank up to her thighs, but she bullied through, trenching out a path to Casey's snowmobile. "What should I do?"

"Dig under the nose!" Casey was stamping snow, beating out a trail. "We got to pack down the snow, then roll it onto the runners and get it pointed downhill."

No time. Rima could barely move. With every step, the treacherous snow grabbed and pulled, and she was conscious of the fog boiling across the night, pressing against her back. They only had maybe a minute, if that, before the fog reached them. "Casey, there's no time!"

Casey tossed a wild look over his shoulder. His face glistened with sweat. His teeth were bared in a grimace of fear and frustration. "Damn it. All right, leave it; come on, let's flip it!"

They wallowed around to the downhill side, and then Casey backed into the sled, hooked his hands under the seat. Rima slid her left shoulder under the left handlebar, felt the snowmobile rock to the right and then try to tumble back, but she dug in and heaved. The snowmobile tilted, and she nearly slipped as the sled wobbled and then did a slow, heavy tumble onto its runners.

"Come on, get on, but don't sit down!" Straddling the seat, Casey waited until she'd scrambled onboard before pulling up the kill switch, twisting the ignition key, yanking on the start cord—once, twice . . .

Hurry. Rima shot a quick look over her shoulder. The fog was still coming. *Hurry, Casey, hurry, hurry, God, come on, come on!*

The sled's engine sputtered, caught. The machine gave a sudden lurch, and Rima tumbled forward. With a cry, she made a wild grab, snagging Casey's tattered parka just as they began to move.

"Okay, *down!*" Casey shouted. "Rima, sit down!"

Arms wrapped around Casey's middle, Rima obeyed, dropping onto the seat. The sled roared out of the gully, a rooster tail of snow flying behind, and then they were streaking across a sparkling plain of silver-blue snow. With no faceplate for protection, Rima gritted her teeth against bitter air that cut like a bristle of knives.

"Hang on!" Casey shouted as they banked into a tight, fast turn. She felt the back of the sled swing, and for a heart-stopping moment, she thought they'd spin out. But Casey wrestled the handlebars back to true, and the sled spurted over the snow with a roar. He shot a quick glance over his shoulder, and she felt his body go rigid. "Shit, *shit!*"

"What?" But even before she looked back, she knew. The fog was there, a seamless curtain stretching from the sky to hug the snow, chasing after them in an inexorable tide: two hundred yards back and gaining. One-fifty, a hundred yards, eighty. *Fifty . . .*

Casey, I'm sorry. Squeezing her eyes shut, she buried her head into his back, hugged him tight. *If it hadn't been for me, you would've gotten away.*

The fog slammed down.

EMMA

Black Dagger

1

ON A STREET drawn from that terrible summer of *The Bell Jar* when Emma will become so lost in that book, she will think she really might be better off dead; as she stares at the jacket photo of a McDermott novel she's never heard of—the hand in the photograph moves.

Horrified, Emma watches those bizarre fingers unfurl and stretch and sprout talons. Its talons lengthen like a cat's claws. Oozing over the windowsill, the hand slithers down the apron, and now Emma can see that the skin is as scaly and cracked as that of a mummy. The hand bleeds onto the photograph in an inky stain, a black blight, and Frank McDermott . . .

McDermott—the McDermott captured in the picture— comes to life. As if suddenly aware that there is a world outside that photograph, Frank looks straight out to throw Emma a wink.

"Ah!" With a wild, incoherent cry, she stumbles back, her half-finished Frappuccino flying in a fan of whipped cream and mocha-flavored coffee from her left hand. *The Dickens Mirror*, a book that shouldn't exist from a series that was never written, flutters to the pavement like a wounded bird. Around her neck, the galaxy pendant suddenly smolders.

"Hey," Lily says.

"Emma?" Eric—a boy she has yet to meet, who shouldn't be here—reaches for her. "What's wrong? Are you all right?"

"No! No, you're not real! This isn't right!" Emma flinches away. She turns, her treacherous feet trying to tangle, trip her up, spill her to the sidewalk. "Get away from me, get away, don—" Backpedaling, she blunders from the curb into oncoming traffic on East Washington. A horn blasts as a car churns past, its hot breath swirling around her bare legs, snatching at her sundress. She can hear the sputter of the car's radio through an open window: *Investigators continue the grisly task of removing the remains of at least eight children believed to be the latest victims of—*

"No, stop, I'm not listening, I don't hear you, *I don't hear you!*" She takes a lurching stutter-step and tumbles to rough asphalt. As she hits, the fingers of her right hand reflexively close around something hard and jagged.

She looks—and every molecule in her body stills. Everything stops.

The dagger of glass is absolutely flawless and wickedly sharp—and she knows this shape. It is nearly identical to the shard she will fish from that discards bucket and turn over and over on that afternoon when she feels Plath's bell jar descending to engulf her mind in a dense, deathless fog. When she will think, *I didn't see anything, there was nothing down in Jasper's cellar; it was just a crawl space, there was nothing inside, I didn't find . . .*

But there is a difference. This dagger isn't clear but smoky and black, polished to a mirror's high gloss. Her reflection within this black dagger is so crisp she can make out the terror in her eyes, the curve of her jaw, every glister and sparkle of that galaxy pendant.

It's a piece of the Mirror. She is jittering so badly her breaths come in herky-jerky gasps, and she thinks she might be one second away from passing out. *It's from the Dickens—*

A sudden bite of pain sinks into her left wrist, bad enough to make her cry out. What *was* that? *God,* that hurt. Her eyes shift from the black dagger to her wrist—and then a scream blasts from her throat.

A thick, stingingly bright bracelet of blood has drawn— no, no, *is* drawing itself, inch by inch, across the skin of her left wrist.

"N-no," she says. It's like watching someone unzip her. She still clutches the black dagger in her right hand, and a single glance is enough to show her that the glass is pristine, not a splash of blood on it at all. *And anyway, I didn't, I didn't, I don't do it! I only* thought *about cutting my . . .*

"*Aahhh!*" Another slash of pain, on her right wrist this time, the lips of yet another slice gaping open. She shrieks as the moist tissues pull apart to reveal a silvery glint of tendon and deeply red meat. Blood instantly surges into the belly of the wound, pumping and slopping from slit arteries, *splish-splish-splish-splish*, surging with her heart. A nail of panic spikes her throat. The warmth drains from her face, her lips, and her guts are ice. Her vision's going muzzy, and in the black dagger, her reflection's turned runny, the features shifting and melting as a new and different face knits together: same eyes, same golden flaw in the right iris. Same jaw and chin. Only the hair, wavy and golden blonde, is different. Still, she knows who this is.

I'm Lizzie? A violent shudder makes the reflection jitter. *We're the* same *person?*

"NO!" A shriek scrambles past her teeth. "No, I'm me, I'm *Emma!*" Still screaming, she hurls the black dagger away. It cuts the air, flashing end over end like a scimitar. Both her arms are spewing blood now, and as Emma scuttles back on her hands like a crab, vivid red smears paint the road, marking her path. There is blood everywhere, too much, a whole lake of it. Anyone who's bled this much ought to have fainted— hell, ought to be *dead*. For that matter, she's landed in the middle of a busy street. She should be squashed under a bus by now, or flattened by a car.

But there are, suddenly, no cars, no people. No taunts from a radio. When she glances back at the bookstore, she sees that Eric and Lily are gone, too.

It's like House. Terrified, her aqua sundress purpling with her blood, she clamps her torn arms to her heaving chest. Her eyes skip from store to store. *No people.* Except for BETWEEN THE LINES, the other stores are only blank fronts with blacked-out windows. Her gaze falls to the curb, the gutter, then drags up to the trees silhouetted against a milky sky that she knows was blue and bright only minutes before. *No trash, no dead leaves. No sun.* Yet not everything has vanished. *The Dickens Mirror* lies on the pavement, facedown, its covers in a wide splay.

There is movement out of the corner of her eye, on the grimy asphalt. Glancing down at the growing pool of her blood, she sees a glimmer along the crimson surface, which quivers and gathers itself—into a long, rippling red worm.

Oh. All the small hairs on her neck and arms rise. Her scalp prickles with horror, and she can feel her titanium plates, the lacy one on her forehead and its twin at the very base of her skull, heating beneath her skin as if a switch has been thrown and a connection forged in her brain. *Oh, this can't be happening.*

But it is. Her blood is alive, slithering, eeling from side to side, snaking its way over gritty asphalt. Frozen in place, she watches the red slink as it seeps across the road, never spreading, never veering, but creeping up the curb and onto the sidewalk, heading straight for the book. As soon as her blood touches the cover, dragging itself like a moist crimson tongue along the edges, curls of steam rise—and the book . . . quickens.

It's like my blink, *when I saw Lizzie's dad—Frank McDermott—at the Dickens Mirror.* Except it is a book, not a strange mirror, drinking her blood, greedily sucking and feeding, the pages pulsing and swelling, the covers bulging . . . And then she spies . . .

Oh God.

2

THE SPIKE OF a claw rises from the book, like a trapdoor has suddenly opened to let something deep underground find the surface. And then she sees another claw. And a third.

"No." The word is no more than a deathless whisper. Trembling, she watches as the taloned fingers of whatever is living in that book hook over the cover's lip. It is as if *The Dickens Mirror* is not paper sandwiched by cardboard but a mouth, the rim of a deep well, a pit, a cave. A second stygian hand snakes free to clamp onto the edge. The razor-sharp claws clench; and now two spindly and skeletal arms appear. They bunch and strain, the elbows straightening like a gymnast's working parallel bars, as the thing living inside strains to be born. It boils from *The Dickens Mirror*: first the head and now shoulders and a leathery scaled torso, which is now green, now silver, now black. The book-thing twists its long, sinuous body right and left, corkscrewing its way from the page. Then, it pauses as if gathering its strength—or maybe only deciding what it ought to do next.

Quiet, be quiet. Clamping her lips together to corral the scream, Emma holds herself very still as the rounded knob of its head lifts, the thing seeming to taste the air, sniff out a scent. *Don't see me, don't taste me, don't smell me.*

But then . . . it *turns.*

No. Please, House. A dark swoon of terror sweeps her mind. Her skull plates are so hot her brain ought to be boiling. *Please, show me a door, House. Sweep me away in a* blink. *Do something, do anything, but please show me a way out of here!*

House, if it is listening, does nothing. And this thing is . . . not *quite* formed, not yet. It has no face. Where there should be eyes, a nose, a forehead, a mouth, there is only an ebony swirl. A nothing. A blank. But Emma knows: somehow, it *sees* her.

There you are. The voice ghosts over her brain in a whisper that is the sound of brittle ice; of glass frit spilling over a metal marver. *I've wanted to play with you for such a long time, Emma.*

Come. Staaay. Stay and plaaay, Blood of My Blood—

She drags her voice up from where it's fallen. "N-no. No, you're not real. This isn't happening. I saw this in a *blink*. It was just a—"

All at once, the thing's eyes pop into being, but not on its face. Two eyes stare from its hands, one on each palm, and they are not black but blue as sapphires. They are *her* eyes. Even at this distance, she can see the golden flaw floating in the iris of the eye on the right.

Get up, Emma. Somehow, she has pulled herself into a crouch. Her arms are no longer bloody; in fact, there are no wounds at all, not even a scratch. *Get up, Emma, get—*

Too late: in that churning, rippling blank of a face, a third cyclopean eye—as dark as black smoke—peels open.

Blood of My Blood. The thing plants a webbed foot on the sidewalk. Something is happening in that third eye, too; the black blank is eddying and bunching, pulling together, molding itself. *Breath of My Breath.*

That is when she remembers what she's already been shown.

Get up, get up before it really sees *you, the way it did McDermott!* Her brain screams the words, but she's frozen in place. Where could she possibly go in a nightmare, anyway? But she has to move. There is no one to save her. She must get out of here before she ends up *in* the eye.

Come and play a game, Emma. The thing spiders, legs and elbows bent, body crouched low on the sidewalk, its position a mirror image to her own. Boring into her, looking deep, its third eye churns as, within, the glassy oval of a face begins to waver and shimmer up, the way a drowned body floats for the surface—and she knows she only has seconds left.

Come play, the whisper-man sighs. In the third black-mirror eye, lank tendrils of dark hair swirl about a face that now shows the faintest impressions of eye sockets and the swell of lips, like molten glass being worked and molded by a jack—and now there is the ridge of a nose, the slope of a forehead. *Come with me through the Dark Passages to the Many Worlds, into* Nows *and times . . .*

"No!" The paralysis that has gripped her breaks. Emma surges to her feet. "No, I won't let you!" Whirling on her heel, Emma bullets across the street and

EMMA
Them Dark Ones Is Cagey

AND NOW, EVERYTHING has changed.

Madison is gone, yet a clot of heat—the galaxy pendant from the *blink* or hallucination or whatever the hell that illusion of Madison was—rests between her breasts. But that day or vision or room into which House has let her wander . . . all that is over.

Now, instead of an aqua sundress, she wears a thick white nightgown. Barefoot, she stands on a scratchy rough carpet covering a long hallway with a dark wood floor. Above, the ceiling is slightly ridged like the planked hull of an old boat, and that's when she realizes that what she's looking at are whitewashed iron plates. Ceiling-mounted lights hang from rigid metal rods, and give the space a sterile, institutional look, although the air is close and stuffy with a sewage reek, as if all the toilets have overflowed and no one's slopped up the mess of old urine and runny feces.

As if to counter the stink, the hallway is also lined with cheery, flower-filled vases, hanging baskets, and porcelain figurines. Framed pictures of flowers, done in intricate needlework, hang on the walls. Exotic stuffed birds—colorful parrots, a snowy cockatoo, a white dove—perch on artfully arranged branches beneath glass bell jars. The walls are seafoam green, and there are many shuttered windows and dark wooden arched doors with tarnished brass knobs, set slightly back in cubbies like the openings to catacombs but bolted tight with queer rectangular iron locks. The gallery is ghostly, lit by hissing lamps that spill wavering gouts of light and shadow at regular intervals. The whole setup could be from a museum, like one of those exhibits where you stand behind Plexiglas and peer into places where people lived and died long ago.

This hallway. She tips a look to a table just a few feet off to the right where a staring stuffed toucan perches on a fake branch of wire and silk leaves beneath a clear glass dome. *I've been here before, in a* blink.

"You see her, Mrs. Graves?" The voice is male and rough, the accent like something from Monty Python. Startled, she looks up. Perhaps thirty feet away, in what had been an empty hall only seconds before, stands a trio of burly, mustached men in rumpled white trousers and shirts. One clutches a smudgy, sacklike dress of strong, heavy, flannel-lined wool. The dress has no buttons but long ties that run up the back and around each wrist. A pair of padded leather gloves bulge from the pockets of a second attendant a step behind the first.

Strong dress. They'll tie me up in that thing. And then she thinks, *What? How do I know that?*

The attendant with the strong dress says, "You got her in your sights?"

"Indeed I do, Mr. Weber." An older woman, with a grim

set and clipped tone, steps toward her in a swirl of floor-length navy blue crinoline beneath a tightly cinched white over-apron that reaches to her knees. She would look like a fancy cook if not for the stiff, crisp nurse's cap tacked to her head like a cardinal's biretta. A large ring of bright brass keys jingles from a chatelaine at her waist, and the outlines of a small watch are visible, tucked in her blouse's watch pocket and secured by the delicate links of a brass buttonhole chain, from which hangs a tiny, smoky agate fob. Threaded beneath a high, starched white collar, a strange pendant dangles on a red silk ribbon over the shelf of her breasts: some kind of polished black disk set in brass.

But it is her glasses that grab Emma's attention. Rimmed in bright brass, the spectacles are not round or oval but D-shaped lenses. Each lens is hinged at the temple to allow for a second to open and shield the sides of either eye. The four lenses are not clear glass either. They are, instead, a storming magenta swirl.

Purple glasses. Emma hears herself hiss a breath. *Panops?*

"She got a hanger-on?" Weber, the attendant, says. "Anyone else fall out?"

"Thanks heavens, no, not that I see. Come now, Emma. Time to return to your room." The woman—Mrs. Graves—extends a weathered hand, its knuckles swollen with arthritis and age, but her voice is as starched as her collar. "Let's not make this more difficult than it need be."

Nurse's cap. Locked doors. *A hospital?* No. Her gaze clicks to the strong dress Weber holds, those bulbous, too-large gloves. *Jesus, this is a psych ward, an asylum.* But Weber's accent and Mrs. Graves's brusque tones . . .

Wait a second . . . I'm in England?

Emma's stunned gaze jerks to those hissing lights of glass globes and brass pipes. Now that she knows *how* to look, Emma spots inky smudges on the sea-foam wallpaper: soot from brass wall-sconces. *Gas lamps. Oh my God.* Her chest squeezes with panic. *I'm in the* past, *like something straight out of Dickens.*

"How'd she fall out is what I wants to know," Weber says. "You sure she didn't lay her hands on one of them marbles?"

Marble. She nearly reaches for the galaxy charm but catches herself. *He's talking about the pendant?*

"Yes, I'm *sure*, Mr. Weber." Graves's own jet pendant winks a weird, smoky green in the gaslight. With her spectacles in place, her eyes are bruised sockets. "I fear she's stronger. If this keeps up, she might not require a cynosure at all to make the leap."

Cynosure? Emma's pulse skips. *What is that, some kind of tool? Is that what Weber meant by a marble?*

"What'd I tell you? Them dark ones is cagey. Why we're bothering altogether, seeing as how them and their kind bring the plague . . ." Weber's face screws with suspicion. "We ain't never going to understand how to use them tools right, which of them dark ones is safe, so best to do away with the lot, I say."

"Might we have this discussion later, Mr. Weber?" Graves's eyes shift back, her mouth thinning to a crack above a sharp chin. "Emma, please, you're working yourself into a state. Come along. You're safe with us, dear."

"N–no," Emma says, and yes, this is *her* voice: no accent, nothing different about that at all. "Please, I just want out."

"Now, now." Graves moves closer, accompanied by the jingle and chime of brass keys. Her jet pendant gleams. "Let us take care of you, and in turn, you can help us."

"Help?" The thought that she *is* insane—that she really *must* belong here—sparkles through her mind, because she does have a dim understanding of what will happen next. If the nurse gets a hand on her, if the orderlies get close enough, they'll manhandle her into that sack of a dress, jam her hands into gloves, and truss her up before marching her down to a windowless cell deep underground where only the sickest, noisiest, most violent patients live. Someone will force open her mouth, then pour something thick and rust-red and too sweet down her choking throat. They'll pinch her nose if she won't drink; they'll suffocate her until she does. Swallow that tonic, and a thick, cloying fog will descend over her mind, and she'll float away on the breath of dreamless sleep. This, she *knows*—and if that's so, she must belong here. She's crazy. What other explanation is there?

It's how I felt reading The Bell Jar. *But that must not be a real book.* She stares at the stuffed birds trapped under domes of clear glass. *Those jars . . . I've slipped in real details from* this *place, the way you do in dreams.* Everything she thinks she knows: Jasper and Madeline Island; bookstores and Holten Prep and icy, sweet Frappuccinos. *I've hallucinated the future of a girl who doesn't* exist?

At that instant, the blister of a bright pain erupts between her eyes as a headache thumps to life, and she raises a tentative hand. The deep gash she got when her van jumped the guardrail and tumbled into that lost valley is gone. *But of course it would be, because that never happened.* Yet there *is* something there. Slowly, she traces the hard, unyielding, perfect circlet of lacy metal, and suddenly, she thinks, *Wait.* She can feel her heart ramp up a notch as she reaches around to sweep through her hair. *Matching plate, at the base of my skull.* This one is harder to feel because of all the muscle, but she knows exactly what that edge is—and there is hash-marked scalp, the network of scars thin and minute. *Wait a second. That's not right.*

"Oh dear." Graves glides a little closer. "Another of your headaches? Come, let me give you your medicine, dear. A nice tonic, a little cordial for what ails you. How does that sound?"

The titanium skull plates and screws don't belong. They haven't been invented yet, but . . . "Jesus," she breathes. She has no accent, she *thinks* with different words, and these skull plates shouldn't exist. *Which means that I'm still me. What I remember is* real. But she is awake now and aware in a way she's never been in a *blink* before. *Maybe this is like Madison. House is showing me something for a reason.* She doesn't know why she thinks that, but she senses she's on the right track—but to where and why? *The Lizzie-blinks and everything that's happened in House feel like building blocks, one brick being added at a time.*

"Mrs. Graves?" A new voice: another man, his tone peremptory, authoritative. "Do you have her? Did anyone else get out?"

Her thoughts scatter like a clutch of startled chicks. A knife of pure panic slices her chest. Stunned, she gapes as two men angle through the orderlies. Both sport old-fashioned suits with high collars and silk waistcoats, although one is bearded, darkly handsome, and decked out in an expensive-looking tailcoat and black gloves. With his gold fob watch and walking stick, he looks like he's been pulled away from a fancy party or the opera.

"No, sir," Graves says, without looking away. "Our Emma has managed it all on her own, it seems."

"Oh dear." The bearded man tut-tuts. "Emma, *why* do you insist on making such a scene? They're trying to help you."

"Best let me." The doctor's head swivels as he searches her out. He is older, and his eyes are deep purple sockets, his glasses identical to Mrs. Graves's. "Now, Miss Lindsay, are we having a bad night? What do you say we go to my office for a chat and have ourselves a nice hot cup of tea?"

No. A thin scream is slithering up her throat, worming onto her tongue. *No, no, no, it can't be.*

The bearded man in evening clothes is Jasper.

And the doctor is Kramer.

RIMA

Where the Dead Live

"**WHERE ARE WE?**" Rima asked. Casey's snowmobile was still running, the engine chugging between her legs. Yet everything else had changed. The fog was everywhere. The whiteout was so complete, Rima felt as if they were marooned in a small pocket of air, trapped beneath a bell jar at the bottom of a viscous white sea. The night was gone. The sky—well, *up*—was the milky hue of curdled egg white and bright as a cloudy day with the sun at its height. The fog was brutally cold and smelled odd. *Metal,* she thought. *Rust?* "Are we still in the valley? How did we even get here?"

"I don't know." Casey's voice sounded odd: curiously flattened, paper-thin. His face was mottled from windburn, his many scratches and scrapes rust-red, his right cheek and jaw as purple as a ripe plum. "It sure feels different, too. Like the fog grabbed us, and we got beamed to some other planet or something. You know?"

Or maybe we're only a different place inside *the fog.* She wasn't even sure why she would think that, or what it meant. "What do we do?"

"I don't know. I don't think we should stay here." Casey threw an uncertain look over both shoulders. "The problem is, without knowing where we are, I have no idea where we'd be headed. There are no landmarks, just . . . *white*. We could drive around in circles until I run out of gas, and then we're screwed."

"*If* we run out of gas." When he turned to stare, she said, "I don't know if regular rules still apply."

"Like the gas from the van," he said.

She nodded. "There was too much, and the way the snow turned to ice and that monster . . . None of that belongs in—"

"The real world." He paused, then said, slowly, as if testing it out, "It's like this valley is the *fog's* world, and it wanted to make sure we left the piece we were in." He shook his head. "That sounds pretty crazy."

"Not to me. But assuming we could go somewhere, can you even drive in this?"

"Oh sure. How fast we go depends on how far ahead I can actually see." Her arms were still wrapped around his middle, and now Casey put a hand over hers and squeezed. "I'm going to get off the sled and walk a little ways, take a look, see what I can see."

"No," she said, alarmed. She felt Taylor's death-whisper squirm against her chest. *Easy, honey,* she thought to the girl. *I know; we're in trouble.* To Casey: "I don't think we should let ourselves get separated, even for something like that."

"Don't worry; I won't go far. If it helps, I'll walk backward, okay? That way, you keep me in sight, I can't disappear, right?"

Well, unless something snakes out from the fog and grabs you. But she said, "How long?"

"The second I start to fade out, you give a shout, and I'll stop. But I got to know how far we can actually see in this mess."

He was right, but she didn't have to like it. Perched on the sled's runners, she held her breath as he backed up a step at a time. He never looked away, and she didn't dare. The fog seemed sticky somehow, like a cloud of cobwebs, dragging over Casey in fibrous runnels and cloying tendrils.

"Burns," he said, backhanding a clog of fog from his face. "Really cold." His nose wrinkled. "Does it smell funny to you?"

"Yes." She watched as more fog wreathed his chest and twined like ivy around his legs. The fog wasn't grabbing hold so much as—okay, weird thought here—*tasting* Casey, the way a rattlesnake gathered information through its tongue. "Like rust."

"No." Working his mouth, Casey spat and made another face. "Like blood."

She thought he might be right about that. "Okay, stop. You're starting to gray out."

"Yeah, you're getting kind of fuzzy, too. So"—he cast a critical eye to the snow and then back to her—"thirty feet maybe and . . ."

"What?"

"This is snow, right?" He gave her a strange look. "So why am I not sinking?"

She didn't understand at first, and then, staring down

at the sled's runners and his feet, she did. If this was snow, there should be clumps humped over the runners; Casey's feet should break through the surface, but they hadn't. There was no snow on his boots either. "Is it ice?"

"Nope." Squatting, he scooped a handful and studied the white mound, tipping his glove this way and that. "Looks like snow." He gave a cautious sniff. "Doesn't have a smell the way the fog does. This only smells . . . *cold*. Like it's someone's idea of snow, know what I mean? Like a movie set."

"Really?" She took a careful step off the sled's runners. "Then why would the fog—"

The shock as her boot touched the snow was like the detonation of a land mine, an explosion that ripped from the snow to scorch its way up her legs and rupture her chest. Digging in, Taylor's death-whisper shrieked against her skin, the pain like knives, and Rima let out a sudden, sharp shout.

"What?" Casey said, instantly alarmed. Five long strides and his hands were on her shoulders. "Rima, what's wrong?"

"The snow." Gasping, groping for the sled, she stumbled back onto the runners. Taylor's whisper relaxed, but now that she knew what lived in this weird snow that wasn't, Rima imagined all those death-whispers shivering up the sled to seep through the soles of her boots and into her bones. "I . . ." Bowing her head, she swallowed around a sudden lump of fear. "I f-feel something."

"Feel something? In the snow?" He threw a quick glance at his feet as if expecting something to swim out and crawl up his legs. "Rima, what are you talking about?"

Now that she'd begun, she couldn't simply brush it off. *Just say it.* "People."

"People." He waited a beat. "In the snow?"

"Yeah." She wet her lips. "The snow's full of dead people. I feel them."

"You *what*? You feel—"

"Yes, Casey, I know it sounds crazy, but the dead live in the snow. I feel their . . ." She broke off, remembering how Casey had *been* Big Earl, shedding his father's death-whisper as easily as shucking the man's shirt. *He must not know; can't sense the change much at all and only half-remembers. He just becomes.* She gasped. *And if the snow's where the dead live . . .* "Casey." She snatched his jacket and yanked. "Casey, get off the snow, get off *now*!"

"Wuh—" Off-balance, Casey reeled and lurched forward, his hands shooting out to grab the sled's handlebars. "Okay, okay, I'm coming, *relax*." She wouldn't let go until he was straddling the seat so they faced one another. "All right, I'm on," he said. "What's the matter with you? What do you mean, you *feel* people?" Then his brows wrinkled, and he glanced away, his mouth working the way it had when he tasted the fog on his tongue. "You know, I . . . I remember something you said. It's . . . *foggy*." He let out a breathy laugh. "Which fits, I guess. But I *do* remember a little. In the car . . . I wouldn't let you in . . . and I started hurting . . ." He raised a hand to that livid, swollen splash of purple-black bruise. "You said I needed to fight—"

"I remember what I said." She took his gloved hand in both of hers. "It's something I'm . . . I'm able to do. I know you'll think I'm crazy, but just listen." As she talked, she saw the growing doubt and disbelief. Well, she knew how to fix that. "So," she said, "that's how I know about Big Earl: that he's dead. That's why I told you to fight him."

Yup, that did it. An expression first of blank surprise and then a swell of shock, hot and scarlet, flooded his face. "What?"

"You heard me." She paused, then added, softly, "I know what Big Earl did to you. I know Eric didn't mean for it to happen, but he had no choice. He was protecting you. If he hadn't swung that bottle and put Big Earl down, I think you'd both be dead."

"How?" The question came as a harsh, hoarse whisper. "How can you *know* all that?"

"Your shirt. It was your dad's. That's why I didn't want you to touch me, Casey. Because whenever you did, I felt it, *him*, Big Earl's death-whisper . . . and you, when you were wearing the shirt, you were different. You were mean. Didn't you feel it? You feel the difference *now*, right?"

His eyes faltered, his gaze sliding from her face to the snow. Some part of his mind *must* register the change. Perhaps he even knew but tucked that knowledge away in some dim corner where he would have little excuse to look.

"Yes," he said, finally. When his eyes again met hers, they were much too bright and pooled. "Before, when I looked at you and the others? I heard *him* talking to me, telling me what to think. But now I . . . I see *you*, like there's no fog, nothing of Big Earl between us. It's like I'm meeting you for the very first time."

She opened her mouth to say . . . something, she didn't remember what. The words slipped right off her tongue, because that was when she got her first good look at Casey's eyes as they were now. They weren't just bright with tears.

They were *different*. When he had worn Big Earl's shirt, Casey's eyes were a muddy brown. Now they were stormy. Not gray, exactly, or blue or brown or green. His eyes were all colors, and no color, nothing fixed. His were the kind of eyes that, depending on the light, were green one moment and hazel the next. Even blue.

What does that mean? Another thought: *My God, maybe he could get to the point where the change would be permanent and he'd never find himself again.*

"How did you feel then?" she asked. "When you had that shirt? Do you remember?"

"Angry," he whispered. "Mad at everybody, everything, even Eric. I didn't like the feeling, and I heard Big Earl in my head and it . . . *he* was bad. Evil. Remembering him crawling around like this black spider, it makes me feel dirty. That's never happened before either. I'd never had him in my head. Hell, I used to think someone had made a mistake. How could Eric and I *have* a father like that? It never felt like my dad belonged in our lives; he was a mistake, an outsider. Like . . . like this *virus* you just couldn't shake and . . ." Casey let out a trembling breath. "*Ohhh-kay*, that sounds pretty crazy."

She shook her head. "You've never met my mother. She and I don't look at all like we belong to each other. Sometimes I think I popped out of nowhere or someone switched me at birth and my real mom's got this awful kid. I don't even like touching my mom. She feels"—she hugged herself—"like there's something rotting inside. All the drugs she does, that's probably pretty close."

"So if *you* feel dead people, their . . . *whispers*, like the little girl in your parka, Taylor? Is that what *I'm* doing?"

"I don't know." She bent her head to study the snow. "Whatever it is, you seem okay now, but I think you should stay off this stuff until we can—"

When she didn't continue, Casey said, "Rima, what . . . oh, Jesus."

"Uh-huh." She tried to say more, but all the words balled in her throat. In her parka, Taylor's whisper tightened in alarm. *I don't know, honey; I have no idea.*

But she thought they better figure this out, and fast.

RIMA
Tell Me You See That

AT THEIR FEET and all around the snowmobile, the snow suddenly bloomed with oily splotches. *Like something's leaking up from deep underground—or we're on top of something and the snow's melting, giving way.* Her eyes ticked from the snow immediately around their runners to as far as she could see. *It's everywhere.*

"Rima." Casey's voice was library-quiet. "Tell me you see that."

"I see it." The splotches stretched, seeming to sprout legs to creep over the snow. *Like what happens when ink drips onto white paper,* Rima thought. *It seeps along the fibers.* The spider-stains stretched and lengthened and merged. The fog was no longer gelid and still but swirling now, the turgid scent of blood-rust growing stronger. The snow began to shift and hump as black waves rippled all around the snowmobile.

Then, with a monstrous scream, the ebony snow broke, splintering in a shuddering convulsion—

"Ah!" Shrieking, she threw her arms around Casey as

hundreds and hundreds, *thousands*, of crows bulleted from the snow: pulling together out of that weird oil, spinning in a screeching black funnel cloud, hurtling into that blister of a glare-white sky.

"Where did they come from?" Casey shouted over the screams. His storm-gray eyes were jammed wide with shock. "What do they *mean*?"

Death. Stunned, she followed the scrolling tangle of birds as they drew their black calligraphy onto the sky: arabesques and whorls and swoops and slashes and arcs. *Crows are death, and there is so much here, more than we can imagine.* Tightening her arms around Casey, she felt his slip about her waist, and wasn't sure if the shudder working its way through her arms and into her chest was only hers. Yet, as frightened as she was, she was suddenly more afraid for him. It was crazy, stupid, something you did if you were major crushing on someone. *But this is so dangerous for you, Casey; there is something here that wants you, will* take *you, if it can. I feel it.*

She had to get him out of here. Now that the birds had cracked out of their icy shell in their mad flight, the snow—if that's really what it was—was pristine and white once more. *All right; that's a start.* Maybe slide onto the snow, see if she felt anything now. If not, they needed to move, get out from under these birds if they could, put some distance between them. But what if the birds followed?

One step at a time. She tipped her head back to that roiling sky. "I can still see them," she said. The birds' ebb and flow was almost as hypnotic as the sea, or like staring into the swirl of an ebony whirlpool that endlessly circled round and round and round. *Like a black hole, the kind that ought to exist in outer space: you could trip over the edge and fall forever.* "So maybe the fog's burning off. Casey, you think you can drive the sled—"

"Rima." At his tone, she pulled her gaze from the sky. Casey was staring over her shoulder. "Behind you," he said.

She craned a look. A slit had appeared in the thick mist, as if someone had drawn a very sharp knife through taut white fabric. The lips of the cut drew back, and then this rent widened as the fog retreated. When she stopped to think about it later, the effect was like the parting of a curtain on some bizarre stage. Beyond the mist lay a thick forest, dark and very dense, that hemmed the snowfield on three sides.

"Like walls," Casey said. "Like we're looking into a room."

That was exactly right. She watched as the fog wavered and glimmered—and then another shape pulled together, the fog sewing itself into something solid and blocky: red brick capped with a spire. A rosette window blossomed above a set of thick wooden double doors.

"It's a *church*," Casey breathed. "And look, there, to the left."

"Cemetery." The tombstones were a jostle of rectangles and squares, listing like broken teeth. Beyond, she spotted . . . was that a snowplow? No, that wasn't right. The blocky vehicle was outfitted with treads, like a tank, and the discharge chute of a snowblower reared like an orange smokestack to the left of the cab. Instead of a blade, the huge, sharp corkscrew of an auger was mounted at the front of the vehicle.

I know this. The certainty was so bright, it was like a searchlight had flared to life in the center of her brain. *The church, the cemetery, and that thing with the auger is a snowcat, and it's all important. But why? Why do I recognize thi—*

A scream, short and sharp, ripped through the air, followed by a loud, rolling *BOOOMMM*.

Rima knew, instantly: not thunder, or an explosion.

A shotgun.

Coming from the church.

EMMA

A Bug Under a Bell Jar

1

"NO. JUST STAY away from me." Cringing from Kramer's outstretched hand, Emma slides a slow step back and then another, the rough carpet scratching her bare feet. She is suddenly very cold, and from the heavy overcoat Jasper wears, that faint sparkle of snowmelt on his shoulders, she thinks it's probably winter.

Of course it's winter, you nut. Clad only in a coarse flannel nightgown, Emma shivers. *It was* snowing *in the valley. Lily and I crashed in a blizzard.* This hallway, this asylum, these people, all belong in a nightmare, a *blink*, a dream, a hallucination—or it's House that is peopling this illusion, pilfering her memories for details: the embroidered pictures of flowers, the bowed ridged ceiling with its gas lamps, the low pedestal table to her immediate right with that stuffed toucan trapped under a glass dome.

How could House build this from my mind? She doesn't know or recognize this as a real place, or from any book. Now, that day in Madison, the one she just left, she almost understands.

The bookstore exists; she *had* bought *The Bell Jar* that day. The broader details, even her mocha Frappuccino, were correct.

Yet, unless she was taking a cue from all those Dickens novels and stories they listened to when she was young, she has never imagined Jasper as a bearded, middle-aged man in expensive evening clothes, complete with a walking stick. And Kramer, so different: no longer the Great Bloviator in prissy Lennon specs but a Victorian-era shrink decked out in purple panops. It's as if she's exchanged one monster for another.

And I've never been here before, except in a blink *I barely remember. I don't know anything about asylums except what's in* The Bell Jar, *do I? Did Dickens ever—*

"Come with me, Emma." Kramer's tone carries a note of command. "You and I will go to my office and sort this out"

What, and then you'll accuse me of stealing a dead guy's story? She fights for control, her eyes stinging with frightened tears. *Stop it; this is a dream, a* blink; *that's why it echoes. House is build-ing this from your memories. This isn't real.* But she's hip-deep in it; this is like being chased by a monster in a nightmare—and, yes, isn't that *exactly* what's happening? *You have to run in a nightmare; you don't know you're in one until you wake up.* She can't chance that House will rescue her.

"No. I don't want to *sort* it out. I'm not going anywhere with you." Call it a hunch, but if she lets him take control in this hallucination or *blink* or whatever it is that House is doing, it's the end. She'll be trapped here. Behind her—and don't ask her how; she just knows—this very long corridor is nothing but a blind alley, a dead end.

Which means the only exit from this floor is the way that

Jasper and Kramer came in. *How am I going to get past them?* Kramer is the point of the spear; Jasper hovers just behind Kramer's left shoulder. Another foot or so back, Graves stands to Jasper's right. But Weber, the thickset attendant with the strong dress to Jasper's left, is the one she has to worry about. Her eyes fall to Jasper's walking stick with its carved ivory handle, and she thinks, *Right-handed.*

"I will go only if Jasper comes, too, and *only* him," she says to Kramer. "But the rest of you back off, okay?"

Kramer hesitates, and Graves, the nurse, says, "Doctor, I don't think—" at the same moment that Weber grunts, "Them girls know how to make trouble."

"*Those* girls? I'll thank you to remember that you're speaking about *my* ward. Of course, Emma." Arms open, Jasper's already stepping past Kramer. "You'll come to me, won't you? No more fuss, eh?"

Oh, just watch me. "No more fuss," Emma says, and then she darts forward, her left hand reaching for the walking stick. Startled, Jasper flinches, but he's too slow.

"No!" Reaching for Jasper's shoulder, Kramer tries to pull the other man back. "Emma, stop!"

But she won't; they can't make her. Wrenching the stick from Jasper's fingers, she whips it around like a club in a fast, high, whirring backhand. She feels a jolt in her wrist as the heavy ivory head connects, and then Kramer's head snaps back, a spurt of blood jumping from a gash on his jaw. Stumbling, Kramer falls into Jasper, who tries an awkward catch and misses. The two of them go down in a tangle. Behind them, she sees Weber start with a rough exclamation, *"Oi!"* and then recover, gathering himself to charge.

"Restrain her!" Kramer shouts, a hand clamped to his jaw. He is struggling to find his feet. "The door! Don't let her off this ward!"

Thank you. He's just told her: the door is open. Still clutching the walking stick, she sprints to her right, sweeping porcelain bowls and the stuffed toucan from its low table in a clash of glass and metal. Weber makes a lunging grab, but she is smaller and faster, and dodges. She feels the drag of his fingers, and her scalp gives a yelp of pain, but then she's dancing past, with the fleeting thought that whoever said girls with long hair would never survive the zombie apocalypse probably had something there.

"Miss *Lindsay*!" Flanked by the other two attendants, Graves is stepping to block her way. "Stop this at on—" Graves lets out a breathless grunt as Emma rams the cane's ivory head into the woman's belly. Staggering, Graves takes an attendant down with her as she falls, and then Emma is sprinting for the exit in a swirl of white flannel. The hall is enormous, infinitely long, and alive with the muffled cries and catcalls of patients, the slap of hands on stout wood. *Like feeding time at the zoo.* Behind her, she hears heavy footfalls coming closer and Kramer's shouts: "Miss Lindsay . . . No, Jasper, stay here . . . *John*, no, please remain on the ward and let me attend to this . . . Miss Emma! Emma, wait, *wait!*"

Dead ahead, she spots an arched entryway, but . . . is that a curtain, or . . . ? *Oh shit.* Her heart sputters as she realizes what she sees is a floor-to-ceiling iron grate, like the bars of an ancient jail. *Which is exactly what this is: a prison for nuts, lunatics, the mad. I'm trapped.*

Then she remembers: *Kramer didn't want me to get to the*

door. Her eyes fall to a heavy wooden door set in the grate on iron hinges. Of course. You wouldn't swing open the entire grate; there had to be a separate door that would allow doctors and nurses and patients to get in and out.

Without pausing, she stiff-arms the door at a dead run— and screams as a lightning bolt of pain shoots up her arm. Gasping, she reels, her right hand singing, and nearly falls. The door is very heavy, nothing she can easily smack open. Hit that thing at the wrong angle or any faster, she might have broken her wrist. Blinking away tears, she staggers back and shoulders her way through. The door gives by grudging degrees, groaning open six inches, a foot. *Wide enough.* Plunging through onto a large stone landing, she turns, plants both hands, and muscles the door shut. It claps to with a loud bang.

Through the open grate, she can see the others coming, Kramer in the lead. There is blotch of bright red blood on his white linen shirt. *Got to stop them, slow them down . . .* Across the landing stand identical iron grates and doors at nine and twelve o'clock, closing off yet more patient galleries, and the same to her immediate left. In all the corridors now, there is movement: the flow of long skirts and clump of heavy boots as the night nurses and attendants hurry to see just who has gotten loose.

Got to get out of here. She should block the door behind her, if she can. Throwing a frantic glance at the large cast-iron square lock, with a keyhole directly beneath a brass knob at the upper right, she feels a sudden kick in her chest. *Whoa—* her eye fixes on that bright brass knob—*wait a second.*

Attendants are shouting at her from the other galleries; there is the muted tinkle and shake of keys, but she barely hears. Staring at the knob, what she feels is *recognition*, a sense of something clearing in her mind, as if all the pieces to a tough physics problem are beginning to click.

That's the knob House showed me on the slit-door. "Oh Jesus," she whispers, and another fit of trembling sweeps through her as her mind jumps back to her first thought when she found herself here. What if *this* is the real-world detail House plucked from her mind? *Skull plates or not, what if I really* belong *here?*

"Emma!"

Kramer's shout breaks the spell. Her head jerks up, and she sees the men only twenty feet away. There are more crowded at every single grate. *Figure this out later, you nut; move, move!* She spots a small latch-bolt protruding from the bottom edge of the lock-plate and thinks, *Push it.* Jamming the small bolt to the left with the ball of her thumb, she hears the lock catch with a crisp *snap*.

"Emma, stop!" Kramer says as he and the others crowd against the iron grate. Shaking out keys, Kramer reaches through the grate. There is a scrape of metal on metal as his key stutters on iron, and she realizes that she must have hit some kind of dead bolt that can only be opened from her side.

"Emma." Jasper wraps his hands around the iron bars. "Please, let them help you."

"If you refuse to listen to me, pay heed to John, your guardian," Kramer says, still struggling with fitting the key. "You're only making this more difficult for yourself, Emma."

Oh, I don't think so. Wondering, though: *John?* Why had Kramer called Jasper by that name? *Something important there . . .*

But she has no time to think anymore about it. Turning, she

scuttles to the grate to her immediate left and jams the privacy bolt to. That will have to do; no time for the others. From all the wards now come muffled hoots and shouts and bangs as patients hammer their locked doors. Behind her, Kramer is shouting, "Porter! *Porter!*" and Emma thinks: *Uh-oh.* Scurrying to the head of the central staircase, she makes out denser shadows hustling over marble: the night guards coming to get her.

And there is yet one more sound, distant but so familiar, that snags her: a kind of mad, booming, howling chorus rising from the depths of this building to seep through brick and open-worked iron grills: *Matchi-Manitou, in his cave under Devils Island.* And then she thinks, *What?*

Out of the shadows below, a phalanx of seven men swarms for the stairs like an army of black spiders, and she backs away. *Can't get out that way.* She won't let them take her either. She won't go down there. Down may be the way out, but *down* is also bad. Deep underground, in the dank basement of this asylum, there is . . .

Matchi-Manitou, in his deep dark cave . . .

A room, a *sundry room,* the words suddenly popping in her brain with the clarity of a flashbulb. The sundry room is padded with cork and India rubber for violent people like her. There is the rotary chair and thick, sickly sweet rust-red medicine and cold-water baths and more that is much, much worse.

But how do you know this, Emma? And why is she thinking of Devils Island? That's in Wisconsin, and she's . . . She doesn't know where she is, but she can feel the scream rising from her chest. *How do you know what happens here?*

"Here now!" From far below, a very large man, round as

a billiard ball, leads the charge, lumbering up the stairs and using a heavy stick for balance. "Stay there, Miss!"

No way in hell. To her left are arched windows, and because there is so little light behind her, she makes out the open space of a very large courtyard or garden. Protruding immediately below is the snow-covered roof of some other building she can barely see. Flanking the garden on either side are extremely long wings, which must be more wards.

I'm on the second floor. Her hand tightens on Jasper's sturdy walking stick. *Break a window. Climb down.* And then she thinks: *Seriously?* She was no monkey in gym, and even if she manages it, she has no way of knowing how far the grounds extend and she can't go fumbling around in the dark. It's winter; she'll freeze. Barefoot, she won't get far anyway, and snow means tracks. *But I have to get out, find a road and people. Figure out exactly where I am.*

Sprinting right, she pelts along a side landing toward the next flight of stairs, trailed by Kramer's bellows, nurses and attendants trapped behind gated iron grilles, and the porter's shouts. Wheeling around a marble newel post, she catches a glow of streetlamps through high windows and, closer, the wide columns of this building's massive portico—and she falters. *That's the front of the building.* So why is she heading up and not down? Okay, *down* is bad, and yeah, the front doors might be locked, and there's the little problem of getting past all those men. *But what are you doing, Emma? Why are you running* up? This is a *blink*, a nightmare, and forget the stupid brass knob on the lock, how detailed this is, how *real*, and all that shit. She's got to believe she's still inside that creepy little house, the near twin to Frank McDermott's home, and House has created this.

I could do nothing. Eventually I'll wake up or blink back. I always do. Yet even as she thinks this, she has the queasy sense that this would be the wrong move.

Must go up. It isn't just the steady throb of her headache, the burn of her titanium skull plates impelling her to *go, go, move.* It's as if she's being guided by an internal compass, an invisible hand that prods the nape of her neck to urge her on, force her up, up, *up.*

God, Emma, you nut, I hope you know what you're doing. She vaults up another flight. The hard stone is cold on her feet. Dead ahead, she can see that the layout above is identical to that below: four gated wards, two on the right and two on the left. There's movement as the shouts trail and attendants hustle out of wardrooms, where they've been dozing, to see what's going on.

How many floors are there? From her brief glimpse of the flanking galleries, she thinks not many, maybe only four. As she pivots around another newel post for the next flight of steps, she can hear Kramer and the others now: the clap of boots on marble and men's shouts.

"Shit," she breathes. *They're out. No more time.* She is committed now. "Emma, you better be right." Scrambling up this flight, she sees the same layout of wards on either side. *Third floor.* If it's like this on the fourth, she's screwed. As she bounds up the next stone staircase, however, she sees an immediate difference. Despite the gloom, it seems a little brighter up here, and then she spots the arched door at the very top of the steps. As she hits the landing, she pauses to throw looks right and left. No galleries. No wards. End of the line.

Please, please . . . Leaping for the door, she slots her hand through a curved iron latch and gasps. The iron's so frigid it burns. *Good. It means this must open to the outside.* But is it locked? Below, she hears distant bangs, and then Kramer's voice, louder than before but also . . . stranger, more of a gargled, strangled choke, as if he's shouting from a deep, dark well: "Emma! Emma, there's no way out! Come back!"

Shit. Come on. Mashing the thumb plate, she puts her weight into it, shoving, *pushing* with all her strength. *Please, please, please, don't be locked* . . . A little cry jumps from her mouth as the wooden door, so warped and weighty it groans on its hinges, *squawwws* over stone. A gush of wintery air splashes her face, and she thinks, *Roof. I'm out!* She bullies through a narrow wedge between the door and wall . . .

2

AND INTO A huge, soaring space that is utterly and completely without light, as dark as a cave.

Oh shit, where am I? In the hush, she hears her heart thud. *What* is *this?* Turning a complete circle, she strains to make out details. The darkness is close and cold, but she detects that faint silvery glimmer again: light, spilling down from somewhere high above. Tipping her head, she spots a parade of tall arched windows marching all the way around a . . .

A *dome?*

"Oh God." Now other details are materializing in the dim light. On this main floor, there are rows of wooden benches. They look familiar, not because she's necessarily seen them before *here*. But *I know what you are.* She brushes a hand over the hard back of one bench; in the well, near the floor, she spots a folded wooden bar. *A kneeler, which means . . .* Dead ahead, there is a dais on which rests a carved pulpit. Turning, she faces the door through which she's come—through which the others will be on her in a heartbeat, because she can hear them getting closer and louder—and sees high up and just below one of those arched windows, a large, long, rectangular plaque: probably stone, and the kind of marker you'd inscribe with the names of benefactors or Bible verses.

Pews. A pulpit. Next to the door, she now sees a low cabinet filled with books. *They must be hymnals.* Turning back, she lifts her eyes to a spot immediately above the pulpit on its gated dais—*no, not gates; they're communion rails*—and spots the hulking saw-toothed pattern of an organ's pipes. Of course: if you're going to sing something from a hymnal, you'll need something to keep the mad in tune and the lunatics on track.

She knows now, exactly, where she is.

She's in a domed chapel for the insane—and trapped, like a bug under a bell jar.

RIMA

What She Was Made For

THE ECHOES OF the first blast hadn't quite died when there was another thunderous *boom*. Still perched on the snowmobile, Rima felt her heart give a quick, convulsive flutter, like the wings of a startled bird. From the church, another scream tore through the fog.

I've got to go into the church. But why should she do that? Rima didn't know, yet she could feel her body obeying some call she couldn't quite hear and didn't understand. *Got to get inside.*

"Rima!" Casey said, as she swung off the sled and onto the snow. Scrambling after, he grabbed her arm. "What are you doing?" Then he seemed to realize what he'd done, because he threw a fast, nervous look at the snow. "We need to get off this stuff."

"No." She stared down at the white beneath her feet. No death-whispers now. *The birds are psychopomps; they must be carrying the whispers with them.* Or maybe the birds *were* the whispers. She didn't know. "They're all gone. But I think . . ." Tugging free, she took a halting, tentative step. "I have to . . ."

"Have to *what*? Where are you going?" Casey said. He reached for her, but she angled away and left him grabbing air. His gloved hand balled in frustration. "Rima, talk to me. We have to stay together. What are you *doing*?"

"I don't know." She looked back at him over her shoulder. "I'm sorry, Casey, but I think"—she could feel her legs tense, and realized, with a touch of wonder, that she was getting *ready* for something—"I think I'm supposed to . . ."

"No. Rima, no, *wait*!" As if sensing the danger, Casey started for her.

He was a second too late. "I . . . I *can't*!" And then she was suddenly darting across the snow, heading for the church, even as a small voice of sanity screamed, *What are you doing, what are you doing, what are you* doing?

"Rima!" Casey cried. "Rima, *stop*!"

She couldn't. A crazy compulsion had grabbed hold, dug in its talons, and wouldn't let go. This was her destiny, what she was made for, what she had always done. She churned over the snow. The church rushed toward her out of the fog, the distance between them collapsing, the fog folding to bring her closer as if they were points at either end of a single line now drawn together. One of the church's heavy wooden doors was ajar; the spicy scent of incense and spent gunpowder bit her nose.

She flattened herself against an outer wall. The brick was cold as metal. Across the snow, she could see Casey coming, and knew she was almost out of time. Casey would fight to keep her out of the church, and probably win.

Go, before he stops you. She gathered herself. *Go now, go go go!*

She vaulted for the door.

EMMA

This Is *Your* Now

1

SHE MIGHT HAVE stood there, dumbfounded, until they caught her, if not for the bangs and shouts. Heart leaping, Emma shoots a glance at the chapel's door. *Got to block it. Then find a way out.* Not much time either, but she has to. All these windows, and she's in a dome.

"So outside those windows is the roof." Saying the words out loud centers her. She can break her way out and then climb down from the roof, unless there's a very long drop to the roof or a ledge, but she pushes that away. Her fist tightens around Jasper's walking stick. *Break a window. Climb out. But do something,* anything, *and do it now.*

Dropping Jasper's walking stick on the last pew, she rushes to the door and strong-arms it shut. Eyeing the freestanding cabinet, chock-full of books and immediately to the right of the door, she thinks, *Yeah.* Hurrying to the far side, she wedges her shoulder against it and pushes. Jumping over stone with a loud *screee,* the cabinet wobbles, and for a heart-stopping instant, she thinks it's going to fall back on her. *No, no.* She butts against it, digging in with her toes to stop it rocking the wrong way. *Come on, come on . . .*

"Emma!" From where she stands, she can't see the door, but there is a dull yellow glow now, and she hears both the swell of Kramer's voice and a rougher mutter of other men bunched on the opposite side of the chapel's door, which is only just swinging in with that grating *squawww.* "Emma, there's no place left to . . ." Whatever Kramer's about to say ends with a yelp as the cabinet suddenly topples with a huge reverberating crash that bounces back, the echoes caught and doubling on themselves in the cup of the dome.

Just in time. Through the three-inch gap, she can see Kramer's face, the glistening wound where she hit him, the glint of lantern light off his panops' brass frames—but not, she sees, mirrored in the purple lenses at all.

"You think this is the way?" This close, she can hear the gurgle. Kramer's voice is so thick, it sounds like he's got terminal pneumonia. There is an enormous *bang* as he slams a fist against the door. "This is where you belong, Emma, whether you know it or not."

How about not? Hooking her hands on a pew, she drags it back with a grunt, leaning on her bare heels. If possible, the pew's even heavier than the cabinet. *Thank God they didn't bolt these things to the floor.* When she's lined it up, she races to the opposite side, then strains on the balls of her feet. Her calf muscles cramp as she pushes and hammers the pew over stone, until the end of the pew jams against the fallen cabinet to form the long axis of a T. *There.*

Another *bap* as Kramer thumps the door. "Emma, this is futile," he says in his harsh, gargly croak. "You can't get out.

You don't think we have such things as axes or even a stout log? Or manpower? Or another way in? It's only a matter of time—"

Yeah, yeah, resistance is futile—she tunes him out—*blah-diddy-blahdiddy-blah-blah.* Man, if she ever comes out of this *blink,* she is *so* dropping this class. Then, as a butterfly of a laugh flutters in her throat, she thinks, *Emma, come on, don't lose it.*

She's only bought herself a few minutes, if that. Swallowing back that bright burn of hysteria, she turns aside from the still-fuming Kramer and tries to remember why she thought this was such a good idea. *Okay, this is a chapel; it's got an organ.* Which means there has to be a way up to the organ's console. And in the next second, she spots it: a narrow curlicue of a whitewashed spiral staircase to the right. Behind her, she hears bangs and grunts, that fingernail-over-chalkboard grate of wood against stone, and knows that despite her barricade, time's on Kramer's side.

But that *organ* . . . Retrieving Jasper's walking stick, she scuttles down the center aisle, dodges around the communion rails, and bounds onto the dais. Sweeping a hand over the low altar, she feels her fingers close around heavy velvet. *Yes.* Gathering the altar cloth, she jumps off the dais and heads for the spiral staircase. She takes the steps two at a time, her feet cringing away from cold iron. Ducking through a narrow trap, she pushes onto the second-floor loft, which is only long enough to accommodate the organ and, to its immediate right, another cabinet for books and music. Left of the organ are several ranks of folding chairs with cane seats and backs for the choir. If she thought it would help, she might toss chairs down the iron staircase or try barricading the trap with the cabinet, but she doesn't have that kind of time. Besides, she wants that cabinet for something else entirely.

Centered beneath one of the dome's many windows, the organ's pipes form several clusters. The thickest, largest pipes in the center are all much too tall for her to get a step up. To her right, however, a series of smaller, thinner pipes start low at the center and end higher next to that cabinet. *Right there.* Her eyes click to the pipes and the cabinet, and then she's moving before she can think of all the reasons this won't work. *So long as I don't pull it down on top of myself.* But she can't climb holding on to Jasper's walking stick, and for this to work, she needs it. Clamping the wooden stick between her teeth, she knots the altar cloth around her waist. Then, sucking in a breath around Jasper's stick, she climbs onto the organist's seat and plants her left foot on the highest of the organ's three keyboards. She expects a breathy run of notes, but nothing happens. Straddling the gap between the organ and bookshelf, she hangs on to the pipes with both hands as she reaches with her right foot, groping with her toes.

"Emma." Kramer's voice is very loud now, and echoes, and she thinks they've nearly got that door open. "Stop. What do you think you're doing?"

What does it look like, asshole? With the stick wedged in her mouth, she can't answer anyway. Instead, she spiders up, bracing herself on the pipes to her left as she scoots up the cabinet on her right. Even though she's careful not to let her full weight drop on the shelves, there is a subtle shift under her feet, the soft rickety squeal of stressed wood. But the cabinet's as heavy and solidly made as the one on the main floor. *Lucky they didn't have Ikea back then, or I'd be sunk.* With a grunt, she hauls herself the last few inches to crouch on top of the cabinet. She can feel the outside air spilling in a frigid waterfall over the windowsill, which is less than six inches to her left. With a small flare of alarm, she realizes that she never stopped to wonder if the window's muntins are wide enough. *Jesus, if I knock out a pane, will there be enough room for me to climb through?*

Only one way to find out. Bracing the palm of her right hand on the dome's wall, she turns her face away and whips Jasper's walking stick around by the business end. There is a watery splash as the carved ivory head smashes a pane, breaking open a foot-wide maw bristling with glassy teeth.

Time for one more, and then it had better be enough. Kramer is shouting again, and from the corner of her eye, she sees other men, who must've come in a different way, running for the spiral staircase. She swings. The remaining glass explodes, and this time the muntins surrounding this pane, as well as the ones immediately to the left and above, simply fall out. *They're wood, not metal.* Through the huge gaping hole, she could hear the faint *hoosh* of the wind.

Far below, the chapel door finally grinds open, and she pauses just long enough to look down as Kramer and the others clamber over the felled cabinet and scattered hymnals. She sees Kramer raise a lantern, the light cutting deep shadows over his face as he cranes a look. She doesn't even wait for him to ask her what she's doing before she does it.

Unknotting the altar cloth, she snaps the heavy fabric like a sheet. The cloth snags on minute jags of glass but holds. Still clutching Jasper's stick, she reaches with her left foot, plants it on the sill, then shifts her weight to thrust her head and shoulders through the broken glass. *Easy, easy.* Stabbing down, she feels the moment that the tip of the walking stick hits and steadies against stone, and then she leans into it, trusting in the sturdy wood to hold her weight as she pulls her right leg through the window.

"Ahh!" she groans as her bare foot sinks into snow, then flinches away at a sharp bite of glass in her heel. *Go, go, muscle through this. Come on!* Gritting her teeth, she pulls her left leg after and clambers out of the bell jar and into the storm.

2

INSTANTLY, SHE SINKS to her ankles in snow. She stands on the narrow ledge that surrounds the dome. Through a wavering curtain of whirling wet flakes, she spots the curved rails of an iron ladder bolted into the stone. *Must be the way down.* Below, the asylum's roof is a wide, flat, white expanse edged with a decorative marble cornice.

So now what? Where is she supposed to go? For a stunned moment, she can only huddle against the icy dome. Snow blasts over her skin. The wind cuts, ripping the breath from her mouth, and she can feel her determination, the certainty that *this* was the right and only way, beginning to bleed away.

"So now what, House?" She watches the wind fling her words into the storm. "What was the *point*? Why are you showing me this?"

Only the wind answers, in a howl. A dullness settles in her chest. Either she stands here until Kramer or one of his men finds a ladder and comes through that broken window, or . . .

I am *insane.* Floundering, her feet beginning to numb, she gropes her way to the iron ladder and carefully lowers herself a rung at a time. At the very bottom, she pauses, looking up at the massive bell jar of the dome hunched against a moonless night with no stars. Icy pellets of snow needle her cheeks and sting her eyes, which are starting to tear. She is here to find something; she has to believe that, because the alternative is just too awful.

So what is it, House? What do you want me to see, to do now? Dropping into snow, sinking up to mid-calf, she grimly slogs toward the marble cornice at the front of the building. Walking against the wind is like shoving her way through pins. The dome rises off her right shoulder. Far below and across a long, very black expanse that must be the asylum's front grounds, she can just make out the faint glow from gas lamps mounted on high iron posts to either side of a wide gate, and at ground level, the flicker of a lamp inside some kind of structure that reminds her a little bit of those ranger kiosks at park entrances. Raising a hand to shield her eyes, she squints against a pillow of wind-driven snow. *Gatehouse?* Beyond are other lamps, spaced at long intervals on tall posts along an empty street fronted by dark shops. Above those, lozenges of fuzzy light spill from apartment windows where anyone sane is riding out the storm. To the far right, through a distant tangle of bare tree limbs, she spots a glister of many colors, faint and fractured. *Stained glass,* she thinks. *That's a church.* But where in England is she, exactly?

At that, the storm seems to pause a moment, or maybe it's only the wind deciding to pull in a breath, because the snow shifts. Now, to her left and in the distance, she spots the dark spear of a tower thrusting above the far trees—and its clock face, bright as a moon.

All right, that answers that question. Other than Dickens and that crazy stunt where Queen Elizabeth parachuted into the Olympics with Daniel Craig, she might not know much about England, but she recognizes that clock tower. Everyone does. *Big Ben.*

That's when she remembers something else, from a Lizzie-*blink*: a *different* London. Lizzie had thought that; her parents had mentioned it directly. But what did that mean—*another* London? Or would a little girl like Lizzie see the past as a different place, a separate *Now*?

Or maybe it's both. Her eyes snag on a furred arc of green-white balls of light strung between the clock tower and the bank opposite. *What if we're talking about not only travel between two points but also different* times?

Her thoughts suddenly fizzle and her vision seems to waver as the darkness ripples. For an instant, she thinks, *Shit, can't pass out now.* But then, when she doesn't and the darkness stops moving, her mind simply blanks.

Because there, hovering just beyond the decorative marble cornice at the roof's edge, is a tall jet slit, narrow as a lizard's eye and outlined by the glister of a blare-white glow.

No. You're not real. Squeezing her eyes shut, she flutters them open again to find that the view hasn't changed. If anything, the glow is stronger. *Why did you make this, House? What do you want from me?*

"Emma."

At the sound of her name, her heart catapults into her

mouth. *I think about times and* Nows, *and House makes the Mirror appear.* Gulping against a sour surge of fear, she turns. *House makes* him.

Kramer is there, not far away, on the roof. His body is a well of shadow, the details indistinct. But like that slit-mirror that cannot *really* be there, Kramer is backlit by a faint, undulant luster, as sickly green as an old bruise. In a way, Kramer is the Mirror in human form: a blank daguerreotype, a cutout with no face and nothing she recognizes. But, oh, she knows that gargle of a voice that is one and many, because she has heard it before: in a Lizzie-*blink,* and on a Madison street conjured from memory.

"There's nowhere in this *Now* left to run," Kramer says, his voice burring and humming as if the words are being run through a faulty synthesizer. "Or rather . . . you have a choice of where and in which *Now* you choose to be."

Where and in which Now? Having rested long enough—allowing her to see what it is that House wants her to know—the greedy wind starts up again to grab her gown, snatch at her hair. Glancing back over her shoulder at the hovering slit-mirror, she feels that familiar burn in her forehead, which had ebbed as soon as she bashed out that window, beginning to brighten and sting, coring like a laser through her brain.

"I'm not going anywhere with you." She eases back a slow step and then another, her bare soles digging troughs in the snow. "Just let me go. I want to go home. I want out of this valley and this creepy house with its weird doors and rooms. I only want to wake up."

"Emma, this is your home and where you belong," Kramer says. "*This* is your *Now*."

"I don't believe you." Between her breasts, the galaxy pendant on its crimson silk ribbon smolders and heats. *I have plates that haven't been invented; I carry the memory of the future.* "If I'm only crazy, how come *you* know about *Nows*? You're a liar. I'm still in the valley. I'm in House."

"Touché. But did I really say something just now?" Kramer cocks his head. "Are you sure you're not imagining that I said something you'd like to hear? Even if I *did* speak, it is my word against your very intriguing delusion. Tell you what: if I'm not real, come to me." Arms spread wide, Kramer starts toward her. Where she's struggled and slipped on fresh-fallen snow, he seems to glide, and that is when she sees that his shoes aren't sinking. She isn't altogether sure his shoes even touch the snow at all. Something is also gathering . . . *behind* him? No, *Kramer* is shifting, going fuzzy at the edges, his body beginning to steam. "Come," he says, skimming over snow. "Come with me."

Her voice locks in her throat. She is too frightened to scream. Her heart is thrashing in her chest, and the pendant is a scorching, calescent blaze.

Run. Run now. Go through the Mirror before he—

A blackness darker than night swarms over Kramer's body, knitting itself into a tangle of scaly arms and spindle legs; into the thing that pulled itself from the book on the street she's just left. *Peekaboo, I see you.* Its voice, whisper-man black, sweeps through her mind, working its fingers into the folds and crannies of her brain. *Stay, Breath of My Breath. Drink, Blood of My Blood. Stay and plaaay through tiiime—*

"Get out of my head, get out of my head, get out of my *head*!" With a shriek, she whirls around and pelts across the roof, slip-sliding on ice and slick slate. She feels the whisper-man fling itself after, but she is running, running, running, and there is the black mirror, rushing for her face as the pain flares between her eyes and the galaxy pendant seems to explode against her chest, as hot and dazzling as a nova—and there is light, a wide blinding bolt that shoots from the pendant, unfurling itself in a path: light that is so strong and steady and sure, it's as if she's running on a bright, unerring seam.

Forget what Einstein said about light. It's not solid; you can't run on light. *It isn't there and neither is the Mirror,* a tiny panicked voice jabbers in her mind. *Follow this and you're dead. You'll go over the edge, because you're crazy; the doctors were right, Kramer's right, and this path is not there, it doesn't exist, it isn't—*

Screaming, Emma plants both hands on icy marble, swings her legs, and then she is sailing for the mirror, following that ribbon of light, and crashing through in a hail of jagged black glass, and then she is falling, screaming, *falling . . .*

EMMA
The Opposite Ends to a Single Sentence

ONTO A ROAD.

London is gone. Her clothes are . . . regular clothes. Normal jeans, although she's now wearing the turquoise turtleneck House let her find. Her head kills; that metal plate is gnawing a hole in her skull. She has brought nothing from the past except the galaxy pendant, which is, weirdly, still there and warm against her chest. Otherwise, she's fine.

Well, considering all this fog.

Oh shit. Her eyes lock on the wreck of a car, crumpled against a sturdy tree, and then she knows exactly where—and when—she is. *No, this is* Lizzie's *life,* her *past, not mine; this has nothing to do with me.*

Suddenly, space wrinkles. The pendant fires and Emma rushes toward the wreck, though she hasn't moved a muscle. It is as if she and Lizzie have occupied the opposite ends to a single sentence and someone has carved away everything in between. The degree of separation is now no more than a sliver of White Space between two adjacent letters in the same word. Or is she still, somehow, caught in the Mirror, between worlds? Between *Nows*?

Or is this like the bathroom in House—she reaches out and feels her palms flatten on an icy, hard, impenetrable, invisible surface—*and I'm on my side of the glass?*

Another thought, stranger still: *Is this one of those places where the barrier's thinnest?*

Beyond, on the other side, Emma can see Lizzie's mother. Meredith's head lolls; the air bag's painted a slick red. The impact has displaced the engine block, the dashboard has ruptured, and the steering wheel has actually moved, jamming into Meredith's body, tacking her to the seat like a bug to cardboard.

Lizzie's mother lets out a long, *long* moan.

"M-m-mommmm?" Lizzie's head is muzzy and thick.

Wait a second, Emma thinks, on her side of the barrier. *I feel her, like I'm in her head, in two places at once. How can that be?*

"Mom," Lizzie whimpers. The car's hood is an accordion, the dash only inches from Lizzie's chest. Lizzie might be able to slither sideways, but there is nowhere to go. "M-Mom?"

"L-Liz . . ." The word is a hiss, but this is not the whisper-man. This is the voice of her mother, and she is dying; Lizzie knows that, and there is nothing Lizzie can do, no way to fix this.

Trapped on the other side of this nightmare, Emma thinks, *It's like I'm bleeding into her life.* She remembers Frank cutting himself, the sound of his blood squelching over the Mirror. *I'm bleeding into her.*

"Mom?" Lizzie's voice thins with grief and terror. Bright red blood jets from her mother's chest and *splish-splish-splishes* onto vinyl. The steering wheel has done more than pin her mother against the seat. The wheel is broken, and the jagged column has punched through like the point of a lance. With every beat, Mom's heart empties her veins just a little bit more.

Please, House, get me out. Emma watches as the fog gushes into the car, swirling up in a whirlpool past Lizzie's feet, her hips. *You showed me the way out of that asylum. So, show me* now. *Get me out of Lizzie's head, please.*

"L-Lizzieee." Mom's voice is weak, no more than a halting whisper. "G-get . . . a-awaaay . . ."

The phone is still beeping. The fog has crept to Lizzie's chest and continues to rise, snaking higher and higher, coiling around her shoulders in a white rope to hold her fast.

Got to finish the special forever-Now, Lizzie thinks. The symbols she's already formed are starting to fade, the purpling mad bleeding away like her mother's blood. *Got to make the last symbol.*

Symbol? Emma no longer wonders how she knows what Lizzie feels or thinks. She only wants this to end. *What symbol?*

"R-run." Mom coughs, and crimson gushes from her mouth. "L-Lizzie . . . h-h-h-hide . . ."

"Momma, I . . . I *can't.*" The lick of the fog, bright and cruel, is cold enough to burn, and very strong, stronger than Lizzie, and the phone is still ringing, ringing, ringing. The fog's tongue tastes Lizzie's chin. Its ice-fingers tickle her nose. She twists and turns, she holds her breath, but the fog doesn't care. It slips in; it slithers up her nose. Its fingers crawl over her brain and dig into the meat and worm behind her eyes. Lizzie has one last symbol to make, only one, but whatever it was, she can no longer see it in her mind. No, no, it's not fair, she is so *close*; she was almost done! If only she hadn't waited! The fog plucks at the cords of her nerves and muscles. Her legs flop; her arms jitter and twitch—

I've got to do something, Emma thinks, frantically. *I'm so close, just a sliver of White Space. There's got to be* something *I can do.*

Through Lizzie's eyes, Emma watches the day gray as the darkness that is the fog flows over and through Lizzie's vision like black oil, like something out of *X-Files*, when the aliens slip inside and hijack a ride.

And then the light is gone, and Lizzie is blind. She opens her mouth to scream—and can't. Her mouth is stitched shut. No, no, that's not right. Lizzie's mouth is no longer *there*.

Oh my God. If Emma's heart still beats, she no longer feels it. *Lizzie's face, her* face*!*

Lizzie's face is going blank and whisper-man black, the way the words on a page are erased and scrubbed away, one by one, letter by letter, word by word, line by line.

Then, the cell phone ceases its relentless beeping.

Time's up.

A moment's silence. A pause.

Then, a *click*.

And then,

a soft . . .

       tiny . . .

             eep.

And the phone says . . .

EMMA
Space Tears

1

"NO!" EMMA SHRIEKS. Her palms flatten against the edge of White Space. "House, stop this! Don't listen, Lizzie, don't *listen!*"

House does nothing, and Emma knows there's no more time for words. The galaxy pendant around her neck is a bright beacon, like a searchlight telling her mind where to go and what to do.

Bridge the gap. Cross the space. This is like the mirror in the bathroom; this has to be why House showed me how to do this in the first place: to get me ready, prime my brain to believe I can. Just reach out and pull her across and do it now, do it now!

So Emma thrusts her hand, hard; feels the White Space resist and deform and rip and then—

Then there is pain.

Oh God. She opens her mouth to scream, but her lungs won't work. *What* is *this?* This isn't like the bathroom mirror, where it was only cold and then burning. She isn't prepared for how much this hurts, as if the glassy teeth of the broken window from that domed chapel for the mad have snagged her after all. This is altogether different than what she's just done: crashing from the past through a phantom black slit-mirror to this *Now*. That didn't hurt at all. One minute, she was in the snow, on the roof, sprinting from the spidery thing erupting from Kramer's body—and then she was on a road.

And this is not even close to what happened years ago: when she was twelve and found something down cellar in Jasper's cottage that she's determined not to think about. Because that might prove that, really, she's only crazy.

Now, the White Space rips. It gapes in a fleshy wound, and Emma is suddenly teetering on the lip between two worlds, two times, two stories. The Space tears, and she tears with it, her skin ripping, flayed from her bones the way paper splits along a seam. She can feel her heart struggling in her chest in great shuddering heaves, and then there is no thought at all, only a blaze of white-hot agony.

Too late to go back, even if she wanted to: there is the car and Lizzie, right in front of her. She stretches, gropes for a handhold, as the gelid fog burns and scores her flesh. Her fingers slide over something solid: a small wrist, slick and tacky with blood. Her hand closes around Lizzie, and then she is pulling with all her might, dragging the girl from the car and away from the greedy fingers of that murderous fog, reeling her across shuddering time and shimmering White Space, bridging the gap between two letters, two words, two *Nows*. The White Space flexes, folds . . .

2

AND THEY TUMBLED back in a heap.

Emma was knocked flat, smacking what little air she had left from her lungs. For a moment, all she could do was lie there, gulping like a hooked fish flipped onto a dock. Her heart hammered against her ribs. Blood bounded in her neck and head, her pulse beating time in her throbbing temples.

The downstairs hallway, where she'd come back to find herself at that slit-door, was gone. She now lay on plush white carpet in a room with blush-pink walls edged in white trim. To the left, a pine loft bed hovered five feet off the floor. A dollhouse huddled just beneath, and a wine-red tongue of quilt, speckled with colorful glass, dangled over the lip of the bed.

"Oh boy." Sprawled on the carpet to Emma's right, Lizzie lifted her head and said, weakly, "Wow, Emma, I thought you were *never* going to figure it out."

RIMA

Something Inside

DUCKING AROUND THE cold red brick of the church, Rima scuttled through the open door and fetched up against the last row of pews. The church was a ruin. The altar had been junked; a huge wooden crucifix lay in two jagged splinters as if snapped over a knee. Beyond the altar rail, an over-large Bible with gilt covers flopped facedown in a colorful halo of shattered, bloodred stained glass. A body, all in black, lay beyond the chancery railing where it had fallen back against a lectern, which was splashed with gore and liverish chunks of flesh. But there was something off about the body, too. The hands didn't seem . . . quite right.

There was the slight grate and pop of glass on stone as Casey came to crouch alongside. "Why did you run? Wha—" He sucked in a small gasp. "You hear that?"

She did: a small mewling, hitching sound. *Somebody crying.* "Tania?" she whispered.

"Who?" Casey asked.

"Tania," she said, as if that should be explanation enough. At his frown: "A *friend.*"

"A friend from *where*?"

"Here." They were wasting time. Leaning out a little further, she called again, "Tania? Tania, it's me."

A pause. The scuff of a boot over stone. "R-Rima?"

"Yeah. I-I told you I'd come back." The words just flew into her mouth, as if she was an actor dropped into a scene from a well-rehearsed play. But now she began to remember bits and pieces. She and Tania had been working in the school cafeteria when . . . when . . . She skimmed her lips with her tongue. *When what?*

"Is it safe to come out?" Tania asked. "Did you bring the snowcat?"

"The what?" The boy shot her a bewildered look. "What is she talking about?"

"The snowcat," she said, relieved. *That's right; I snuck out and found the snowcat. I drove it over.* Her hand strayed to the front pocket of her parka, and her fingers slid over the jagged teeth of a key. *I grabbed a gun and I left it in the snowcat.*

"What snowcat?" the boy asked.

Instead of answering him, she called to her friend, "Yeah, Tania, the cat's outside." The words still felt strange in her mouth, but somehow she knew that these were the *right* words, filling in the blanks of a story still taking shape in her mind. "I found a rifle in the equipment shed, too. It's in the snowcat. Come on, before they find us."

"Rima," the boy said, urgently. "Rima, what rifle? Who are they? What are you talking about?"

She fired off an impatient glance—and then felt a sudden jolt of panic. The boy's face seemed familiar, especially his eyes, so stormy and gray. But she didn't know him, couldn't remember his name. *Who is he? Do I know—*

"Rima?" The boy reached a hand to her shoulder. "Are you all right?"

Casey. The name flooded into her as if flowing from his fingers. "Yes, I–I'm . . . Casey, I'm fine."

"Then what is this?" Casey asked. "Who's Tania? Who are *they*?"

Dangerous, that's what they are. "Casey, I don't *know*, I'm not sure." *But this is right; this is the right story.* "All I know is, this is what's supposed to hap—" She caught movement near the chancel rail, a flicker of shadow, and then a girl's face, white and drawn beneath a thatch of wild black hair, slid above the edge of a pew. "Tania," Rima said, relieved. "Are you all right?"

"Yes." Tania's eyes, little-girl wide, flitted from her to Casey. "Who's he?"

"Casey. He's a friend."

"From where?" Tania was standing now, a shotgun clearly visible, the barrel pointing at Casey's chest. "I don't remember him from class."

Neither did she, exactly. She improvised. "I found him wandering around when I got the snowcat." From the corner of her eye, she saw Casey turn another look, but she pushed on. "I couldn't just leave him there."

"How do you know he won't change?"

Change? The word chilled her blood. *Change into what?* Then she remembered the broken body in the chancery, and those hands that weren't quite right. "Who is that? Who did you shoot?"

"Father Preston." Tania's chin quivered. "I couldn't stay in the gym, so I ran to the church and Father Preston was here, only he . . . he . . . I didn't want to, but I *had* to!"

"Stay calm, Tania. It's okay," Rima said, and then she was up, breaking out from cover and going to her friend. Casey said something, but she barely heard, couldn't really understand the words. "Come here," she said, gathering the weeping girl in her arms. "It's okay. It's going to be all right."

"Nice that you think so." Tania smelled of charred gunpowder, the oil the groundskeeper—*Fred,* Rima thought, *his name is Fred*—used to clean the shotgun, and sweat. Turning her head into Rima's shoulder, Tania slumped into her. "I'm so *scared*."

"It'll be okay." Rima slid the gun from Tania's slack fingers and handed the weapon to Casey. Casey's face was a mask of confusion, but she could tell from the firm set of his mouth that he would follow her lead.

"Rima, I . . . I don't feel so good," Tania moaned against her shoulder. "I think I'm going to be . . . I think I might be s-sick."

"We just have to get you out of—" Then Rima felt Taylor's death-whisper flexing and bunching with alarm along Rima's arms and around her middle, and that was when Rima's mind registered what her hands—so sensitive to the whispers within—were telling her, what *Taylor* sensed.

There was something else here, under her hands. Not in Tania's soot-stained parka or whispering in her clothes, no. Rima saw Tania's face twist as another pain grabbed her middle.

There was something inside Tania.

EMMA
Just One Piece

"COME ON!" LIZZIE sprang to a sit. "We got to get the others, quick!"

"No, wait, wait a second," Emma said. Her head ached, and a slow ooze of something wet wormed from her right ear. When she put a hand to her neck, the fingers came away painted bright red. From the pain she'd felt as she reached through White Space, she thought her skin would be torn in a dozen places, but other than the gash on her forehead she'd gotten when the van crashed, there wasn't a scratch on her. The pendant wasn't around her neck anymore either. Just another part of her *blink*, she guessed, like the flannel night-gown and Jasper's ivory-handled walking stick—and good riddance.

Now that they were in the same space, in the same room, Emma could see that, really, they didn't look all that much alike. Lizzie's face was oval, the blond pigtails giving her the look of a pixie. Falling to the middle of her back, Emma's hair was very dark, lush, and coppery, and her face was square.

What are *you?* Emma's gaze fixed on the golden flaw in the little girl's right eye, embedded in an iris that was a rich, lustrous, unearthly cobalt. *Same flaw, same eye, identical color.*

"I'm not going anywhere with you," she said, and thought, with an unpleasant little ping in her chest, that this was the same thing she'd said only minutes ago to Kramer or the whisper-man or whatever the hell that had been. All these repetitions and echoes were starting to drive her crazy. It was as if she existed in multiple places at once, the lines slotting into her mouth depending on which choice she happened to make at that instant.

And then she thought, *Whoa. Wait a second . . . multiple places?*

"You have to," Lizzie said. "I can't do this alone. The others are lost; they've fallen between the lines. I couldn't hold on to them all."

Okay, so the kid was as crazy as she suspected *she* was. Not too comforting, that. "I'm not going anywhere until you tell me what's happening."

"I'll explain everything, I promise," Lizzie said, scrambling to her feet. "But we have to get them now." When Emma still made no move to follow, the little girl said, impatiently, "Why did you reach through White Space if you didn't want to help?"

"I didn't know what I was doing." That was almost true. The impulse had been instinctive, no more mysterious than rescuing a baby bird fallen from its nest. "You were in trouble and . . ." *And I was in your head, which was just too freaky-weird.* "I just knew I could."

"But *why?*" Lizzie pressed. "Why did you *really* do it?"

"Because . . ." She bit off the rest. *Oh, come on, what do you care if she thinks you're nuts? Just say it.* "I saw your dad, at the Dickens Mirror, in my *blinks*, and I did the same thing because House showed me: in the bathroom, at the slit-door to the . . . well, I think it's a library. And I . . . I was in your head just now. It felt like we were the same somehow, like echoes or twins or . . ." She made an impatient gesture. "Only we're not. I was wrong. I don't look anything like you. You're a little kid. I'm seventeen." *And I'm nuts and you're . . . okay, maybe you're nuts, too.* "Whatever," she said, and huffed out in annoyance. She was *so* taking her meds from now on. "I'm not *you.*"

"No, you're not," Lizzie said. "You're just one piece. You all are."

RIMA
I Don't Know Who You Are

NO, GOD. NOT *Tania, too.* Cold sweat slicked Rima's skin. The whisper of something unspeakable moved in a darkling roil deep within Tania to shiver and squirm beneath Rima's hands. *It can't be happening to Tania, not when we've come this far.*

Tania sensed something, because she drew back, her frightened eyes shimmering with tears. "What's wrong?"

"N-nothing," Rima managed. She was aware of . . . of that boy. Her mind blanked, as if all the words she'd been thinking were suddenly erased. The name that had been on the tip of her tongue only seconds ago vanished like smoke. The boy, that kid with her: *What's his name?* She couldn't remember. He didn't even look all that familiar.

What's happening to me? A bolt of panic shuddered through her chest. *I remember Tania. I recognize the church. I know where I am. So why can't I remember him?*

"Rima," the boy said, "I don't think we should stay in here."

He knows me. Anything she might have said knotted in

her throat and wouldn't come out. She felt as if her mind was being swallowed a bite at a time. *How can he know me if I don't recognize him?*

"Rima?" The boy reached to touch her, then seemed to think better of that. "You've . . . you brought the snowcat, remember?"

Right. She almost let out a giddy laugh. *The cat, I remember that.* She was freaked out, that was all. Who wouldn't be? After the carnage in the cafeteria, where the pimply guy with the dweeb hairnet in the serving line, Victor, suddenly howled and sprouted *claws* . . . who wouldn't be spooked? *Worry about this later. Just move, get out!*

"Yes," she said. "Right outside. We better get going."

"Wait." The boy was clutching Tania's shotgun in one hand and now shucked in a shell, the pump making a loud, echoing, ratcheting, insectile sound. "Tania . . . Tania?" When the girl dragged up her head to look at him, the boy said, "How many shells are in the shotgun? Do you know? How many shots did you take?"

"T-two," Tania said, then shook her head and moistened her lips. "N-no. Three, I . . . I th-think. I d-don't know."

"All right. It's okay." To Rima: "Let me go first, all right? Just in case. You take care of your friend." Without waiting for her to agree, the boy turned and hurried up the center aisle.

"Come on, Tania. We're almost out. Just hang on." Threading an arm around the moaning girl, Rima staggered after the boy. Leaning so heavily against her that Rima was practically carrying her, Tania stumbled along, nearly doubled over with pain. Ahead, at the front entrance, Rima saw the boy put up a hand and then slide to the open front door. "Anything?" she whispered.

"No. Here, she's too heavy for you. Let me help." Darting back, the boy grabbed Tania's other arm and took most of the girl's weight. "She'll fall otherwise."

"Thanks." And then Rima blurted, "I'm sorry. I don't know who you are. I don't remember your name. Isn't that weird? I *think* I knew, but now . . ."

"I'm Casey." The boy's voice was calm, which surprised her, because his eyes, their color, were so strange: stormy and indefinite, as if they hadn't quite settled in his face just yet. "It's okay, Rima. We've had a really rough night so far."

"Yeah?" Rima tried a shaky smile. "Feels like it's been pretty bad."

"And then some." A brief smile flickered over the boy's lips. "Come on."

With Tania lurching between them, they wobbled outside and over the snow in an ungainly jog. At the sight of the blocky orange snowcat only a short distance away, Rima felt the cobwebs of uncertainty in her mind being swept away by relief. *I know this. I recognize this.* She also knew that there were two distinct parts to the vehicle: a glassed-in, two-seater forward cabin for the driver and a larger passenger cabin just behind that, like a smaller version of a semi-tractor trailer.

Turning to the boy—*no, Casey; he's Casey*—she said, "Let's take Tania around back. There's a door there and more room for her to lie . . ."

There came a sudden hard *bang*, not the blast of a shotgun but the slam of stout wood against brick. With a jump of alarm, Rima turned and saw a dark blur—something with a head and arms, a swirling black torso—storming, insanely fast, from the church. In the blink of an eye and before she even had a chance to pull in a breath, the thing was there, right on top of them, *looming* over Casey, who was only just now beginning to turn, and there was no time to get to the snowcat, no time!

"Casey!" Rima shouted. "Casey, *look out!*"

EMMA
Find Your Story

"A PIECE." EMMA stared. "A piece of what?"

"A piece of me," Lizzie said. "I've been trying to pull you closer . . . gosh, *forever*. It's way harder to grab someone who's popped right off the page than you think."

"What?" She felt the burn of a scream trapped somewhere in her chest. "You," she said to the little girl, "are nuts. What are you talking about? That's just an expression. All I want is to wake up and fall out of this *blink* into my life. I want you to get House to let me go." As soon as she said that, she thought, *Okay, that sounds pretty crazy, too.*

"This isn't a dream, or even a *blink*. I wish it were. It would be easier, maybe." Lizzie looked suddenly . . . tired? No. For a brief second, her outlines seemed to glimmer, her eyes to actually . . . *smoke*, and Emma thought, *Oh holy shit.* But then the moment passed, and Lizzie was only a little girl with shock-trauma eyes: a kid who'd seen and been through too much. Like Emma, come to think of it. She didn't like looking at the few pictures of herself before Jasper had the doctors surgerize her brain and repair her head and face. It always felt as if that little girl was a freak, a clay doll badly in need of molding, caught halfway between a formless nothing and something only vaguely human.

"I don't know any other way to explain it," Lizzie said, her cobalt eyes so dark and shadowy and haunted, they'd have been at home in an *X-Files* episode. "You're a piece. Part of me is in you, like your eyes."

"My eyes are just *blue*," Emma said. "Eric's eyes are blue. So are Rima's." Weren't Bode's eyes blue, too? Tony's and Chad's, she couldn't recall, and Casey . . . maybe green? Brown? Hazel? She wasn't sure.

"Yeah, but the others' eyes aren't *exactly* the same, not like ours. We've both got that birthmark, that little speck of gold? We've got our dad's eyes," Lizzie said.

"*Our* dad? That's crazy. I don't know who my dad is, and I'm not *you*." Emma clambered to her feet, a move she regretted a split second later when her head swirled. Wow, it was like she was waking up from a bad fever. *Or like I still got one.* She put a hand to her forehead, but her skin was cool and dry. "I'm me."

"Yes, yes, you *are* you, but . . ." Lizzie darted to her bookshelf. "Let me show you."

"*Ohhh* no, no," Emma said, as Lizzie tugged down not a book or a folder but a scroll tied with purple ribbon. "No more books, no more monsters slithering out of pictures and people morphing."

"You're in my room," Lizzie said. "It can't hurt you."

"What are you talking about?" she said, but she almost understood. House was an island, the only place where light shone in this darkness. House had the power to whisk her places, or keep her in a single room. Jesus, what if Lizzie wasn't here either? What if this was all House's doing and just one more thing she was being shown for whatever reason?

I could go round and round this thing until my brain ties itself into a knot. Just got to accept something as a given, and I know I'm real. Yeah, but she'd interacted with Kramer; the snow had been freezing cold against her bare feet; the window-panes smashed with the right sound in the right way. So had that been real, too? *No, I know that was a blink because I'm pretty much back where I started: not out of the valley but back in House. Whatever House thought I needed to see and experience, I have.*

"Did you make this place?" she asked. "This is the special forever-*Now* you were thinking about, isn't it? That's what those weird symbols were about. Is this what you were trying to make right before the crash?"

"Yeah, it is. It's worked . . . okay, I guess. Here." Lizzie unrolled the scroll. "Read that."

"Wait a minute." She didn't make a move for the proffered roll of white parchment. "What does that mean, it's worked *okay*? How is it supposed to work?"

"Too much to explain now, Emma, and you're wasting *time*." Lizzie thrust out the parchment. "*Take* it."

It was on the tip of her tongue to say something snarky, like time was relative, but she thought, *Oh, cut it out; she's just a little girl.*

The scroll was very strange, not yellowed with age or crackly but smooth and velvety soft. She'd never felt anything like it. The parchment was also completely blank, front and back. "Read what?" she asked, turning the scroll over and then back. "There's nothing there."

"Sure there is. There's White Space."

"Yeah, I see that it's white, but that's because it's blank, Lizzie. I can't read *nothing*."

"You still don't get it, do you? The words are *there*, in White Space. Haven't you been paying attention? House showed you over and over again. You don't *put* words on White Space; you *pull* them out. It's like what our dad did with the Dickens Mirror."

"No, it's not," she said, and wondered why she was bothering to argue this. "I remember what you saw, at least a little bit of it. He pulled out a *thing* . . . or the thing got into him." She stopped, frustrated, wishing the memory of that *blink* was clearer. "Look, I'm sorry, but this is only blank parchment, and don't give me that gobbledygook about how *special* your dad's parchment was."

"Well," Lizzie said, "it *was*. It *is*. Wait, here, I know what you need." Reaching on tiptoe, the girl yanked the coverlet from her loft bed. "Hold on to this. Honest, it'll help a lot. I use it all the time to find you guys."

The memory quilt: Emma recognized the swirl of colors, the rattle and chink of glass. She backed up a step. "Are you crazy? After what happened? I'm not touching that thing."

"But Mom sewed on the Sign of Sure, and that will *help*." The little girl thrust the quilt out to Emma. "Everything that's important to a story is on the page. It's already *in* White Space. All you have to do is follow the path, the same way you do when you go between *Nows*."

"Path?" But she remembered: on the roof, her galaxy

pendant suddenly growing hot and then the leap of a bright beam. *Light that was solid, like a path. I even thought about it that way.*

"Yes. Use that to find the story and pull out the words."

"Lizzie, you *write* on paper. There's nothing magical about that, and no matter how special your dad's parchment or ink, there are no words *in* this thing."

"Yes, there are. You've just never thought of building a story this way before, that's all."

"But—"

"Emma, will you stop *thinking* so much?" Lizzie rapped, with an air of angry impatience that was, eerily, a bit like Kramer's: *I didn't say* steal. "The others are in trouble, and you're wasting time! Now shut up and find your story."

She gave up. The kid was nuttier than she was. No, no, the kid wasn't real. This was a dream, a *blink*, or just another illusion conjured up by House. Eventually, she'd pop back into her life, and this would all be nothing more than a hazy memory, a vague uneasiness. She could live with that. Swear to God, she'd take the damn meds, too.

For something that wasn't real, the scroll freaked her out. That velvety white was the color of the snow and the fog. It was the same color of white that hid Jasper-nightmares. Wait, was white a color? Yes and no: visible light was all wavelengths, all colors, combined. To see them, you had to use a prism, a specially fabricated piece of glass, to separate them into their component parts. Otherwise, white light was . . . white. It was nothing.

But still full of color, just waiting for you to use a special tool to pull them out. Then: *Stop it. White light is white. Jasper slathered his paintings with white paint. This is only a blank parchment scroll.* She studied the quilt. *And this thing is only bits of cloth and glass sewn into pretty pat—*

"Patterns," she said, her breath suddenly balling midway between her chest and mouth as her eye fell on something she recognized and knew she shouldn't. This was a quilt that belonged to a strange little girl stuck in an even odder house at the bottom of a valley Emma had the feeling didn't exist anywhere on earth.

Yet there was no mistaking that glass sphere sparkling in the center of an elaborately embroidered spiderweb.

There, stitched into Lizzie's memories, was her galaxy pendant.

CASEY
What Killed Tony

CASEY'S BREATH CLAWED in and out of his throat as he staggered and lurched over the snow and away from the ruined church toward the waiting snowcat. His left hand was clamped to Tania's right arm; in his right, he gripped the shotgun. God, he wished Eric was here. His brother knew weapons; Casey knew . . . well, the theory. Rack the pump, point, shoot. Pray you hit something. Hope to hell you don't run out of cartridges before you do.

Rima didn't recognize him. But how could that be? High above, the roiling sky was still black with crows. This new girl, Tania, someone Rima knew and had a history with, was moaning, nearly doubled over. Rima was murmuring encouragement, telling Tania, *Hang on, almost there.*

Rima knows her *but not me.* He had the disorienting sense of walking into a movie already half over. *Rima knew what was happening* before *we even got here.* No, that was wrong: before this place made itself out of the fog. Could *Rima* be doing that? No, that was crazy.

Or was it? This was the nightmare of Tony on the snow, déjà vu all over again. Casey hadn't told Rima—there'd been no time—but he'd *recognized* that thing, with its bulbous body of writhing tentacles, that bristly maw, those myriad mad eyes. He had glimpsed it only moments before, not as a living thing but a drawing: a creature that existed on the cover of a paperback. Something by Lovecraft, wasn't it? Yes. Tony had tossed the well-thumbed novel onto the Camry's backseat, where Casey had also found some very old vintage comic books.

The reality was this: what had torn Tony apart was something Tony knew well, because he'd read about it, over and over again if that dog-eared paperback was any indication. What killed Tony was a monster that leapt off the pages of a book.

And what about me? What Rima had said about whispers, and his own transformation, a taking-on, taking-*in*, to become his father when he'd slipped into Big Earl's shirt . . . No, that wasn't exactly right either. *Dad wore* me, *instead of the other way around, like I was the shirt, and he had to fill me out in all the right places.* A grab of fear in his gut. So what did that mean? His memories of the last few hours were so hazy they felt as if they belonged to another boy's dream. Did he even *remember* if something like this had happened before? *God, do I even know what it feels like to be myself?* So weird. He wasn't . . . sure. But how could he *not* be?

Stop it. You're Casey. He was freaked, that was all. This *place* freaked him out, especially the fog. He lifted his eyes to the crows overhead; thought about the church behind and how Rima seemed to be . . . slotting herself in? As if the fog was really a . . . a *thing* that could spin itself into the intricate web of your personal nightmare.

What are you? He eyed the fog, thick and bunched and viscous, which had peeled back to hover above the distant trees, and he thought of the types of coverings used to protect furniture. *Do you read our thoughts? Can you* hear—

A loud, hard *bang* jolted him back. *Uh-oh.* That sounded like it had come from behind. The church? *But it was empty. There was just that body.*

"Casey," Rima suddenly shouted. "Behind you! Look *out!*"

Something clamped onto his left shoulder, and then Casey let out a startled yelp as his feet left the ground. The world spun in a sudden, drunken whirl. He felt the whip and bite of cold air, heard the whir as he bulleted around, and then whatever held him let go, as if some little kid had gotten bored and flung this toy aside.

Casey went flying. As he hurtled through the air, he heard Rima scream again, a kind of decrescendo wail like the shrill of a passing ambulance siren. Flailing, he plummeted to this strange snow that had no give, no play at all, but was hard as packed earth. At the last second, he managed to twist, taking the brunt on his left shoulder, before turning in a somersault to slam onto his back. The impact jarred air in a great whoosh from his lungs. A streamer of hot pain scorched his spine, then licked down either leg, and he went instantly numb. For a trembling moment, he could only lie and stare at the crows oiling over the sky.

Breathe. His lungs were on fire, no air in them at all. He couldn't make his chest work. *Breathe, got to breathe, got to*— With a giant effort, he sucked in a deep, gurgling gasp, felt a violent ripping in his chest, and then he was coughing out a scream of crimson mist. Something wrong with his chest, something *broken* . . . His lips were wet; he tried to gulp air but choked on another gush of warm blood.

The thing heaved up from the snow. It seemed to grow, as if the snow had split to spit out a monster caught somewhere in the middle, no longer a man and only halfway into becoming. The thing's face, studded with bony spikes, twisted in a grimace. Pale lips peeled back to reveal a bristling forest of very sharp, very pointed teeth.

What is this thing? Casey's stunned gaze tracked to a gory thumbnail of Roman collar around its throat. He thought back to the tumble of limbs and black cloth in the chancery and what Tania had said: *I shot Father Preston.*

Her aim had been spot-on. The thing's chest was a wreck of mangled and splintered bone and moist, bloody tatters of flesh, but the body itself was rippling, the chest shimmering and boiling. Its skin seemed almost molten, sloughing in elongated runnels that somehow curled in and around pink fingers of revitalized muscle and glimmering silver ligaments of tendon and gristle.

It's repairing itself. A black fan of horror unfurled in Casey's chest, crowding out what little breath he managed as the thing bellowed and reared over him. Where was the shotgun? He didn't have it. *Must've lost it when it threw me.* He was going to die here. All that thing had to do was reach down and—

The air shattered with a sharp *CRACK*. Flinching, the thing bawled and then spun around, clawed hands splayed, slavering jaws open in a vicious snarl.

"Over here!" It was Tania, somehow upright, and leaning out of the snowcat's passenger's side door. Brandishing a long gun in one hand, she waved something else—a hammer?—in the other. "Come on, you son of a bitch," the girl shouted. "Come and get me!"

Wheeling around with a roar, the thing that had been a priest sprinted away from Casey in a mad, ravening dash. At first, he thought it was heading for the snowcat, but then he saw it suddenly veer in a sharp dogleg left and away, toward a distant wall of dark trees. It was, Casey saw now, trying to get *away*.

And that was when the snowcat began to move.

EMMA
All I Am

1

"WHERE DID YOU get this?" Emma's tongue was thick and awkward. From its place on Lizzie's memory quilt, the glass galaxy of lush cobalt and fumed silver gleamed. Beneath a transparent shell, tiny people and creatures floated in a writhing gorgon's knot. "I haven't made this. I don't know how. I'm not good enough yet. It's just an idea."

"Our mom found it." Lizzie stroked the pendant with a reverent finger. "Of all the glass, this is the one with the most magic. It's the Sign of Sure."

"Sign . . ." Mrs. Graves's pinched, disapproving face suddenly swam up from memory, and she could hear Weber's broad, almost comical cockney: *You sure she didn't lay her hands on one of them marbles?* "My God, not *Sign of Sure*. You mean *cynosure*. A guide, a . . ." Oh, come on, what was the right word? "A *focus*."

"Well, yeah." Although the little girl might as well have said, *Duh*. "I just said that. It's how you don't get lost and end up in the wrong *Now*."

She didn't pretend to understand any of this. But any kid who'd suffered through PSAT prep knew what a cynosure was. *A focus. A lens.* Couldn't it also be a beacon?

So, go with this: Lizzie used this to focus her mind? Or bring something distant *into* focus, like the lens of a telescope? What had the kid said? *I use it all the time to find you guys.* Emma thought back to the bright, unwavering, seemingly solid path of light that had sprung from the pendant as she vaulted off the roof toward that apparition of the Mirror. *Some kind of mental flashlight?* If that was true, the cynosure was a way of seeing through to, well, somewhere and, maybe, a somewhen.

But a flashlight worked both ways. Whatever lived in the dark might not see you exactly, but they sure had a pretty good idea of where you *were.*

So did it work that way when you were trying to find the words to your story? Would the words . . . well, *find* you if only they had some help figuring out where you were?

This is crazy. "What do I think about?" Emma skimmed a hesitant thumb over the pendant in its brightly colored web of embroidery. "What am I supposed to see?"

"You. Read *you* like you want to find out more about your book, as if you want the words that are your story to make sense in your head, to bring them all closer from way down where you can't see them." Lizzie nibbled on her lower lip, then brightened. "Like an ocean, you know? White Space is like water that's way deep. Just because you can't see what's way down there doesn't mean things aren't swimming around, right? So, pretend you're fishing or the pen you're using has no ink, and you want to hook the words."

"I don't have any bait," Emma said flatly. "Without ink or

pencil or crayon or paint, you can't write anything."

"Emma, *you're* the bait. That's what the Sign of Sure's about. You could write this if the pen *pulls* instead of *puts*," Lizzie said. "Like when Dad reached into the Dickens Mirror, he was the bait. Pretend you're *that* kind of pen."

Oh well, that made things so much *clearer*. She wouldn't have been surprised if Keanu Reeves popped by for a visit: *There is no spoon.*

And then she thought, *Wait, wasn't that almost* exactly *what I thought when Jasper talked about White Space and Dark Passages?* An eerie ripple of déjà vu wavered through her—this feeling that everything in her life was the echo and twin to something else: Emma taking a right turn here, a left turn there, going up here, down there—and all simultaneously.

How could Jasper have known anything about this? The guy piloted chartered fishing boats and pickled himself until he stroked out. But this clearly couldn't all be coincidence. That weird obsession Jasper had for Dickens's novels and stories—had Jasper been looking for clues, trying to find the Mirror? To do what?

What she knew was this: Jasper had talked about White Space and Dark Passages. Jasper painted nightmare creatures and then—she wet her lips, tasting salt on her tongue—then he covered them over with thick white paint. She stared down at the parchment. *With his version of White Space.*

"What's between the *Nows*?" She cleared the frog that had suddenly decided to squat in her throat. Graves had panops, and so did Kramer. Weber said something about *hangers-on*. "There's something there, isn't there? In the Dark Passages?" *Jesus, I'm starting to sound as crazy as Jasper.* "What was your dad really doing? He wasn't just pulling out words to a story."

Again, she saw the little girl's face darken and glimmer, her haunted cobalt eyes grow shadowy and somehow opaque as something ghosted through. It was as if, for just an instant, a mask slipped, and Emma got a fleeting peek at what she thought was the much older girl and woman, scarred by loss, that Lizzie would become, and felt a tug of sympathy.

"I'm just a kid," Lizzie said. Her chin trembled. Blinking furiously, she looked away. "I don't know everything. He was doing something . . . *bad*, all right? Okay? Can we just not talk about that? This isn't the same thing."

"I'm sorry," Emma said. "I just want to understand."

"What's to *understand*?" A huge tear rolled down the girl's cheek. Another tear chased it, and then more. "I've told you what you need to know. House keeps showing you. Now just *do* it before it's too late and the others get hurt! They're in big trouble, and I can't get them without your help."

Eric. Her stomach squeezed. "Big trouble? Get them from where?"

"Would you shut *up* already?" Lizzie dragged an arm over her streaming eyes. "Just do it, Emma! Look at the scroll and find your story!"

"Okay, okay." The last thing she wanted was to deal with some little kid's meltdown, and if Eric and the others were in trouble . . . *Find my story? Use myself as bait?* She cupped the galaxy pendant in a palm. *Okay, so . . . I want the beginning of my story, how about that?* But what really was the beginning of her story? Jasper? She stared at that expanse of blank white parchment. Probably. She didn't really know anything about her parents.

All of a sudden, she felt a familiar ache between her eyes, that same burn she always got before a *blink*. In her hand, the galaxy pendant warmed, and then, from the white of that blank scroll, a light pinkish blush began to waver into being, like the stubborn echo of a bloodstain on a collar that just won't come out.

"Oh my God." She was so startled she nearly dropped the parchment. On the skin, that weakly scarlet blush shimmered and began to dissolve as if she'd somehow lost her grip on whatever was shuddering its way to the surface. Against her palm, the galaxy pendant began to cool.

"Don't worry, it'll come back," Lizzie said, her voice still a little watery and oddly indefinite. "Remember, you're the bait. Everything you need lives in you. Just find your words, Emma. Let them come. You're not like Mom. You don't need the purple panops to see that far down or between."

Panops. All-seeing. Her chest tightened. *Kramer had purple glasses. So did Graves.* But to see what? She opened her mouth to ask but then felt her questions fizzle as a familiar tingle she always felt before a *blink* swept through: a sense of falling and space opening up. In her hand, the cynosure burned but not as hot or bright as in the London *blink*. Nothing solid, no path of light leapt to show her the way.

Maybe that's because it's functioning as a lens now, bringing something into focus.

Something was definitely happening. On the parchment, that pink smudge was deepening and becoming more distinct. It was, she thought, like watching Jasper prep a design onto a primed canvas, except there was no hand other than the one in her mind, drawing and pulling out meaning. In the next instant, a snarl of brilliant red bloomed over the page, spreading over the surface in the complex tangle of an intricate calligraphy, spinning into letters and words, and she read:

McDERMOTT-SATAN'S SKIN-FOLIO 45

Everything she knew about her bio parents fit the back of a stamp, with room to spare. Dear Old Drug-Addled Dad tried a two-point set to see if Baby really bounced against a backboard. (Uh, that would be no.) Mommy Dearest boogied before Dad . . .

2

***NO.* SHE COULD** feel a fist of dread close around her throat. *No, this isn't happening.* This was Kramer's office all over again, just a different story this time. Her eyes flicked to the header: *Satan's Skin.* That was the book where *her* story came from, the one she'd written for Kramer's class. So what was *she* doing in the same manuscript?

It can't be. All the air whistled from her lungs. She hadn't written herself into her story. All she'd done was dream up the characters. *McDermott's novel fragment,* Satan's Skin, *is a about a demon-book written on demon-skin. Kramer said the gist of the plot is that characters don't stay put in their own stories. They keep jumping out.* Then: *That's what worried McDermott. He said that if the characters' stories didn't resolve—*

"I remember when Dad said he'd give you my eyes." Lizzie's voice reached her from what seemed like another planet. "If you know where to look, you'll find my whole life in Daddy's books."

But not my *life.* She smoothed the scroll to bring the words into greater clarity, her clumsy fingers fumbling as the White Space resolved into crimson blocks of text:

> *Cue ten years of Child Protective Services and a parade of foster parents, group homes, doctors, staring shrinks, clucking social workers. Her headaches got worse, thanks to Dear Old Dad . . .*

> *Jasper said the island got its name from the old Ojibwe legend that Matchi-Manitou, some honking huge evil spirit, was imprisoned in a giant underground cave at the entrance to the spirit worlds, and only the bravest warriors could pass through the black well at the center of the island to fight the thing, blah, blah. Some vision quest crap like that. The only well she knew on that island was near an old lighthouse and keeper's cottage. Still, whenever there was a really big blow, the roar and boom of the sea caves—of big, bad Matchi-Manitou . . .*

She felt her knees trying to buckle. *This is like that John Cusak movie where the characters are nothing but alters, hallucinations. But my life is mine, I'm me, I'm real.*

And then her gaze snagged on this line, floating on its own like a crimson banner dragged by an airplane:

> *One June afternoon, Emma wandered down cellar for a book and*

3

AND. SHE WAS panting now, chest heaving. She stared so intently at that parchment, the scroll should've burst into flames. *And?* "And *what*?" she said, and shook the parchment as if she could dislodge the words stuck between the lines. *"And WHAT?"*

"Emma?" Lizzie's voice filtered through a high burr. "Are you okay?"

No, I'm nuts. I'm insane, and this is about down cellar. Her hands shook. *This is about when I was twelve and found that door. No one knows about that.* But there it was, in screaming red calligraphy spidering over white parchment.

"Where's the rest?" Her voice grated like an engine that just wouldn't turn over. "The sentence just *stops*. Why is that? What happens next?"

"Don't you know?"

"Yes. I mean . . . I don't like thinking about it, but . . ." She clamped her lips together, willed herself to get out a complete sentence. "Why isn't it here? How can it just stop like that?"

"Because that's where our dad stopped. It's as far as he got before Mom . . ." Lizzie's eyes pooled again. "Before she did what she did."

"Where he . . ." The memory quilt slipped in a muted tinkle of glass from her trembling hand, followed a moment later by the flutter of the parchment scroll filled with that bloody scrawl. She put a trembling hand to her mouth. "I thought your dad's notes and unfinished novels were locked up somewhere."

Lizzie nodded. "But he couldn't help himself from starting

again, even though he promised. He said books were like really bad colds you just never got over until you wrote them down and got them out of your blood. Maybe he put so much of me in you, it was harder for him to stop himself, but I don't know. Anyway, he just never finished you, and that's why you got out. But that's also what makes you really special. You're not like the others, especially the guys whose stories are over."

He never finished *me? She means, there's no period to the end of that sentence; there's no* The End. *But* I *know what happened after I went down cellar. I'm not twelve anymore; I'm seventeen, and I have memories and a life and I go to school.* Then she thought, *Oh my God. Eric.*

"Special." Her voice came out in a croak. "Not over yet? What is this?" She grabbed her middle with both arms, trying to hold it together. She was going to be sick; she was going to lose it; she was losing it; she could feel the burn flickering up her throat. In another second, she would break a window and go shrieking out into the snow. No wonder it was called Alice in Wonderland syndrome: *This is just like London, because we're all mad here.* "What do you mean, I'm closest to you? That I got out? Out of *where*? What are you saying?"

"Emma, you've got the most of me in you . . . you know, like our eyes and stuff. You pull words from White Space. The Sign of Sure recognizes you just like it knows who I am. So I figured you were special enough to help me hold all the others in place."

"The most of y-you. The guys whose stories are o-over."

"Uh-huh." Lizzie nodded. "You know, like Rima and Bode and Tony. They're harder to do because they're over and can't change much."

Oh shit, oh shit. She was gulping now, her breath coming in jerky, shuddery gasps. *God, please, please,* please *let me wake up.* "Different books. You're talking about characters from different books, from your dad's *books.*"

"Well, sure," said Lizzie. "I just had to show you how to do it by opening the right books and dropping you into different book-worlds until you figured out how to pull me into your White Space, your story. Oh boy, it took you long enough."

"Opening the right . . . dropping me into book-worlds . . ." Emma choked. All her blackouts. She looked down at the parchment scroll, with its unfinished story of her life. All those *blinks* when she lost time; when she saw things . . . "Are you s-saying . . . are you t-telling me that all I am is s-some *character* from a goddamned *book*?"

"Well, yeah." Lizzie's lips wobbled. "Kind of."

RIMA

The Thing That Had Been Father Preston

"GO!" TANIA DROPPED into the passenger's seat. Whiter than salt, her face glistened with sweat. Another spasm of pain grabbed the girl's middle, and she grunted through gritted teeth, the knuckles of her right hand tightening around the rifle, as she clicked her shoulder harness home. "G-go, Rima, g-get us moving!"

"Hang on!" Mashing the accelerator, Rima felt the hard knock of the snowcat's engine throttling up to a full-throated roar. The vehicle surged forward in a squalling grind of grating treads and screaming metal. Through the windshield, she could see the thing that had been Father Preston sprinting away, his cassock unspooling like a cape, flowing around his ruined body like black oil. Preston was moving fast, faster than should be possible for a man, almost skimming over the snow.

"Get him, Rima!" Tania straight-armed the dash against another wave of pain. "G-get that son of a b-bitch," she panted, sweeping a hank of sweat-dampened hair from her forehead. "Go, Rima, g-go!"

Go. Rima rammed the joystick. Dropping on its hydraulic slave, the snowblower came alive with a mechanical scream, the massive orange auger chewing and biting snow that, finally, had decided to *behave* a bit like real snow. The discharge chute belched glittering arcs of pulverized ice. Rima gunned the engine, and the machine lunged forward like a ravening insect, steel mandible ripping, tearing. *Go, go, go, go!*

The thing was now past the cemetery, almost to the woods, but *they* were gaining. Sixty yards . . . fifty . . . *thirty.* They were so close now that she could see the thin puffs of ice crystals kicked up by the thing's mad passage. The edge of the snowblower's casing was ruler-straight, and as they neared and the thing that was once a man—a gentle priest who believed that touching whispers was a gift, and not a curse—dropped below this new horizon, Rima shouted, "We've got him, we've got him, *hang on!*"

They hit: a sudden, jarring blow. Both girls slammed forward. Tania managed to hang on to the shotgun but lost her grip on the hammer, which clanked off the windshield and went spinning to the floor somewhere behind them, in the passenger cab. With a gasp, Rima threw up her arms as she catapulted forward and saw the wheel rushing for her face. At the last second, her shoulder harness caught and held, jerking her back like a hooked fish. Above the cat's stuttering clank and roar, she heard a long, bubbling, unearthly wail. Beneath them, the snowblower seemed to stagger and mutter a stuttering, muted gargle, like a person simultaneously trying to breathe and talk with his mouth full.

"No no no no no." Rima stiff-armed the cat's balky controls. "Don't you quit, don't you *quit!*"

With a choked bellow, the cat coughed a mucky jet of macerated flesh and bone from its discharge chute. Blowback splatted against the windscreen, but instead of the moist red and purple and pink of a man's blood and tissues, what hit that glass was viscous and black as oil and no longer human.

Choking again, the cat lurched and clanked to a shuddering halt. In the cab, the sudden stop catapulted the girls forward once more, and this time, Rima's shoulder harness failed. Pain exploded in her right cheek as she slammed into the steering wheel, and her vision sheeted red.

"Rima?" Tania's voice was tight and breathless. "R–Rima?"

"I'm . . . I'm okay. I'm fine," she lied. Her cheek felt like a bomb had detonated and blown a hole through the roof of her mouth. She felt the warm spurt of blood on her cheek and down her neck, and there was more blood on the steering wheel.

"N–no," Tania said in that same cramped voice. "That's n–not what I meant. Look, Rima." She pointed. "L–look at the windshield."

Rima did—and then wished she hadn't.

The windscreen was a nightmare of steaming flesh and ropy streamers of black blood.

And all of it was moving.

EMMA

Whatever They Make Will Be *Real*

1

"KIND OF?" EMMA'S chest imploded. This was insane; she might be nuts, but she was real, she did things, she could *feel*. "Is that kind of *no*, I'm *not* a character in a book, or is that kind of *yes*?"

"I mean, *kind* of." Lizzie's face was a tiny white oval. Her cobalt eyes were dark as India ink, the shadows that ghosted through before somehow even more pronounced than before. That birthmark glittered as brightly as a finely cut yellow diamond. "It's sort of like that—"

"*Sort* of? *Kind* of? What are you talking about? I have a *life*!" Her hands flashed out to grab the little girl's shoulders. Crying out, Lizzie tried backing away, but Emma wouldn't let go and shook the kid, hard, like a floppy rag doll she was suddenly very tired of playing with. "Stop this shit! I have a *past*! I go to school! I watch *X-Files* and *Lost* and write stupid papers about crazy dead writers! I drink goddamned mocha Frappuccinos!"

"I kn-know! I've v-v-visited!" Mouth sagging open, Lizzie

was bawling her head off, sobbing the way only little kids do. "The words are al-all th-there!"

"Stop *saying* that! I'm not just words on a page!" Her chest was going like a bellows, the air scouring her throat. She felt the prick of furious tears. Of all the things her mind could light on, this is what she thought: *Kramer would just love this. This is so Philip K. Dickilicious; I write this up, and I'll get a damned A for sure.*

Then she thought about that fragment of a sentence penned in red ink, a sentence that refused to resolve: *Wait a second. There's no period. Nothing comes after.*

"What about all the rest of my life? Is Kramer in your dad's story?" Her voice came out sounding as dry and raspy as shriveled cornstalks stirred by an October wind. Her fingers dug until she felt the girl's bones. "Is Holten Prep? Is Star-bucks?" *Is Eric?*

"No. That's one of the reasons you're so special, Emma." Tears gleamed on Lizzie's cheeks. "You did all that by your-self."

2

"I . . ." SHE COULD feel the kid's words like something physical, a slap, hard enough that she let go of the little girl and actually took a staggering step back. "I . . . I *what*? I did *what*?"

"You heard me." Lizzie's eyes glimmered again with those odd, curling, smoky, *X-Files* shadows. "You got loose and wrote yourself. You're *still* writing yourself."

"That's crazy." The words came out raspy and harsh, as if they were glass ground on a Dremel or abrasive stone. Her eyes dropped to that limp tangle of parchment. That had been blank, but she'd pulled McDermott's words, *what Lizzie said was a story that he never finished,* from nothing. "This isn't *The Matrix.* I'm not Neo. I'm a real person."

"And what's *that*?" Lizzie said. "Maybe you're only real because you think you are."

"Don't be ridiculous. You can't prove something like that. You just *know*."

"But what's *that*?" Lizzie pressed. "What's *knowing*? It's still all just stuff that happens in your head, right?"

"Come on, there's more to it than that." Emma felt a sweep of . . . not déjà vu, exactly, but a feeling that she was having an argument with some older version of herself: a girl who wouldn't let the Great Bloviator off the hook. *No, stop that; you are not her.* She put her hands on her cheeks. "I *feel* my face. I've got a real cut from a real steering wheel." *I got a girl killed. I've got titanium skull plates and scars.* "I hear you. I see you."

"But the tools for all that are in your head. Like you *touch* something, but then you give it a name." Lizzie picked up her memory quilt. "This is a quilt because we say it is. That's how you write yourself—don't you get it? Everything you know is because of what happens inside your head. Without your brain to turn *this*"—she gave the bunched quilt a shake that made its glass tick and chime—"into cloth and stitches and glass, you wouldn't know what it was."

"No. Thoughts and perceptions aren't *tools*. They're not really *real*. You can't hold or even see them." Which wasn't exactly true, she knew; you could take a picture of the brain and see what parts were firing when, say, you saw a pencil or tasted an apple. "I mean, when I think about making or writing something, it doesn't just happen. First, I have to have the idea, and then do something with it. The idea comes first. Ideas are . . ." She groped for the right word while at the same time thinking how odd it was that she was having this conversation with a little girl who couldn't be more than five years old. "Ideas are *energy*. When you strip it all down, thought is just a bunch of the right cells firing at the right time in the correct sequence. That's all ideas are. Thoughts are physics and chemistry."

"Emmaaa." Lizzie did an eye-roll. "What do you think thought-magic is? A pen and paper are just tools to make thought-magic real, but that doesn't mean they're the *only* tools." She held up the galaxy pendant, stitched into its spiderweb. "The Sign of Sure is a *tool*. It helps you find your way between *Nows* and *see* better. Dad's Dickens Mirror, and his special paper and ink, and Mom's panops—they were just different *tools* for grabbing and fixing thought-magic. And even then, it's why Mom had to make Peculiars to hold the extra thought-magic, so everything stayed where it was supposed to."

"Stayed where it was supposed to. You mean, on the page," Emma said. Weird how talking this out, actually *thinking* about it, calmed her a bit. *Maybe because thinking and science are what I'm good at.* She *almost* understood this, too; she could feel her mind inching toward some kind of comprehension, the way Meg Murry had groped after that tesseract and what made a wrinkle in time work. The whole character-from-a-book thing, she didn't buy. She was a person, and that was that, right? Right? But she'd *felt* the heat from the galaxy pendant, that cynosure, feeding off her thoughts, her intentions.

And in the blink *or whatever that was at the slit-door, I felt a click, a change, like House was trying to hammer it home through my thick skull: the Dickens Mirror is a tool.*

Or a machine?

And what's a story but symbols penned in black ink on white paper? The symbols wouldn't mean anything if there wasn't White Space, that blank page. It's the emptiness *that defines the shape, that tells me that the symbol I've just written is an* a *or an* s.

"So the . . . the *fog* that came after you and your mom," she said. "That wasn't *just* the thing your dad pulled through the Mirror?"

Lizzie shook her head. "Mom said that when the Peculiars melted, all the thought-magic that wasn't able to go anywhere got loose. So the fog's all of that tangled up with the whisper-man and . . . and . . ." Lizzie's lips shook and her face tried to crumple again.

"And your dad?" Thinking, *It's like burning a log. The wood vanishes, but it doesn't really go away. Its energy is released as heat. The energy changes form, that's all. So the fog is . . .*

"Yeah," Lizzie whispered. Her eyes glistered and wavered like cut blue glass in deep murky water. "The whisper-man and my dad are all mushed together, tangled up. They were like that even before I finished my special *Now* and swooshed the fog here so it couldn't go anywhere else. The whisper-man and . . . and Dad . . . they're *part* of the thought-magic now, the *fog*, except the whisper-man is way stronger. I don't know exactly why, but he can use the thought-magic, and I can't stop him. The only good thing is this is pretty much the only place he can use it."

"Because we're in your special forever-*Now*? Something

like your mom's Peculiars?" She thought about the snowy, frigid valley. Something about cold was important . . . something in chemistry . . . no, physics? *I know this; thought about this same thing not too long ago. But what, when?*

Instead, she said, "That's why there's House. You had to make a safe place for yourself to stay. So this, the bedroom, the House, is kind of *you*, but everything else belongs to the . . . the whisper-man? The fog?" When Lizzie nodded, she went on, "You said the others, Rima and Eric, Casey . . . you said they've fallen between the lines because you couldn't hold on to all of them. But Lizzie"—bending, she retrieved the parchment with its unfinished story of an odd girl with even odder gifts—"there's only White Space between lines."

"I know that," Lizzie said. "Why do you think it's so important to find them? They're between the lines of this *Now*, and the *Now* is full of the fog, and the fog is thought-magic. They're in *nothing*, and that's bad because the really strong ones will make it into *something*."

"Wait, wait." She held up a hand like a traffic cop. "You're saying that wherever they are, the others will use the . . . the thought-magic, the energy, to make their stories?"

"Right." Lizzie's face flooded with relief that Emma seemed to have finally caught on. "Especially the ones whose stories are done. They're the strongest because they're set."

Set. "You mean *set* as in a period, the end of a story," Emma said. "Their stories are like road maps that they *must* eventually follow, no matter where they are. Only what happens won't *just* be words on a page. If they're in the fog, whatever they make will be *real*."

"Uh-huh," Lizzie said. "With teeth."

CASEY AND RIMA
Fight

1

MOANING, CASEY ROLLED to his hands and knees. When he gave another moist, ripping cough, the spray that spattered the snow reminded him of those red sprinkles they put on cupcakes. Whenever he moved, it felt as if the bones of his ribcage were grating together. With every breath, a glassy, jagged pain hacked at his lungs.

To his left and very far away, easily a couple football fields, and almost at that distant black wall of trees, he saw the silent snowcat crouching in the center of a goopy, slimy mess that was a little like the tar they used on roads in summer. Spatters of the same goo glopped over the driver's cab.

Out of the corner of his eye, he caught a small flick, and turned a look. Something was out there, just sliding from the trees. He squinted, trying to bring whatever it was into focus—and then his heart skipped a beat.

This time, instead of one thing racing for the snowcat, there were three.

2

MY GOD, IT'S *moving.* Rima's stomach turned a slow, gurgling somersault. On the windscreen, the glistening, shredded, oily chunks of the thing that had been Father Preston pulsed and quivered in a slow, shambling creep. Ropy clots of black blood eeled like inky water snakes. *Like in biology, when they make you cut up a worm; only the worm doesn't glue itself back together.* She could *hear* them, too: a high-pitched *SMEEE-smeee, SMEEE-smeee,* a sound of fingers smearing steam from a bathroom mirror. Horrified, she watched as two pieces met, their seams thinning and mending, the bits of raw stygian flesh sewing themselves together into a much larger chunk that squirmed off in search of another mate. The entire windscreen was alive with shivering, creeping flesh laboriously knitting together bit by bit.

"R-Rima?" Tania's voice trembled. She pointed, using the rifle she still clutched in her right hand. "It . . . it's re-repairing itself. It's m-making itself all over again." She stared at the rifle. "I bet I could shoot it a hundred t-times and it would . . . it would . . . God, how do you *k-kill* something like that?"

"I don't know." She cut her eyes away from the mess and toward her friend, then started back in alarm. "Tania! At the window! Look out!"

Too late. The glass on Tania's side exploded in a hail of gummy fragments. Two arms—long, lean, impossibly strong—thrust into the cabin. Both unfurled hooked claws. One latched onto the rifle, yanking it from Tania's hand; the other lashed out.

"OHHH!" Tania shrieked. Bright red blood jetted from her right shoulder. She tried twisting away, but that clawed hand only dug in, slashing deeper, and gave her another mighty yank, tearing her halfway from her seat.

"No!" Rima lunged. Snatching double fistfuls of Tania's parka, she braced herself, planting one boot against Tania's seat, the other against the transmission box, and heaved. "I've got you, Tania! Pull, Tania, pull!"

"I c-can't—*aahhh*!" Jammed against the shattered window, unable to pull free, Tania screamed again. Her shoulder harness had snapped. The only thing saving her from going through altogether was that the window was just a touch too small. "I can't, Rima! It's too *strong*, it's too—"

Going to lose her, going to lose her! Or whatever had her would tear Tania apart a piece at a time. Frantic, Rima tried to think of what to do, something she could use. The rifle was gone. There was the dropped hammer, but she would have to loosen her grip on Tania to find it, and patting around the foot well would take precious time she didn't think they had. So what else was there? More tools in the equipment lockers in the passenger cab? Maybe, but there was no time, no *time*!

So she let go of Tania and did the only thing left.

3

EVERY STEP BROUGHT a blast of fresh agony, but after the first five steps, the pain wasn't worse, just constant. The important thing was Casey was on his feet, and he'd found the shotgun. Ahead, he saw the things swarming over the snowcat;

heard the explosion as the glass let go and then a scream. Why weren't they *moving*? He was still too far away to do any good with the gun, and he couldn't afford to waste shells, especially since he didn't know how many he had left. *Tania took two shots, maybe three, in the church.* He was pretty sure there was a round in the chamber; he'd racked the pump, but he didn't know all that much about guns. God, he didn't even know how to *check*. How many shells did a shotgun hold? What if there was no shell in there at all?

Just got to hope there is, and that I'll have time to get close enough for one good shot. To do that, he'd have to get right on top of them, because he was pretty sure that shotguns weren't as good as rifles, didn't have the range, and he didn't much trust his aim anyway. If he could just get there in *time*.

Then, he heard the snowcat's engine grind, and felt a burst of elation. *Yes, yes, come on, Rima; get it going, get it—*

The cat turned over once, twice, coughed, and then revved to a howl.

"Yes!" Casey cried, ignoring the fresh lancets of pain that stabbed at his chest. He pumped his fist. "Hit the gas, Rima, hit the *gas*! Go! *GO!*"

4

WITH THE CAT still in neutral, Rima stamped on the accelerator. The engine responded with an earsplitting clatter, followed by a bark that ground and gathered itself in a whooping crescendo shriek—and then she slapped the transmission lever with all her might. The cat dropped into drive and surged forward, its treads ripping snow with a great, shuddering roar.

Through the shattered window, above the clatter and squeal of the cat's treads, there came another, new note: a high, shrieking wail as the thing that had Tania lost its balance on the running board. Too late, Rima thought, *Oh God, don't foul the treads!* She held her breath as the cat lurched, that side bumping up and then crashing down—

5

ON THE SNOW, now no more than seventy yards away, Casey watched as the cat swung round; saw clearly—and heard—the moment when the man-thing was reeled, squealing, beneath the cat's treads. Its shriek abruptly cut out as if hacked by an ax.

Yes, *yes*! But where were the other two? Shaken off? Run away? No, they wouldn't leave; he knew that. So where? His eyes raked the snow and then sharpened on the cat once more.

"Rima!" God, could she *hear* him over the engine roar? He was running as fast as he could, but he was still managing nothing more than a staggering stumble that was slow, much too slow! "Rima, the *roof*! There's one on the—"

6

GOT YOU. **EASING** back on the gas, Rima felt the growling cat grind to a halt. She was shaking all over. *I got you.*

Tania moaned, and when Rima got a good look, that fleeting sparrow of triumph fled. The other girl's parka was scarlet. More blood was spurting from Tania's right shoulder, the entire arm only just hanging on by a thread of torn flesh and splintered bone.

"Rima." Tania's voice was less than a whisper, and so weak there was barely any sound at all. Already whiter than salt, her face was going translucent and glassy, the color bleaching away. "R–Rima?"

"Oh God." Rima started to unwind Tony's scarf, still knotted around her neck. If she could slow down that bleeding, get them to someone who could help. *In the school, the nurse's office, there's got to be—*

There was an enormous, splintery *crash*, followed by the instantaneous *hoosh* of cold air. Rima's eyes jerked front, expecting to see a fist pistoning for her face. But the windshield was intact. *Oh shit.* Heart thudding, Rima inched round to look over her shoulder and back toward the passenger cab. In the next instant, a thin, strangled, squeaky sound midway between a moan and a scream dribbled from her mouth: *"Ohhh!"*

This second man-thing was much taller and beefier, with a dense, furry ruff sprouting from its neck and glistening skin as slick as a black grub's. When it saw Rima look, the creature's yellow eyes lit with a feverish, feral gleam. Its lips skinned back from a bristle of teeth and a tongue as ropy and muscular as a black snake.

Time seemed to hesitate for a span no longer than the pause between two heartbeats. In that moment, Rima heard the splash of Tania's blood and her faltering breath growing weaker and weaker; she could smell the man-thing, wild and animal and utterly alien, and taste it, too, rank and raw in her mouth. She even had time to wonder about Casey, who must be dead by now, torn apart, because where there was one thing and then two, there were probably a lot more.

And she had time to know this: she could run or she could fight, simple as that.

Without taking her eyes from the thing, she squatted, reached down—and felt her fingers close around the hammer.

Fight.

BODE
Whatever This Place Makes Next

"**WHAT IS THIS** stuff?" The billowing fog surrounding the Dodge sponged up all sound, so that Chad's voice came out flat and, Bode thought, a little dead. "Can't see for shit. You ever seen anything like this, Bode?"

"Nope, never, not me, not even after they drop smoke, you know?" As soon as the fog swallowed them, Bode had taken his foot off the accelerator, but the Dodge still thrummed, the engine having settled down to a steady rattle. He took a sniff and grimaced. "Smells weird. Not like phosphorus or how napalm stinks when it's cooking off. Like burnt diesel."

"Naw. This smells like"—Chad's blade of a nose wrinkled—"like, you know, *blood*. And I don't mean cooked neither, like from an explosion, but fresh. Man, I don't know *what* this shit is."

"Do you?" Shifting his gaze to his rearview mirror, Bode saw two faces: Eric's, pinched with strain but intent, and the blasted ruin no one else could see that was Sergeant Battle. He said to Battle, "You know what's going on, Sarge?"

Got some ideas. Battle's face twisted, but given that half the sergeant's head was blown apart, his left eye dragged on his cheek, and his brains slopped over his neck in a wormy pink goo, Bode couldn't be sure if Battle was frowning—or cracking a grin. *None of 'em you're going to care for.*

"Yeah?" Bode eyed the white world beyond the Dodge. He really couldn't tell whether they were still on the snow, on a road, or hanging in midair. The truck was nowhere—and *nowhere* was deep within the fog, which boiled and curdled and rushed by in dense clots. He understood the Dodge wasn't going anywhere and only the fog was moving, but the optical illusion was disorienting, like sitting by a train's window as another train the next track over pulled from the station. "Well, I don't much know if I care for what's going on now. You want to give me the straight dope?"

Wouldn't believe me if I told you.

"Try me," Bode said.

You're not ready to hear it yet. The mortar had chunked a blast crater just above the sergeant's left ear, so that when Battle shook his head, Bode saw straight through to the fog. The view reminded him of peering out the murky window of a Huey flying low and NOE, nap-of-the-earth, through the tangles of a jungle's early morning mist. *Same way you didn't listen outside that honky-tonk. Told you to let it go, but no . . . you just had to pull that trigger.*

"Let it go? Let it *go*? Oh, that would've turned out really great." Bode snorted. "Sorry, Sarge, but a court-martial wasn't in my plans."

If they catch you, son, it's the firing squad for sure. You're supposed to kill the enemy, not your LT.

Yeah, yeah. The problem was, Sarge couldn't know what it was like to *be* Bode. The man was dead, after all, and what did ghosts know about being haunted? Bode could mute Battle's voice with drugs. In 'Nam, there'd been pot and hash and Binoctal and booze, but opium was best, Bode's consciousness floating away and Battle's face pulling apart on a cloud of sweet-smelling smoke. Stateside, opium dens were scarce, but you could score all kinds of drugs if you had the dough and knew where to look and who to ask. Things got dicey, though, when your prick of a lieutenant followed you into a bar and threatened to turn you in.

From the backseat, Eric said to Bode, "Well, we can't just sit here. As crazy as this sounds, we got to get moving. The others are still out here."

"Where you want to go, huh?" Chad flapped a hand toward the windscreen. "*How?* Inquiring minds want to know."

"Maybe we could check how far ahead we can really see," Eric said.

"Yeah, you go right ahead, be my guest." Chad was *pick-pick-picking* at his mouth sore again. "I ain't going out in that. I say we sit tight, wait it out. Shit's got to go away sometime. Just gotta, you know, wait for the sun to burn it off."

"Forgetting for the moment that less than a half hour ago, it was *night*," Eric said, "I don't think that's too likely, Chad. This isn't any kind of regular fog. You saw how it came after us. It ran us down."

"Yeah, thanks, I was there. So what are you saying?" Chad twisted his head around to scowl at Eric. "You saying it's *alive*? Like it ate us for food or something?"

In the rearview, Bode saw Eric glance askance, as if

searching for the right words. "No." And when Eric looked back, Bode read the dread. "But it *wants* us for something." Eric's darkly blue eyes searched out Bode's. "*You* feel it, right?"

"No," Bode said, uneasy. For a kid he'd only just met, Bode still trusted this devil dog; felt as if they shared something in common besides uniforms. "What do you feel?"

"You're listening to this guy?" Chad demanded.

"This"—Eric bunched a fist over his chest—"*pull*. Like something's digging in, trying to hang on or get a hold. I'm not really sure."

"Yeah, I'll bet. *You*," Chad said, "are so frigging stunned, man. Got yourself into some, el Diablo, you ask me."

"What?"

Listen to the devil dog, Battle said to Bode. *You know he's right.*

Bode frowned. "But Sarge, Chad's also right. I don't feel anything like what Eric's saying."

That's because he's got more of a connection. He's not set the way you are.

"Set?" What did *that* mean? "Connection? Sarge, connection to what?"

Not what. Battle raised the charcoal smudge of his remaining eyebrow. *Who.*

"All I'm saying is, I think we need to get moving." Eric licked his lips. "And we need to do it *now*, before the fog decides for us."

Chad opened his mouth to object, but Bode said, "Yeah, it's not a bad idea. I hate just sitting on my ass, waiting for something to happen. Here." Bode reached across Chad, pawed open the glove compartment, and pulled out a flashlight. "You take that, Eric, see how far you—" He broke off as the Dodge's engine suddenly revved.

"Man, what are you *doing*?" Chad said.

"Nothing, I'm not doing anything. My foot's not even on the gas." Bode stamped the brake. "We're just—"

"Starting to move," Eric said.

He was right. The Dodge hitched and staggered, the wheels seeming to spin on ice—*or thin air,* Bode thought—and then the tires found and caught on something, as if a road had suddenly materialized, making itself out of the fog. The Dodge started to roll, the tires beginning to hum, and the hum rising to a steady high note.

"Well, do something, man!" Chad braced himself as the Dodge picked up speed. "Try the emergency brake, try—"

You can't stop this, Battle said. *It's using you, gathering you together. It's forcing her to try and pull you through onto the same White Space.*

"What? *Who?*" Bode asked Battle. "Try what? What the hell's White Space?"

"You can't fight it." Eric's hand closed over Bode's shoulder. "The fog won't let us stop. We're being pulled toward something for a reason. I *feel* it, this . . ."

"Tug," Bode said, because he felt it now, an insistent finger hooked in the meat of his brain. "In my head."

"You guys serious?" Chad looked from Bode to Eric and back again. "You're serious. I don't feel *anything*, except like I might take a dump in my pants, man."

Eric ignored him. "Bode, please, give me a weapon. The

shotgun, the rifle, I don't care, but give me something and do it now."

"What?" Bode asked. "Why?"

"So I can fight." Eric's skin was so dead white he seemed a creature spun of fog. "So I can kill whatever this place makes next."

CASEY AND RIMA

Look at Her Face

1

HANG ON. TOO far away to help when he'd spotted the man-thing breaking into the snowcat's passenger cabin, Casey was closer now, running as fast as he could, grimacing at the grab and tear in his chest, trying to look everywhere at once, the pain stinging his veins. Thirty more yards, twenty, ten . . .

A howl blasted from the passenger cabin, followed by a shriek. *No, God, please.* "Rima!" Hooking one bloodstained hand on the jamb, he wheeled round and onto the steps, and then he was bursting through, bringing the shotgun to bear. "Rima! Get—"

The thing barreled into him. Crashing to the metal floor, Casey screamed as a swoop of pain churned through his chest. He made an instinctive move to cover up, protect himself, raise the shotgun, but the thing swatted the weapon away. Before he could do anything to save himself, the thing clamped its powerful hands around his throat and dug in.

No! Panicked, pulse galloping, fingers scrabbling for purchase over furry knuckles, Casey surged, tried bucking the man-thing off, but it was too heavy, and he was only sixteen, not very tall, and already hurt. The thing was shaking him hard enough that the back of his head thunked and clunked and bounced on metal. *Losing it . . .* His arms were going as limp as overdone noodles. Wavering blood-spiders unfurled in front of his eyes, his vision going blotchy before suddenly squeezing down to a pinprick: red spangles going to black, diminishing to a single bright speck, like the end of a very long tunnel. The world muted, flattened, and he thought, stupidly, of that deadening fog. And then even that was slipping away, and Casey saw nothing, couldn't hear anything other than the feeble thump of his heart, and that was dying, too.

But then . . . something happened. He felt the thing jerk, but the sensation was very far away, a whisper that his brain didn't seem to have the will or energy to hang on to. Another jerk, a faraway flop, the way a fish struggled to free itself from a hook.

All of a sudden, the pressure around his neck was gone.

He wasn't thinking anymore, didn't know what was going on. What happened next was instinct, reflex. He heard, very dimly, a tortured, wheezy caw, the rasping cry of a bird fighting the jaws of a cat with the last of its strength. A razor of cold air sliced his throat. In the next instant, his chest exploded a bright hot burn as his tortured lungs struggled to inflate. Casey's eyes snapped open, unseeing, his vision still blinkered, patchy, and molten, and he began to retch. Gawping, he managed another stinging, croaking bird's caw of a breath, and another—and then, above the thunder of blood in his ears, he made out a very strange sound: a hollow, dull *thuck!*

Running over pumpkins. The thought was hazy, hard to

hang on to, like trying to cup a fine mist. *Running over pump-kins on Halloween.*

2

"AH!" RIMA SWUNG again, with both hands, bringing the hammer whizzing down. Its black claw whickered, cleaving air. She'd gotten it between the shoulders the first time and was aiming for the head now, but even hurt and surprised, the thing was fast. At the last second, it flinched away, and she missed, the claw whizzing past, pulling her off-balance. She stumbled, her right knee banging into an equipment locker. Gasping against a starburst of pain, she caught herself on her hands, the hammer gripped in her right hitting the lid with a dull clank. To her left, the man-thing let out a huge bellow that she *felt*, blasting over her back and humming through metal.

Stand up, get up! But she already knew she was too late. She was turned around, facing the wrong way. From the corner of her left eye, she saw the thing rearing up, large as a mountain. Shifting the hammer to her left hand, she put her weight into it, whipping the hammer around and up in a vicious slice.

The creature never saw it coming, and then, in the next instant, it couldn't, at least not from that left eye. Rima felt the bone give as the claw slammed into the ridge above the socket. Gravity and momentum did the rest. Snagged on shattered bone and soft tissue, the claw tore out the socket. The eye burst in a sludgy spray of gelatinous yellow muck. Bawling with rage and new pain, the thing reeled, pawing at the ruin as snot-colored goo slithered down its snout.

She cringed back from the mess. She couldn't help it; it was automatic, a reflexive moment of disgust and horror; and so she didn't understand her mistake until a half second too late—because the thing still had that one good eye.

With a roar, the man-thing drove its fist, hard and fast as a piston. The blow slammed just above the bridge of her nose, and pain detonated in her forehead to spread in molten fingers. It felt like he'd broken every bone in her face. Her mind skipped a beat, and she stumbled, her consciousness suddenly slewing to one side like a car sliding off an icy cliff.

Stay with it. Fight. But her hand was empty. *Hammer . . . dropped it . . .*

Another blow, solid as a battering ram, drove into her belly, punching out her breath and what was left of her strength. Doubling over, trying to pull air into lungs that would not obey, she simply crumpled.

Get up. She knew her feet were moving, but only in a useless shuffle. Her head felt as if someone had buried the business end of an ax in her skull. Her grudging lungs balked. *C'mon, get up, get—*

There was a sudden blinding flash of yellow light, firecracker-bright, as a deafening *ba-ROOM* filled the cab. The blast was so strong she felt it shiver through the deck and into her teeth.

The thing's chest erupted in a liquid black halo. An oily rain of blood and mangled flesh sheeted over the walls and fell on Rima in a viscous shower. For a moment, she was too stunned to do anything, much less understand. The roar had been replaced by a muzzy, muffled *hoosh*, like water rushing past her ears. But then she felt something: a slick creep along her skin, a worming sensation over her clothes, eeling through her hair.

"Ahhh!" Rima clawed her way to her feet. To her left, the man-thing splayed, its chest replaced by a huge crater of obliterated bone and tissue. Frantic, she began swatting at the mucky bits of the monster's flesh squirming over her chest and arms and hair. "Get off, get off, get them off!"

Through the *hoosh*, she heard someone say, "Rima, what is it?" Then: "Casey, are you . . . Jesus, what the *hell*?"

Still disoriented, she turned a wild look. An older boy, with dark hair and eerie blue eyes, crouched in the entrance to the passenger cab. Openmouthed, the boy stared at the wriggling bits and shivering globules of black blood. "My God, its *chest*," the boy said. "It's *moving*."

"Re-repairing it-itself." Her voice felt rusty, her tongue thick. From where she stood, Rim could see strings of the thing's chest muscles nosing and then coiling together. Closing her eyes against a bolt of nausea, she pressed her trembling lips together and gulped against the sudden acid bite on her tongue. Something squiggled on her thigh, and she swatted it away in a fast sideswipe. The black slug of muscle sailed across the cabin to hit the far wall with a moist *splot*. For a second, it clung there, trembling as if trying to clear its head, before beginning a slow slither toward a neighboring splotch. She turned aside with a shudder. "Just like Father P-Preston."

"Who?" Shotgun still in hand, the older boy was helping Casey ease to a sit against an equipment locker. "What's going on? What *is* this thing?"

"D-don't know." Groaning, Casey clamped an arm to his left side. "My th-throat f-feels broken," he croaked. "H-hurts to . . . *ahhh!*" He threw his head back as the other boy probed his chest, and Rima saw a necklace of purple-black bruises ringing Casey's neck. "God, Eric, *d-don't.*"

Eric. Of course, his name is Eric. He and Casey are brothers. She put a hand up to her throbbing forehead and felt the beginnings of a knot. *Why couldn't I remember? What's wrong with me?*

"I'm sorry, Case," Eric said, calmly enough, although Rima saw a ripple of fear as the older boy touched a gentle hand to Casey's bruised jaw. "My God, what happened to your face? Can you walk?"

"Y-yeah. It's a long story." Wincing, Casey backhanded a trickle of blood from the corner of his mouth. "Where's Emma? How did you guys find us?"

"She's back at this farmhouse we found. The fog pulled us here, me and these two guys out in the truck . . ." Eric made a face. "That sounds pretty nuts."

"No, it doesn't. Fog got us, too," Casey said, then looked up as Rima dropped to her knees by his side. "Rima, are you . . . God, you're hurt."

"I'm fine." She covered his hand with hers. An impulse, not something she really thought about, but which, once done, felt entirely right. "Thank you for coming, for not letting that thing g-get . . ."

"Would never l-let that happen." His eyes fastened on hers, and she could feel a slow flush working its way up her neck. He turned his hand over, palm up, and gave her fingers a squeeze. "Tania?"

"Who?" Eric asked.

"Oh God." She felt a pang of guilt. In all the commotion,

she'd forgotten. Hurriedly pushing to her feet, she edged past the thing, sparing it a swift sidelong glance, then stopped dead and gave a much longer stare.

"What?" Eric was there in an instant. "What is . . . oh shit."

"Yeah," she breathed against a clutch of dawning dread. A moist mesh of fresh connective tissue had already formed; a toothy cage of remodeled bone arced over a gray sponge of new lung. Whips of thickening muscle waggled, and she swore she saw that thing's left hand convulse in a sudden spasm.

"I think we're out of here, *now*," Eric said, and moved to help Casey make his feet. "What about your friend? Is she . . . ?"

"Just a second." Dead ahead, the pudding that remained of Father Preston was still *SMEE-smeeing* over the windscreen. She wondered what they could possibly be rebuilding themselves into. The snowcat's auger had chopped the priest to hamburger. Could *all* those pieces be finding their way back together again? How could you kill something that kept regrowing like those nematodes Rima had sliced and diced in eighth-grade science?

Betcha fire would do it. Steeling herself, she worked her way around the driver's side transmission box. *Cook those suckers.*

Then she forgot all that, pushed it away as irrelevant, when she got a good look at Tania's face. The girl's skin was the color of cottage cheese, and her lids drooped, the whites showing in half-moons. Her ruined right arm was dusky, and her lips were purple. She wasn't breathing. Blood saturated her clothing and had gathered in a crimson lake on Tania's seat, spilling over into the foot well.

"Rima?" Casey called.

"Just . . . just give me a second." She closed her eyes against the prick of tears. *Come on; do what you have to.* Steeling herself, she opened her eyes, blew out a hard breath, then touched her fingers to the angle of Tania's jaw below her left ear.

A second later, over the sudden slam of her heart, she heard Casey: "Rima?" When she didn't answer, Eric said, more sharply, "Rima, what's wrong?"

"Oh my God," she said. "Look at her *face.*"

RIMA
Doomsday Sky

1

RIMA! RIMA! SOMEONE . . . Casey . . . was shouting, and now another voice, Eric's, joined his, both boys screaming from the back of the passenger cab and a million miles away: *Rima, get down, get down, get out of the way!*

But she couldn't move. She was beyond shock, into deep-freeze. Her body was icy, numb, like that little kid with the splinters of an evil mirror in his heart and eyes; a child fit only for the world of the Snow Queen. Rooted in place, she could only stare at Tania, her face, her neck, and if she thought at all in those first few seconds, it wasn't in words so much as sensations: the skip of her heart, the slickness of new alien blood on her fingers, the hard scent of iron and blasted flesh and spent gunpowder, the airless dead space in her lungs as they emptied.

And the boys, of course, still screaming from so far away: *Rima, Rima, get down!*

Tania's throat and face were moving, not twitching but undulating and worming as something eeled just beneath the surface, the suddenly elastic skin puffing and then deflating, over and over again, as if Tania were growing gills. Trickles of black leaked from the dead girl's nose and dribbled out of both ears. Fat, ebony pearls swelled from the half-moons of her eyes. A deep ripple worked its way across Tania's face from right to left, from one cheek to the opposite, skimming under and lifting Tania's lips as if the girl were dragging a thick, fleshy tongue over and around her teeth.

Tania's mouth suddenly sagged, the jaws unlocking—and at that, Rima's brain eked a single, small *oh*. Then she blanked, her mind blinkering white with terror as a nightmare of legs, jointed and bristled as a tarantula's, unfurled from Tania's lips like the spiky petals of an alien rose. Deep in the heart of this bizarre flower, two sets of long, pointed fangs clashed, working from side to side like a spider's mandibles, grating together with a coarse rasp, like the grind of metal files.

Rima felt a crack of horror, like a jag of lightning, scorch through her mind to burn from her mouth in a high, terrified scream as Tania's eyes snapped open. The whites were a jet-black sea of hemorrhage. The pupils belonged to a lizard, a snake, the vertical slits narrowing as Tania let go of a shrill, chittering squeal.

"Rima!" There came a hard jolt as someone crashed into her from behind, a solid body blow that knocked her to one side. Panicked, taken by surprise, she flailed, but Casey grabbed her arms and then he was bullying her back, slamming her flat against a far wall, covering her up, using his weight to hold her in place, screaming, "Shoot! Shoot it, Eric, shoot it!"

The cab flooded with bright yellow light, and the roar from

the shotgun was so huge Rima thought her eardrums would explode. The blast punched whatever Tania had become in the chest, but it wasn't like the movies. Instead of flying back, Tania, who also had a new gaping hole where her heart used to be, blundered back to crash against the cat's transmission box. But she didn't go down, not the way the man-thing had. Still pinned, Rima watched as Tania made a left-handed grab, steadied herself against a seat, and pulled upright. Another roar from the shotgun, and all of a sudden a spool of guts boiled in wet spaghetti tangles. This time, Tania lost her feet, coming down hard and with a sodden splash. Almost at once, she rolled onto hands and knees and then clawed her way upright again.

"Jesus," she heard Casey say, his voice catching with pain, and she realized just how much wrestling her out of the line of fire had cost him. Slick with sweat, he was panting, his breaths shallow, his stormy eyes wide with shock. "Look at how *fast*."

She saw. The damage to Tania's chest and abdomen was already repairing itself, the tissues knitting together at a ferocious rate, so fast the skin seemed to boil. The entire interior of the cabin was now alive with squirming tissue, creeping blood. On the deck, she saw the man-thing shudder with a fresh convulsion and thought they had only a few seconds left.

"Case! Rima! *Now!*" Eric was suddenly there, expression taut. He hooked a hand under Casey's arm. "Shotgun's dry. You're out, too, Case. Come on, we go to go."

Of course, the guns are out of ammunition. She darted a look at Tania, who was setting her feet. The hole in her chest was gone, and as Rima watched, the last loop of intestine, not pink or white or blue but smoky gray, was sucked back in the way a kid slurped up that last juicy noodle. Even Tania's nearly severed arm was stitching back into place. Eric and Case could pump out shots all day, maybe even make oatmeal out of Tania's head and brains, and the end result would be the same. As she crowded after Eric and Casey, she half-expected the jittering man-thing to grab her by the ankle, but she swept past and then she was out, bolting from the cabin, hopping to the snow, running from the nightmare.

Wondering if the fog would let them go.

2

"THIS WAY!" A boy's voice, coming from her left. Turning, she spotted a rust-red truck, its gray-white exhaust pluming in the still, frigid air. Eric and Casey were nearly there already, although Casey was listing now, leaning heavily against his brother. Two other boys stood on the running boards. One, so lanky and thin he was like the slash of an exclamation point, hoisted a rifle in the air one-handed, like a cavalry commander ordering a retreat. "Over here, come on, come on!"

Rima sprinted for the truck. Above the shriek of her breath, she heard the birds, still crowding the dome of the sky, but the grating, mechanical clacks of their cries seemed closer than before. Flicking a quick glance, she heard herself gasp, and for a second, she actually faltered and slowed. Maybe it was an illusion, but was the sky *lower*? She thought so. It felt as if the glowering, inky sky was beginning to crouch and crowd down. Or perhaps there were only more crows whizzing back and forth, coming together in darker clots before unwinding in screaming spirals to sweep over the trees—where, she saw, the fog huddled. *Drawing down the death,* she thought, not really understanding what that meant but knowing it was true because the death-whispers she'd sensed before were still gone, taken away when the crows spumed from the snow.

"Come on, come on, move it!" The wiry kid who'd called was already dropping into the passenger seat. "We got to boogie!"

Running out of time. Tearing her gaze from the crows winging over that doomsday sky, she got herself moving. But her chest was fizzing with panic, suddenly filled with a terrible foreboding. The space of this place was being closed up, pinched off, *extinguished* the way an upended jar smothered a flame.

Eric had just slotted in the two empty shotguns and was helping Casey clamber through the back passenger's side door, so she rounded the nose for the opposite side. She wheeled around the back door just as the driver craned a look—and she almost screamed. Because this was another boy she already knew, had met before, and she thought now as she had then: *What are you?*

"Get in!" Then a look of shock swept through the boy's face, and Bode's mouth unhinged. "Whoa. What the hell, what are *you* doing here?"

She almost said, *Trying not to die,* but the lanky kid—Chad, she remembered now—interrupted. "Oh shit." She looked and saw Chad staring back the way she had just come. "Aw, Jesus," Chad said.

From his place directly behind Chad, Eric said, "What?" Rima saw his head snap a look, and then his body stiffen. "Oh God. Bode. Bode?"

"Yeah." Bode's tone was grim. "I see them."

So, now, did Rima. Tania was on the snow and so was the man-thing Eric had shot. Instead of coming for them, both Tania and the man-thing were heading toward those distant woods, and she thought back to Father Preston's lightning dash. Tania and the man-thing weren't exactly running; even half-mended monsters must have a few residual aches and pains. But they weren't tottering, shambling zombies either. Still, hit the gas, and the truck would leave them in the dust, no sweat.

The problem was . . . how the hell to outrun the others.

RIMA
Think My Hand

THE DENSE WOODS beyond Tania and the man-thing and the stalled snowcat, and over which the fog brooded, were alive with creatures—hundreds, *thousands* streaming from the trees. They were like the crows that had bulleted out of the snow, and Rima watched, stupefied, as they joined into broad, sweeping formations, spreading out to flank the truck like an army. They were a wall, a tidal wave of death, and all the more terrible because they came in absolute silence.

"Rima!" Casey grabbed her wrist and pulled. She tumbled in, and then Casey was reaching past her, dragging the door shut with a *chuck* as Chad screamed, *"Go, Bode!"*

"We're gone!" Bode hammered the gas, the sudden acceleration throwing Rima back against her seat as the Dodge surged forward with a throaty *vaROOOMMM*. But Rima felt the change almost instantly, after less than twenty feet: how the truck balked and tripped and stumbled, as if they'd hopped onto railroad tracks by mistake. After another moment, the Dodge bogged down even more, suddenly churning what felt like taffy, the tires miring in deep snow that had been as solid as ice only two seconds ago.

"What the . . ." Cursing, Bode butted the stick into first and gunned the engine. This time the Dodge jolted forward by less than a foot.

"Aw, *Christ*," Chad said. "Look, right under us. Look what's happening to the goddamned snow."

Rima plastered her face to the window glass and peered down. The snow was no longer unbroken or a vast white expanse but seamed with jagged cracks growing wider by the second. Yet a quick glance past Eric and toward the trees showed the snow there to be intact and unchanged. Beneath the truck, more splits appeared and the seams became ruts that rapidly filled with gelatinous ooze, like lava bubbling from the deep heart of a volcano. Except this lava was black and boiled up so quickly, it overflowed and began to spread over the snow in a tarry lake. It didn't seem to be hot, but Rima thought it was the fog's dark twin: quivering and molten, sucking at the truck's tires to hold it fast. Looking back across Casey and Eric, she saw the creatures still coming, but now those fissures and cracks in the snow were spreading out, stretching in jagged fingers.

We're the focal point. It's all centered on us. It was as if they were the spider spinning a fractured web. Above the woods, the birds were still drawing down in an obsidian curtain, blacking the sky, shutting the lid on this day, this place, their lives. *We're causing this,* making *it happen. But how?*

"Bode, do something. Get us moving!" Chad screamed. "The things are almost here, man, they're almost *here*!"

But they may not be able to get to us. Rima saw that, further away, the snow seemed to be pulsing, the swells widening in ripples like a pond after you heaved in a heavy stone. *Like Tania's face, her neck.* She eyed a swell, saw how fast it raced under the snow. Even at this distance, she could see Tania, who'd now linked up with the creatures, stagger.

"Can't!" Bode yanked the truck's gearshift, dropping them into first and pumping the accelerator, fighting the black lava's grab, trying to rock them the way you might try to jump a car out of a deep rut. The truck's engine whined, its growl rising to a high howl, and *still* they were only crawling over the snow, going nowhere fast. Now Rima could smell something burning. The pistons, the engine block itself—it didn't matter.

"Is there anything we can do?" Eric asked, tensely. "Bode?"

"I got nothing, man," Bode said, tersely, teeth bared. Sweat beaded on his forehead. "We're sitting ducks. I don't know what else I can do. I'll keep *fighting* this hunka junk, but . . ." There was another tremendous grind of gears. "How you and your brother set for ammo?"

"My gun's dry," Eric said. "Case is out, too."

"Which leaves the Winchester with five"—the Dodge bucked as Bode fought the stick—"and eight in the Colt. Plenty to go around."

"Plenty? Aw, man, you crazy?" Chad moaned. He'd clapped both hands to his head. "Thirteen measly shots or thirteen hundred, there are too many of them, man."

"He's not talking about enough bullets for *them*," Eric said.

There was a moment's trembling silence, which the birds' shrills filled, as the Dodge's engine muttered a basso counterpoint. "Oh no," Chad finally said, shaking his head. "Bode, you are out of your mind. If you think I'm gonna eat a bullet . . ."

"Better than them eating you," Bode said.

"We're not there just yet," Eric said.

But we will be soon. Rima felt Casey's hand find hers. "Do you know what's happening?" he asked.

She shook her head. But God, she thought this might be her fault. *She* knew Tania; *she* knew about Father Preston, the church. And for a while, that world was so *real*, as if *she* had pulled something together out of her mind, or memory, or both, knitting a world as surely as those creatures could remake and mend their flesh.

Then stop this. She closed her eyes. *Please, Fog, or whatever you are . . . please stop or show me how. Even if I have to stay. Please.* She pushed out the thought as hard as she could, wondering if there really was anything to hear it. *Let the others go. I don't want Casey to die.*

"Hey, hey." She opened her eyes to find Casey staring, her hand clutching his in a death grip. "Don't worry," he said. "I won't let go."

"Casey." She swallowed. "I think . . ."

"Guys?" Eric broke in. "Look."

About fifty yards away and all around them, the creatures were at a dead stop, gathered in a silent, milling throng at the edge of that advancing flood of coal-colored goo. Rima could see Tania pacing back and forth, looking for a way across, as the black tide lapped and gurgled around her ankles. Several of the man-things were actually backing away, and most were stumbling as the snow continued to fracture.

"Man, you know," Chad said, "if it's not hurting *them*, maybe be better to take our chances."

"I wouldn't base anything on what happens to them," Eric said. "I blew holes in that girl and she——"

All of a sudden, Tania let out a bawling screech so loud it cut through and over the birds' cries. Rima heard herself gasp as Tania gave a sudden, violent lurch, as if she'd been grabbed around the ankles. Her hands flew up as she dropped, straight down, the dark liquid instantly closing over her head.

"Jesus," Bode said. "Like quicksand."

"No, it's too fast," Casey said. Outside, more and more of the creatures had wheeled around to try and run, but what was left of the snow was breaking apart under their feet, the surface crumbling and collapsing. Silent before, the creatures now brayed in rusty barks. Black sludge steamrolled over the snow in a remorseless juggernaut, slopping over and slurping up the white. The crazed, ravening birds were so low now, they swarmed directly overhead, thick as blowflies over dead meat. "They're not sinking," Casey said. "It's like they're being pulled *back*."

"Or down," Eric said. "Like something's *grabbing*——" He broke off as a violent shudder vibrated through the truck. "Oh boy. Bode, *Bode*."

Chad's eyes bugged. "What the *hell*?"

"Oh God," Rima said, and then screamed as the vehicle suddenly jolted downward, canting at a crazy angle. "It's happening to us."

"We're sinking!" Chad braced himself against the dash. "Jesus, it's got us, we're sinking, we're *sinking*!"

"Can you get us moving, Bode?" Rima said. The boy shook his head, and, as the truck rose, Rima's stomach swooped, then tried cramming behind her teeth as they plummeted on the other side of a swell. "Then what do we *do?*"

"I know what *I'm* doing!" Chad popped his door. "Bode, we got to go, we got to go, we got to go go *go!*"

"*No, Chad!*" Bode and Eric screamed at the same time. "Chad, stop!" Bode shouted. "You can't go out there!"

"Well, I'm not dying in *here!*" Chad shouted, and then he was flinging himself out of the truck.

"Get him!" Rima shrilled, even as Chad tumbled out. She tried springing over the backseat, but Casey grabbed her waist and held her back. "Casey, no, we have to get him! Bode, don't let it touch him, don't let it—"

But Chad was out. The moment his feet hit the churning black, Chad . . . didn't sink. The surface actually *stilled*, as if it were holding itself steady in order to make sense of this strange new taste. *Maybe I was wrong.* Still hunched up against the Dodge's ceiling, with Casey's hands battened onto her waist, Rima stared as Chad cautiously straightened. *Maybe it will let him go. Maybe it senses that we're different.*

Then she saw how the surface shuddered, just a bit, and what echoed through her mind then wasn't a sight but a sound: that squeaking, wet-fingers *SMEE-smee* of Father Preston's meat inching over glass. "Chad!" she said.

"H-hey," Chad exhaled, as if suddenly realizing what he'd just done. Turning, he looked back and spread his arms. "L-look, man, it's coo—"

Flashing out from the murk, a black tendril shot out like the sticky tongue of a chameleon unfurling to snatch a moth on the fly. Chad shrieked as it roped around his left leg.

"*Chad!*" Bode bawled.

"God, get it off, get it off!" Chad wailed, struggling to

pull himself free. His clothes were cooking, the steam rising not in white but black curls. As he bent to snatch at the black tongue around his leg, another spun out to wind around his right wrist. *"JESUS GOD!"* Chad threw back his head in an agonized scream. The first tentacle had coiled all the way up his leg to his groin, and Chad's pants were shredding, dissolving to threads. The flesh of both his left leg and right arm began to bubble, as if Chad were a plastic bag filled with water reaching the boiling point. Then, all of a sudden, fountains of blood jetted in pulsing red ropes from where the flesh had been burned, and Chad let go of a wild shriek: "Bode, it's burning, it's *burning, IT'S EATING ME!"*

Of them all, it was Eric who reacted first. "Oh my God, oh my God." He swept Rima out of the way and scrambled into Chad's seat. "Chad, Chad, grab my hand, grab it!"

"Eric!" Letting go of Rima, Casey lunged for his brother, and just in the nick of time, because Bode, wide-eyed and ashen, was still paralyzed, seemingly unable to move. As if sensing what Eric meant to do, the inky tarn gave a mighty *heave*, and the truck dropped again with another stomach-churning lurch. Off-balance, only inches from the open door, Eric pitched forward. With a yell, Casey made a snatching grab, hooking Eric's waistband, and then he was working his way up Eric's back, hugging Eric in a tight embrace. "I got you, but hurry, Eric, hurry!"

"Chad!" Eric had stretched himself on the seat until his chest hung over the pulsing muck, now less than a foot from his face. Maybe a taste of Chad was all it had needed, because the black goo had morphed into a writhing sea of muscular, ropy tentacles that coiled over and around Chad to burn into his skin and draw out his blood. Everywhere they stung Chad, fresh black steam smoked, drifting up in an inky cloud toward the birds, which were so close and thick, it was as if they *were* all that was left of a sky.

"Chad!" Eric shouted again, and thrust out both hands, straining as far as he could. "Chad, grab my hands, give me your hands!"

Saturated with blood, blind with pain, his skin steaming and bubbling and tearing open, Chad tried. He was crumpling now, not sinking so much as being eaten alive, dissolved in a vat of black acid, but his left arm was still free. Twisting, Chad made a frantic grab—and missed.

"No!" Eric shouted. Rima thought he would have leapt from the truck if not for Casey and now Bode, who finally seemed to have snapped out of it, was dragging back on Casey to keep them both from falling. "Chad," Eric screamed. *"Chad!"*

Shrieking, Chad fell, dropping into the embrace of a thousand stygian tentacles. One snaked over his eyes, and yet another probed at Chad's mouth and slid inside—and then Chad was no longer screaming but choking as the tentacle worked and wormed into his throat. Chad's skin was turning, going from white to a deep plum and shading to black, as if the tentacle were a hose, pumping ink—or dissolving Chad from the inside out.

The truck jolted, the engine died with a gurgling rattle, and now, groaning, the Dodge listed in an excruciating slow roll, like a boat beginning to founder. Crying out, Rima jammed her left foot into the back of the front seat and the other against the raised ridge running up the center of the floor. The truck was too old for shoulder harnesses or hand loops, so she spread her arms and flattened her palms on the roof. The truck was now canted at a forty-five-degree angle, far enough that she was afraid to let up with her legs. As it was, if they tipped much more, she'd be practically standing straight up.

"Oh Jesus." Both Bode's fists, trembling with strain, were clenched in Casey's parka. "Kid," he grunted, "I'm slipping, can't hold you! Eric, shut the door before I lose him, man! Shut it before those things get a taste of you, too! Come on!"

"Can't!" Beyond, Eric had planted his boots to either side of the open door and was bracing Casey, trying to keep both his brother and himself from falling out. The waving, searching tentacles of that black anemone were probing the bottom right corner of the truck door, as if deciding whether they liked the taste, the sound a moist but hollow *splot-splot-splot-splot*. Chad was completely gone now. Either swallowed or dissolved . . . Rima thought it didn't much matter. "We've rolled too far," Eric said. "It's too heavy, I can't *do* it."

"Man, we're done, it's over," Bode said, and yet his body didn't seem to believe that, because, if anything, he pulled even harder on Casey, eking out every last second of life. "Come on, kid, help me. *Pull.*"

"I'm *trying.*" Casey's voice was as gray as his face. He flicked one quick look back at her. "Rima, if you can, pop your door or unroll your window and climb out, get on top of the truck."

"He's right." Sweat coursed down Bode's cheeks. "Get outta here, Rima. Maybe you can find your way out of this." When she made no move to do so, he barked, "Rima, *damn it,* go!"

"Forget it," she said, thinking she sounded braver than she felt. "I'm not leaving you guys. There's no point." Even if she could bully the heavy door or lever herself out the window, she could picture herself balancing on an ever-diminishing island of metal until the ooze finally took her, too. Worse, she would hear the others—hear Casey—as they died before her, and know she was powerless to help.

"Hey, we're not sinking as fast," Eric said. He sounded breathless, like he was churning through wind sprints. At his feet, the tarn kept on sampling the truck, the *splot-splot-splot-splot* of little black tongues flicking along the bottom edge of the door, working toward the hinge, as the truck slipped deeper by slow degrees. Eric managed another inch back. "You feel it? We're still going down, but . . ."

"Good." Bode's teeth were bared. "Hope it's got a stomachache. Hope it *chokes*."

"But it was so fast before," Casey said in as breathless a tone as his brother. "What's it waiting for?"

"Maybe it's playing around." And then Eric grunted at the *splot-splot* of a tentacle over the door's running board. "Maybe it likes it when we scream."

And then, out of nowhere, Rima thought she heard something: slight, airy, the thinnest sliver of sound. *What?* That wasn't a scream. Craning, she looked to her right and through the truck's rear window. It was now very dark in the truck and outside, the coil of birds blotted out whatever sky remained. If anyone could look through all those birds—say, the way you could through the clear glass shell and into the intricate design at the heart of a paperweight—it would probably seem as if the truck were a small bubble of metal and glass, and they, the creatures trapped inside. *Like one of those old-fashioned diving bells, the ones open at the bottom but filled with air.* Other than the birds, there was no one out there.

Then, she heard that sound that almost wasn't again, and this time she recognized a word.

"Do you hear that?" she said.

"Hear what?" Casey asked.

"Someone just called my name." She twisted a look over her left shoulder, craning up through the passenger's side door. More birds. "I think it was *Emma*."

"What?" Bode said.

Rima. Still tentative and evanescent, but now somehow more intense to Rima than simply empty air, as if Emma was honing in on them. Then: *Eric.*

"What?" Eric said. His head jerked up. "Emma?"

"You heard that," she said. "You heard her?"

"What are you guys talking about?" Casey asked. "Where?"

"I don't know." Rima threw a wild look around. "Emma?" she called. "Emma, where . . ." She listened again, and then heard Eric answer: "Bode and Casey."

Another pause, and then Emma's voice again, so insubstantial you might mistake it for the sough of a light breeze that held no meaning at all, saying something else.

"Jesus," Bode breathed, at the same time that Casey said, "God, I heard that."

"Yeah, but what's White Space?" Eric said. "And what does she mean, *think my hand*?"

RIMA

The Thickness of a Single Molecule

1

"MAYBE THINK *ABOUT* it?" Casey said.

"I don't think that's what she means," Rima said. Was White Space something on the other side of this place? She looked at the way this world was shuttering: the birds, drawing down death, obliterating the horizon, as if an eyelid were closing. "Maybe what she means is we should *think* her hand; not what it *is*," she said, "but what it *does*. Like it grabs, it . . ." She felt the rest wick away on a gasp. "Oh my God, *look*."

Just outside her window, hovering against all that blackness as if suspended from an invisible string, was a luminous silver-white slit so bright it almost hurt to look.

"Is that the fog?" Bode said.

"No. I think it's a *door*," Eric said, still stiff-arming the frame to keep from falling out. The tentacles had swarmed past the running board, and were now licking at the interior edge of the foot well. The outer corner of the door was already under. "That's what she means by White Space."

"Okay, but so what? How do we get through? It's not wide

enough; it's a nothing," Bode said. "We can't even *get* there. It's not a single step. So what would we hang on to?"

"We hang on to Emma. We let her pull us," Rima said, and looked back down at them. "We're inside something or on the other side of a mirror, in the glass, looking out like Alice in Wonderland. What we see through the slit is the . . . the wrapping paper, the *skin*, like on a baseball or a clean sheet of paper with no words on it yet. That's where she pulls us, onto that page, where *she* is."

"What?" Bode said. "How do you know this?"

"I *don't*, okay? It's just a guess. But Bode, do you want to stay *here*?"

"She's right," Casey said. "I almost see it, too. But Rima, I still don't understand how we can use it."

"Me neither," she said, and then popped the lock of her door.

"What are you *doing*?" Bode said.

"What does it look like?" She shoved as hard as she could, felt the door open by six inches. *Heavy.* "*Help* me," she said to Bode.

"What?" Bode turned a swift glance back at Casey. "Can you hold him?"

"I guess I'd better," Casey said.

"Go, Bode," Eric said, with a tense jerk of his head. "I don't understand this, but I know we're all dead if we don't do something."

"Go. I can hold him," Casey said. "Just do it."

"All right, I'm letting go," Bode warned, and then took away his hands. At the end of the seat, Eric's legs, spread in a wide V, suddenly quivered with the additional strain, and at Casey's hard, sudden gasp, Bode said, his voice rising with alarm, "Kid?"

"Got him." Casey's voice came out strangled. "But *hurry*. Do it, guys, do it *now*."

Without another word, Bode turned in his seat, bunched his arms, and gave his own door a mighty shove.

"Wait," Rima said, "what about—"

"Faster this way than the back door." The words squeezed out on a grunt as Bode heaved. There was a loud, piercing, metallic yowl that Bode matched with a drawn-out jungle yell of his own, and then the door was open and he was swarming over his seat, turning around until the weight of the door rested on his back. "Come on," he panted, and extended a hand. "Come on if you're coming."

Trusting in Bode's strength took an act of will. If he slipped, she wouldn't fall out, but she'd knock Casey. Then Eric would slip . . .

As if she sensed Rima's fear, Emma came through: *Hurry, Rima*. And: *All of you at once*.

"She's crazy. How are we supposed to do that?" Bode said, as he hauled Rima over his seat in a half slide, half fall. Turning her body around, Bode got her facing out. "Okay, you're here. Now what?"

"Now we all think her hand," she said, taking one of Bode's in hers. She didn't dare look away from that slit, which was either dimming or being covered over, she couldn't tell. "Grab Casey."

Emma: *Hurry*.

"I got him," Bode said. "Do it, *do it*."

"You have to help," Rima said. "It's a leap of faith. *Think* her hand, *think* of her pulling us, and don't anyone let go."

Come on, Emma, come on. Rima fixed her eyes on the sliver of White Space. *Do you feel us? Pull us, pull us now.*

For a very long second, nothing happened except the slow but inexorable slide of the truck, and she thought the muck might win this tug-of-war after all. *Emma.* Panic boiled in her chest. *Emma, please, help us. Where are you?*

"I'm right here, Emma," she heard Eric say. "Concentrate on me, feel me; I'm here, I'm *here*. Pull, Emma, *pull*."

At that, there was a sudden rush, a whirring. Rima felt herself moving, and she thought, *Go. Trust her. Go now.*

She stepped

2

OVER SPACE THAT was truly a blank—not black, not gray or white, but *absence*—and into a flat, hard cold of nothing.

If Bode's hand was still in hers, she did not feel it. Instead, her body compressed. She was passing *through* something, but didn't know what. She could feel her heart struggling in her chest. She opened her mouth to scream, but nothing came. It was as if she was shifting not from a place but from one *thing* into another, the way water rearranged into ice or steamed away as vapor, and her one thought, as thin as a plank of wood shaved to the thickness of a single molecule, was . . .

PART FOUR

HELL
IS
COLD

EMMA

Outside of Time

"I BELIEVE YOU," Rima said. She studied Lizzie's crazy quilt, with its intricate stitchery, oddly shaped blocks of fabric, colorful glass beads, and dangling pendants. Her fingers skimmed a large orange tabby cat embroidered onto a trapezoid of green felt. "I don't understand it all, but I believe you." She paused, then added, "I think."

"Well, *I* don't." Bode was leaning against the mantelpiece of a hearth in which orange-yellow flames crackled and danced. They were gathered in a front family room that Bode didn't recall seeing in the house, and that Emma was pretty sure hadn't been here at all, and certainly not *this* way—strewn with comfortable furniture, a fire already lit—until she and the others trooped down from Lizzie's room.

"*This*, I believe in," Bode said, rattling open a box of matches. Selecting one, he struck it. "Something I can touch and feel," he said, as the flame gobbled up the match nearly to his fingertips. Wincing, he flipped what was left into the fireplace. "See, *that* hurt. That was real. So *I'm* real. I'll believe in time travel before I believe this other extra-universe crap."

"Multiverse." From her perch on an ottoman near Lizzie, who was hunkered on the floor, Emma said, "So, forgetting what just happened to you guys, the *reason* you're in Wisconsin instead of Wyoming—"

"You just said you don't know *where* we are. Why can't we be in Wyoming?"

"Whatever. How about the fact that you started the day in *1967* but ended it almost fifty years later? And this is because . . . ?" When Bode didn't reply, Emma said, "Feel free to jump in anytime."

"Well, first off, I'm not saying I have all the answers. Second, I could say the same right back to you guys. Like, maybe *you're* back in sixty-seven with me, see? It's all in how you look at it." Scowling, Bode scraped another match to life. "Real is real. This guy, Tony? Rima and Casey said he got chewed up and then blown to pieces. I *saw* Chad die. We all nearly got killed."

"I didn't *say* we weren't real. I said that *we*—that is, the energy that's us, our . . . *essence?* Our souls? Whatever you want to call it, I think the core of who we are and how we think of ourselves, might be in a different timeline or alternative universe, or even outside of regular time the way we know it."

"See?" Bode waved a dismissive hand. "It's all voodoo. You're just guessing, and I don't even understand what you just said. Our *essence?* Outside of time? And what timeline? What other universe? I'm *here*, it's *now*, I'm real."

"He's got a point." Casey lay on a sofa as Eric knelt

alongside, gently finger-walking the patchwork of ugly bruises on his brother's chest. "How does some weird theory explain . . . *Ow.*" Casey fired a glare at Eric. "That *hurt.*"

"Sorry, Case." Eric made a face. "I think maybe two, three breaks? Or only cracks . . . I learned battlefield stuff, the basics, but I'm no medic."

"It jab when you breathe?" When Casey nodded, Bode said, "Yeah, they're probably broke. Not a whole bunch you can do, and they'll heal up on their own okay. If they got tape in this place, I can show you how to splint them, maybe make you a little more comfortable. Duct tape'd be good." Bode's eyes drifted over to Lizzie. "I don't suppose you're smart enough to whip up a little first aid kit?"

"Don't be such an asshole," Emma said.

"I don't know if there's a kit, or . . . *duck* tape, whatever that is." Lizzie's arms tightened around her knees. "I've never needed any band-aids or iodine or stuff. Maybe there's something in one of the bathrooms, or kitchen."

"I'll be okay." Grimacing, Casey slid his arms into a faded denim shirt Eric had unearthed from an upstairs bedroom. "But I'm with Bode," he said, gingerly touching a large purple splotch of bruise splashed over his jaw. He hadn't said how that had happened, but the way he and Rima had glanced at one another when Eric asked made Emma wonder. "My bruises feel pretty real," Casey said as he flexed the swollen, split knuckles of his right hand.

"And see, that's just wrong." Bode struck another match. "The kid's all beat up. Pain and getting hurt and *dying* kind of go against this whole we're outta some book shit."

"Not just *some* book." Emma pulled *Echo Rats* from the

McDermott novels she'd taken from the library that had just . . . appeared? Been behind that slit-door all along? Or was the library made as this family room had been: when House decided she needed it? The slit-door was also gone, replaced by an ordinary wooden door with an ordinary knob. Inside was a normal, ordinary library with floor-to-ceiling shelves crammed with books. Only one detail in that room gave her pause: a copy of some painting of Dickens, mounted next to shelves crammed with the writer's works. The only picture in House she'd seen so far, the painting featured Dickens, napping, in his library. Floating all around were various characters from his novels and stories, but the piece looked unfinished. Only a portion had any color: Dickens, a few of the characters, some of the books. The rest was nothing more than an outline, a compositional rendering. She really recognized only one character hovering above Dickens's right hand, because it was one of the most famous: Little Nell on her deathbed.

So what . . . this was a clue? No Mirror in the background that she could see. Perhaps one of Dickens's own books was important? Or a character? Well, hell if she knew, and they had bigger problems.

But she'd also noticed something else: no radio in that library, or anywhere. In fact, she hadn't heard that scratchy static-filled broadcast about murders since she'd pulled the others into House. Didn't know what to think about that either, or why that broadcast, so constant across situations—whether it was with Lily or in House, or way back, down cellar—had dogged her in the first place.

"*This* book," she said now, holding up the novel. Two red

eyes, with slits for pupils, stared out from the center of a pitch-black cover. "*Your* story."

"We don't *know* that," Bode snorted. "So the guy used my name. Big deal. Don't tell me you never saw your name in a book and didn't get a little weirded out."

She knew what Bode was saying. The effect was jarring, a mental hitch, like blundering over an exposed root. The paper she'd written for the Jane Austen unit in English last year was torture, like analyzing a weird, alien twin. "This is different, Bode. You must feel it, even if you don't want to believe it. What other explanation is there? And don't say drugs or you're drunk or something. This would have to be the most detailed bad trip of all time, and you know it."

"I don't know anything, and neither do you. You're spouting theories." Bode's jaw set. "Point is *I'm* me, right here, flesh and blood. You read that book? Is this crazy valley in there, or you guys? This house?"

"I don't know. We didn't go over *Echo Rats* in class. But I doubt *we're* in there, or this situation. The jacket says the novel takes place in Vietnam and Wyoming."

"Where you said you and Chad were this morning," Eric put in.

"And still could be now," Bode said.

"No," Lizzie said. "We're not anywhere, really, or any-when."

"What does that mean, Lizzie?" Rima asked, at the same time that Bode rolled his eyes and drawled, "Oh yeah, that's *so* clear."

God, the way certain things kept repeating and echoing was starting to weird her out. "What about this?" Flipping the book over, Emma quickly jumped her gaze from that black-and-white photo to the blurb. She doubted any scaly-armed monsters would suddenly corkscrew free, but you couldn't be too careful. "The blurb *says* 1967, Vietnam, Seventh Cav, C company, black echoes . . ."

"Black echoes?" Casey asked.

"VC tunnels." When Casey looked blank, Bode amplified. "Vietcong?"

"Who?"

"Guerrilla force for the North Vietnamese Army," Eric said. "It's, like, ancient history."

"Not to me. Echo Sector's lousy with tunnels. Blacker than pitch," Bode said. "Just like on the cover."

"You *crawl* through enemy tunnels?" Casey said. "In the *dark*?"

"Get shot if you use a flashlight."

Flashlights. Getting shot. Emma felt that queer mental jolt. *That's exactly what I was thinking earlier. What does that mean? That we're really all linked because of Lizzie?*

"Yeah, tunnel rats," Eric said. "I read about you guys."

"That's us. Dropping into a black echo's the only way to kill Charlie before he kills us." Bode's tone was matter-of-fact. "Look, for the sake of argument, let's say you're right. Well, why can't that book be from one of those . . . those universe things? Like *it* came *here* to us? Know what I'm saying?"

"Well—" Emma began, and stopped. That all these books existed in an alternative timeline had never occurred to her.

"Ah. *Ah.*" With a wiggle of his eyebrows, Bode used a thumbnail to scratch a flame from another match. "See? Gotcha."

"It's not a contest," she said, although she felt as if she'd lost a point. Why hadn't she considered that? Bode was absolutely . . .

"He's right." When she turned to look, Eric shrugged. "Well, he is. Why can't someone have written about us in one timeline and painted us onto canvases in another, or . . . I don't know . . . made us into toys, or something? I can buy multiverses. The theory's there. I've read enough science fiction. For all we know, this could be a simulation, too, right? Like *The Matrix*?"

Yet one more echo, but Eric, she almost understood. Didn't like that she did either. "Yes, but . . ."

"So leaving aside the *how* of getting here for a second, Lizzie finds and then brings us"—Eric looked over to Lizzie—"through these, ah, Dark Passages?"

"No, Eric, I *told* you," Lizzie said. "Except for Emma, you guys came from book-worlds. The Dark Passages are what's between the *Nows*."

"See?" Bode threw up his hands. "This is exactly what I'm saying. The Dark Passages are between *Nows*, and what's between *Nows* are the Dark Passages . . . That's like saying something's a cat because it's a cat, but it doesn't tell you *anything* about what a cat really is."

"Tautology," Eric said, then waved that away. To Emma: "My point is that there are a lot of possibilities, but let's just go with what you're proposing, okay? In that case, what Bode said could be true. Why *couldn't* we be *ideas* in one alternative universe or timeline and real people in another?"

"Like the soldiers in one of Tony's comics." At Eric's puzzled look, Casey said, "They were in his car. There was this

Twisted Tales about soldiers fighting giant rats. The soldiers turn out to be toys, but *they* think they're real." When Bode opened his mouth, Case said, "Yes, I know. You're real. I got that, but get *this*. The comic was *new*, like he'd just pulled it off the rack, only the date was April. Last time I looked, it was December."

"So? Big deal." Bode blew a raspberry. "It's a real nice drugstore. They take good care of their merchandise. April was only a couple months ago."

"Only if this is 1983. I read the date." Casey frowned. "Come to think of it, Tony's car was *really* old, and he played cassette tapes, not CDs."

"CDs?" Bode asked.

"A compact disc, for digital data . . . You can put music . . . Never mind." Emma waved the explanation away. "It's not important. What he's saying is, Tony was from the past." She paused. "Well, okay, *our* past, same as you."

"Or you're all from my future."

"Whatever. I'm not sold we're in a specific time," Eric said.

"He's right. You're not." Lizzie laid her cheek on her knees with a sigh. "You're outside of a regular *Now*. You know, where there are things you guys call today and tomorrow and next week." It might have been the dance of shadow from the fire, but for a brief moment, the little girl's eyes did their odd glimmering shift again. Emma couldn't tell if Lizzie was only tired, or depressed. Or—here was a crazy thought—*bored* and a little exasperated, as if she'd seen this play a thousand times before and was simply waiting for the characters of this particular drama to get it out of their systems, think it through, and catch up already.

"There's just this special forever-*Now*," Lizzie said. "And it's like this big house, with a lot of rooms and no hallways in between."

"Separate . . . rooms?" Rima said. "You mean, where things happen depending on who's there?"

Lizzie nodded. "That's the way it is here because of all the thought-magic. And it's always night and really cold."

"Hell is cold," Eric muttered, and when Bode gave him a look, he added: "Dante. We read *Inferno* in school. The ninth circle of hell is a frozen lake."

"I remember that," Emma said. "Lucifer's trapped in ice up to his waist."

"And shrouded in a thick fog." After a pause, Rima continued, faintly, "We read it, too."

"Dad liked that book," Lizzie said. "Not the God stuff, but he and Mom said the ice was close to what it was like in a Peculiar: really, really, *really* cold."

"Yeah, that explains a lot." Grunting, Bode scraped another match to life. "Thought-magic."

"Bode, all she's talking about is *energy*," Eric said. "You took high school science, right? Heat is energy. Those matches? Friction on red phosphorus is enough to turn it, chemically, into white phosphorus, which ignites in air and releases heat. Take away heat, you bleed energy, which means that things cool down. You ever seen ice?"

"Of course. So?"

"Ice is solid because it's been cooled," Casey said. "Energy's been taken away. Add energy, *heat*, the molecules speed up and ice melts. It becomes liquid. Heat it enough, it turns to steam. It just depends on how much energy you add. If I know that much science, Bode, so do you. I think what Lizzie's saying is that the inside of a . . . a *Peculiar*? This kind of special container? It's cold for a reason."

"That's right. All the thought-magic slows down. It still *does* things, but it can't get out." Lizzie looked at Rima. "Like what happened to you guys. I know that was really bad, but not as terrible as it could've been. In a Peculiar, the thought-magic's not as strong."

Oh my God. Emma felt a flutter, like the wings of a trapped butterfly, in her throat. She'd spouted the same thing to Kramer. *Drop the temperature enough . . . She's saying that a Peculiar creates the conditions for a Bose-Einstein condensate.*

"So after Mom blew up the barn and everything," Lizzie said, "all that thought-magic from the whisper-man and my dad and all those Peculiars, which were full of extra thought-magic left over from your book-worlds—"

"Stop, stop," Bode said. "What do you mean, extra?"

"I mean . . . *extra*. Leftovers. Like, you know, you made too much macaroni and cheese." When Bode looked blank, Lizzie said, impatiently, "Well, you don't just leave leftovers out on the table or the floor, right? You put leftovers away, *into* something. Mom did the same thing with the thought-magic that Dad used to pull stories onto White Space. She had to, or the stories wouldn't stay on the page. So all that extra thought-magic in the Peculiars got loose and tangled up, all mixed together, with my dad and the whisper-man and became, you know, the *fog*."

There was a moment's silence. Emma didn't know about the others, but her head was crammed with so many questions, she wasn't sure in which order to ask or even think them. Having skimmed shelves of McDermott novels, she knew this much: there was a Bode novel, a Rima book. *Now Done Darkness* was Tony's story, and she'd counted twenty-two other novels. If he'd kept it up, McDermott might be into Stephen King territory by now.

But in all of that, there wasn't one completed book about—

"Why isn't there a book about us?" Casey suddenly asked. "We're here, but there's no Eric book, no Casey book."

"Terrific." Bode snorted. "Which means you guys are the only *real* people?"

"I *told* you, I don't know anything about that," Lizzie said.

"There's no Emma book either," Eric said.

"Not exactly," Emma said, and gestured at the parchment she'd brought down from Lizzie's room. She'd half-expected that red spidery scrawl to have disappeared, but it hadn't: *One June afternoon . . .*

"I think Emma's book was the one my dad was working on when Mom . . . when she . . . you know." The little girl pressed the heel of a hand to her pooling eyes. "There was a whole bunch of thought-magic spilling out all over the place, and that's when Emma got loose."

"'One June afternoon,'" Eric read, and lifted his eyes to hers. "It says that you went down cellar for a book. Did that happen?" When she nodded, he said, "Can you tell us what happened next? Do you remember?"

Oh yeah, in spades. The family room seemed suddenly much too hot. She didn't want to talk about this, and not only because it had scared her silly. Talking would make it real, because she would be putting words to an experience that felt like the distant cousin to what was happening to them now.

And everything—my blinks, *my blackouts—all that started where McDermott's fragment ends.*

She cleared her throat. "Like it says, I was a kid. I decided to forget it, try never to think about it. Most of the time, it's muddy, like a dream. But what the parchment says is right. It was June, a week after I turned twelve," she said, "when I went down cellar to look for a book."

EMMA
Down Cellar

THE FIRST THING she notices down cellar is the icy tongue of a draft licking her ankles.

Well, that's weird. Emma frowns. The cellar's got two rooms. The first has nothing very interesting: a boiler, a washer and dryer. But this second room is like a cave filled with treasure, chockablock with boxes and shelves and heaps of novels, including a special glassed-in cabinet of first-edition Dickens books Jasper keeps here, down cellar, where the temperature is always cool and the air kept very dry. There are also old comic books and stacks of science fiction, as well as tomes on science and history and art. There's a massive antique rolltop desk, too, locked up tight. She's run her hands over that thing a dozen times, searching for a hidden catch or knob that might release the rolltop. Her jewelry box has a secret compartment, so maybe there's some über-secret way of getting into the desk, too, but she finds nothing. Picking the lock also turns out to be way harder than in the movies, and she's finally let it be. Probably Jasper doesn't remember the desk's even here, hunkered in the dark.

But the draft is really strange. It doesn't belong at all. Inching on hands and knees, she follows the chill behind a tower of boxes butted against the south wall. There, etched on the wall and along the floor, is a perfect two-foot square. Instead of the gray wash used on the rest of the cellar's cinderblock, however, *this* square is a blinding, featureless, bone-bright white.

She rocks back on her heels, the better to study that blank. There is no doubt in her mind that Jasper has slathered the same paint here that he does on his canvases, but why? Is something beneath this? A painting on the cinderblock? She wouldn't put it past him. But the idea doesn't feel quite right.

Then her eyes catch a slight wink of brass, and she sees a pull-ring on the right, about midway down. The pull-ring is Emma-sized, just right for her hand. Had that been there a moment ago? She isn't sure. But there's no doubt now.

Wow. A little mouse of excitement scurries up her spine. *A door? Another room?* She laces her fingers through the pull-ring—and hesitates. She's not an idiot. There might be spiders, or bats, or dead things with gooshy innards waiting in the dark. Maybe Jasper's hidden this door for a good reason. Nightmares live under the white paint on his canvases, for heaven's sake.

Still, she can't resist, and pulls. At first, nothing happens, and she is about to pull harder when small flakes of white paint begin to snow in a fine flurry to the cool concrete. She feels the door gasp and shudder, as if suddenly waking from a deep sleep. Then the door gives; it *yawwwns* open on a silent, rushing exhalation of pent-up breath, the way she porpoises out of Superior's blue-black waters on a hot summer's day.

But behind the door, there is nothing. It is Pitch. Black. Just an inky square. The darkness almost doesn't look real. She can't see an inch into all that nothingness, and it smells funny: like when she scraped both her knees bloody the day she took a header off her bike.

Light. She races back upstairs, then pulls up and tiptoes into the front parlor. In the kitchen, the radio is yammering to itself, the reporter excitedly talking about police and victims and *murder*, but she doesn't care. Jasper is gone; probably sketching but mainly boozing before heading off to make arrangements for a kayak trip they'll take in a week's time to Devils Island. Sal's taken the truck to town for groceries. So Emma's safe, at least for the rest of the afternoon. Perfect. Stretching up on her toes, she filches a pack of matches from the fireplace mantel. In the kitchen pantry, she finds a plastic bag of used candles—Sal's *such* a cheapskate—and fishes out three blue stubs left over from her and Jasper's birthday cakes the week before.

Back downstairs again, lickety-split. She strikes a match: *psssttt!* The match head splutters to life, and then she raises her tiny torch to the dark. The blackness does not give. Inky shadows flee *from* her, splaying over the cement behind, but no light penetrates this third room. At. All.

Okay, that's even stranger. That's not the way light works. Or darkness, for that matter: if the room is empty, then nothing should prevent light from penetrating.

She reaches a tentative palm, like a mime tracing an invisible door, and instantly snatches it back. Whoa, *cold*. She *haahs* warm air onto her fingers, shaking her hand until the feeling needles back in darts and tingles. What she's felt is so frigid it burns—and hard, like a pane of black glass. Yet in that brief contact she felt the darkness, well . . . seem to *give* a teeny, tiny bit: as if the glass, smooth as a sheet of quartz crystal, morphed to a dense yet pliable cellophane.

But there *is* something else: a sound, scratchy with distance, seeping from that gloaming. What is that? She cocks her head, straining to tease out the components. The sound is as crackly as the weather band radio Jasper listens to whenever there's a big blow and Superior gets wild. So someone left on a radio? Like Sal has done upstairs? That doesn't make any sense, not even for Jasper. Probably just hearing a weird echo. And yet there is *something* making noise in there. No matter how hard she tries to pull the sound to her, however, all she gets are static-filled whispers, like the hiss of sand spun into a dust devil.

Whoa, wait just a second. The hairs on her neck suddenly spike with alarm as another thought occurs to her. What if there's someone *living* under Jasper's house? That stuff can happen. Over on the mainland, down around Ashland, bums hole up in broken-down shacks all the time. The news says so.

I shouldn't go in there, she thinks. *What if there are snakes? Or rats? Or something worse, like monsters and shadows, in the dark?* That could be. Maybe that's why Jasper's walled this up, so what's inside can't get out.

Or what if the black *is* the monster?

"That's just silly," she says. "It's your imagination. It's like when you listen to a seashell and hear the ocean. You're listening to air, that's all."

Candle in one hand, she reaches for the blackness, wincing

as her fingers meet that icy, glassy darkness, but forcing herself not to flinch back—and this time, there's a difference. This time, she hears the faintest, tiniest *click*. Like the snap of a light switch or the sound her little jewelry box makes when she reaches underneath and presses the little brass nib and—*snick-click*—the hidden compartment springs open.

Oh! Her heart does a spastic little flip. Now the glassy black membrane seems too thin and gives easily, and she watches as her hand and the candle slide into the dark.

Almost instantly, the flame dies and goes out.

What? Maybe the draft blew it out. But when she pulls out the candle, the yellow arrow of its flame still flickers. *Huh?* She eases the candle in again, and right away, the flame disappears—and so, she notices now, does her hand. Yet she still feels molten candle wax spilling onto her fingers. The sensation is distant, the wax's warmth leeching away quickly, as if sucked into a deep well. No pain, though. Just *cold* and—

And then, something inside hooks her wrist and *tugs*.

"Oh!" Emma ekes out a tiny, wheezing cry. *"No!"* She tries taking her hand back, but this something only tugs *harder*. From deep inside, the whispers suddenly swell, growing louder and more excited, the sound like the *scritch-scratch* of rats scurrying over glass. Stifling a shriek, she plants her feet on either side of the door and *pulls*. The darkness gives like grudging, soft taffy and then lets go with a sensation like the snap of a rubber band: *ka-twannnggg!*

She tumbles back, gasping. Her hand is still attached, all fingers accounted for, but the tips are white and icy. The candle's dead. A thin streamer of smoke curls from the blackened wick—and the molten wax has *frozen*.

There really *is* something—someone—in there. She sprawls, unmoving, paralyzed with fear, her heart going *thumpity-thumpity-thumpity-thump* in her chest. She felt a *hand*. There were *fingers*, and she *heard* it . . . *them*. They almost got her.

And what about the candle? Her hand? Once she pierced that darkness, she hadn't been able to see either. She's paid attention in science: no light + brain-freeze cold = . . . outer space? Or a really cold vacuum? But neither makes sense. There can't be a black space-hole under Jasper's house.

Then her mind jumps: *Matchi-Manitou, in his deep dark cave.* The Ojibwe say there's a big evil demon in a huge black cave under Devil's Island. Jasper goes over there all the time. He paints nightmares and then covers them up. He boozes and babbles about White Space and broken *Nows* and Dark Passages.

So maybe this is one of them, a Dark Passage, and this is like Devils Island. Her lungs are going so fast she's dizzy. *Catch a clue, Emma. You* live *in a cottage overlooking Devil's Cauldron.* So is this a tunnel that connects the two? Is *this* the Dark Passages Jasper's so scared of? No wonder Jasper's covered this over. He doesn't want whatever's in there getting out. *Or me or anyone going in. Something grabbed me. Something's whispering.* If Matchi-Manitou had gotten a really good grab and—*bam!*—she'd gotten hooked and reeled in like a salmon, what then? Would she have been able to see at all? Maybe she wouldn't want to. She'd be dinner. Matchi-Manitou would drink her blood and crunch her bones and eat her up, *munch-munch-munch.* Even if she'd managed to get away, where would she be? What if she ended up somewhere—some*when*—else?

You are not going to think about this anymore. The sweat pops on her forehead as she levers that door, really throws her weight against it. *You are going to forget all about this. Stick your fingers in your ears and la-la-la-la all the way back upstairs.*

The door is pissed. Doesn't want to close at all, nosirree-bob. She can feel it protesting, or maybe that's only what lives inside the dark exerting some force to keep her from closing it off again. From deep within, the whispers seethe, but there are so many she can't make out the words, which she thinks is probably good. She doesn't hear them; she's not *listening*, la-la-la-la . . .

Finally, grudgingly, the door grumbles shut. She doesn't dare look at that white blank too long either. If she does, she might see the ring again, and then the urge to pull open the door and *push* against the dark would be too strong.

Nope, no way, not going there. She works fast, wedging all those boxes tight-tight-tight against the white cinderblock. She covers that door and blots it from view. Hours later, when Jasper stumps back in, reeking of fish slime, bourbon, and the turp he uses to clean his brushes, she's at the kitchen table, an untouched glass of chocolate milk she doesn't want in her hands, as the radio yammers on and on about death and murder and blood, so much blood. Lost in a boozy fog, Jasper doesn't spare her a glance, and *she's* not telling. In fact, she decides right then and there not to . . .

EMMA
All Me

"... **THINK ABOUT IT,**" she said. "Until today I was doing a pretty good job, too. But some of what's happened *echoes* and circles back to that, even down to that little click. I heard the same thing at the library door." And in the vision of that insane asylum, come to think of it, when she'd locked the door in that iron grille.

"What if what you found was a force field put up by some machine?" Eric asked. "Like a . . . a device or *tool* or something?"

"That's what Dad called the Mirror," Lizzie said. "Same with the panops and Sign of Sure. He said they were all tools from a long time ago and another *Now.* I never thought of it before, but the time I saw my dad at the Mirror? When he . . . when he c-cut himself?" She knuckled her eyes, but Emma saw the tears starting again. "When he t-touched the M-Mirror, *it* made a c-click."

"But I didn't cut myself," Emma said. "It just *happened.*" Then thought: *Force field or barrier might be right, too. I keep thinking about where the barriers are thinnest. What would happen if those went away or sprang a leak?*

"Might work like a fingerprint ID for a computer," Eric said.

"You're saying the machine *recognized* me?"

"It kind of fits, doesn't it? Whatever was down cellar let you . . . well, log on."

"What?" Bode asked. "What a log got to do with anything? A log's just wood."

"It's just another word for a special kind of key," Casey said. "Only this key unlocks a machine."

Key. Emma felt the word hook her attention. *Lizzie said . . . or was it her dad . . . one of them mentioned a key.* But hadn't Frank McDermott also said that this key was something they'd read? *Yes, he said manuscript, and they found it in London.*

"But log on to a machine that can do what?" Rima asked. "Draw out energy that you can use to make a book? Or glass?"

"Or anything." Eric ran a hand over the hard edge of the coffee table. "Even something as simple as this. In the real world, the one we all think of as real, the only reason this wood table *stays* a table is because the energy required for wood and iron to hold their shapes is exactly right—*for that reality.* Add more energy—say, touch a match, start a fire—you destroy the wood's ability to hold that shape. You've added too much energy to the system and initiated a different reaction."

"Like the phase transition of ice to water, or water to steam," Emma said. "To *fog.*"

Eric nodded. "So I guess this . . . this Dark Passages energy stays put in our reality only if you use a certain amount and no more."

"You *know* . . . what happened out on the snow—those creatures just appearing, the church, Tania?" Sliding a copy of *Whispers* from the pile of books, Rima studied the cover art: the portrait of a girl with wild, staring eyes as black as oil and a frill of spider's legs blooming from her mouth. "If I let myself just accept the idea for a second that my story's already been written and the fog *is* energy waiting to be used and molded and fixed . . . it kind of explains a lot."

Bode barked a laugh. "How?"

"Look, outside this house, there's fog. Call it thought-magic, call it energy . . . whatever. Casey and I started out caught in a whole lot of *nothing*. Just . . . just fog," she said, although from the look she shot Casey, Emma almost thought she had been about to say something else. "But then *I* made things out of the fog because of who I am," Rima continued, skimming a light finger over the portrait's forehead as if trying to smooth back the girl's bangs. "I *made* Tania, and I did it because Lizzie's dad had already written it all out for me. I made . . ." She offered up the book with a slight shrug. "I made the *story* that I came from, or it built itself around me."

"But then why did it get so crazy?" Bode asked. "The way everything fell apart on the snow like that? Is *that* in the book?"

Lizzie sighed. "I *told* you. The book-world *Now* that she made broke. I think there were too many of you guys all together for too long on the White Space of the wrong story. Dad said that whenever a lot of book-people end up on the same White Space, they break it, because the stories can only go in certain directions. It would be like everyone all piling into a car and wanting to go his own way. But you've only got the one car," Lizzie said, like a kid regurgitating a lesson she's gone over so many times she could recite it in her sleep. "He said the wrong characters are like, you know, the things that give you a cold."

"You mean viruses? An infection?" Eric asked.

"It actually makes sense," Rima said. "That world was going pretty strong until you and Bode and Chad showed up and brought the . . . the *energy* of your stories. Like what you just said about adding energy to ice or wood? Only it was the *world* I was building from my story that broke."

"So where'd Chad go?" Bode said. "He's dead, right?"

"No. Well, sort of," Lizzie said. "He's just gone from *here*, this whole *Now*. He's back where he belongs, in his book-world."

"But Tony . . ." Casey nudged out *Now Done Darkness*, a book whose cover art—a bulbous, slimy-looking monster, with more tentacles than an anemone and what seemed a million eye stalks, chewing its way out of a woman's stomach—made Emma actually ill. "We saw him die. So, is he really dead? Does he die in his book?"

"No," Lizzie said. "I've visited that book-world a bunch of times."

"But he's *dead*," Casey repeated.

"Yeah, kind of," Lizzie said. "He got killed here, so he's *gone* from here. But he's not *dead* dead. Just who he was *here* is gone."

"What?" Casey said, but Rima interrupted, "I think there's a difference between dead and gone. I know what we saw, but . . ." Rima's fingers crept to a crocheted scarf wound in a loose cowl around her neck. "His whisper, in the scarf?

And his mother's? They just disappeared, as if they'd been erased, and that never happens. Taylor, for example." Rima stroked an arm of her ratty parka. "She's still here. Even when her whisper finally fades, there'll still be the tiniest trace, like a watermark. That makes sense because she's written into my story already. But there's *nothing* in this scarf. Tony isn't tangled up in my book, and if he was never a *person* but just the *idea* of one—the energy it takes to make a person come to life on a page—maybe that's why. It's like his chapter closed. Tony was never supposed to be here permanently." Rima nodded at *Now Done Darkness*. "*That's* the version of Tony we met, and he belongs *there*."

Lizzie's mouth worked. "I just *said* that." .

"But then how come he showed up to give Rima a ride?" Bode said. "That was still her . . . what? Book-world or something? And she and I met at the rest stop."

"That's because I was starting to pull you guys all together," Lizzie said. "It's hard, and I sometimes drop you where I don't mean to. Things would've fallen apart if I hadn't separated you all again. Right after that, all of you . . . you know, you think you drove here, but really, I dropped you into this *Now*."

"How do you *do* that?" Casey asked, as Eric said, "So can you get Tony again?"

"No, I can't," Lizzie said, choosing Eric's question. "Once you die in this *Now*, you can't come back here. You can be in other *Nows*, just not this one, or any *Now* where you get killed."

"Wait a minute." Bode frowned. "So let me get this straight. Tony's alive. So are Chad and Emma's friend?"

"Yes, Chad is in his book-world and"—the little girl waved

a hand through the air—"other *Nows*, but only one Chad is allowed in a *Now*, no matter if it's a book-world or, like, you know," Lizzie said, "a regular *Now*."

So this wasn't like *The Matrix*. Frowning, Emma worried the inside of her lip. Which would make sense, because the film was about a simulation: a Neo-avatar slotting into a computer program. In a regular *Now*—call it an alternative timeline—if she died, she was gone from that timeline, period. That didn't mean there weren't a lot of other Emmas and Bodes and Erics and on and on, like an infinite number of Xeroxed copies. But which was the original?

"Why do you call them that?" Bode frowned down at Lizzie. "*Nows*. I don't get that."

"Gosh, you *guys* . . . You're thinking in straight lines too much. Look. Here's the difference." Sweeping up *Echo Rats*, she cracked open the covers and jabbed a page. "*That's* a book-world *Now*." She flipped two-thirds of the way through. "Here's another *Now*." She turned the page. "This is another book-world *Now*," she said, stabbing the left-hand page and then the facing page, "and that's another." She riffled the pages in a fan. "All of these, the pages, they're all book-world *Nows*. There's no *yesterday* in a book-world. There's no *tomorrow*. There is only the page where you start reading, and you can skip around back and forth and start wherever you want. Do you get it? You can read a book from what you *think* is the beginning to the end—go on, follow all the stupid numbers—and then start all over again, or in the middle; it doesn't matter. You can *decide* where the beginning is, because the book-world is the book-world. It *never* changes. That's not the same as a *Now* where there's Christmas and stuff and people get older and things like that, but there are lots and lots of different *Nows* and you can visit them by going through the Dark Passages."

"To visit different timelines," Eric said, "or alternative universes."

"Fine, *whatever.*" Sudden tears pooled in Lizzie's eyes as her lower lip quivered. "What's so *hard* about this?" Lizzie hurled *Now Done Darkness* across the room, the book doing an awkward cartwheel to crash against a wall. "For book-people who are all *me*, you're so *stupid*!"

After a moment, Bode said, "All *me*? Say what?"

EMMA
Tangled

THE CRAZY QUILT was a rainbow riot: scraps from every bit of clothing Lizzie had ever worn, decorated not only with the Sign of Sure in its web but very special glass figures and alphabet beads Meredith McDermott had used to spell out Lizzie's full name:

ELIZABETH LINDSAY MCDERMOTT

These same beads had been rearranged to form other names, too, and in various combinations:

There were more names, too: EARL and ANITA, LILY, even MARIANE. Emma picked out SAL *waaaay* off in one corner of a sliver of black velvet. There were still many others she didn't know: BETTE. ZANE. DOYLE. BATTLE. All characters who existed in other book-worlds but had no part in her story.

But if I'm writing my own, and part of me is tangled up with Lizzie . . . Emma's eyes crept back to the glass beads that spelled out ERIC. *I can only imagine so far, and no further?* No, no, wait a second, wait just a minute . . . that couldn't be true. Her gaze swept across the quilt, and then she felt the air ease from her throat. Okay, no KRAMER. No JASPER either, not that she could see right away. The quilt was about half the size and length of a twin bed, and it would take time to pick over and parse out everything. But she knew on a deep, gut level: Jasper just wouldn't be there.

There's no J in Lizzie's name, and she said I made Kramer myself. So, did I also make Jasper? That thought promoted another, something that had bothered her but which, at the time, she couldn't afford to dwell on because she'd been running for her life: *In that insane asylum, Kramer called him John, like that was Jasper's first . . .* She felt her heart kick start in her throat. *No, no, that can't be right.*

At her sudden intake of breath, Eric threw her a small frown, but she only shook her head, not trusting in her voice. *And I don't even want to know what this means.* Because she had finally put something together, a puzzle over which her mind must've been working, like a computer laboring, quietly, toward a solution at once inescapable and irrefutable.

2

IT WENT LIKE this.

Jasper was obsessed with a lot of things: the Dark Passages and horrific nightmarish creatures and *Nows*—and Dickens. So Emma knew a fair amount about the writer, including this: sometime in the mid-1860s, Dickens, along with his mistress and her mother, was in a catastrophic train accident that should've killed him. Of the train's seven first-class carriages, Dickens' car was the only one *not* to plunge from a viaduct and into a river at Staplehurst in Kent. For hours after the accident, Dickens tended the injured. Some died before his eyes.

The accident was something academics like Kramer loved to point to as the metaphor for Dickens himself: imperious, selfish, bombastic, a bit of the egomaniac whose life was going off the rails. At the time of the crash, the writer had been in the middle of *Our Mutual Friend*, which might have been lost if Dickens hadn't remembered to retrieve the manuscript from his overcoat, which he'd left in the railway carriage, before boarding an emergency train to London.

Badly shaken and already in poor health, Dickens actually lost his voice for several weeks. His kids and friends said he never fully recovered, would get the shakes on any but the slowest of trains. Worse, Dickens struggled to finish *Our Mutual Friend*. Never at a loss, his next installment was several pages short. Either he was used up or traumatized—probably a bit of both; the guy was pretty manic to begin with—but his best writing days were behind him, the crash the beginning of the end. *Our Mutual Friend* bombed, and Dickens didn't attempt another book for five long years. But when he did, he decided to try something that, for him, was pretty radical: a murder mystery. He decided on *The Mystery of Edwin Drood*.

But he never finished. Exhausted from grueling reading tours in the intervening years, Dickens keeled over from a stroke at his Gad's Hill estate after a day's work on *Drood*, and that was that.

She and Jasper used to try to work out the rest of the story, figure out whodunit, just for fun. So did a lot of people; several authors had taken stabs. Some literary groups and fan clubs still held *Drood* competitions as part of Dickens festivals.

And way, way back—early 1900s, she thought—there was even a mock trial, where a bunch of famous people, like George Bernard Shaw, got together and heard evidence about the character that Dickens hinted in a letter to his biographer, Forster, was the murderer.

She might be writing her life, yet one thing was now dead certain: if Jasper was a creation, he wasn't hers. In fact, she now wondered why she'd never noticed this before.

Because Edwin Drood's killer was John Jasper.

3

OKAY. HER HEART was galloping in her chest. *Calm down. Think this through.*

Say, for argument's sake, that Eric was right. In *this* universe, she was like Jasper, a character created under very special circumstances with weird tools and constructed of a bizarre sort of energy that had gotten loose to write her own life. She—and maybe Jasper, too—was unique because certain, very special machines recognized her: the cynosure, for example, and whatever lurked in Jasper's cellar. The Dickens Mirror might have responded to her as well, if Lizzie's mom hadn't destroyed it.

But *why* would it? Because she had too *much* of whatever McDermott had pulled from the Dark Passages? Meredith McDermott always sealed extra energy away in a Peculiar, a Bose-Einstein condensate that rendered the energy inert, unable to . . . well, get free, do damage, whatever. So the machines recognized her, one of their own, because she was unbound, unfinished, filled with just enough juice? And if the energy to make her came from the Dark Passages, did that mean these devices originally belonged to whatever lived there?

Lizzie says tangled *a lot.* If she followed Rima's reasoning— that the versions of Rima and Tony and Bode she was seeing now were set because they'd come from a book-world—then Lizzie's finding and hanging on to *her*, a character who was unbound, ought to be a lot harder. *Unless this version of me, the one McDermott was writing, is tangled up with all the other book-worlds, as well as Lizzie, her dad, and the whisper-man.* Following Lizzie's loopy logic, that meant *she* had McDermott in her, too.

Just as Jasper had some of Dickens in *him*?

What did that mean? Could McDermott have actually *known* Dickens in that other London? And what about the fact that there was no KRAMER on Lizzie's quilt? She supposed not every single character in every single McDermott novel could be modeled on or incorporate bits of Lizzie. But if you believed the academics, writers always slotted in portions of their lives into their work, whether they knew it or not. So could Kramer be a piece of—or stand-in for—something or someone else? McDermott, perhaps? *His first name was Frank . . . no, Franklin.* So that *would* work; all the letters you needed to make KRAMER were right there.

Following that reasoning, *she* ought to have pieces of *all* of them: Bode, Tony, Rima, Chad, and on and on. So would that same *tangled*-ness make it easier for the machines to recognize her? It might even explain these weird echoes—how they all tended to use the same phrases, for example.

Whoa, wait. What if *she* was the one making up all of them? What if *she* had dreamed up Lizzie? But why would she do that?

Well, Jesus, all she had to do was think about her so-called life. She'd taken that psych course. Why did any little kid dream up imaginary friends? *Because she's lonely. No one wants her.* She fit the bill: cast-off, ugly, traumatized, all-around weird. Sure, Jasper pulled a save, got her fixed up, made her . . . well, into a normal-looking person, a girl someone might even think was halfway decent-looking. Maybe.

But had she made herself a protector—because she'd desperately needed one? *John Jasper was Edwin Drood's uncle, and his guardian.* So had she heard or read the story and then somehow brought John Jasper, unbound and unfinished, *to* her? Conjured up *these* people and this situation because she wanted friends? It fit. Wasn't she the one lusting after an imaginary guy whose story she couldn't finish?

Wait, wait. Slow down. She could feel the heat in her cheeks. Yes, Eric was nice; he was perfect, exactly what she'd always imagined. She felt the connection, this *pull.* Look how he'd risked his neck to come after her and Lily. The way he looked at her made her feel . . . special.

But there's Casey; don't forget that. She gave herself a mental shake. *Eric knows him. Casey's his brother. So that clinches it right there, you nut: you can't possibly be causing this. Stop freaking yourself out. For God's sake,* you *didn't dream up Frank McDermott or purple panops or a cynosure or a Dickens Mirror.*

Had she?

4

"SEE?" LIZZIE SAID to Bode. "That's what I mean. You're *all* me, some of you more and some of you less. It's the way Dad wrote you. Emma's just got more of me in her than the rest of you do."

"Wait a minute, wait a minute," Bode said. "Putting aside the fact that, you know, I'm a *guy* and in the Army, and you're just this little kid . . . so you filch a couple letters and spell my name. So what? Those are beads. They're glass."

"No. They're Mom's thought-magic." Sniffing, Lizzie smoothed the quilt over the hardwood floor. "It's like Daddy said: look hard enough and all the pieces of me—and all of you—are tangled up, right here, forever and ever."

"No." Bode folded his arms over his chest. "It's bullshit. I don't buy it. I don't see that this proves anything. You could make my name out of . . . *Beauregard.*"

"Sorry, dude," Eric said. "No *O.*"

Bode flushed an angry plum. "You know what I'm saying. C'mon, Devil Dog, why are you so ready to believe all this?"

"Because." Eric threw up his hands. "I want to move on already. Enough emo, guys, really. Fussing about this isn't going to change the fact that we're stuck here and have to deal, period. The sooner we get past this, the sooner we can figure out *why* we're here and then get out."

"I can dig that," Bode said. "But I don't have to believe this to—"

No, I think, actually, you do. The rules here were so different, they wouldn't get far if they couldn't start thinking outside the box. "Bode," Emma said, "what's your last name?"

"What? Well, it's . . ." After another moment, Bode's face darkened. "What kind of stupid question is that?"

"Stupid"—Eric hunched a shoulder in an apologetic shrug to Emma—"but she's right, dude. Your name tape says BODE. Is that your last name, or first?"

"It's my name," Bode said.

"And you know that because . . . ?"

"Because I know it, all right?" Bode touched the name tape with a finger. "Says so right there, and it's . . . you know . . . in my head."

Casey glanced at Rima. "Can you spell *tautology*?"

"Yes." But she wasn't smiling. Rima's hand had crept to her lips, and she looked as if she might be sick. "It's not funny, Casey."

"Yeah," Bode said, but without a lot of muscle behind it.

"Okay, so it's on your uniform," Eric said. "Then it has to be your last name, right? So, what's your first name?"

"It's . . . it's . . ." Bode shot Eric a thunderous look. "All right, I don't know. I don't *know*. I'm *Bode*, okay? That's who I am."

"Oh God." Rima's skin was pale as porcelain. "You know, until Emma asked, I didn't realize, but . . . I don't remember my last name either. I'll bet if Tony were here, it would be the same for him, and Chad." She looked at Eric and Casey. "What about you guys?"

Eric and Casey looked at each other, and then Casey's mouth dropped open. "No," he whispered. "Eric?"

"I'm sorry, Case," Eric said, "but I don't know either."

Emma kept her mouth shut, grateful that no one asked her. After all, her last name, Lindsay, was right there in a scream of big block capitals. *My last name is her middle name. No wonder she says we're the closest, that I have the most of her.* Come to think of it, she didn't know Sal's last name, or Mariane's. Kramer was only Kramer.

Stop. Eric's right. I could go around and around forever, but I've got to start with a given: I'm real. *No matter what Lizzie says, I'm not words on a page. I like cherry sundaes in tulip glasses, and I save the whipped cream for last. I drink mocha Frappuccinos. I remember blue candles on birthday cakes and watching 9/11 in school and . . .*

Her thoughts hitched up then, because she realized that she didn't know something else very, very important. "Lizzie, when did your dad die? What year?"

"I . . ." Lizzie licked her lips. "I don't remember."

"How can you not know?" Bode asked.

Lizzie was very pale. "I just *don't*, okay?"

"When's your birthday?" Emma asked.

"That's easy," Lizzie said, with more than a little relief. "June ninth."

"What?" Bode came out of his slouch. *"What?"*

"That's *my* birthday," Rima said, faintly. "Bode?"

He looked away, but Emma saw the small muscles ripple along his jaw. "Same day," he said.

"Mine too." Eric paused, and then he looked at Casey. His

eyebrows folded in a slow frown. "But yours—"

"I don't know." Casey gave Eric a wild look. "I should *know* my own birthday, but I . . . I don't remember!"

"What about you?" Bode said to Emma.

"Same." Jasper and she shared the same birthday, which she'd once thought was just, well, coincidence. But now . . . *Except for Casey, we've all got blue eyes, too. Lizzie's and mine are exact matches. All of us are the same because we're tangled up together, with Lizzie, and, through her, with her dad. All except . . .*

"I don't *know* when I was born," Casey said again, and Rima reached for his hand. "I don't even remember the *year*. But I know I'm sixteen. So what the hell, why can't I remember?"

"What about you?" Emma said to Lizzie. "What year were you born?"

Lizzie opened her mouth, then closed it. A look of absolute bewilderment flooded into her face.

"You don't remember," Bode whispered. "Jesus, you don't *know*."

"Easy," Eric said, though even he looked a little shaky. "She's just a kid."

"Yeah. Okay. Easy. Let's . . . let's take it . . ." Bode raked both hands through his dark, close-cropped hair. "Jesus, I can't deal with this anymore, okay? What's the bottom line? Why did you bring us here, and what the *hell* we got to do to get out?"

"It's like I told Emma." Lizzie's cobalt eyes dropped to her hands. "I need you to get my dad. If we can, then I think he can help us."

"What do you mean, help us?" Bode said. "We were fine

until *you* got it in your head to put us in this mess!"

"Oh yeah," Eric said. "Shot at by Vietcong and crawling through tunnels full of booby traps. You were doing great."

"How can we get your dad, Lizzie?" Casey said. "He's dead."

"No." Lizzie shook her head. "Not really."

"Dead is dead," Bode said. "Gone is gone. You just *said* . . ."

"Like I don't *know* that." Lizzie's expression darkened with anger, and her eyes deepened to that odd and smoky sapphire glimmer Emma had trouble reading. "He's gone from that Wisconsin," the little girl said, "but he was tangled up in the whisper-man, and the whisper-man's in my special *Now*."

As are you, and yet . . . Putting aside how bizarre this all was, Emma felt this tickle of uneasiness along her neck. Lizzie could obviously leave this place long enough to grab them. *Yet if she and her dad and the whisper-man and the leftover energies from every Peculiar are tangled together* . . . She could feel her brain inching toward something else she could *sense* but didn't quite know yet.

"So, your dad's *here*?" When Lizzie nodded, Bode said, "Where?"

"He's the barn," she said.

"The one outside?" Bode turned a frown to them before looking back at Lizzie. "So what's the problem?"

"I can't find him. Whenever it sees new people, it adds rooms and I get lost."

"What? A barn can't make more rooms."

"Sure it can," Lizzie said, "if it's alive."

ERIC
What Does That Make Us?

"SO WHAT ABOUT the snowmobile?" Yanking open another cupboard, Bode stared at the shelves crammed with Kraft macaroni and cheese. "Man, I see one more Blue Box, I'm gonna pound somebody."

"There's a loaf in the bread box," Eric said. He was sitting on a kitchen chair, with his right leg propped on another. Emma had eased up his bloody jeans to the knee, exposing an ugly eight-inch rip in the calf he'd snagged on that ruined guardrail . . . God, *hours* ago, from the feel of it. *Days.* The deep gash was ragged and crusted with old blood. Emma had dug up both a first aid kit in a downstairs bathroom and a half-bottle of antibacterial soap under the kitchen sink, which was, Eric thought, a little odd. *Almost like the house knew we might need it.* "Couple jars of peanut butter in the pantry."

"Christ no," Bode said. "Only thing peanut butter's good for in Charlie rats is stopping you up if you got the runs."

"Charlie rats?" Emma looked up, a crumpled gauze,

spotted with bright red blood, in one hand. "What is it with you guys and rats?"

"What?" Bode looked confused. "No. It's short for C-rations. Rations. Rats?"

"You mean, MREs?"

"No . . . ah . . . you know, MCIs." At her blank expression, Bode said, "Meal, Combat, Individual? Canned food? It's what the Army gives us for chow."

"Cans?" Emma said.

"We use plastic now, and they have a different name," Eric said.

"Really?" Bode's eyebrows arched. "Cool. How do they taste?"

"Uh . . . well, you know . . ." He bit back a grunt as Emma touched moist, soapy gauze to the torn meat of his wound. His mangled muscles twitched as if jumping out of the way. Between the pain and the gasoline reek from his and Emma's parkas, which they'd draped over some spare chairs, he was starting to get a little woozy, too. He cleared his throat, grimacing at the faint chemical taste on his tongue. "I've only had a couple, in basic, but they're okay, I guess. Although they still put in peanut butter, so you'd probably still hate them."

"Naw, nothing's worse than ham and motherfu . . . uh, lima beans," Bode said, with a sidelong glance at Emma. "Anything else in this place?"

"Oreos in the cookie jar and *bags* . . ." His thoughts derailed at another jab of pain. "Bags of M&Ms in the pantry," he finished in a gasping exhale. To Emma: "Go easy. Feels like you're scraping bone."

"Maybe because it's *deep*," she said. "Hold still. I've got to clean it."

"That's it for food?" Bode said.

"Stop complaining. Those are all the important food grou—*aaahhh*." At another knifing hack of pain, he gripped his chair seat with both hands. "Jesus."

"Stop being such a baby," Emma said, adding the soiled gauze, now the color of a cranberry, to a growing pile. "Just a little bit more, and then I'll rinse it out, smear on some ointment, and bandage it up." Tearing open another pack, she dipped the gauze into a small bowl of warm, sudsy water, then carefully spread the wound with the fingers of one hand. From where he sat, Eric saw pink muscle and a minute layer of yellow fat curds just under the skin. "You really could use some stitches, though."

"I could do that, no sweat," Bode said.

"No thanks. I *know* where you got your training." He smeared pain-sweat from his forehead with the back of one hand. To Emma: "You seem like you know what you're doing."

"Mmm. Lots of practice." The corner of her mouth quirked in a grin. "My Uncle—well, guardian—Jasper was always getting dinged up on his boat. Once he hooked himself with this big old nasty barb right here." She pointed to her left cheek. "Just missed the eyeball. *That* was fun. He blamed it on the group he took out that day; said they brought bananas. If he'd known, he'd never have let them on."

"What's wrong with bananas?" he asked.

"Bad luck for boats." Emma shrugged. "Don't ask me. Anyway, he wouldn't go into the emergency room. Made me take it out right there at the kitchen . . ." She suddenly straightened, the grin slipping off and a look he couldn't decipher creasing her forehead and cutting small lines at the corners of her narrowed eyes. "At the kitchen table." She paused. "Just like now."

"Hey." Leaning forward, he touched a finger to her right forearm and felt her shiver. "You okay?"

"You look kind of peaky," Bode said.

"No, it's . . ." Shaking her head, she exhaled. "I'm fine. Just a little déjà vu."

"So what *about* the sled?" Bode asked, returning to his first question. "Can we use that to get out of here?"

"We've been over this . . . Hey, Case," he said, as his brother wobbled through the kitchen door. "Where's Rima?"

"Upstairs," Casey said, gingerly lowering himself into a straight-back chair. "Lizzie wanted something from her room, and Rima didn't think she should go alone."

And you let them go? Alone? That they weren't all in the same place where they could keep an eye on each other made him uneasy, but he kept his mouth shut. Casey had been so edgy before, not himself. The way his little brother looked now only scared him more. The hollows beneath Casey's eyes were as livid and purple as the bruises on his neck and that huge lump on his jaw. God, had Big Earl punched Casey before, back at the cabin, and he'd just not noticed? And that thing in the snowcat choking the life out of him . . . *Too close. A couple more seconds, Casey would've . . .*

"Did I hurt you?" Emma said, suddenly looking up.

"What?" He had to work to look away from visions of Casey lying dead in that snowcat, or broken, his blood seeping between the warped boards of that damned cabin, as Big Earl bellowed.

"I asked if I hurt you," she said, her careful eyes on his. "You jumped."

"No, it's okay," he said, but he heard how rough his tone was, and swallowed. "So, Case . . . how you feeling?"

"Betcha still hurting," Bode said. "You're pretty beat up, kid."

"I'm okay," Casey said, though a small grunt escaped as he shifted on his chair. "Is there anything to drink?"

"Moo juice in the fridge." Bode opened a cupboard. "Or you gotchyer Kool-Aid, gotchyer Swiss Miss, and we got water."

Casey made a face. "That's it?"

"Not unless you can figure a way to suck macaroni and cheese through a straw. What'll it be, kid?"

"Hot chocolate. I can get it," Casey said, half rising and then cautiously sliding back onto his seat as Bode waved him down. "Okay, if you're offering. Thanks."

"You sure you're all right?" Eric heard the slight nagging note, but he hated this feeling of helplessness more. "Emma, is there anything like aspirin or something in the med kit?"

"Yes," she said, giving him a long look he couldn't read. "Some Motrin, too."

"What's that?" Bode asked.

"Ah . . . like aspirin, only not." She looked back at Casey. "Might make you feel better."

"No, really, guys, stop fussing. It's not like I'm a doll . . . What?" Casey looked from Eric to Emma and back. "What'd I say?"

"Déjà vu all over again," Emma said, and hunched a shoulder. "We seem to keep repeating some of the same phrases, that's all."

"If we're as tangled as Lizzie says, maybe that's what happens," Eric said.

"Naw, come on." Bode flapped a hand. "They're just expressions."

"You really believe that?" Emma said. "Still?"

Casey filled the small silence that followed. "So why were you guys talking about the sled?"

"Bode wants to bug out," Eric said.

"Hey, Devil Dog." Bode ran water from the tap into a kettle. "When you say it like that, sounds like I want to cut and run just when things are getting hairy."

"Well, you do."

"Then what would we do about Lizzie?" Casey asked. "We can't leave her here."

"Watch me." Bode set the kettle on the stove, then turned on the gas. A hiss, and then a circlet of blue flame sprouted. "Now, see, that's just wrong. Where's the gas *coming* from? What's powering the lights?"

"Everything. This place, the fog . . . that's how it works here. Or just think of everything as energy, just in different forms." Emma paused, her eyes ticking back to Eric's again. "Even us."

The same thought had occurred to him. Odd, how the two of them seemed to be on the same wavelength. But it was a good feeling, one he'd never had before. "I don't see it happening any other way."

"You know, you guys keep looking at each other like

that," Bode said, prying the plastic cap off a can of Swiss Miss, "one of you's gonna catch fire."

Eric saw the spots of sudden color on Emma's cheeks as she ducked her head. "No," she said, carefully drying his wound with clean gauze. "I was just thinking about how this must work, that's all."

"Uh-huh," Bode said, spooning cocoa mix into a mug. "You keep telling yourself that."

Eric changed the subject. "Look, Bode, if I thought we stood a chance on the sled, I'd try, but we don't, because there are too many of us, and I'm not leaving anyone behind. Even if we *could*, where would we go? We might wander around for hours and be right back where we started, or lost in the snow, which would be ten times worse—if the fog even lets us get that far."

"He's right." Emma squirted a thin worm of clear antibiotic ointment into Eric's gash. "We're not going anywhere until we finish this thing."

"Whatever *this thing* is," Bode said. "Me, I personally don't get it. What's so hard about getting her dad out of some creepy old barn?"

"Well," Casey said, blowing on his hot cocoa, "obviously something. Eventually, we're going to have to go over and find out what."

"Aw, no." Bode raised his hands in a warding-off gesture. "Count me out. Let the kid fight her own battles."

"So what, you're going to sit here, eat macaroni and cheese, and complain?" Eric said as Emma began to wrap a gauze roll around his calf. "That's your plan?"

"For that matter, what makes you think House or the

fog will let you?" Emma looked up at Bode. "House created rooms and sent me places. So we're doing the barn, Bode. It's only a matter of when . . . and who. I don't think we can go out one at a time either. She brings people over in groups for a reason, probably trying to find the right combination."

"Of what?" Bode asked.

"Skills? We all must have something. Rima's got that whisper-sense going. Emma can use the memory quilt, and she pulled us here," Eric said.

"Yeah, well . . ." For an instant, Bode's eyes unfocused, flicking left before firming on Eric's face. "*I'm* nothing special. What about you and the kid?"

"Beats me." Although he thought he saw a shadow whisk through Casey's face. "Maybe it depends on what the barn throws at us."

"So you think the barn's like House?" Emma said.

"Has to be." He'd been thinking about this. "Remember what Lizzie said: not *my dad's in the barn*. She said *he's* the barn. It's kind of subtle, but given your experience in this house . . ."

"So what?" Bode said.

Eric watched Emma think about this, then give a slow nod. "You mean that the barn was his space. It's where her dad worked. So the barn is . . . him? A manifestation, a way for her to see him?" she said. "Or only a product of how she thinks about him?"

"Maybe all those things," he said.

"Then why not just make him a person?" Casey asked.

"She might not be able to. She keeps saying *tangled*. Maybe that barn's as much of her dad as the fog allows her to see." Of course, this begged the question of just how *they* were supposed to untangle the guy's, well, energy or essence or whatever.

"Huh." Casey took a meditative sip of his cocoa, then stared into his mug. "Kind of makes you wonder what this house is. Or who."

"It's probably like the barn. Not one thing or person, but pieces all mixed together."

"But with one dominant personality, maybe," Emma said. "As scary as the rooms and visions have been, every-thing I saw and did was built upon what came before it. Every situation put me into another where I was given an example of what I had to do and then"—Emma seemed to test the word before she said it—"*prompted* to do exactly what I'd been shown. Sort of okay, here's *how* and now *you* try. I don't know if House was playing with, showing, or training me up until I finally got the idea of what I was here to do. Just like Lizzie said."

"Could be all three." He'd thought about this, too. *Emma has to be part of this, somehow; the* reason *the rest of us are here.* It was the only thing that made sense. Lizzie tried various characters in various combinations, so they must each have a part to play—but Lizzie said that Emma was more *tangled* with her than the rest of them. Only Emma had been shown the memory quilt. If that cynosure was a machine, it recognized Emma, and she'd used that to reach through and pull them here. This house showed Emma something very much like this Dickens Mirror.

Emma has to be the key, a focal point.

Which made him wonder: assuming Lizzie had always known Emma was more tangled than they, had Emma been here before, with others, but failed? *Or maybe only they died in this place, but Lizzie somehow got Emma out?* That actually might be just one more component to Emma's strange seizures or fugues, those *blinks.*

She might have been here before, but when she wasn't ready or hadn't acquired the necessary skills. He studied Emma as she snipped paper tape to secure the gauze wrap around his leg. *So what if all this—the crash, this valley, all this death—what if this has been designed for Emma, too?*

Aloud, he said only, "The house might have a lot of her mom in it."

"Or what a little kid would wish for and associate with her mom. Lizzie said Meredith died before Lizzie could finish this place." Emma paused, then added, with a shrug, "On the other hand, no one ever found a body, so it's a decent thought. House is the only place with light. It's warm. There's food."

"So if a piece of her mom, or the *idea* of her, takes care of Lizzie and makes food, gives us a place to rest and be safe," Casey asked, "what does her dad . . . what does the barn make?"

"Maybe what Frank McDermott made best," Eric said.

"Books?" Bode asked.

"No." Emma shook her head. "Monsters. Death. Things that live in the dark."

"Hell," Bode said after a pause, "you're talking about a tunnel. A lot of nightmares in a black echo, and they aren't all human."

"For *you*," Eric said, and glanced at his brother. "I'll bet it's a different nightmare for each of us."

"Different characters, different books." Emma gave them

all a strange look. "I wonder if that's why the others Lizzie brought here before failed."

"How do you mean?" Bode asked.

"I get it." As soon as she'd said it, Eric knew what she was driving at. "Once they hit the barn, they must meet up with their monsters."

"Jesus." Bode's eyes widened. "You mean they *die*? Like that kid, Tony?"

"I don't see how it can be any other way," he said. "Otherwise, the people she's brought before would still be here, trying to figure a way out."

"Aw, man." Bode hooked his hands around the collar of his BDU as if it was a ledge and he was hanging on for dear life. "Aw, *man*."

"Eric, if that's true, and we're all . . . you know, *his*, like he's our *father*"—Casey shot him an anxious look—"then what about *us*? What does that make *us*? If everything is all tangled here, doesn't that make us a little like him, and *all* the monsters? And God, what does that make Liz—" Breaking off, Casey frowned up at the ceiling at the same moment that Eric heard something: sharp but short, as if cut in two.

"Did you—" Emma began as Bode said, "Hey, you hear . . ."

But it was Casey who moved first. "Oh God," he said, bolting up from the table so quickly his mug overturned with a slosh. "That was Rima."

RIMA

A Safe Place

"**WOW, GREAT ROOM,**" Rima said, and meant it. She took in the plush carpet, pink walls, the litter of toys. "I've never seen a loft bed before."

"It was my idea." Lizzie was crouched beneath the bed, fiddling with a wood box overflowing with various miniature Ken and Barbie-like dolls clearly meant for play with that dollhouse. "I wanted a private space just like my dad, so Dad got it built for me special, same as my dollhouse."

"It's really nice." Rima knelt beside the little girl. The dollhouse was a painted lady: a riot of Victorian bric-a-brac, with gabled roofs and turrets. "So, is this where you spend most of your time?" Odd. She hadn't thought about that until now, but here was this ageless little girl stuck where time had no meaning and there was virtually no sense of place. *It's like being locked in a padded cell on a mental ward.* She eyed the toys. *Or trapped in a dollhouse.*

"Some." Lizzie hunched a shoulder, her attention focused on sifting through and pulling out very specific dolls that, at a glance, seemed oddly mismatched, as if they came from many different sets. "I like to play, but I'm not always here. I can leave for a little while."

"Leave the house to come get one of us from a"—she stumbled—"a book-world." She *did* believe the girl's story and Emma's theories, but only because arguing against what was going on didn't change anything and she knew what she'd experienced. *And I have to believe that Tony, or some version of him, is alive somewhere.* If Emma and Eric were right about alternative timelines, Tony could be anywhere, even lurking in a future chapter of her own story. Casey, too: slotted into the life she knew as a boy she simply hadn't met yet.

"Yeah," Lizzie said. "It's kind of hard, but I can do that. I can visit, too."

"Visit?" She blinked. "What do you mean?"

"You know . . . come over and visit. To *play.*"

"A . . ." She fumbled. "Like a playdate?"

"Yeah. I play with most of you guys, but mainly Emma." Lizzie was unwinding a miniature scarf from a girl doll's neck, spooling and unspooling it around a finger the way a chameleon shot and then recalled its sticky tongue. "I only come when you're asleep, though."

"When I'm . . ." Her heart did a quick, surprised fillip. "Why? I mean . . . why when we're asleep?" *And what do you mean, we play?*

"Because you guys are harder. You're, you know . . . you're *set.* Emma's way easier. She and I play a lot. In a way, it's nice when you're set the way you are, because it makes you easier to see and find. But it can also be a bad thing."

"How come?" She couldn't believe she was actually having this conversation, although she wasn't sure that while she could say the words, she understood their meanings. *See us better because we're set?* "Are you saying that it's easier to find us on the . . . the page? In the book-world?"

"Yeah. I mean, it's not *super* easy, because for a book-person, the book-world *is* the *Now*. It's all you know, but you can still go a lot of places in it. Dad called them subplots and subtexts and things that happen off stage. They're like . . . hidden compartments in a jewelry box or something. In a book, you can read about a book-person's day or one *hour* out of a day or *five minutes*, and then—*poof*—a chapter later, or the very next page or paragraph, it's the day before or after or next week or even two months later, a *year*. You could be on a different *planet*. But what about all the time and space in between, see? Those are the hidden, secret parts, all the good stuff between the lines nobody ever thinks about but that has to be there. Book-people can find their way there and do all kinds of things, especially when they've got parts of what lives in the Dark Passages in them. That's why people liked my dad's books so much; the book-worlds were so *real* they could get lost in them. Dad said the stories got under their skin and lived inside. A ton of people even wrote themselves into the book-worlds and dressed up like their favorite characters and went on and on and on, sometimes for their whole lives. Dad called it"—Lizzie screwed her face in thought—"fan fiction."

The whole universe between the covers of a book. But parts of what lives in the Dark Passages? Did she mean the energy in the Dark Passages . . . whatever *that* was?

"But it's also kind of bad, too," Lizzie continued. "To grab the book-world you, I mean. It's like you're wearing a big old sign: *I'm Rima.* That makes it way easier for the others in the Dark Passages to notice you. Then they try to grab on, like catching a ride, and oh boy, you don't want that."

Forget words she could say: she felt like she'd stumbled into a blurry foreign film from Outer Mongolia with no subtitles. "Others? You mean like what grabbed Emma when she was a little girl?" Then she thought of something else: "Wait a second, you said you came to visit book-worlds, right? But Lizzie, you said a book-world's not a *Now.* A . . . a timeline is a *Now,* an alternative universe. And the Dark Passages . . . you said they were big halls between *Nows.* There aren't Dark Passages between you and book-worlds, right?"

"Right, only between the *Nows,* and they're big, long, *really* dark halls," Lizzie said, "with lots and lots of shadows and places to hide."

Places to hide? "But Lizzie, if you can only grab book-people with some of *you* in them and *they* only know book-worlds, even the books with lots of hidden compartments . . . how are the book-people getting into the Dark Passages?"

"Because I take them."

"But why? How? Don't you need the Mirror for that?"

The little girl gave Rima a *no, silly* look. "I've never needed the Mirror to get from one *Now* to the next. All I have to do is think a *Now,* then the Sign of Sure shows me and I go and play for as long as I want. Well . . ." A finger of dark oil seemed to glimmer through her blue-blue eyes. "I *used* to be able to stay a long time. I can't now. Like I said, I always get pulled back. It's *never* long enough."

"Oh." She swallowed. "What lives in the Dark Passages? It's not, ah, just energy?"

"Oh, it's energy all right, but really bad energies, like the whisper-man. When they notice you, they try to grab and hang on so you'll pull them through, too."

"And that's not good for a *Now.*"

"Right. Too much of their kind of energy is *terrible* for a *Now*, like an infection. It can break the *Now.* That's why it's important to play with you book-people while you're sleep-ing. That way, you don't see them, and they can't see you very well either."

"Why?" But she thought she understood. No science whiz, even she knew that large portions of the brain shut down with sleep.

"Because part of you, the one that says *hi, I'm Rima,* turns off. Even if they do manage to get their hands on you and I drop you along the way—like into a strange *Now?* It's still okay because you're asleep and everyone expects dreams to be weird. I always find you guys again because we're tangled, so that's okay."

"Oh." She was starting to feel dizzy. Emma and Eric might get this, but physics had always given her a headache. Had Lizzie just said book-world people like her *could* go to different *Nows? She somehow takes me* out *of the book-world?* How would that work? *And God, what* does *go on between the lines?* "So when you come to . . . to play . . . if we're . . . we're turned off, what do *we* do?"

"Not a lot, but that's also because I always put most of *you*-you in a safe place, anyway. It would be really bad for you to wake up in another *Now.*"

"What?" She was startled. "What do you mean, you put me in a safe place? How can you both visit and then put me somewhere?"

"Easy." Lizzie's blue eyes, dark as India ink, were surprisingly calm. They were, Rima thought, very deep, as if filled with water found only at the bottom of the sea. "I *can* . . . if I trade places with the part of you that's mostly Rima and just play with . . . you know . . . the outside."

"The outside. You trade . . ." The words knotted in Rima's throat. "Places." She swallowed against a rising dread. *Isn't that what Emma thought happened with this girl's father and the whisper-man? Something Emma says she saw in one of her visions?* "You mean you take our place? Like a substitute?"

"No." Lizzie's face gathered into another *you silly*, and then she pinched her own left forearm and levitated that with her right hand, the way a puppeteer manipulated strings. Rima saw that Lizzie had wound that tiny doll-sized green scarf around one finger, the way you'd knot a string so as not to forget something. "I take *you*."

"Take?" A slow horror spread through her chest. "You . . . you live *inside* us? But . . . but . . ." *You can't take a whole body across.* Could she? Wow, she really could use Eric or Emma; this was so *Star Trek.* Then the idea—intuition, really, a leap—popped into her brain to spill from her mouth: "You're not taking my body, are you? You're taking the essence, the *energy* that makes me Rima. That's what you bring to different *Nows.*"

"Yeah, that's right." Lizzie beamed. "Only I don't take the whole *you*-you. I can't. Well, I *could*, but then it gets too crowded and another Rima would go crazy, and that's not fair.

Really bad things happen then. I remember a couple times, when I wasn't very good yet? Other Rimas and Emmas and stuff tried *killing* themselves because of all the noise in their head. Some of them even ended up in the *hospital*."

"Another . . ." *Different timelines. Alternative universes.* When she put her hand to her lips, she felt the shuddering *thump-thump-thump* of her pulse. *She's talking about slipping part of me and herself into another,* different *Rima.* While that Rima was asleep? *No, that must be what she means by* crowded, *why she says the* other *Rima would go crazy. You'd have two minds—three, if you count Lizzie—occupying the same body.*

"Anyway, it's not for very long," Lizzie continued in that chatterbox little-girl way, but now Rima thought she detected the hum of another lower, darker, subterranean note. "Like I said, I always get pulled back here. I visit Emma the most because she's the closest to me. Her lives are kind of cool."

"Lives?" she said, weakly. *Other timelines. Other universes. Other Emmas.*

"Yeah. Well, except for homework. I let her do most of that because she's way smart; I just have to kind of turn off parts of her so she doesn't wake up all the way—except sometimes when I think she needs help. Like writing her story for this class? I did that for her; she was too freaked. The rest of you guys are way harder to live inside when we play in your book-worlds, because you're all written out already. Unless we go between the lines and into secret subtexts and stuff, we don't stay in your book-worlds that much. Not that you're a bad person or anything, but your book-world life is pretty ooky, Rima." Lizzie's too-blue eyes, tinged now with that strange smoke, fixed on hers. "Too many bad feelings, and your mom is kind of, you know, messed up."

There was more to this, much more, but she had to get out of the room and back down to the others. "We should . . ." She slicked her numbed lips and tried to get up, to push herself from the floor where she'd knelt next to the little girl. *Little girl, my ass, there is definitely something . . . something . . .* But her legs trembled and felt as weak as water. "You know," she said, finally planting a foot solidly to the floor, "I think we really should go downstairs . . ."

Her voice choked off as her eyes fell to the dollhouse—and really *noticed* the dolls over which Lizzie had been so engrossed for the first time.

There were six: three boys, three girls. One boy had short, muddy-brown hair; a mass of brown curls topped a second; and the third was a wispy blonde. One girl was a luxuriant copper, while the other sported a wild, unruly shock of shoulder-length honey-blonde curls. The third doll was a very light, corn-tassel blonde.

But their faces, their hands . . . Rima's heart was inching up her throat. *They're not Barbie or Ken dolls. They're porcelain. They're glass.*

The dolls' clothes were all wrong, too. With that Victorian dollhouse, they should've worn crinolines and petticoats and lacy fans and velvet trousers with cummerbunds and top hats adorned with diamond stickpins. Instead, the dolls were dressed in jeans, sweaters, jackets, and . . .

Fatigues. Rima felt the blood drain from her cheeks, and her arms prickle with a forest of gooseflesh. *Bode's wearing olive-green fatigues. So was Chad. Tony's hair was curly and brown. Bode's hair is dark brown.* Her eyes zeroed in on the girls. The copper color was right. She hadn't gotten a good look at Lily, but she'd bet the girl had been a blonde. *And* my *hair . . .* The trembling had moved from her legs to her chest and arms . . . *I never can get those curls to behave.*

The fingers of a shiver tripped up her spine. Casey said the soldiers in the comic were toys. This wasn't a coincidence, but still her mind insisted: *No, no, don't be stupid. It can't be.* But Lizzie had said it: *I always put most of* you-*you in a safe place.*

And then, through the swell of her horror, she realized who *wasn't* there. *My God, where's—*

"So, Rima." And then she was staring into Lizzie's eyes, or they hooked hers, because Rima could feel the *grip,* the *dig.* The beginnings of the *pain,* like a thousand sharp pincers biting her brain. That odd glimmer spread from Lizzie's eyes and overflowed, rippling through the little girl's features, which began to shimmer, to smoke. To run together. Lizzie's cobalt eyes shifted, darkened, deepened, *oiled . . .*

Get out, Rima thought. Her mind was racing; she could hear the shriek in her bones, feel the twitch of her muscles trying to obey, but she couldn't move. *Run, Rima, run. Get out while you still can. Get out before her eyes change, before they change all the way!*

"So," Lizzie—or whatever this thing really was—said in a whispery voice from a faraway place Rima was certain she had never been, "what game should we play next?"

PART FIVE

WHISPER-MAN

EMMA

Remember Him

1

"IS ANYONE ELSE freaked out?" Bode's voice was hushed, as if they'd crept into a cemetery or haunted house instead of onto the porch. The big boy hefted a stout leg from one of the kitchen chairs he and Eric had broken up for clubs. "Because I'm completely there, man," he said.

"I hear that." Letting out a long breath, Eric peered over at Emma. "You have any ideas?"

"Other than *everything's* been swallowed up?" Huddled in her still-damp parka, Emma hunched her shoulders against a shiver of dread. "Not a clue."

After storming upstairs and finding nothing in Lizzie's room but the dollhouse and that scatter of toys, they'd swarmed out of the house to find that, once again, everything had changed. Now, the fog was everywhere: a solid white wall that hemmed the house in all the way around. No breaks. No thin spots at all.

She was also bothered by something else she *hadn't* seen. Earlier, as the others bolted from Lizzie's room, she'd paused, her eye falling on that box of porcelain dolls and the pile of six set off to one side. *If we're book-world characters, this almost makes sense.* It would be like playing with Ariel from *The Little Mermaid*, or Frodo. Or a Captain Kirk action figure. At Holten Prep, there was this one guy who was so seriously obsessed with Stephen King, he snapped up a pair of Carrie action figures for a couple hundred bucks just this past year. She bet there were McDermott fans who did the same. So the dolls weren't *awful*. What made them unusual was that they were porcelain. Glass.

And if she *was* right about what they were and represented . . . two were missing. Two dolls that should be there weren't.

"What do you mean, it's disappeared?" Casey's skin was drawn down tight over his skull. Purple smudges formed half-moons in the hollows beneath his stormy eyes. Wound around his neck like a talisman was Rima's scarf, which she'd left in the downstairs family room. "The barn's got to be there. We've searched the whole house. The barn's the only place left to look."

"Then we got this huge problem, don't we?" Bode waved his club at the fog, which hadn't spilled onto the porch but simply *stopped* at the very edge. "That stuff's pea soup. You could wander out five feet and get lost."

Walling us in. The air was rich with that same metallic stink, too: crushed aluminum and wet copper. It was the smell of blood and this weird snow and the blackness down cellar. *Everything that's happened before keeps happening over and over again.* Clamping her hands under her arms, she shivered, hugging herself harder. *But I don't understand what the point is.*

"It's daring us to come and get them," Eric said, and she

had the weirdest sense he'd somehow provided her with an answer. "Rima and Lizzie are insurance, that's all."

"Then why cover up the barn?" Bode asked. "Why make the fog worse?"

"Upping the ante. It's another test." Eric looked at her. "You said that everything you've done is preparation for the next step. What if this is it?"

"Crossing through the fog?" She frowned. "What kind of test would *that* be?" What he'd said also made her think of something else: what if House *wasn't* all Lizzie's mom, or even a healthy chunk? They'd assumed House was a safe haven. *I'm missing something.* "I guess I could try finding them with the cynosure and pulling them through?" She heard the question and made a face. "Somehow I don't think that will work. I really think we're supposed to do exactly what Lizzie wanted: go over there."

"So can we stop talking and spouting theories that get us nowhere and just *do* something here for a change?" Casey's voice hummed with frustration. "God, Lizzie was right. You guys are overthinking this! Come on, let's just *go!*"

"Not so fast, kid." Bode reached for Casey's arm, but a single black glare from the younger boy, and Bode thrust his hand into a jacket pocket. "I know you're hot to trot, and I don't blame you. But we got to think this through. Remember: other characters . . . other *people*, have been here before," Bode said, grimly. "Things haven't turned out so great for them. If we're walking into a fight, we need more and better weapons than the crap we've found so far."

Crap was right. While the boys had been dismantling kitchen chairs for clubs, Emma had unearthed three flashlights, a lighter, and a packet of birthday candles (blue, of course). Toss in the box of fireplace matches and Eric's Glock, and that was it for weapons. All the long guns— Bode's rifle and shotgun, the shotgun Casey had retrieved from that church—were gone, left behind in the doomed truck. Not that it would've mattered, anyway, because they had no ammunition.

Emma watched as Eric stepped to the edge of the porch and looked down to where his snowmobile ought to be. A thoughtful expression drifted over his face. "What?" she asked.

"Got an idea. Wait a second." Darting back into the house, he returned a few moments later with a can of Swiss Miss in one hand and the lacy curtains that had hung from the kitchen window bunched in the other.

"Hey, you want to kill someone," Bode said, "you go for the Nestlé Quik."

"Ha-ha." But Eric was grinning.

"What's the can for?" Casey asked.

"Gas," Eric said. "There's a siphon and an empty can in the rumble seat of the Skandic. Big Earl used to . . ." He stopped, his jaw hardening. "*We* always carry them, just in case. And there's a whole quart of oil, too."

"So what?"

"So we fill up this Swiss Miss can and maybe a couple more. The gas might come in handy."

"Well, you and Emma are kind of walking gas tanks already," Bode observed. "But yeah, I see where you're going."

"*I* don't," Casey said.

She did. "Fire. Bombs."

"Bombs?" Casey gaped. "You mean, like Molotov cocktails?"

"Well, not exactly," Eric said. "We don't have the right bottles."

"What about the peanut butter?" Emma said. "We could empty the jars."

"For a Molotov?" Bode made a face. "Might work, but the mouths are really wide and you have to score the glass to get it to blow up right. We don't have that kind of time anyway."

"How do you guys *know* these things?" Casey asked.

"Books," Eric and Emma said together.

"'Nam," Bode said.

"Gas burns and so does oil." Eric cocked his head back at the house. "Grab a couple sheets from the beds upstairs, tear some into strips to wind around these chair legs, soak 'em in oil, and then we have torches."

"But we can't see the snowmobile," Bode pointed out. "The same thing you're worried about with the barn could happen here. Get yourself turned around, might not find your way back." He paused. "Or it could be like what went down in the truck."

"The fog swallowing and then taking me somewhere? Possible, but I have a feeling this is the end of the line. Anyway, we know where the snowmobile *was*." Eric held up the curtains. "Tie these together, make ourselves a rope, I'm good to go."

"Not alone, you're not. I'm coming with you." When Eric opened his mouth to protest, Emma put up a warning hand.

"Don't even start. We've already seen what the fog can throw at us. There's no telling what could come out of it. You can't siphon and watch your back at the same time."

"Emma, the chances of anything bad happening to me are small," Eric argued. "I'm not trying to leave. I only want another weapon."

"Which it may not want you to have."

"You popping off shots in a whiteout—"

"Is a terrible idea," she finished for him. "Promise, I won't do that."

"But I thought you didn't like guns," Bode said.

"And I still don't." She hefted a chair leg. "Let's go."

2

"KEEP TALKING." ERIC was looping a last knot of lacy curtain around his middle. "It'll keep me oriented. If I don't answer, give me a chance to tug or something. If you don't get anything, then you guys pull us back. Whatever you do"—he gave the knot a final yank—"for God's sake, don't let go."

Bode tightened his grip on the very end of the makeshift rope. "We're on it."

"What do you want me to say?" Casey said, paying out lacy curtain from the coils in his hands.

"I don't care." Eric shuffled to the first step with Emma, one hand hooked into his waistband, a half step behind. "Sing. Tell jokes. Whatever."

"La-la-la-la," Bode droned.

"Something with a beat would be nice," Eric said.

"Row, row, row your boat . . ." Bode might be a decent soldier, but his voice made Emma's brain hurt.

"Oh, that's much better," she said.

"MERRILY, MERRILY, MERRILY, *MERRILY*," Bode boomed. "Life is but a—"

"Shut up." Casey's skin was white as salt. "Just shut the hell up. This isn't funny."

"Easy, Case," Eric said.

"You shut up, too," Casey said. "If it was Emma, you'd be the same way."

Despite everything, her neck heated and she was grateful that Eric didn't look her way. After a small silence, Bode said, "I'm sorry, kid. I was just blowing off some steam."

"Yeah." Doubling up on the makeshift rope, Casey set his feet and lifted his chin at Eric. "Go. And be careful." He looked at Emma. "Don't let anything happen to him."

She only nodded, then looked to Eric, who stood to her left, and raised her eyebrows. "Ready?"

"Uh-huh." Eric's mouth had set in a determined line. "You stay close."

"Don't worry about that." Her fist tightened around the chair leg. "Any closer, I'll be on *your* left."

At the edge of the porch, Eric hesitated, then put out a gloved hand. Emma watched the fog swirl and then cinch down around Eric's wrist as if Eric had stuck his hand into a vat of whipped cream. "What's it feel like?" she asked. "Is it cold?"

"Not really." Eric's eyebrows tented in a bemused frown. "Kind of thick, though. Almost . . . molten."

"Can't see your hand from here, man. It's like it got

amputated," Bode said, passing Emma a flashlight. "I don't think the light's going to do you any good. That stuff's too soupy and the light will scatter. But I'm curious how far you can go before *we* lose it."

The answer was about five feet. On the first step, Emma could still look back and see two hazy shadows. By the second step, Casey and Bode had disappeared.

"It's totally weird." Casey's voice was flatter than paper and as insubstantial as mist. "We see the rope, but it looks like it's holding itself up."

With Eric's left hand wrapped tightly around the porch railing, they eased to the third step and then the fourth; at their feet, the fresh-fallen snow humped and sifted. Yet the snow made absolutely no sound at all. The air was still and silent. Eric was right, too; she felt the fog as something turgid, like tepid Jell-O just beginning to set.

Or blood on the verge of clotting. The hairs on her neck prickled; a scrape of fear dragged over her chest. *What are you doing?* Annoyed, she clamped her jaws until the small muscles complained. *Stop it, you nut.*

"Guys." Casey's voice reached them from what sounded like very far away: "Found it yet?"

"Not yet," Eric said.

"Eric?" A beat, and then they heard Casey call again: "Eric?"

"I said, not *yet!*" Eric called.

Bode: "Barely hear you, man. You guys sure you're still by the house?"

"About as sure as I can be." Eric stretched his right hand, groped through the white muck, and shouted: "I feel the hedges. The sled's got to be maybe ten feet in front of me."

"What if it's not here?" She thought she saw something flit past to her right, but when she darted a look, there was nothing but the fog. Weird. She was certain she'd seen a figure. A man? Rima?

No. She reined in on the images that tried forming right behind her eyes. *Don't do that. Don't think of a specific person or try to pull meaning out of this stuff. That's what it wants. Remember what happened to Rima and Casey.*

"It's here. I know it's right . . ." Eric let out a sudden grunt and hitched up so fast Emma piled into him. Gasping, she tripped, lost her grip on the club, and stumbled just as Eric twisted and made a grab.

"Gotcha," he said, reeling her into a bear hug. "You okay?"

"Yeah," she said, a little breathless. Their faces were inches apart, so close her eyes nearly crossed. "Guess we found the snowmobile."

"Yup." His arms tightened, just a tad. "This is kind of nice. You realize they can't see us."

Or hear them, probably. Her heart gave a little kick. "I should get the club."

"It's not going anywhere, and . . ." His sapphire-colored eyes fixed on hers. "Things have been so crazy, happened so fast, I want five seconds. Just five seconds where I'm not running or fighting or worrying and freaking out."

She felt her body relaxing into him, just a smidge. "You never seem freaked out."

"I am, though, all the time. About Casey, mainly. Learned how to hide it early, though, on account of my dad." His shoulders moved in a small shrug. "Don't show a bully how scared you are because it only makes him want to hurt you more." His eyes drifted to the fresh bandage she'd put over her forehead. "I wouldn't have hurt you, you know."

It took her a second to realize what he meant. "Oh. You mean, after the crash?" From the tingle, she knew her cheeks must be red. "I know. I'm sorry I wouldn't let you help. It's just that I . . ." She hesitated, then thought, *Oh, just tell him.* "I have these metal plates. You know, screwed into my skull, into the bone? They're actually pretty easy to feel, and I guess I'm kind of self-conscious about them."

"Plates?" His eyebrows crimped. "Like for a skull fracture?"

"Yes. I mean, that's another thing they can use them for. The plates are small, but . . . yeah."

"Do they hurt?"

It was not the question she'd expected. No one at school knew, but a couple clueless security guards and TSA people wanted to know: *Hey, how'd you get those?* She hated their eyes most of all, the curiosity, the kind of *greed* for a good story about somebody else's bad luck: *So I met this kid . . .*

"Sometimes. Mainly, the one right here." She touched the bandage. "I get headaches. Anyway, I didn't want you to feel them and"—*think I was a freak*—"get weirded out."

"I wouldn't have, and I'm not weirded out now. Can I feel it?" He read her hesitation and said, "Will it hurt? I don't want to hurt you."

She'd never allowed anyone to touch her face. Not that there'd been guys lined up, waiting their turn. "Give me your hand." She guided his fingers. "There. That circle?"

"Yeah." He pulled in a small breath. "Is it metal?"

"Titanium. That one's got this lacy pattern, kind of steampunk, actually. And there's another one"—she pulled his fingers to the back of her head—"right here."

"Hmm." His hand buried itself in her hair, and she could feel him probing. The pressure was . . . nice. "Hard to feel that one through the muscle."

"There are new plates, ones that will absorb into the bone, but I don't want any more operations."

"Is it because of scars?" She saw how his eyes sharpened a bit as his fingers found a thin, firm ridge of scar. "You don't have that many."

"Yes, I do—tons—but they're up here." She pressed his hand to the crown of her head. From his expression, she knew when he found the fleshy seams. *Like Lizzie's crazy quilt.* "It's weird. They're hidden, but I always see them anyway."

"*I* don't see anything but you." His dark blue eyes searched hers. His hand moved to cup the back of her head. "Emma, do you . . . do you think that when this is over and we get out of here, we could . . ."

"Yes." Her heart was a fist knocking against her ribs. *This should be a dream, but it's not.* She thought of his mouth on her neck, his hands in her hair. *This is like a dream I've been waiting to have my entire life.* "I'd like—"

Their rope of linked curtains suddenly jerked hard, once, twice, three times. They jumped and looked at one another, but neither made a move to pull away. Eric gave an answering yank and turned a grin. "They probably think we're dead."

"Maybe we better get that gas," she said.

"In a second. I think . . ." Eric brushed a strand of hair from her cheek. "Yeah, I think I definitely need to kiss you now."

"Yes," she said, but he was already pulling her mouth to his before she got the word out. His lips were very warm and full and as soft as she'd imagined. They were perfect and so was he. He was everything she had ever wanted or dreamed of. Her skin was electric; her eyes closed as his tongue traced her lips. There was a fluttering in her chest that had nothing to do with fear but was, instead, a sweet ache, a longing; and then she was sighing into his mouth, and they breathed into one another, moving together, her body fitting to his so perfectly that there was no space at all between them and only this moment: in the fog, on the snow, with him.

"God," he whispered, breaking the kiss, leaning back just far enough to look into her eyes. His cheeks were stained with color. His breathing was ragged. "I've wanted that for . . . God, *forever*, from the first moment. When I saw you, I felt this sense of . . ."

"Finding." She was close enough to see his pulse bounding in his neck. "Of finally finding something."

"Someone." His hands framed her face. "This is like one of those stupid books, you know? Teenage insta-love. But this is so different. It's like I was born for you, for *this*. When you talk, your voice is already in my head, and I'm thinking the end of the sentence *with* you. Isn't that weird?"

"No," And then her mouth was on his throat, and she tasted the salt of his skin, heard his gasp as her lips moved on his neck, felt the hum of his blood against her tongue. Then he was saying her name and covering her mouth with his, and they were kissing again, drinking in each other.

Don't ruin this. Emma felt her whole body give something close to a sigh, and then it was just the two of them, cupped in fog as time stilled. If she ever found a way to encase a universe within glass, this was the perfect one, the only world and moment she wished to inhabit. *Right here, right now, hang on to him and remember this. Remember how he feels, his taste, his arms, his mouth. Remember this.*

Remember him.

3

THERE WAS ENOUGH oil for three torches. As Casey filled the Swiss Miss can and two empty peanut butter jars, Bode and Eric tore the sheet from Lizzie's bed into strips. "This way," Eric said, as he knotted and cinched a strip into a belt around Emma's middle, then slid in the chair-leg club, "our hands are free . . . No, you take that," Eric said as Bode held out the Glock. "I have nothing against guns, but I never liked that thing."

"Whatever works for you, Devil Dog," Bode said, tucking the pistol into the small of his back. "We still got a problem, though." Bode slipped a gurgling jar and the gas-filled Swiss Miss can into a pillowcase that he knotted to a belt loop. "There's no way we're gonna find enough sheets and blankets to get us through that fog and into the barn."

"There's got to be a way," Casey said, tucking a pair of blunt-edged child's scissors Bode had used to hack sheets into a hip pocket.

"There is." Eric looked down at Emma. "Pull us through. Use the cynosure the way you did before."

"That was different," she said, running her hands over the beads and glass of Lizzie's memory quilt. "I was on the other side. I knew where I was and where I wanted you to be. I was pulling you, not *throwing* us inside a place I've never been. I don't know if it will even work in the same world," she said, thinking, *I can't believe I just said that.* "Lizzie talked me through it."

"What did you do before?" Eric asked.

Her fingers ghosted over the beads that spelled his name. "Concentrated on all of you." She felt the flush creeping through her cheeks and dropped her eyes to the quilt. "It was weird. You think you remember what someone looks like, but all you've got are outlines, a fuzzy snapshot. I just kept concentrating on filling you in, but it was really hard." She looked up to find Eric's eyes, intent, on her face. "Even with the cynosure, I'm not sure it would've worked if you hadn't . . ." She slicked her lips. "If you hadn't called me." *If you hadn't told me to* feel *you.* She remembered that moment so well: groping around in the dark with her mind, trying to conjure up his face or Rima's. Then, that indescribable sensation of something flooding her brain—Eric's voice, his . . . *energy?*—and then it was like something out of that unfinished painting of Dickens surrounded by the ill-defined outlines of his characters. Eric faded *in*: first a suggestion, then an outline, and finally him.

"When you did that, and I got a sense of you," she said, "I gave you color, and then there you were."

"So do that again," Casey said. "Give Rima and Lizzie color."

"But that was to bring you guys to me," she said. "This would be *going* somewhere and trying to take you along." *Without dropping you on the way.*

"Our only other alternative is walking into that fog, either one at a time or all together," Bode said.

"And we know that won't cut it," Eric said.

"I could get us all killed." Her hand closed over the Eric beads. "I should do this alone. If something happens, then you guys figure out something else."

"Not a chance." Eric cupped the back of her hand in both of his. "She brought us in combinations for a reason. We stick together."

"Damn straight," Bode grunted. "I don't buy all this multiverse jazz, but if we're all part of each other? We're stronger together."

"He's right. Give Rima color." Casey's voice hummed with urgency. "Please."

"Okay." Letting go of a long breath, she searched the quilt until she found what she wanted. "Casey, let me see those scissors for a sec."

Casey handed them over. "What are you doing?"

"I don't think the entire quilt is necessary. Lizzie might need it because she's only five," she said, taking the proffered scissors, then picking at the web of thread cupping the galaxy pendant. "The beads and fabric might be prompts."

"So you think the cynosure is the *only* device?" Eric asked.

"Pretty sure. It's the only thing on this quilt that keeps popping up in everything House shows me." Teasing the glass orb free, she watched how it shimmered in the fan of weak porch light. Now that she actually held it, she saw that its designer had done a pull loop. Clearly, the cynosure was to be worn like a pendant on a necklace. "This is exactly what I was going to make, but I'm not nearly skilled enough. It would take me years of flamework to make glass sculptures this detailed. But the urge to do it has been eating at me for a long time, like insisting it gets done, you know? Can't be a coincidence."

"Here, use this." Eric reached a hand beneath his collar. There was a muted clack of metal as he reeled out a beaded chain. "Safer than your pocket."

"Aren't you supposed to wear them all the time?" she asked as he threaded the pendant onto the chain. The glass butted against Eric's dog tags with a dull tick.

"In the field. Technically, I'm not supposed to wear them when I'm not in uniform, but I just like them." His lips flickered in a brief smile. "I trust you to give them back."

"Thank you," she said, hoping the heat she felt at the back of her neck hadn't crawled around to her cheeks. She let her palm linger over his dog tags, still warm from his body. *This is real, too.* She held out her hands. "Lizzie's always talking about dropping people."

"Hey, I hear that," Bode said, taking her left hand in his rough, callused paw and reaching for Casey. "Hang on ti—" He broke off.

"Bode?" Casey turned the older boy a curious look. "You okay? You just about jumped out of your skin."

"Yeah, I'm cool." Yet a sudden strain arrowed through Bode's face, and Emma saw his eyes dart a question at the younger boy. "Just . . ." Bode's throat bobbed in a swallow. "Let's go, okay? The sooner we get this over with, the better."

"You can do this," Eric said to her. His grip, sure and warm, tightened around her right hand.

Glad you think so. She closed her eyes. Her thoughts would not be still, flitting from one image to the next, and she felt a splinter of panic. What should she think about? Rima? Lizzie? No, this was the reverse: putting *them* onto and into a blank. She thought of the door down cellar; watched the memory of her hand reaching toward that inky cold; remembered the blackness dimpling as her palm pressed that odd, glassy membrane.

But the candle flame was still there. I felt it. This would be the same. The trick would be filling *them* in, making *them* visible. She let herself see the barn as Lizzie had described it: a black void into which she could drift, like slipping in on the breath of a dream. *Now*—she felt Eric's hand in hers—*start to fill them in; draw us onto and into the space.*

There came the familiar tingle of a *blink* ripsawing through her skin, a lancet of white pain as the bruised lips of that spiky maw parted in the dark before her eyes. A red rose of heat bloomed on her forehead. Between her breasts, there was a sudden warm flush, and she knew the galaxy pendant must be glowing. A jolt crackled in her chest, an atomic bomb of light and heat that lashed down her arms and out her fingers. Someone gasped. Casey said, wonderingly, "Did you feel . . . ?" But Emma barely heard, was suddenly past hearing. In the blackness of her mind, behind her eyes, she saw them all—Casey, Bode, Eric, *her*—as cutouts edged with the same kind of glow that had haloed Kramer. *His* had been the color of a sick, creeping evil, but theirs was true light spun in pulsing filaments from their fingers, knitting their hands together with . . .

Colors. It was Eric, not speaking but floating in her mind nonetheless. *Emma, do you see this?*

Man. Bode. *It's like a spider's web, tying us together.*

Eric's light was a deep cobalt blue, a near match, although hers was edged with a golden nimbus finer than lace, as fiery as the sun's corona. Bode's color was very strange, deeply vermillion, but blurry and indistinct, as if whatever Bode was bled and oozed like an open wound. For a second, she could've sworn that Bode was not a single color but two.

But *Casey* . . . Casey was many and all colors, a nacreous, wavering shimmer that was now rose, now sapphire, sulfur, violet. Casey was anybody, anyone.

Her ears filled with the rush of a thousand birds, as the colors looped up their arms, drawing them tight, tight, and ever tighter, as woven together as the glass creatures knotted in her galaxy pendant. Then she felt a swooning, the earth dropping away, which swept through her like a chilling wind, and they were suddenly falling, their light tangling to a streaming rainbow. The galaxy pendant fired as space folded, flexed, and then . . .

EMMA
Monsters Are Us

COLD. DARK. SHE felt the press of the black, heavy as an anvil.

She opened her eyes, then fluttered them in a rapid blink because, for a second, she wasn't sure they were actually open; it was *that* dark. Then, from the *nothing* in front of her eyes, she teased their colors, faintly luminous, misty as frayed cobwebs. For the moment, they were still linked, their circle unbroken by their passage into whatever space she'd hurled them.

Yeah, but are we inside? Is this the barn? There was something solid beneath her feet, icier than a tombstone, and she thought, *Oh crap, I dropped us in the wrong place.*

Casey's voice reached out from the dark. "Did we get in?"

A scuffling sound, and then their circle winked out as Bode let go. "Oh yeah," Bode said. "I know *inside* when I feel it. Just like dropping into a black echo. Man, you don't know what bad is until—"

A whisper of alarm sighed across her neck. Why? Something Eric had said that, now that she thought about it, echoed a *blink*; the way McDermott had talked about stories and how ideas were infections . . . *And we wondered what the barn might make.*

"Until you've run into these *things*," Bode continued, "big as your—"

The monsters are us. The thought was sudden, immediate, explosive. *Bode's story is written, and the monsters are in—*

"Bode!" she shouted, frantic. "Bode, *no!*"

RIMA

Blood Have the Power

"DON'T FIGHT IT, baby. Look what you're doing to yourself. You're bleeding." Anita's skin was pasty and her breath fruity with cheap wine. "Trust your momma, honey, and this will be over quick. You've got a black stain on your soul, only I'll wash it clean. Take care of that stain once and for all."

"M-Mom," Rima rasped. She had come back to herself as she was now: spread-eagled, on her back, in no place she recognized. The ropes around her wrists and ankles were very tight, tied off to stakes driven into rock that was strangely smooth, glassy, and very black. There was light, but it was a pallid, bony glow. The ceiling soared to some point high above, where the air was choked and clotted: a dark, shadowed space that swam with what she thought were birds. She could hear the dry, papery rustle of their feathers, and smell their wild animal stink. "Mom, please, let me go. You don't want to do this."

"Oh, honey." Anita's voice choked off in a sob, and then she was tipping the bottle to her mouth, her throat working as she took another pull. Swallowing, Anita sighed, then wiped her moist, slack mouth with the back of one hand. Her eyes were black holes on either side of her nose. "It's been so *hard*. I just can't deal with it anymore."

"That's why I *left*." Rima felt the sob welling up in her throat and forced it back down. Crying wouldn't help. She had to keep Anita talking, or else . . . Her gaze flicked to the glint of a very long, very sharp boning knife Anita had in her right fist: the same knife that had carved a red necklace the night her mother had pinned her to the bed and come within a whisper of killing her. "Mom, please, just let me go. I'll leave and never come back, I promise."

"Blood have the power." The voodoo priestess was as Rima remembered her, too: hatchet-faced and hungry. The woman lit five fat yellow candles—one at each point of a pentagram—and then began to drizzle a small stream of black sand onto the rock. "Blood *binds*. When you ask the voodoo for something, you must make sacrifice. The spirits live in the sand. Feed the spirits, and the power come full circle."

"So I'll be able to kick it," Anita said, her words beginning to slur. Her hair was plastered to her forehead in oily ropes. "I'll get clean. Don't you see, honey? Bringing you up has been so hard, and I'm just not that strong. I give and give, and you take and take."

"Mom, that's not *true!*" She didn't know what she felt more, fear or rage. "I've done *everything*. I've cooked and cleaned, I get food, I—"

"I know," her mother said, and her voice rode on a sudden growl, all weepy sincerity forgotten. "That's because you've drawn on *my* strength. You've always taken what you wanted.

What do you think a baby is? Huh? A little parasite, that's what. You've got no control. The baby's inside, growing and taking and swallowing, *needing* . . ." Her mother's features twisted to a monstrous gorgon's. Rima turned her face to one side, but her mother's claw-hand shot out and clutched a handful of Rima's hair, twisting until Rima's scalp burned and she cried out; until she was forced to look back at her mother, and nowhere else. Anita's face cramped with fury. "Well, what about *me*? Who takes care of me? Who gives me back what you've *stolen*?"

"I . . . I didn't m-mean . . ." Rima's voice came in a broken, hitching whisper. "Momma, I was just a *baby*."

"Just a *baby*," her mother spat. She fisted the knife, holding it in a perfect vertical, the point quivering an inch from Rima's right eye. "No *baby* ever *drew* the dead."

Rima's mouth dried up. She went still, although her mind was gibbering: *No no no no.*

"You started even then, filling me up with death-whispers. I could hear them inside, like beetles scratching in a paper sack, *scratch, scratch, scratch, scratch.*" Anita's face twitched as if hearing that terrible sound all over again. "Now's the chance to let all that blackness out of you, out of *me*—because you've touched me, you've been inside, *scratch-scratch-scratching* my soul with your *filth*."

"Not yet." The priestess wrapped her skeletal fingers around Anita's wrist. Rima drew in a sudden gasp as the knife wobbled. "Only the blood work," the woman said. "Blood binds. Kill her too fast before the blood draw, and the blackness stay in you, stain you, doom you." Small, straight knucklebones cored through the woman's earlobes, and a long necklace of bird skulls chattered and clacked. "Spill the blood, and the black flow out and the spirits drink. You drink, and then the blackness leave because the girl's blood is strong."

There was a long, breathless moment, and then Anita wrenched free. The blade whickered, shaving air above Rima's face, but Anita was stumbling to her feet now, and Rima remembered to breathe. The bottle winked in the candlelight as her mother drank again. Watching the white length of her mother's throat convulse and swallow, move and slide, Rima thought back to the fight on the snow and what Tania had become: the way her throat had pulsed and heaved before that bloom of jointed legs erupted from her mouth like a gruesome black rose.

Oh my God. She felt a bubble of hysterical laughter pushing against her teeth. *Tania* was *Anita*: one and the same. Like Lizzie's crazy quilt, names made out of letters rearranged to be both different and yet parts of a whole. Her mother was the monster. She was every monster Rima would ever fight, and always had been.

She thought of poor little Taylor—where was her parka now, anyway?—and how shocked that little girl had been when her father morphed into a monster capable of hurling his child from a balcony. Taylor blamed herself, but what had happened wasn't her fault.

And this isn't mine. Rima felt the sting of tears and then the slow trickle as they rolled down her temples and soaked into her hair. *The real poison is if I let my mother convince me that it is.*

She watched as the priestess began to dance: a slow, rhythmic shuffle. Her mother followed in a drunk-stumble, slashing the air with that knife. *Have to do something.* Rima's heart battered her ribs. *Can't just lie here until Anita decides she can't wait.* But what did she have to fight with? She wasn't stupid enough to think she could *will* this away; this wasn't like the fight on the snow, and even then, once set in motion, that story would unravel to its conclusion. She suspected only Emma had the power to jump through one space and *Now* to another. So what could *she* do? All she had was a touch that soothed and took away whispers.

Wait a minute. She felt everything inside, even her breath, grow still. *I take.*

She had to call twice because Anita was that lost, that out of it. "What?" Anita said. Her mother's words were mushy, and that anger, fiery and a bit insane, had died a little, but Rima knew the embers of her mother's resentment wouldn't need much coaxing.

So she chose her words very, very carefully. "Mom, I won't fight you anymore. I can't. You're my mom, and I know you're only trying to help."

"Thass righhh, baby." Anita's slushy voice went maudlin. A rill of shiny snot slicked her upper lip. "Thass righhh."

"I know, and I love you, and I'm scared." She was aware of the priestess's coin-bright eyes, and somewhere, overhead, the ceaseless churn of the birds, but Rima fixed her gaze on Anita and did not look away. "I'm scared, and I need you. So, please, would you hold me? Would you please hug me just this one last time?"

BODE
Either Way, You Lose

1

BATTLE WAS GONE —and what the hell was that about?

It had happened back at the house, right before Emma did her crazy . . . well, whatever that was. Soon as Casey touched him, Bode felt the sergeant go, just *whoosh* away like Bode'd gotten a sucker punch to the gut.

That tripped him out. After, Bode had been distracted, worried about what the sudden silence in his head meant. So when they'd materialized in the dark, Bode hadn't been on top of his game. Just said the first damn thing that came to mind. Stupid. Like popping out of a spidey hole without tossing out a rock first, seeing if anything up there took the bait and blasted that rock to itty-bitty ones. You never made that mistake twice, because after the first time, you were dead.

Emma's shout still rang in his ears, but Bode felt the change happening a split second later. The darkness collapsed in a rush, the black slamming down, flattening the space above and all around as if the barn were being squeezed by four giant palms: above and below, right and left.

"Down, get down!" he shouted, dropping to his knees. The darkness heaved, the floor's texture changing from something smooth—*poured concrete*—to the unmistakable grit of earth over rock.

No, no, no. Can I think it away? He was gasping, his chest heaving like bellows, trying to pull in air that dwindled by the second. *Forests; I like trees and open sky and water.*

But that's not where his nightmares lived, and it was too late anyway. The blackness was hardening, his monsters taking their shape. He heard the others thudding to the dirt as the darkness rushed in, growing close and tight, cinching down, clenching and knotting to a fist. For a split second, Bode thought the black space meant to flatten them. Then, the sense of pressure eased as the ink of this new space stopped flowing.

Casey: "Has it . . . it's over, right?"

"I think so." Emma sounded as out of breath as Bode. "It was like the roof collapsed."

"It's not a roof." Bode raised himself to a squat, relieved that his head and shoulders didn't meet up with anything solid. Fumbling out a flashlight, he thumbed it to life. A spear of blue light pierced the black, and he saw exactly what he expected. Of course he would.

This was a nightmare he knew by heart.

2

THE TUNNEL WAS not perfectly round. No VC tunnel ever was. The spider holes where snipers and guards waited were two-foot squares cut out of camouflaged earth, wide enough for a very small guy like the average VC or a runt like Bode. Big guys only got hung up. This was good for Charlie, but bad if you were an average Joe looking to make it back to the States in something other than a pine box shoved into luggage class.

Once past the spidey holes, the tunnels opened up a little to a max width of about three or four feet, but they went on forever in a multilevel rock warren of passageways and larger rooms where up to a few hundred VC lived for months at a time. The air was normally very bad, too, smoky and stale and heavy with the odors of human waste and the stink of too many people coughing, breathing, pissing, shitting, spitting in too small a space.

Barely enough room to turn and fight. Bode felt sweat bead on his neck and face and between his shoulder blades. He was very conscious of the club stuck at a now very awkward and uncomfortable angle in his waistband. Slipping it free, he choked up on the wood, but even his reach was too long. Try to take a swing, and he'd be chunking out earth.

"This tunnel's pretty tight," Eric said in a tone that had about as much heat as a weatherman's. "Are they all like this?"

"No, they get worse," Bode said. Lucky to have that devil dog along. Guy had the temperature of a flounder, or a lot of experience roping back fear. Whatever his story, that Eric stayed calm helped Bode keep his cool. "Down deep, you're on your belly the whole time. If this *is* the same, though, we'll get to rooms, eventually, and they open right up." He paused. "We should probably cut the lights."

"Why?" Casey asked.

"Because they're like wearing a sign: *Shoot me.*"

"How are we going to see?"

"We don't. We go by feel."

Eric shook his head. "I honestly don't think a guy with a gun is the worst thing we're going to run into down here. We'll make better time if we leave the lights on. Besides, I'd kind of like to see what I'm up against, if you know what I mean."

Because we will *have to fight.* Eric didn't have to say it for Bode to know he was right. "But we don't even know if Rima and Lizzie are here. This is from my head."

"They're here," Casey said.

"Yeah?" Bode looked at Casey with fresh curiosity. *When he took my hand; it happened when Casey touched me.* "How do you know that?"

"I just know." Casey's face was a glimmering silver oval. "Lizzie, I can't tell, but Rima is close by." He fingered the scarf. "I just *know*," he repeated.

Eric regarded his brother for a long moment. "Can you tell us which way, Case?"

Casey's tongue flickered over his lips. Then he gave a jerky nod and pointed to the tunnel beyond Eric. "Down there."

They set out, Bode in the lead with Casey on his heels, then Emma and finally Eric, bringing up the rear. They shambled like hunchbacks, their boots grinding and scuffing against the hard-packed earth; the pillowcase, with its gasoline-filled Swiss Miss can and peanut butter jar, sloshed and gurgled against Bode's left thigh.

Emma's voice reached him from behind. "Hey, guys, the tunnel's getting larger. I can stand up, and it's not really all dark. Look at the walls."

She was right. The walls glowed: not brightly, but with

'a soft green luminescence that bled from the blackness itself.

"That's so weird," Eric said, and then gave a soft laugh. "Well, *weirder*. Bode, you ever seen a tunnel like this before?"

"No." Bode thought about those muscular tentacles that coiled up from the inky snow to drag Chad to whatever lived beneath. "Is this thing going to break up? Like, are there too many of us in one spot?"

A pause. "I don't think so," Emma said. "You go to the trouble to take Lizzie and Rima, and *then* you kill us all at once? Makes no sense. This is about something else."

"A test?" Eric said to her. "To see if you can get us here?"

"But we *are* here," she said.

"Can you get us back out the way we came?" Bode asked. Stupid; he should've thought about that earlier. "You know, do that color thing?"

She made a face. "I don't think so. Don't ask me how to describe it, but this doesn't have the same feel of . . . of potential. Like energy you can mold and use. I think this place is set." She peered at him through the gloom. "Don't beat yourself up about this, Bode. If it wasn't you, it would've been one of us."

"Then what is this?" asked Casey. "A way of picking us off one by one?"

No one answered—mostly, Bode thought, because, yes or no, either way, you lose. Although he agreed with Eric. This had the *feel* of a trial by fire of some sort. He wished Battle would tell him what. For a dead guy, Battle knew a great deal about life. But the sarge, who had lived inside Bode's head for so long, was silent and had been for quite some time now, even before the barn. Yet he'd *been* here; Bode could always feel him, this quiet burn in his head like the flicker of a pilot light. After the fight on the snow, though, Battle had only . . . listened? Maybe not even that; Bode just couldn't tell.

And then Casey touches me—and Battle's gone. I felt him go. Bode armed sweat from his forehead. *So where is he? Why did he leave?* His stomach pulled to a knot of anxiety. *Sarge, I need you. Please, talk to me.* If he *was* hovering somewhere around, however, Battle remained mute.

Ahead, Bode saw that the tunnel was now very wide and much higher, enough so he had clearance for a good round-house swing. He'd be able to take a pretty good shot at whatever might hurl itself from the dark.

That's all wrong. It shouldn't be this way. This isn't like any tunnel I've ever seen, or worried about.

A soft sound drifted out of the dark: a whispery rustle that was not the sharp scrape of a boot. He pulled up so suddenly that Casey smacked into him. "Hey," Casey said.

"Quiet!" Bode held his breath, trying to listen above the boom of his heart. He probed the darkness with his light, but there was nothing in front, on the floor, or behind. Yet the sound kept on, papery and dry and somehow not only louder but *larger*: a scurrying, rhythmic shush that grew and grew and . . .

"What *is* that?" Emma whispered. "Where is it coming from?"

"I don't know." He didn't want to think about rats or snakes or . . .

Then his heart stuttered as he heard something new: the spatter of pebbles raining like fine hail onto rock.

Oh shit.

He aimed his light straight up.

BODE
Dead End

THE ROCK DIRECTLY overhead was alive—with scorpions.

Big as rats, with bulbous black bodies and pincer-claws long as fishhooks, they seethed over the stone. Diamond teardrops of glittering poison dripped from enormous barbs at the tip of shiny, curled tails. But instead of mandibles, these scorpions' heads were unformed and smooth as mirrors. Then, in the next instant, gashes appeared and split to become mouths.

Jesus. Bode felt the cracks in his mind widening, his thoughts splintering. The glassy surfaces peeled back to reveal eyes: dead eyes, black eyes, the eyes of cobras, the eyes of nightmares. *Faces, they have* faces.

"*RUN!*" he screamed, much too late.

As one, the scorpions dropped from the ceiling. Bode felt the hard bodies bouncing off the padded arms and shoulders and chest of his jacket. They bulleted off his scalp, then slithered over his face. One landed on his left shoulder, hooked, and held on. With a wordless screech, Bode swung the flashlight like a club. The heavy stock batted the thing from his shoulder, and it tumbled, pincers flailing. These just managed to snag his pants, and then the thing's tail was stabbing him again and again, the pointed barb working to pierce the tough olive canvas of his fatigues. Still shouting, Bode battered at the thing with the butt of his flashlight. Losing its grip, the thing did a flip and landed on its back. Its spindly legs churned, the pincers snapping uselessly at air. Its many eyes glared up at Bode, and it let out a rasping, almost mechanical chitter that sounded eerily like an M16 cycling on full auto.

"Die!" Bode brought the sole of his boot smashing down. He felt the soft belly give as the scorpion's body burst in a viscous spray of thick, yellow fluid. Cursing, he ground the thing into paste. The others were screaming and flailing and stamping; the floor was turning sludgy with slick, gooey, foul ichor. The only reason *they* weren't dead—not yet, anyway— was their clothing. But their faces were exposed, and their hands.

"Get them off!" Emma shrieked. Her hair was a living tangle. "Get them off, get them off, *get them off!*"

"Emma!" Spinning her close, Eric swatted scorpions with his bare hands, crushing them like overripe grapes beneath his boots.

"Bode, we got to go!" Casey bawled. "We got to get out, we got to go, *we got to go!*"

Bode didn't need convincing. "Go back, go back the way we came!"

"We *can't!*" Still hugging Emma close, Eric aimed his flashlight back down the tunnel. "Look!"

Whirling round, Bode followed the light—and what he saw made his guts clench.

The floor was moving now, too. The scorpions were there, a remorseless, black, undulating river. *Driving us forward,* Bode thought wildly. *Just like the fog, making sure we keep going this way. We should be dead by now, but we're not. They're herding us.*

No choice but to keep going. "Move!" Bode grabbed Casey, spun him, and then gave the boy a vicious shove to send him on his way. "Go, kid, go go *go*!"

"Casey, wait!" Eric shouted. "Emma, quick, give me the lighter!"

"What?" Bode asked, but Emma had already tossed the lighter to Eric, who was yanking out his torch. Bode thought, *Yeah.* He grabbed his own unlit torch. "Emma, the matches!"

She jerked out the box; the dry chatter of wood inside cardboard was like dice on stone. She worked out a match, struck it; the match flared, and then her torch caught with a small *hoosh* as flames fled up the rags in liquid, orange-yellow runnels. Eric was already swinging his. The creatures didn't like the fire; rearing on their hind legs, they hissed. Their pincers *snick*-snapped, the clawed jaws clashing like scissors. A few got too close, and then the air was alive with a *pop-pop-pop*, the scorpions bursting in sprays of stringy yellow mucus. Several tried shooting beneath the flaming arc of Eric's torch, but then Emma was right there, by Eric's side. Together, they swept their torches back and forth, keeping the scorpions at bay while Bode jabbed at the ceiling.

The things retreated, but Bode knew they couldn't keep this up forever. Their torches were too weak, and the second they turned to run, the scorpions would sweep after them. Then, out of the corner of his eye, he saw Eric strip out of his parka and shout to Emma, "Give me your coat! Take off your coat!"

"Devil Dog!" Bode bawled. "What the hell you *doing*?"

But it was Emma who answered. "Gas!" She yanked off her jacket. "Our parkas are still wet, and we've got a jar of gasoline!"

"Guys, get ready to run!" Tossing their parkas into the roiling mass, Eric threw his torch after, then spun on his heel. "All right, Bode, Casey, go, *g*—"

The parkas went up in a flaring yellow ball with a solid, heavy *whup!* The scorpions' reaction was instantaneous. The ebony wave shied as the air filled with stuttering pops loud as gunshots. The scorpions' screeches became a keening wail as a thick, sooty bloom pillowed through the tunnel. A second later, the jar of gas, still zipped in one pocket of Eric's parka, erupted like a flash-bomb: a great, hard, brilliant *bang*.

They charged down the tunnel, Casey in the lead, boots clapping stone, running so fast the walls streamed and blurred. Their torches guttered, and Emma's died, but no help for that. Bode's breath tore in and out of his throat; he kept expecting the walls to sprout more of those scorpion-things at any second. The tunnel was curving right now, growing ever wider, and he thought, *Got to be a room, there's got to be a junction; that's how these things work.*

Almost before the thought was fully formed in his mind, the maw of a junction pulled apart and firmed to his right. At the same instant, he saw that the way dead ahead was blocked. Again, there was really no choice. They may have stopped the scorpions for the moment, but the tunnel itself would make sure they went in only one direction. "Casey," he shouted, "to your right, that way!"

Cutting right, Casey darted out of sight. Bode followed, the blackness unreeling like a tongue. *Room, room, there's got to be a room; there's got to be a way out of this ma—*

Casey pulled up so fast that Bode couldn't stop in time. He hit the kid a solid body blow, and they went down in a tangle of boots and legs. "You okay, you okay? What the hell, why did you—" The question evaporated when Bode got a good look at what lay directly ahead. A bright arrow of fresh terror pierced his heart. Behind him, over the thud of his pulse, he heard the clatter of boots and then Emma's voice, broken and horrified: "Oh no."

Because she now saw what he did: a rock wall, as glassy and smooth and flawless as a silvery-black diamond, not three feet away.

The tunnel was a dead end.

RIMA
The Worst and Last Mistake of Her Life

"A HUG?" ANITA repeated, as if her brain was a faulty computer trying to process information in a language it had never learned. "You . . . you would *do* that?"

"Yes." The word dribbled from Rima's mouth, pathetic and small. "You're my mother."

"Oh honey." Anita's legs suddenly unhinged. At first, Rima thought her mother might be falling, but then she saw Anita awkwardly catch herself with the nearly empty wine bottle, the glass letting out a dull *chuk* as Anita knelt. "Honey," Anita said, boozily, "you don't know how *mush* I've wanted that. But what could I do? The stain on your soul was *shhho* black, I *wuss* always afraid you'd drag me down."

Of all the things her mother could have said, that actually stroked a bright flare of anger. *Keep it together; only got one shot at this, or it's over.* "That's past now, Mom," she said, not bothering to try to control the shudder in her voice. Anita was so wasted, she would hear it as fear—and oh God, yes, Rima *was* afraid.

"Girl lies," the priestess said.

So did a lot of adults, mainly to themselves. With an effort, Rima kept that thought from reaching her face. Her eyes never wandered from her mother. "I know how hard it's been," she said to Anita. "And I've been so afraid." It helped that this was true. *I don't want to die down here. Please, God, don't let me die here.* She had never been more frightened of her mother than at this very instant. But then again, this wasn't her mother, not really. This was the mother her nightmare had made. *To hell with McDermott and his stories; this is my life; I'm real. I've written my own mistakes, my private nightmares.* What power she had was in her. If this came out of her mind, then the way out must already be inside her, too. She had to remember that. "Mom, if you're going to do this, I think you better."

The knife was already moving, and too late, Rima wondered if her mother understood. The blade flashed down, and then Anita was sawing at the rope tethering Rima's right hand. At that, her heart tried to fail. *I'm left-handed. It knows that's my weaker hand.* So she would have to be very quick. She watched the knife eating the rope; the tension around her wrist eased, and a second later, her hand was free.

A sudden, fierce urgency flared to snatch at her mother, made a grab, *do* something, and Rima had to work hard to muscle back the impulse to knot her fist in Anita's hair. *Wait, be patient. Don't spook her, because you won't get another chance. Wait for it.*

As if sensing some danger, her mother rocked back on her heels. The muzzy look on her face sharpened a moment, and the knife she still clutched twitched, the point moving to hover over Rima's throat.

"Careful of the knife." Rima licked her lips. "You don't want to cut yourself."

For a shuddering moment, nothing happened. The bright spark that was the point of the knife ticked back and forth ever so slightly with each beat of Anita's heart. Rima said nothing, held her breath. Then she heard the knife clatter to the rock, and Anita was leaning forward, practically falling on top of her—and Rima thought, *One chance.*

"Oh, my poor baby, come here," Anita sighed, snaking her arms around Rima's neck and shoulders. "Come to Momma, baby."

"Oh, Mom." Her voice broke as she carefully wound her arm around Anita's thin shoulders. "I forgive you," she whispered—and then she clamped down and felt for the center of her mother with all her might.

In the next instant, when Anita began to scream—when it was much too late—Rima understood: she had just made the worst and last mistake of her life.

Too late, Rima understood everything.

BODE

The Shape of His Future

"**NO, NO, NO,** no, no!" Bode swung his torch right and left, but there were no chinks in the rock, no breaks. The rock was as smooth as a black mirror; his reflection so perfect, it was like staring through a window to a moonless night. "This can't be right!"

"That doesn't make sense," Eric said. The high scream of the scorpions swelled from the mouth of the tunnel. "If the other tunnel ended, how can this be a dead end, too?"

"Because this is where we're supposed to end up." Casey reached for the glassy rock, and his hand's ghostly twin floated to meet him. "*This* is the way it wants us to go."

"Kid, we're not talking fog now. This is solid rock," Bode said. He saw the margins of Casey's reflection smudge and blur—and then the ruddy glimmer of a face suddenly seemed to ooze from Casey's body to appear on the rock's mirrored surface.

Holy smoke. He knew the others couldn't see this. *The kid—*

"But it's the *wrong* rock." Emma's expression was tight, intense. "*Look* at it. This is almost like obsidian, volcanic glass."

"So *what*?" he grated, bunching his fists. His brain was yammering, *Get out, get out, get out!* Despite what he saw in the rock—something that should've reassured him they might still have a chance—Bode was more frightened now than he'd ever been in his life. His back prickled. If you spent enough time worming on your belly through black echoes, you got a sense when there was something coming for you out of the dark, and he could *feel* the scorpions swarming down the tunnel. Those things would rush through the archway in a broad black river, and he would drown in a writhing sea of pincers and stingers. They would slither into his mouth, swarm down his throat, eat him from the inside out, scrape his eyeballs from their sockets. *Got to get out, got to get out.* "What does that matter?"

"Glass isn't an organized solid. Light doesn't show itself until it reflects or bounces off something. That's why you see yourself in a mirror but not necessarily in clear glass. But *look* at us." When she moved her hand from side to side, its mirror image echoed but blurred and elongated into shimmering, smeary trails. "This isn't really reflecting. It's as if the reflection's being . . . slowed down?"

So what? His nails were slicing crescent divots from his palms. *Tell me something I can use!* Bode had to really work at not grabbing Emma by the shoulders and shaking her until her eyeballs jittered. "Yeah? How does that help us?"

"It's like it . . . *traps* the light." Casey's hand was still pressed to his glimmering double. "As if it's coming back to us out of tar or something."

"Emma," Eric said, "what if *this* is the same kind of energy sink that's in the Peculiars? Wasn't that designed as a barrier, a way of containing energy? Look at the smears. Remember what Lizzie said? Her dad said the glass makes the thought-magic slow down."

"What does that mean?" Bode could see now that when he turned his head, his reflection lagged behind, the margins blurring into streamers. "Is that good?"

"No. It means there's something beyond this, inside, the way the Peculiars trapped energy. Anything that can trap energy can trap us." Emma actually backed up a step. "I'm not touching this. We can't go through here. There's got to be another way."

"You know there isn't. Emma, please, *Rima's* on the other side. I *feel* it." Casey's face glistened and more tears streamed down his cheeks. "We have to *help* her!"

"Well, whatever you're going to do, do it now," Bode said. The scorpions' squalls were much closer, no longer only echoes but a shrill of sound as focused and insistent as a drill coring through the bone of his skull. "I'll settle for anyplace those things aren't."

"We got to go for it, Emma," Eric said.

"Eric," she said, "it's an *energy sink*. That means it can steal from me, from *us*. You want to wake up dead inside solid rock?"

"Do you have any better ideas?" Eric said. "You have to get us through, Emma. It's the only thing left."

Well, Bode thought, *not quite.* Emma looked pretty spooked. Even if she *could* do it, Bode still thought it would take her much more time than they had left. But he had the gun. He had the can of gas, and their second jar besides. He had everything he needed, no more and no less.

In that moment, the shape of his future became clear. Shit, the writing really was on the damn wall now, wasn't it?

"Get them through, Emma. You find Rima and that little girl, and then you guys clear out," Bode said—and wheeled back the way they'd come.

"Bode!" Eric and Emma shouted. Bode saw Emma try to spurt after him, but Eric snagged her arms and held on tight. "Eric, no! Bode!" Emma cried. "Bode, stop!"

He did, but only at the bend and just for an instant. "Don't drop them, Emma. Don't let yourself get stuck. Get them out and get them clear, you hear?"

Then he rounded the corner and sprinted down the tunnel as the heavy pillowcase banged his thigh, as remorseless as a countdown.

BODE
Into the Black

1

HE LOOKED OVER his shoulder only once, enough to satisfy himself that they weren't following, and then he dug in, dashing down the tunnel, closing the gap. Ahead, he could hear the tidal wave of the scorpions as they came in a susurrous hiss, like the ebb and suck of waves dragging over the rubble of shattered seashells. When he thought he'd gone far enough, he swiftly untied the sack, took out both the jar and the can, and set them side by side on the rock.

Jar or can? There would be no second chance, so he had to guess right the first time. He settled on the jar; the can was thinner, and unless the glass simply melted, the shards ought to have enough punch behind them to slice through aluminum. Pulling the Glock from the small of his back, he squatted and butted the muzzle against the glass. A bullet alone wouldn't get the job done; that only worked in movie-magic and books and television. What he needed was the muzzle flash.

Sweaty fingers gripping the Glock, he waited through

a long second and then another. Maybe ten seconds left, or maybe less, but a long time to wait alone, a lot of life to try to cram into too short a span: focusing on every breath, the hum of his blood, that steady thump of his heart; paying attention to the set of his body—*this* body—while knowing that each sensation was possibly the last he would ever feel.

Then, in that third second, a voice he knew and had been afraid was gone forever floated through his mind: *Proud of you, son.*

The relief he felt was so huge he could feel his throat ball and his eyes burn with the sudden prick of tears. "Thank you, Sarge." He swallowed against watery salt. "I thought you would stay with Casey."

In a moment. Right now, you need me.

"I needed you before. You could've warned me. You had to know what would happen once I got into the barn."

I'm a soldier, son, and a ghost—not a mind reader.

"That's not all you are, Sarge. I feel it. That's right, isn't it? You l-left me for C-Casey . . ." Faltering, he forced his trembling lips to cooperate. "But you must have some damn good reason. Please, Sarge, help them. Help Emma. You will, won't you?"

If I can. I am as I have been written.

"I don't know what means." But he thought he might. What if *his* life, everything he'd experienced, was in preparation for this moment? If *this* was why he'd been written: to help the others, give them a chance? *And where will I be if—when—I wake up?* If Lizzie was right, he would open his eyes, and there would be jungle and heat and bullets whizzing, the black echoes waiting, and Chad, grousing about no smokes and lousy food. Perhaps he would have no memory of this, or the others, at all. A wash of sadness filled his chest because, of all the things he wanted to forget, these people weren't among them. Theirs was a friendship and bond forged in battle, and he was afraid for them. He was afraid for the kid, Casey, most of all.

Something even worse behind that weird rock. I feel it. They got to protect the kid; Battle must know this.

And would *he* find them again, somewhere else? Was there another Bode, an infinite number of Bodes, living their lives, making their mistakes, writing their own nightmares? Finding these people whose fates were woven with and into his?

Or maybe we're each other's salvation. This might be atonement, too, a way of making things right.

"I'm sorry, Sarge." He didn't bother trying to hold back the tears now. What the hell; he was dead, no matter which way you sliced it. "I'm sorry I got hung up in the tunnel; I'm sorry I was late. You should've left. You should've gone, but you were there, waiting for me." Bode's voice broke. "I'm so sorry I got you killed."

We were at war. My choices were mine. I wouldn't leave you then, and I won't leave you now.

"Thank you." Bode's vision blurred. His cheeks were wet. The air was screaming now. Only a few seconds left. "It's been an honor to serve with you."

The honor's mine. Go with God. Then: *I think now would be a good time, Bode.*

Yes, he saw them coming, almost on him now: a seething, rippling river sweeping from the dark.

Into the black, he thought, and squeezed the trigger.

2

BODE HAD LESS than an instant and barely a moment, but that was enough for him to know that he was wrong. He was not going into the black at all.

Light bloomed, orange and hot, and took him.

EMMA
Push

1

"BODE, STOP!" BEYOND the tunnel, Emma heard the swell of the scorpions, very close now. She tugged against Eric, who still had her arms in an iron grip. "Eric, please, we have to go after him. We can't let him *do* this."

"Go after him for what, Emma?" Eric gave her a little shake. "Think. Bode knows that this is the only way. We don't have a choice and there's no more *time*! Now, *come on*! Don't make this be for noth—"

The room lit with a sudden, brilliant flash. The air exploded with a huge roar. The concussive burst, hot and heavy with burning gasoline, blasted through the mouth of the tunnel, followed a second later by a boiling pillar of oily smoke. She felt her throat closing, the muscles knotting against the acrid sting.

"Em-Emma," Eric choked, and then he was pulling her down. Hacking, Casey had already dropped and lay gasping like a dying fish as tears streamed down his cheeks. The air near the floor was a little better, although she could barely see through the chug of thick black smog. Emma's head swirled, her shrieking lungs laboring to pull in breath enough to stay conscious.

"H-hurry," Eric grunted. "Do it, Emma. Get us out!"

"C-Casey, take Eric's hand," she wheezed, and then she slammed her free hand against this strange black-mirror rock and thought, *Push.*

2

IT WAS DIFFERENT this time, and much, much more difficult.

Her head ballooned; the galaxy pendant, Lizzie's cynosure, heated against her chest. Their chain of colors spun itself to being, and then the familiar tingle of a *blink* began as the earth seemed to shift and yawn. Beneath her fingers, she felt not rock but that thin rime of ice frosting her window, the liquid swirl of the bathroom mirror, that featureless black membrane in Jasper's basement, the thick clot of that murderous fog.

Push. She narrowed her focus. At the same instant, she felt the heat from the galaxy pendant gather, build, surge, and then *rocket* from her mind, as bright and sizzling as a laser beam shot from the throat of an immense generator. *Push, damn it, push,* push.

They passed *into* the wall: not a plunge but a slow and tor-turous ooze, the bonds tethering the molecules of this strange, alien glass teasing and ripping. The black mirror—no, this *Peculiar*, thinned, as if the touch of her mind was a warm fin-ger to frosted glass. Yet the way was not clear; the glass did not melt so much as give and grudgingly deform, the way a too-wet sponge dimpled.

With a stab of horror, she also realized *they* were slowing down. She was still *pushing* as hard as she could, but it was as if she were bogged down in something viscous and gluey, like a woolly mammoth caught in an infinitely deep tar pit. The energy sink was sapping them all. The chains of light linking her to Eric and Casey were beginning to fade, the colors bleaching away.

Emma! It was Casey, his thoughts stinging with red panic. *Emma, I'm slipping, I can't hold on, I can't—*

God, no! But she was tiring, fast, and the harder she fought, the less energy she had. Her mind skidded, her concentration faltering as her hold on the others slipped. The sensation was bizarre, as if her thoughts were clumsy feet trying to stay upright on glare ice.

Emma. Eric, steady and sure. *Look at me.* Feel *me. Let me help.*

Help? How? She saw the cobalt shimmer that was Eric, but that was all, and Casey had his hand so she couldn't really feel Eric either. Casey was still there, but his touch was like smoke against her fingers. Her whole body was going numb, draining to an outline, a silhouette, as the energy sink bled her of color and life.

Eric, again: *Feel me, Emma. Look for me. I'm right here.*

Then she remembered. She thought of their kiss on the snow: Eric's mouth searching hers, his hands framing her face, his body fitting to hers. *Give him color; use the cynosure to fill him in.* In another moment, she saw his face shimmering in the dark of her mind's eye.

That's it. Stay with me, Emma, Eric said, as their chain of three and many colors brightened. *Hold on to me, look at me,* use *me, and keep going; get us through.*

She didn't know why this helped, and how any of this worked. She was only a junior in some yuppie private school, for God's sake. There was no science she knew to explain this, but it was as if she *believed* Eric into being. Maybe it was his faith in her, or only the electricity between two people, the way the air thickens and crackles when they look at each other. The connection is there, and you know it.

But she hung on, and she *pushed*. Her ears filled with a rushing, a whirring, and then they were passing through much faster, the stubborn glue of the energy sink weakening, the bright beacon of Lizzie's Sign of Sure as solid as any path. She felt the space of this bizarre Peculiar dilate like an immense pupil . . .

From beyond its margins, swelling from the dark and whatever waited, she heard a loud, long, bloody scream.

And she heard something clamor in a raucous, cawing chorus. She knew what that was, too.

Birds. Not a few. Not a couple dozen. But hundreds and hundreds of birds.

Dead ahead.

RIMA

Blood Binds

1

ONCE, IN BIO, they'd sat through a gruesome video of some sadist-scientist injecting formaldehyde into a squeaking, thrashing rat. For Rima, the poor thing couldn't die fast enough, and yet that was not what horrified her most. The worst was when the red leeched from the rat's eyes until they were a dead, milky white.

Stealing her mother's whisper was like that.

Anita was screeching. She tried pulling away, but Rima hung on. The sensation was agony, like a rush of liquid nitrogen churning through her body, freezing her mind, icing her heart. Anita began to jitter and twitch as her whisper—her life and what rode in her soul—oiled into Rima.

And then she knew because she felt *it*.

No! Her back suddenly bowing with pain, Rima let out an agonized scream, but it was already too late. *This is what it wanted.* She felt her body expanding and deforming as the whisper-man uncoiled, streaming through her limbs, riding her blood to plump out her fingers, her toes. She felt the bite of rope still cinched around her right wrist and both ankles as the whisper-man squirmed and wriggled and bunched, and then she cried out as the rope split and fell away. For a wild second, she felt a spurt of hope. Maybe she would live through this; maybe she might actually be able to contain the whisper-man without . . .

All thought whited out as a monstrous pain ripped through her chest: not a single talon but razor-claws that dragged and tore and split. Her scream choked off as blood gushed into her mouth, and then it was all she could do to grab enough air.

Can't hold it. She sucked in a gurgling gasp. *Tearing me apart.*

OH, POOR LITTLE RIMA. The whisper-man's voice crawled over her mind. DOES IT HURRRRT?

"Y-yes." Her mouth was sour with the taste of copper and pain. "Pl-please, t-take it back. L-leave me . . ."

TOO LATE. YOU'RE A BRAVE GIRL, AND STRONG, BUT NOT STRONG ENOUGH TO PLAY THIS GAME. IF IT HELPS, YOU'RE NOT THE ONE I WANT ANYWAY. FOR THE MOMENT, THOUGH, YOU'LL DO. NOW, YOU JUST RELAX AND LET ME DO ALLLL THE TALKING.

She felt her consciousness compress as the whisper-man crowded in. She recoiled, tried kicking out with her will, but he was walking over her mind now, insinuating himself into the cracks and crannies and secret places, prying her apart. The whisper-man surged in a river of black through her veins; her heart shuddered with the force of it, and when she looked at her hand, what little breath she had snagged in her throat.

Her skin was moving.

No. She could feel the blackness there, worming and

heaving, those dark tentacles eeling over her bones, seeping into the meat of her. This was like Tania. The same thing was inside her now, balling in her gut, ready to skitter up her throat on its spidery legs.

No, the whisper-man crooned in her mind. *YOU STOLE A WHISPER, THAT'S ALL. A BIG BAD WHISPER, BUT NO MORE THAN THAT. ONLY BLOOD BINDS. ONLY BLOOD WILL DO.*

She was on her feet. When had she done that? No matter. Warm blood trickled from the corners of her mouth and down her neck to soak her chest. Her vision was muddy and her cheeks were wet; when she put a hand there, her fingers came away ruby-red.

Overhead, the birds boiled and screamed. On the rock, at her feet, Anita was as still as a discarded wax figurine. Beyond the magic circle, the voodoo priestess cowered.

"You say you let me go." The priestess sounded both aggrieved and frightened. "You make a promise. You say once you have the power, you free me."

Rima opened her mouth . . .

2

AND THE GIRL'S lips formed words, but the words were not hers, and neither was the voice.

"*YES,*" the whisper-man said. It twisted Rima's lips into a bloody crack of a smile. "*BUT . . . I LIED.*"

Then, it brought down the birds.

EMMA
To the End of Time

1

THE PECULIAR SPAT them out. They tumbled, not falling as much as rematerializing in a stagger, hands still linked: Emma first, then Casey, and finally Eric. A ball of sound broke over them, an echoing scream that rebounded off rock and doubled, and Emma thought, *Cave.* For a second, she thought they might still be in Bode's nightmare: same story, different page. Then the floor undulated and bunched, and whatever else she might have thought after that turned to dust in her mind.

The birds spread in a roiling, living carpet. Emma smelled blood and the birds' feral, almost metallic stink. A thousand glassy eyes glittered; black beaks gaped to reveal pink mouths and yellow tongues. Most were crows, but there were a few owls, their curved talons slick and stained with blood, stringy with dark flesh.

As if responding to some signal, the birds lifted as one in a broad, ebony curtain and shot toward some spot high above, leaving behind shredded clothing and a tumble of stained bone. The birds massed—and then seemed to melt into the ceiling. They fell utterly silent without even so much as a rustle. Yet they were there; their beetle-bright eyes studded the ceiling in an alien galaxy, a splash of eerie starlight.

That was when Emma realized something else: she could *see* herself. Not from their eyes; she wasn't in the birds' heads, thank God. But she saw herself, as well as Casey and Eric, reflected from the rock high above, at their feet, and all around. They went on and on, another Emma/Eric/Casey and yet another Emma/Eric/Casey and another and another and another: an infinite number of Emmas and Erics and Caseys marching away to the end of time.

The cave was an immense black-mirror sphere.

"Emma," Eric said, and pointed. "Look. Inside that circle of candles."

She followed his gaze, and a blast of horror swept through her body.

"No." Casey's voice was an anguished whisper. *"No."*

2

RIMA SWAYED. HER body glistened, as if she'd been dipped in red paint. More blood dribbled in crimson rills from her mouth, her ears, her shredded wrists, and a thousand rips in her skin. Her shirt was a bib of purple gore, and Emma gasped as fresh blood blossomed in a dark rose over Rima's stomach. Blood leaked through tiny fissures in her skin to form rivulets that ran down her legs and dripped from her fingers to puddle on the rock with a sodden, dull *puh-puh-puh-puh*. Rima looked like a porcelain doll done in a fine crackle-glaze: a leaky vessel through which her life's blood seeped and would soon drain away completely.

"We're too late." Casey was trembling. "We're too late; it's *got* her."

"Good for you, Casey!" Rima boomed, although the voice was not hers, or the whisper-man's either, the one Emma had heard in her *blinks* of Madison and that asylum. Definitely a man's voice, though.

Beside her, she heard Eric suck in a breath. "What?" she asked. Eric's skin had gone white as salt. "Eric?"

"Oh God." Eric's face was a mask of horror. "God, no, please don't do this."

"No." Casey tensed, and he might have sprung into the circle if Eric hadn't snatched his brother's arm. "No, *no!*" Casey was crying, trying to fight his way free. "It's not right, it's not *right!*"

"Now, Casey. *Son*." The monster wearing Rima made a *tsk-tsk*. "Is that any way to talk to Dear Old Dad?"

ERIC

My Nightmare

THIS IS MY fault. Beneath his hands, Eric could feel Casey shuddering, a vessel under pressure, ready to explode. *We're in my nightmare now.*

"You're dead!" Casey's hands knotted to fists. "You're *dead!*"

"Why, Son." The thing in Rima, the monster with Big Earl's voice, pulled a pout. A huge, ruby-red tear trickled down her cheek. "That hurts my feelings, it really does."

"I'm not your *son!*" The cords stood out in Casey's neck. "Don't *call* me that!"

"Don't, Casey. That's what it wants," Eric said. Big Earl had been a big man with a large man's bluster, but this was like being caught in an echo chamber. His dead father's voice battered his brain. Eric's mouth filled with a taste of clean steel, and he grabbed onto his hate, hugged it as tightly as he held his weeping, raging brother. Good, stay angry; anger was something he could use. He willed his mind to diamond-bright clarity. *This is the enemy. No matter what its face, it always has been.* "Don't give it any more power."

"Oooh," the whisper-man boomed in Big Earl's voice, "you always were a smart boy, Eric. I guess Emma was a good teacher, huh?"

Emma let go of some small sound, almost the whimper of a trapped animal, but Eric kept his gaze screwed to the whisper-man. "Leave her out of this. She's got nothing to say to you. She's got nothing to *do* with you."

"Oh now, Son, you'd be surprised." The whisper-man threw Eric a wink. "Because she's got *everything* to do with *you.*"

The words barely registered. This thing might have his father's voice and Rima's face; it might enjoy and feed upon this kind of sadistic play, but take away the bluster and it was clear: this thing needed them for something. Not only that: Eric knew, instinctively, that they must be *willing* to give it up. Otherwise, it would have taken what it wanted already, the same way it had snatched Rima and Lizzie.

And where is Lizzie? He risked a quick glance left and right; saw both the ravaged body of what he thought must've been a woman and a lumpy heap of bones, stringy flesh, and bloody clothing reduced to tatters. The skeletonized body seemed small but still too large for a little girl. *What's it done with her?*

"Stop playing games. You need something from us," Eric said. "What is it? Where's Lizzie?"

"A boy with your gifts." The whisper-man tut-tutted. "And you went into the Marines? Such a waste."

"Gifts?"

"Why yes, Son. You're a smart kid; you've figured it out already. Each of you has a special gift, even if you don't know what it is just yet."

"Stop *calling* him that! You're not our father. He's not your son and neither am I," Casey said. "We know what you are."

"OH, CASEY," the whisper-man said, reverting back to its own voice, which wasn't necessarily a relief. To Eric, it sounded like both a gargle and the scream of nails over a blackboard. It felt like knives in his brain. "YOU DON'T HAVE A CLUE, MY BOY. YOU *REALLY* DON'T."

"Fine, then show yourself." Casey scrubbed away the whisper-man's words with an angry swipe of his hand. "Stop playing games. If this is *our* nightmare, you don't need Rima. Let her go."

"OH NOW, I COULDN'T DO THAT—NOT YET, ANYWAY," the whisper-man said. "WE NEED TO COME TO TERMS FIRST. SO I THINK I'LL HOLD ON TO HER FOR THE TIME BEING." A crimson spider stretched along Rima's left side as a fresh seam opened. "A LITTLE COLLATERAL, *DON'TCHA KNOW.*"

"Collateral for what?" Eric said.

"A BARGAIN, OF COURSE. A *NEGOTIATION.*"

"What could we possibly have that you can't already take?" Eric said. "Where can we go? We're in *your* space."

"I want to talk to Rima," Casey said.

"I WANT TO TALK TO RIMA, *PLEASE*," the whisper-man said. "CASEY, WE REALLY HAVE TO WORK ON YOUR MANNERS."

"Where *is* she?" Casey shouted.

"SHE'S RIGHT HERE—SCREAMING HER HEAD OFF, I'LL GIVE YOU THAT. THIS IS THE PROBLEM WITH USING YOU WHEN YOU'RE AWAKE. EXCEPT FOR EMMA, IT'S *MUCH* EASIER WHEN YOU'RE ASLEEP. WHY, IF I WEREN'T SUCH

A *STRONG* CUSS, SHE MIGHT DISTRACT ME."

"What?" Eric heard Emma say; from her tone, he couldn't tell if she was startled or had suddenly found the missing piece of a mental jigsaw puzzle.

"What do you mean, using us when we're awake?" Eric said to the whisper-man. "Why is Emma different? What are you talking about?"

The thing in Rima's body kept on as if he hadn't spoken. "BUT RIMA'S JUST A SLIP OF A THING, AND NOT VERY STRONG. SO SENSITIVE, SO SWEET—AND I KNOW SHE LIKES *YOU*, CASEY. SHE WOULD DO ANYTHING TO SAVE YOU. TRUST ME ON THAT. I THINK THE TWO OF YOU WERE SOMEHOW MEANT FOR EACH OTHER."

"Then please stop hurting her." Casey's lips trembled, but he shrugged out of Eric's grasp and pulled himself up straight. The deep bruises on his translucent skin were as livid as clotted blood. "Let her go before you kill her. You have the power to do that."

"It does, but it won't, Casey. Not yet, anyway. It wants to *play* just a little longer," Emma said. She had gone very pale. Her cobalt eyes were nearly violet in the bad light. "Where's McDermott? Where's *Lizzie*?"

"THAT BRAT?" The whisper-man spluttered a wet, horsey sound. Blood misted in a tiny cloud. "LITTLE LIZZIE WAS NEVER HERE."

EMMA

Monster-Doll

SHE HAD ALREADY half-guessed the truth. The story had spun itself out in her *blinks*: Lizzie's parents, the Mirror, the panops and Peculiars, Lizzie's dolls, the flight from the house, that crash, and that very last *blink* in which Meredith lay dying, with Lizzie not far behind, as the fog leaked and nosed its way inside the little girl. There had been all that talk about *tangles*. But the shock still hit Emma like a slap.

Lizzie had felt it with the monster-doll, which must have been some incarnation of the whisper-man. How Lizzie did it, Emma couldn't guess, but it must be a little like any kid at play: you act out all the parts. You get into the doll's head and lose yourself in a fantasy world. Somehow, using the galaxy pendant, Lizzie must've crossed into some realm. Bypassing the gateway that was the Mirror? Or had she found another machine? For that matter, maybe the cynosure had more than one function, could be used in ways Lizzie's parents hadn't known or understood.

Either way, Lizzie had grabbed a piece of the

whisper-man—or he'd hung on to her; who knew?—and then the whisper-man talked to her in a language she could understand. They'd *played*. They went places; it had shown her how to do things in different *Nows*. Yet, with every contact, untangling who she was from *it* was harder. A bit of Lizzie was always left behind, and vice versa. It had sunk in its teeth, gotten a taste. So when the fog finally caught them after the crash, that enormous tangle of energy—from the Peculiars, the whisper-man, and what was left of her father—invaded the little girl, walked her brain, and *became* her, sliding inside Lizzie's skin to wear her the way you did a glove. It just hadn't done it fast enough, and Lizzie had time to finish her special forever-*Now* and imprison them both.

"I think she was never here, as a girl, for *us*," Emma said, "but she put you here. She made this place out of her idea of a Peculiar, and then she bound you. She was bleeding, and you need that, don't you? It's the actual blood that matters. It's why McDermott cut himself. It wasn't only to activate the Mirror. It was to give you a way in that would stick." *But it must not work all at once unless there's enough time.* What was it that McDermott had said? *A cumulative exposure, something he had to do over and over again. He must've thought that if he cut himself just every so often, took in only a little of its energy, he could use it without it having enough of a hold to use him.*

So was that what London had been about? McDermott taking in too much? But there had been something wrong with Meredith McDermott, too. *Scars. I remember scars on her arms. Her memory was faulty; there were holes, things she couldn't recall. Hadn't McDermott said that Meredith and Lizzie went away? To where?*

"YOU KNOW, YOU'RE VERY SMART, A REAL CHIP OFF THE OLD LIZZIE-BLOCK." The whisper-man gave a sly, ghastly wink. "I CAN SEE WHERE ERIC GETS IT."

"Why do you keep *saying* that?" Eric asked.

Emma kept her eyes screwed to the whisper-man. "We're not talking about that."

"OH, BUT WE ARE. YOU ALL NEED TO UNDERSTAND THE STAKES HERE," the whisper-man said.

"What's to understand?" Casey said. "You're an asshole."

"SO ELOQUENT. EMMA'S GUESSED MOST OF IT, I'LL BET. IT'S REALLY VERY SIMPLE. AFTER THE CRASH, I GOT INTO THAT LIZZIE AND, OH BOY, WAS THAT A MISTAKE. SHE WAS *MUCH* STRONGER THAN EVEN *I* REALIZED AND SUCH A BRIGHT, CREATIVE LITTLE GIRL! YOUNGER MINDS AREN'T BOUND BY LOGIC; NOT EVERYTHING HAS TO CONFORM TO RULES. WHO KNEW SHE'D PAID SUCH CLOSE ATTENTION TO HER MOTHER AND THOSE PECULIARS? OH, I KNEW THE RISKS. SHE WASN'T A PUSHOVER LIKE DEAR OLD FRANK, WHO HAD THE KNACK BUT JUST DIDN'T KNOW WHEN TO STOP. BUT I COULDN'T RESIST. REALLY, AFTER I SAW HOW SHE COULD PULL THINGS BACK INTO HER REALITY—THAT STORM, FOR EXAMPLE; HECK OF A THING—AND WITHOUT DESTROYING THAT PARTICULAR *NOW,* WELL, I KNEW I JUST HAD TO GET ME MORE OF *THAT.*"

"Where is she?" Eric said. "Is she dead? Did you kill her?"

"SON, LIZZIE WAS GONE FROM HERE A LONG TIME AGO," the whisper-man said. "WITHIN MINUTES OF THAT *SWOOSH.* OH, SHE'S ALIVE SOMEWHERE ELSE, AN INFINITE NUMBER OF VERSIONS IN ALL THOSE MULTIVERSES

YOU TALKED ABOUT, ALTHOUGH THAT'S TOO NEW AGE FOR
ME. CALL IT A REALM, OR A *NOW*. EVEN A BOOK-WORLD,
WITH ITS SECRET COMPARTMENTS. IT'S ALL THE SAME
IN A WAY, BECAUSE THE WORLD OF A BOOK IS SO REAL
TO ITS CHARACTERS, AND THOSE WHO READ IT, TRIP
INTO IT, GET LOST."

"Where you can't stay long," Emma said. "*Now* or book-
world, it doesn't matter, because you're bound to Lizzie's story
and she's bound you here. You can be what you want *here* but
nowhere else."

"WELL, IT'S NOT AS LIMITING AS *THAT*. BINDING
WORKS BOTH WAYS. GIVE A LITTLE, GET A LITTLE.
YOU'RE RIGHT; LIZZIE AND I ARE TANGLED, THE SAME
WAY THAT FRANK'S IN HERE AND, OF COURSE, ALL . . .
WELL . . ." It threw Emma another wink, so eerily similar
to the one McDermott had given her in that Madison-*blink*,
she felt a swift, sharp frisson race up her neck. "*MOST* OF YOUR
STORIES, THE ONES STORED IN THE PECULIARS."

"What do you mean, *most*?" Eric said. "There are others?
Ones that aren't finished, like . . ." Emma felt Eric move a
little closer, as if to shield her, too. "Like Emma's?"

In reply, the thing only hunched Rima's left shoulder, but
when it did, Emma heard a distinctive *riiip* that made her flash
to Sal tearing up old sheets for rags. "SO I *CAN* BREACH THE
PECULIAR FOR SHORT PERIODS OF TIME, BECAUSE LIZZIE
HAD THAT KNACK; JUST LONG ENOUGH TO GRAB ONE OF
YOU, WHICH ONLY MEANS THAT I GRAB THAT PIECE OF
HER IN YOU. I CAN VISIT ANY *NOW* AND PLAY WITH THE
VERSION OF YOU—*IN* YOU—THAT EXISTS IN THAT *NOW* FOR
A LITTLE WHILE. TRUE, EXCEPT FOR EMMA, YOU'RE ASLEEP

AND YOU MISS ALL THE FUN; WELL . . . *MOST* OF YOU DO."

All my blackouts. All those blinks. She felt the cold, keen blade of this new horror slice into her heart. *They haven't been fugues or seizures. It's been using me,* wearing *me to visit versions of me in different timelines.* And it could use her while she was awake. Why? *Because I'm my own person: real, not set in a story with an inevitable end?*

"Emma's the key, isn't she?" Eric said. "She's the constant. This has all been a series of . . . of *tests.* You manufactured everything so Emma would eventually learn what to do to get you out of here and into a different *Now.* That's why you kept bringing different people. You had to keep altering the mix to help her get there. That's right, isn't it?"

"What?" Somehow this idea was even worse. "Eric, what are you saying?"

"Think about it, Emma," Eric said. "It's the only thing that makes sense. If it's tangled with Lizzie and McDermott, then it already knew you had the ability. What it had to figure out was who would help you get there. Must've sucked for it, constantly having to hit the reset button."

"You're saying I've . . . I've been here *before*?" Multiple contacts with this thing? In this *place*? But didn't every contact leave a stain? How infected with *it* was she?

"BINGO!" The whisper-man gave Rima's right knee an exaggerated *by-golly* slap that left a palm-sized splotch on her jeans that swiftly turned the color of blackberry jam. "BY GOD, YOU'RE A BRIGHT SONUVAGUN. BUT IT WASN'T AS SIMPLE AS ALL THAT. IT WAS ALSO A MATTER OF EMMA COMING INTO HER OWN, MARSHALLING THE *RIGHT* ABILI-TIES HERE AND, WELL, IN THAT LIFE SHE'S MADE FOR

HERSELF. EACH OF YOU HAS A GIFT, MY BOY, WHETHER YOU KNOW IT OR NOT. BUT ONLY ONE OF YOU HAS THE GIFT I NEED."

"What's that?" asked Casey. "Who?"

"WHY, THE GIFT THAT KEEPS ON GIVING, SON. I NEED SOMEONE WHO CAN CARRY A WHISPER, AN *ENERGY* AS STRONG AS MINE, WITHOUT COMING APART AT THE SEAMS. I NEED A *MIND* THAT CAN ABSORB ME WITH-OUT GOING *TOO* MAD, SO WE CAN PLAY TOGETHER FOR A NICE, *LONNNG* TIME ACROSS THE *NOWS*," the whisper-man said. When it smiled, Rima's lower lip split in two to sag from her teeth. "I NEED THE GIFT, CASEY, OF YOU."

ERIC
Write the Person

"NO." ERIC MOVED to put himself between Casey and the whisper-man. "You can't have him. You can't have any of us."

"OH, I BEG TO DIFFER." Rima's clothes were drenched now, and blood painted every inch of her face. "SEEMS I ALREADY GOT LITTLE RIMA NOW, HAVEN'T I? IF YOU DON'T HURRY, YOU WON'T HAVE TO WORRY ABOUT ME LETTING HER GO EITHER. SHE'LL JUST *DIE*, AND IT WON'T BE PRETTY. OH NO, IT WON'T BE PRETTY AT ALL."

As if to put the period to that, a fresh split opened on Rima's throat with a meaty rip to reveal a faint glimmer of tendon and red, wet muscle. Eric felt a fresh surge of anger at their helplessness—at *his*. No one could lose that much blood and survive. But this thing did have powers. "If you leave, will that save her? Can you heal her somehow?"

"OH, YOU BETCHA." A tremor squirmed through Rima's cheeks, and the whisper-man let out a sudden groan. "AHHH... WHOA, BOY, BETTER HURRY. SHE'S IN A *LOT* OF PAIN."

"Eric," Casey began.

"No. Don't even *think* about it, Case." Eric's heart beat hard and loud in his ears. Cold sweat rimed his upper lip, and a cramp of fear grabbed his stomach. Being scared wasn't bad, was it? His drill sergeant once said that anyone who wasn't a little freaked out was a damn fool. The trick was not to let it paralyze you.

I can do this. I've been fighting one way or another for my whole life—against Big Earl, the odds. Myself. Just one last battle.

"Take me," he said. "Use me."

"No," Emma said. "Eric, don't."

"SORRY, BOY," the whisper-man said. "I DO SO ADMIRE YOU, BUT ONLY CASEY WILL DO."

"It's all right." Except for the bruises, dread had bleached Casey's skin until his face was nearly transparent. "I'll do it."

"Case, you can't." Eric's hand tightened on Casey's forearm. "I won't let you."

"But you heard it. I'm the only one who can save her." Casey's eyes were wet. "You'd do it for Emma or me. Please, Eric. Let me do this for *her*."

"It's a liar, Casey." Emma's tone was steely and sure. "No one can save her now, not even you."

"But it said it would," Casey said.

"YOU HAVE MY WORD ON THAT," the whisper-man put in.

"Screw you," Emma spat. "You don't have that kind of power. If you did, Tony and Bode and Chad and Lily would be here. Lizzie died from the crash; I don't see you healing her. Even if she'd lived, she couldn't have held you forever. Eventually, you would've ripped her apart the way you're killing Rima now. If you could heal like that, you could hop in and out of Lizzie, patch her up, wash, rinse, repeat a hundred times over. You wouldn't need Casey."

"I KEEP—*AAHHH*." The thing grunted. Rima's lips peeled away from teeth tinted orange with blood. Her upper lip trembled, then tore, the skin stretching and thinning and coming apart in wet threads. "I KEEP *FORGETTING*," it said, using Rima's hand to knuckle away blood, "WHAT A SMART LITTLE ORPHAN GIRL YOU ARE. WITH YOUR GIFTS, YOU AND I COULD GO FAR, BUT YOU'RE NOT STRONG ENOUGH TO HOLD ME EITHER. OURS WOULD BE A VERY *SHORT* UNION. LUCKY FOR ME, YOU STUMBLED ON HOW TO WRITE THE PERSON WHO COULD. *OOOPS*." The whisper-man put a mangled hand to Rima's ruined lips in mock dismay. "LET THE CAT OUT OF THE BAG. ME AND MY BIG, FAT, BLOODY MOUTH."

"Write the person?" A feather of alarm stroked Eric's neck. Emma, he saw, had gone very still. "Emma, what's he talking about?"

"WHY, YOUR GIFTS, ERIC," the whisper-man said. "HAVEN'T YOU WONDERED WHY YOU AND EMMA ARE, WELL, SUCH *GOOD* PALS, AND SO SOON, TOO? WHY YOU LIKE HER SO MUCH? WHY YOU ARE SO ATTRACTED, *CARE* SO MUCH ABOUT HER? EVEN *THINK* ALIKE? BET YOU COULD FINISH EACH OTHER'S SENTENCES, AM I RIGHT?"

"Eric?" he heard Casey say, but Eric couldn't tear his eyes from the sudden anguish in Emma's face. "Emma?" he said. "Emma, talk to me. Tell me, you can tell me."

"Please," Emma said—not to him, but to the whisper-man. Her voice was tiny and strained. "Please, don't. Don't do this."

"Emma," he said, a flower of dread growing in his chest. "Emma, no matter what it is, whatever this thing has to say . . . it won't make any difference."

"GOOD, LOYAL, STRONG, BRAVE, SMART ERIC," the whisper-man said. "BUT OF COURSE, YOU'RE ALL THAT—BECAUSE THAT'S EXACTLY HOW EMMA WROTE YOU."

ERIC
The Other Shoe Drops

"WHAT?" ERIC FELT his center crumple, like bricks tumbling from rotten mortar. *"What?"* He looked at Emma but couldn't grab her eyes. "Emma, what's he saying?"

"OH, COME ON, ERIC. YOU'RE SMART ENOUGH TO FIGURE THIS OUT. IN FACT, I ALREADY TOLD YOU THAT IT WAS A MATTER OF EMMA *DEVELOPING* HER ABILITIES, BUT NOT ONLY *HERE*. REMEMBER, SHE'S BEEN WRITING HER LIFE FOR QUITE SOME TIME. SHE JUST NEEDED TO WORK UP THE COURAGE TO TAKE THAT ONE LAST, *EXTRA* STEP." The whisper-man sighed. "HATE TO BE THE ONE TO BREAK IT TO YOU, BUT YOU'RE *NOT* McDERMOTT'S CREATION, ERIC. YOU'RE EMMA'S."

The words seemed to detonate in his brain. He could feel himself beginning to tremble all over from the blasts, the shock. *No, no, no, that can't be. It's lying.* But what if, *what if?* His fists bunched. *So the hell what? I don't care. I have a life. I feel things.* He was real; he was *alive.* He had Casey to fight for, and now there was the promise of Emma to care about. Nothing could take any of that away, least of all this thing.

"I'm *nobody's* creation." He squared off, pulled himself that much straighter. "I'm my own person. I don't care if I don't remember everything. For all we know, that's your doing. But I make choices in a world you know nothing about. You may control this space, but you have no say over me or my life, so fuck you very much."

"BRAVE WORDS, BUT I'D EXPECT NOTHING LESS. BELIEVE WHATEVER YOU WANT, BOY—BUT I'D TAKE A VERY GOOD LOOK AT EMMA IF I WERE YOU. THAT FACE SPEAKS VOLUMES, DOESN'T IT? YOU'RE HER CREATION, ERIC, THE BOY OF HER DREAMS. THAT'S WHY YOU TWO GET ALONG SO WELL. WHY YOU'RE SO *DRAWN* TO HER. SHE WROTE YOU. MADE YOU JUMP RIGHT OFF THAT PAGE, TOO—AND *THAT* WAS WHAT I WAS WAITING FOR."

The whisper-man was wrong; it was a liar and a cheat. Except . . . one look at Emma's pale, stricken face and he knew that the whisper-man *was* telling at least a version of the truth.

Emma wrote me into being? The same way Lizzie used symbols and McDermott churned out novels? No, no. Despite his resolve, he was getting cold, so cold. *Come on, get a hold of yourself. Think this through.*

Emma could have written about a boy *like* him. That could be it, right? Sure, this was a place where the energy of thoughts conjured new realities.

But I am alive *outside this place. I was on a snowmobile. We nearly crashed.*

But what if this thing was telling the truth? Did that matter? What if things had happened the way the whisper-man said?

That can't be right. I hope; I think about the future. When I dream of the girl I want, I see Emma. Yes, but was that because Emma *made* him think this way? No, that couldn't be, because that would mean Emma had written him into a nightmare of abuse and Big Earl and murder.

No, no, that was an accident. The gun just went off. What was he thinking? *Emma would never*—

"But I didn't write *you!*" Emma screamed at the whisper-man. "I never wrote a father . . . a *monster* like you!"

Oh God. As strong as he knew he could be, Eric felt something deep in the center of his being waver. *She just admitted it. She* wrote *me.* He felt Casey's hand on his shoulder, but the touch was distant, nothing more than a suggestion. *She wrote* us. *Everything I think I know, all that I am . . . is because of her?*

"YOU WROTE HIM A FATHER WHO GOT WHAT HE DESERVED. BUT DON'T BE SO HARD ON YOURSELF, EMMA; YOU COULDN'T HELP IT. REMEMBER *YOUR* DEAR POPS AND HIS SET POINTS? MOMMIE DEAREST MAKING LIKE A TREE AND LEAVING HER LITTLE BUNDLE OF JOY IN A MIL-LION PIECES? A TRAUMATIZED, UGLY LITTLE GIRL WITH NO HOPE, NO FRIENDS? YOU CARRY THE PAST, EMMA, AND IT COLORS EVERYTHING YOU TOUCH, ANYTHING YOU DO," the whisper-man said. "MCDERMOTT KNEW: THE MONSTERS OF THE PAST ARE BLOODSTAINS THAT ONLY FADE BUT NEVER DISAPPEAR. HE INFECTED YOU. YOU COULDN'T HELP BUT INFECT ERIC, TOO. WHY ELSE GIVE HIM AN ABUSIVE ASSHOLE OF A DAD?"

What? Through the sudden muddle in his mind, he felt the words prick like pins. *What does he mean, infect?*

"But I never imagined *you.* I never gave you a *name,*" she said, fiercely. "And I know that I *never* even thought of, much less wrote, a bro—" Her mouth clamped shut.

"WHAT WAS THAT?" The whisper-man cupped a hand to Rima's ear, which tore, releasing a gush of fresh blood to dribble along the girl's chin. "SAY WHAT, EMMA, DEAR?"

"*Damn* it, leave her alone!" Eric's rage finally boiled over. "Just shut the fuck up! I don't care, I don't *care*! What does this have to do with her or me or Casey? Huh? If you've got something else to say, *say* it!"

"OH, ALL RIGHT. HERE'S WHERE THE OTHER SHOE DROPS." The whisper-man paused. "OUR LITTLE EMMA DIDN'T WRITE CASEY, ERIC."

Casey's hand was still around his arm, and now Eric felt his brother go rigid. "What do you mean?" Casey said. "What are you talking about?"

"Don't let it get to you," Eric said. The icy dread in his stomach seemed to suddenly thaw. He should've known it was lying. Of course, Emma didn't write Casey: because she'd never written *him*. Daydreaming wasn't the same as creating, and what he felt for Casey was *real* and so intense he could hold it in his hand. Casey was his brother. That was a given. Nothing could undo that. "It's just playing games, Case. This is all an illusion; it's a lie. I'm alive. I'm real, and you're my brother; you've *always* been my brother."

"DID I SAY HE WASN'T? I ONLY *SUGGESTED* THAT YOU BOYS DON'T SHARE . . . WELL, THE SAME *MOTHER*, SO TO SPEAK," the whisper-man said.

"Shut up," Emma said to it. Tears streamed over her cheeks. "Just shut up, shut up!"

The whisper-man ignored her. "I SAID YOU ALL HAVE

GIFTS, ERIC. NOW LET ME TELL YOU ABOUT YOURS. YOU
WANTED SOMEONE TO PROTECT AND LOVE, CARE FOR,
FIGHT FOR. EMMA MADE YOU THAT WAY. SHE SET YOU IN
MOTION, BUT COULD NEVER BRING HERSELF TO FINISH
YOUR STORY, JUST AS FRANK NEVER PENNED HER END.
SO YOU'VE GOTTEN LOOSE. YOU ARE SO VERY MUCH LIKE
HER IN THAT WAY, TOO: A FREE AGENT WITH FREE WILL
. . . WELL, WITHIN LIMITS, BECAUSE, AFTER ALL,
SHE'S HERE, AND SO ARE YOU. YOU ARE ALL BOUND
TO MCDERMOTT AND HIS STORIES, TO LIZZIE, TO THIS
PLACE, AND TO ONE ANOTHER, THROUGH THE *NOWS* AND
ALL TIMES. THE POINT, ERIC, IS YOU CREATED THE
PERFECT VESSEL FOR ME: A YOUNG *MIND*, A CLEAN
SLATE OF A *PERSONALITY* WITH ONLY ENOUGH HISTORY
TO ROUND YOU OUT, MAKE YOU WHOLE. *YOU* BROUGHT
CASEY TO LIFE, ERIC . . . ALL BY YOURSELF."

Eric felt his knees go watery. There was nothing inside
his chest. He couldn't speak, or move. His brain hung in
an airless space, a kind of *between*, like the vacuum between
stars.

"CHARACTERS WRITING CHARACTERS THAT BRING
OTHER CHARACTERS TO LIFE . . ." What was left of
Rima's mouth skinned a grin that was all tattered flesh, smeary
orange teeth, and purple clot. "KIND OF MAKES YOUR HEAD
SPIN, DON'T IT?"

"*Fuck you!*" Casey screamed. He wrenched free of Eric's
slack grip and sprang for the circle. "*Fuck you!* I'll *kill* you, I'll
fucking *kill you!*"

"No, Casey!" Eric and Emma shouted. They surged after,
but Casey was small, fast as a whippet, and he had a head

start. "Casey, no!" Eric cried, as Casey crossed into the circle. "Casey, stop, no, st—"

The air abruptly came alive and swelled with a wild rushing sound that Eric thought was like the roar of water, except it came from somewhere high above. What happened next came so fast that neither he nor Emma could do anything about it.

As one, the birds foamed from the rock and crashed down in a gale.

RIMA

A Whisper, Like Blood

STARING THROUGH THE windows of her eyes, Rima watched as Casey flung himself into the circle—and all that was left of her moaned, *No, Casey, no!* She couldn't help him. She wasn't strong enough to distract the whisper-man for long; it had taken every ounce of her will just to give the lie to the whisper-man's assurances that it could save her. Now, her own life was fading fast; she could feel her mind thinning the way a cloud dissipated under a bright sun. She couldn't break free, but she had to do something, *something.*

She understood now, too, about the dolls this thing had fashioned as receptacles for what it, as Lizzie, called the "*you-you.*" Six dolls, not eight: there was no Eric-doll, no Casey. Neither had a place in McDermott's book-worlds, and of the two, Casey was the *cleanest*, nearly a blank slate, able to absorb whispers and *become* with ease.

She felt the whisper-man crush Casey to her bleeding body in a tight, suffocating embrace. Casey's warm breath slashed over her ruined face, and his own was close, just inches away. She sensed the whisper-man's intent an instant before her own hand tightened around Anita's boning knife, which the whisper-man had slid into the small of her back, and she thought, *No no no no, please don't, don't hurt him, don't!*

Too late, and she had no power anyway. A quicksilver flick, and then Casey gasped as the knife sliced through his coat and slid into his left flank, just below his ribs, slipping through skin, dividing muscle. The tip drove to the artery, releasing Casey's blood in a great, throbbing gush.

No, no, no, CASEY! But Casey was sagging against her now, his life pulsing out in a crimson river.

"Oʜʜʜ, ᴛʜᴀᴛ'ꜱ ɢᴏᴏᴅ." The whisper-man crooned like a lover into Casey's ear: "Tʜᴀᴛ'ꜱ ɢᴏᴏᴅ, ᴏʜʜʜ, ᴛʜᴀᴛ ꜰᴇᴇʟꜱ ꜱᴏ ɢᴏᴏᴅ, ᴅᴏᴇꜱɴ'ᴛ ɪᴛ? Gɪᴠᴇ ʏᴏᴜʀꜱᴇʟꜰ ᴛᴏ ᴍᴇ, Bʀᴇᴀᴛʜ ᴏꜰ Mʏ Bʀᴇᴀᴛʜ. Tᴀᴋᴇ ᴍᴇ, ꜰᴇᴇᴅ ᴍᴇ, Bʟᴏᴏᴅ ᴏꜰ Mʏ Bʟᴏᴏᴅ, ᴏʜʜʜ, *ꜰᴇᴇʟ* ᴍᴇ."

There was one chance, and only one—because she knew what the whisper-man had forgotten. But she must wait, wait, wait. She didn't dare allow herself to think any further than that. If she did, *it* would know. She latched onto a rhyme, a meaningless tune, because she must hide, hide, quiet, quiet: *Mary had a little lamb, little lamb, little lamb. Mary had a little lamb . . .*

Beyond the circle, she heard Eric and Emma both screaming, but couldn't see them at all because of all those hundreds and thousands of crows. The birds—beaks stabbing, slicing, *ripping*—boiled over their bodies. Emma and Eric would be dead, and very soon, if she couldn't stop this.

Hurry, hurry, hurry. Mary had a little lamb, little lamb, oh, hurry hurry hurry . . .

"BLOOD OF MY BLOOD," the whisper-man whispered with the ruin of her mouth, her bloody flesh pressed against Casey's ear. "BREATH OF MY BREATH, I BIND YOU."

Hurry hurry hurry . . .

"I TAKE YOU, OHHH, FEEL ME AS I *FILL* YOU!" It crushed her mouth to Casey's, and then Casey was drinking the whisper-man in, binding the darkness to him.

Yes! The blackness slid away; the whisper-man flowed in a deep riptide from her body. There was no blessed wave of relief; she would not live through this. The icy slush that passed for her blood was gone, but now fire licked through her limbs, throbbing with every beat of her dying heart. The pain was a vice, crushing her chest and forcing out her breath. The cord that had held her up for so long snapped, and she began to fall. But as she did, she realized something else that the whisper-man did not know.

There was someone else—something she half knew and recognized—inside Casey.

Help him. She was sinking fast, hurtling toward that final darkness on legs suddenly no more substantial than air. *Please, whoever, whatever you are, help Casey fight, help him, help . . .*

She knew when her body thudded to that strange, smooth, and glassy rock, but she registered nothing more than a distant thump. Her mind spun. She couldn't think, couldn't put her finger on it. There was something important she had to do . . . but what? *I know this . . . what is it . . . it's import—*

Then, she remembered what the whisper-man had forgotten: that a whisper, like blood, leaves a stain.

Wearing her body, the whisper-man had brought down

the birds. That stain—this ability—was still there, but faint and growing fainter.

Please, God, just keep me alive a few more seconds.

With the last of her strength, she gathered her will and sent an arrow of thought, flying true.

Go. I command you now. Go.

ERIC

To My Heart, Across Times, to the Death

THE MOMENT CASEY sprinted for the circle, Eric simply froze, unable to believe his eyes. What was Casey . . . ? Then his body took over, his mind clamoring: *Go go go!* He lunged after his brother, Emma by his side. He was so focused on reaching Casey before his brother vaulted into the circle that it took him a few seconds to hear the change, the way the air seemed to churn with a weird, freakish rustle.

"Eric!" Emma suddenly gasped. She grabbed for his arm, and he followed her eyes to the ceiling.

Panic slammed into his chest. *"Down!"* he shouted. He tackled Emma, driving her to the floor, covering her with his body as the birds hurtled for them in a black rain of needle-sharp beaks and razor talons. Their bodies were everywhere: a living, ravenous tornado that flowed and whirled over and around. Beaks stabbed at his back, his neck, gouging holes in his flesh. Frantic claws raked his hair, and then he was screaming as blades of pain hacked at his scalp. His parka was gone, and so they were through his clothes in no time, their claws drawing hot lines through his flesh. The birds' claws ticked and skittered over the glassy rock, and there were more birds scuttling over the floor, worming their way to Emma. She was shrieking, and he shouted something wordless, battering at the birds with great sweeps of his arms.

Then a very large crow clamped onto his scalp. Its talons, steely as stilettos, dug in as its beak jackhammered his neck. A red sheet of pain stole his vision. Screaming, he surged up, back arched in agony.

It was, precisely, what the birds had waited for. They swarmed for his face. Nails of pain spiked his cheeks and forehead. One bird swooped in from the side, and he turned his head just in time, as the bird's beak laid his skin open from the corner of his right eye to his mouth.

The crow battened on his scalp was still coring the flesh of his neck, its beak driving and digging. He reached back, his fist closing over slick feathers. The crow slashed at his fingers, flaying flesh from bone. Roaring with pain, he yanked the flailing creature from his blood-soaked scalp, and then the bird was bulleting for his face, its black beak flashing right for his eye.

Gasping, he got a hand up just in time. The bird's beak drove into the meat at the base of his thumb, a shock wave he felt all the way to his elbow. With a cry, he tumbled back as the relentless birds closed over him, ripping and pecking—

Then, as if in response to a silent signal, the birds simply stopped—a fast, abrupt hitch, like the flick of a switch—and then lifted off in a vertiginous swirl, spiraling higher and higher to mass at the ceiling.

For a second, Eric could only lie there, stunned. His body was saturated and slick. Blood ran into his eyes, coated his mouth with a taste of warm aluminum. To his right, Emma was drenched with gore. She lay on her stomach, her face hidden by the dark fan of her hair, and he thought, *God, no, please.* Then he saw her move, and relief surged through his body.

"YOU *BITCH!*" It was Casey, in the circle, bellowing in a voice that was not Rima's or Big Earl's or his own, but the guttural, clotted gargle that was the whisper-man's true voice. "STOP! WHAT ARE YOU DOING?"

Oh, Casey. Eric felt everything inside go dead with despair. His brother's back bowed as if drawn by an unseen archer. Blood stained Casey's mouth and glistened on his palms. His chest was a bib of gore. His shirt was slashed on the left; a large vermillion splash slicked his side as a crimson jet spurted from a wound right below his ribs.

"NO, STOP!" Casey shouted. "LET ME GO!"

Rima? Eric thought with stupid amazement. *She* was doing this? She'd called off the birds? *My God, is she still inside him, too?* There was no way of knowing. Rima's body lay in a still, sodden heap where she had crumpled after the whisper-man released her. He couldn't tell if she was still alive. But *someone* was fighting back. Something had saved him and Emma.

"NO, DON'T! LET ME GO!" Casey roared. "I'M NOT *FINISHED!*"

"*Look* at him." Blood coursed from slashes on Emma's arms and neck. A long rip, the mirror image of his, snaked down her cheek. "Eric . . . there's somebody *else.*"

There was. Casey's stormy eyes—eyes that could hold and

be any color—were churning and changing, growing black as oil.

But now he could see that there was also another: a shadow, much larger, man-shaped, smoky and indistinct, bleeding into being, *steaming* from Casey himself, as if it had been hiding inside and waiting for just this moment.

The whisper-man had said it: *I need someone who can carry a whisper, an energy as strong as mine, without coming apart at the seams.*

There was Casey, the brother for whom Eric would give his life—and someone else, already inside his brother, fighting for him, *with* them. But could Casey and this other *win*?

We can't take that chance. Eric got his feet under him, then grabbed Emma's bloody hand in his. *Blood binds, and I don't think we've got a lot of time.*

"Emma," he said, hoarsely, "this whole room is a mirror. It's a *mirror. It* can't get completely free of the Peculiar's energy sink for long, but *you* can. With the cynosure, you can go to different *Nows*, but you have to cross into the Dark Passages to do it, and that's *where* this thing—"

"Yes." Her eyes met his, and he read that she understood, exactly, what they had to do. "Just hang on to him long enough," she said.

To the death, Emma. I will never let go. There was so much more to tell her, a lifetime of stories they might have written, but there was no more time. *I will hold you both to my heart, across times, to the death.*

Together, they charged into the circle at a dead run.

THE WHISPER-MAN
There Is Another

"YOU *BITCH*!" THE whisper-man raged. Somehow the girl had called off the birds, not that it should have mattered. Once taken in—once invited—the boy should have been helpless, without the strength to resist. Not like Good Old Frank, who knew a trick or two, or his brat, who was more skilled even than her father.

But something was wrong.

THERE IS ANOTHER. This couldn't be. Casey was the perfect creation: an outline waiting for color, a sponge, a *tabula rasa* with even less of a history; and that which Casey possessed—abuse and cruelty, rage and betrayal—was the very kind of horror it liked best. True, the boy had been *infected* by his brother, who had, in his turn, been tainted by Emma. Casey had morals and scruples. He could love. Yet Casey was fresh and strong. As soon as it finished taking the boy, it would bind enough of Emma to gain the one thing it lacked: access to the cynosure, a skill Lizzie had somehow denied it and Emma hadn't possessed until it had shown her what to do. Then it would break free, away from this place. Together, it and Casey would play across the *Nows*.

Slipping inside the boy had been so effortless, little more than a sigh. Just like Lizzie, the boy opened himself, a willing sacrifice for his brother and the Rima-bitch, who should be dead, but she had tricked it, *tricked* it. Still, time should've been on its side.

Suddenly, it felt the red scald of an acid-burn, so stinging and harsh, it let out a howl. What *was* that? Something in the boy, the boy; the boy was *carrying* something!

WHO ARE YOU? WHAT ARE YOU? LEAVE! THE BOY IS MI—
Something axed Casey's legs, and then it was toppling, crashing to the smooth, glassy black rock. Screeching, the whisper-man kicked and spit as Eric wrapped Casey up tight. Eric was alive; he had survived the birds as had Emma, and it knew what she meant to do. It could not fight them all, not at once. No, it would not go back; it would not be *nothing* again.

I WON'T BE LOST AGAIN, I WILL NOT! A great gust of fear, sour and strong, swept through it. The whisper-man gasped in terror, and Casey stiffened with it. *LET ME GO! YOU CAN HAVE THE BOY IF YOU—*

I don't want him. I want you. The intruder battened down with a will that coiled itself in a muscular rope, tighter than any serpent. *I was written for this purpose, this moment. I am your end, and we* will *grapple.*

YOU WILL LOSE.

Probably. I can't match evil for evil. But I have come to do battle. I can delay you, just long enough.

WE CAN SHARE, the whisper-man thought, wildly. *THE*

BOY IS STRONG, STRONG ENOUGH FOR TWO, FOR MANY. TOGETHER, WE WILL—

Beneath Casey's body, the mirror-rock quivered as if with a sudden earthquake. The floor of the Peculiar heaved, gave, thinned. The whisper-man felt Emma's will surge, as strong and sure as Eric's arms around his brother, as the intruder's hold on *it*—and the way began to open.

"No, *WAIT!*" it thundered. "LET ME *FINISH!*"

EMMA
What Endures

1

ERIC CRASHED INTO Casey, smashing the smaller boy down against the rocky floor. Casey's head struck hard; the man-shadow bleeding from his skin swirled and then draped itself over Casey's bulging eyes. From her place by Rima's broken body, Emma had the crazy, wild hope that this—the emergence of this other, the shadow—would be enough. But then Casey screamed again, and his voice still belonged to the whisper-man.

There was a pressure around her hand, and she looked down into Rima's ravaged face. "D-door," Rima whispered. Bright blood-bubbles foamed over her lips. "Make a door into . . . into the D-Dark Passages . . . Eric c-can't . . . h-hurry . . ."

"Emma!" Eric shouted. Casey was thrashing, bucking and kicking, but both the shadow-man and Eric had the smaller boy pinned, and Eric was close enough to touch. The shadow had whatever power a whisper possessed, but Eric was real. He was solid and strong—and more: Eric was the force and the power of love. "Do it now, Emma, do it *now*!"

"I WON'T LET YOU!" the whisper-man boomed. "I WILL BIND YOU, BLOOD OF MY BLOOD, I WILL *BIND—*"

Together, then, and that was as it should be. They were linked in space and time and an eternity of words, bound in a single purpose to a solitary hope. Tightening her grip on Rima, she reached for Eric's outstretched hand. His fingers closed around hers—

And Emma screamed. A stinging red charge, scorpion-bright and viper-quick, *bit* into her mind, because blood—all their mingled blood—*binds.*

YOU SEE? The whisper-man boomed through the cavern of her skull. YOU CAN'T FIGHT ME, EMMA. YOU'RE NOT STRONG ENOUGH, BLOOD OF MY BLOOD, AND I WON'T NEED YOUR BODY. I WILL TAKE WHAT I WANT; I WILL HAVE YOUR ABILITIES. I AM TAKING THEM NOW. YOU FEEL IT, DON'T YOU? MY POWER, MY STAIN SPREAD-ING THROUGH YOUR BODY, AND YOU, BLOOD OF MY BLOOD, I WILL BIND YOU—

Go. Not Rima or even Eric, but the shadow-man, the other whisper, the one concealed in Casey's body. *Hurry, Emma.*

And she thought, *Push.*

The cynosure fired. The purple maw gaped, and she felt the change as the rock thinned and pulled apart, and then the chains of light that were Rima and Eric and Emma and, yes, even Casey's many colors flared to life—but there was a faint smear of red that Emma knew.

Bode? A jolt of surprise and joy. *Bode! Is that—*

In part. I am Battle, and what remains. His secret, and gift. The shadow-man's thoughts were as airless as the fading images of a distant dream. *Hurry, Emma. You don't have much time.*

She saw what it meant, and felt it, too. A seeping black stain was working its way through their chain, because *it* had Casey and so did Eric. So did they all. A whisper left a stain, and they were all bleeding, their blood mingling because they were willing to sacrifice for one another. They were *willing*.

Emma! It was Eric. The blue and gold of their mingled chain pulsed with urgency. *Go, Emma, go! Break this place wide open, and do it now, Emma, do it* now!

She *pushed*, and the mirror-room groaned under the effort. All of a sudden, a door blistered and broke open in a great, convulsive shudder as a glistering bolt of light, more powerful than the hottest sun, erupted from the cynosure. A nanosecond later, the Peculiar exploded, shattering in a blistering halo of energies—

2

AND THEN THEY were through and falling fast into somewhere, some*when*, completely new.

It was like nothing that had come before. There was light, not only the brilliant path laid by the cynosure but the hard, bright diamonds of a crowded galaxy. Those must be the many worlds and times of the *Nows*, and this, the Dark Passages, a hallway with infinite branch-points. Above, below, all around, the way spread itself in a dizzying cluster of galaxies, and they rocketed through, sweeping past worlds; past doors and realms and an infinity of *Nows*. Choose a door, any door, and *push*; pop onto the White Space of another story, a different timeline, a new—

Something nipped her skin. A needle, a sting as viper-quick as the bite of the whisper-man trying to scorch its way into her body—and yet not, because she also *felt* it: a tenebrous *finger* on her arm. She started, her focus wavering. What was that? She thought of the inky tentacles swimming up from snow as Rima's nightmare broke apart and remembered the moment she'd pushed through that black membrane in Jasper's basement: that *hand* swimming around her wrist to pull her in, just as McDermott reached through the Dickens Mirror and pulled something out. It had never occurred to her to wonder if there might be more than one monster.

But now, she remembered what Lizzie said: *You don't want them to notice you.*

The cynosure was a focus and path, a lens and lighthouse . . . and a . . . a *beacon?*

My God. The realization broke like a wash of icy water. *They're the moths, and I'm the light.*

Something shot out of the black and battened down on her wrist. An instant later, something else slinked around her waist, a third teased an ankle, a fourth curled around her right thigh. Whoever these creatures were, whatever lived in the Dark Passages swarmed. Or perhaps they were the fabric of darkness itself, the space between galaxies and all matter: a living web that grabbed and tugged and latched on like leeches; and their sound, the whispers that were a clamor and then a river swelling to a roar, crashed through her mind.

They see the cynosure. She felt the panic scrambling up her throat. *That's why it's so dangerous to cross. They know we're here; we've been seen!*

YOU SEE? YOU CAN'T GET AWAY. The whisper-man was

still strongest in Casey, but despite the shadow-man, its gelid fingers were surer now, beginning to creep over her thoughts, and she knew from the sudden gasp in her mind that Eric felt it, too. Of course it had been there all along; in the illusion of Lizzie, it had touched them all. In a way, it was finding bits and pieces of itself in them. Perhaps its stain—what Frank McDermott had discovered as the twin to all his horrors— was the midwife of the nightmares of all their lives.

FIGHT ME, AND YOU ONLY DRAIN YOURSELF, AND THEN THEY WILL HAVE YOU. STOP FIGHTING, AND I WILL HELP YOU ESCAPE—AND THEN YOU WILL HELP ME. The whisper-man bit down again, and she grunted, her concentration stuttering. Almost at once, the Dark Passages thickened. She was still *pushing* as hard as she could, but it was as if she were bogging down, as she had been in the energy sink of the Peculiar, as mired as a woolly mammoth caught in a deep pit of black tar. The light linking her to Eric and Casey and Rima was beginning to fade, the colors bleaching away as these others, whatever they were, clawed and grabbed. Her mind slid, her concentration—her *hold* on the others—slipping as if she'd stumbled onto a floor made of slick ball bearings.

Help us, she thought to the shadow-man. *Please, if you helped Bode, help us.*

I can't do any more. The shadow-man was a sigh, and already evaporating, slipping like smoke from the chain. *I belong here. You have to do the rest.* The shadow-man was dwindling, fainter than a dying echo. *Don't hang on too long, Emma. Let go before the infection—*

But then the shadow-man, whatever it had been, was gone.

What? Let *go?* What did that mean? No. If she did that,

the others wouldn't make it. They'd be stuck here. Yet where, exactly, *was* she going? They had no place in any world or *Now*, not all together. The whisper-man had Casey, and soon, it would have Eric. She would be next, and Rima, her color already so faint, would die soon. If, by some miracle, Rima lived and Emma could get them all through, no *Now* would be safe, not if they brought the whisper-man, too.

Even if I could get rid of him somehow, if we all end up in the same Now, *wouldn't we destroy it the way the world Rima created from that snow did when Eric and the others found them?*

My God, she'd brought them to the place where they would die. Or drift forever, trapped in the Dark Passages with all these others, whatever they were.

NOT TRUE. The whisper-man pulsed in her brain. LIS-TEN TO ME. I ONLY WANT THE BOY. DO WHAT I ASK, AND I WILL GIVE YOU ERIC. I WILL FREE HIM; I WILL FREE YOU ALL IF—

Emma. Eric—his essence, that *color*—suddenly surged. *We're already free, because we can choose.*

NO NO NO. The whisper-man's panic was electric. WHAT ARE YOU DOING?

Emma. The cobalt edged with a glister of gold that was Eric shone so bright he could've been the deep waters of Superior at sunrise, a *Now*, the promise of a different world— and maybe he was all those and more: not only himself but what endures in memory and across times. *Emma, no matter what . . .*

NO, I WILL GIVE BACK THE BOY! PULL ME THROUGH AND I WILL—

Keep going, Emma. Find your Now. *Find a way out.*

No, Eric, she thought. *We can't. It will still—*

Go where you can, where you have the best shot . . .

NO NO NO NO—

And don't listen to it, Emma. We have the power to choose, and this is my choice. Eric was calm, his thoughts like a long drink of cool water on a desperately hot day. *I choose for you.*

Eric, don't. In that last instant, she finally sensed what he meant to do. *Wait!*

Don't look back, Emma—and then . . .

He let go.

EMMA
Where I Belong

NO! SHE MADE a grab, reaching out with her mind, her hand, her *will*—and missed.

That was enough to break them. Her hold on Rima slipped, and then they were all spinning away from one another in streamers of light, like falling stars. In response, the Dark Passages roiled, swelling as the darkness converged in a tidal surge over Rima, so faint, and the rainbow-swirl that was Eric locked in his fatal embrace with Casey and the whisper-man. The Dark Passages rolled over and swallowed them up, and then she just couldn't see them anymore. The colors died and, with them, Eric's voice. The whisper-man's howls cut out, and then there was nothing: no Casey, no Rima. No Eric.

She tried to stop, slow down, but the cynosure wouldn't let her. Lens and beacon, focus—and a path now, one *she* couldn't leave. Later, she thought Eric himself gave her that one final *push* as he broke away, so she wouldn't be able to stop even if she knew how. But she didn't, and now these beings were swinging around. Sniffing her out. She could feel them *noticing* the beacon from the galaxy pendant, and knew she was almost out of time.

Got to get out. But how? Where could she go? If these really were doors to other *Nows*, then she—or a piece of her, another version—must exist in each. She belonged everywhere and nowhere. Would she, on her own, break a *Now* to pieces? What would happen if she met up with or even slipped *into* herself in another *Now*?

Can I do that? Maybe. She was different. The whisper-man said so; it had taken her while she was awake, dropping her into her many alters, because she was a creation with no set path.

Then put me where I belong, she thought fiercely. She felt the cynosure crackle with a new and vicious heat. *Drop me into the* Now *where I'll find them again: Eric and Casey and Rima and Bode and—*

PART SIX

THE
SIGN
OF
SURE

EMMA

Elizabeth

1

"ELIZABETH." A SLIGHT buzz to the *z*. Whoever this man was, he had a lisp, so the name seemed to have been mouthed by a rattlesnake: *Elisssabess*. A pause. "Elizabeth?"

"Wh-what?" The word burred on her tongue, slow and hesitant. She sounded like a Little Mommy My Very Real Baby Doll with a faulty motherboard. Or HAL, from *2001*, getting his memory banks yanked. "Whaaat?"

The same man said, "Elizabeth, is that you? Can you hear me?"

"H-hear?" She *felt* the sounds as much as she heard them, a kind of fading in and out, there and gone, as if her brain were an ancient radio and she had to feather the knob to get the scratchy broadcast bounced halfway around the world to gel. She realized, belatedly, that she was standing. Swaying, actually. Worn wool chafed her bare feet. A sheet, or maybe a very long nightgown, clung to her legs, chest, and back. Her skin, hot and damp, smelled sour, and her lank hair reeked of sweat and grime. *Bad dream?* Her chest, her stomach, the inside of her skull . . . felt very strange: flat and hollow, a limp glove of a girl—all skin, no innards. The last time she'd felt this wan and washed-out was when she was ten and coming out of anesthesia after the surgeons put in her plates. Then, her mind had slowly bled back into her body, the blood inching through to plump up arteries and veins and the pink sponge of her brain and guts, the way air leaked into the nooks and crannies of a deflated Macy's Day Parade balloon. *I've been sick?* Where was she?

"Who's Eliz . . . I'm . . ." She lost the thread of the question and her answer, the words unraveling on her tongue. Her head ached. Eyes watering with pain, she tried to bring the world into focus, but it was foggy and fuzzy, a chaotic blur seen through a broken kaleidoscope, the colored bits of glass refusing to arrange themselves into patterns. The only thing she recognized with any clarity was a yawning chasm, an inky hole at the center of her vision. The edges of the gap wavered, as if the world around it was only an uncertain outline and just now on the verge of becoming.

That must be the way I came in. She was in a new *Now*? The hard eye of her titanium skull plate burned. Wincing, she pressed the heel of her left hand to her forehead, then heard herself drag in a sickly gasp. *No gash.* She pressed harder, her fingers searching through muscle and skin. *Wait a minute, where's—*

"Now, now, are you in pain?" A different voice, female, much clearer, the static starting to fade. The words were clipped, a little dry. "Another of your headaches?"

Oh God. Her heart iced. Was there an accent? *No, you're imagining things; this is House, up to its old tricks.* With a fresh blast of panic, she pressed harder, using the fingers of her left hand and the heel of her right because she was . . . clutching something, a pen or stick or maybe a fork. She couldn't tell, but for whatever reason, she didn't relax her grip; felt as if that was the wrong thing to do. *Where is it, where is it?* It had to be there. She *felt* the plate burning in her mind. Give her a pen and she could ink its exact margins, every curve, even where the screws were. But under her fingers there was only skin and muscle and bone.

No plate. How can that be? I feel *it.* Gasping, she fought a rising tide of black horror as she ran her fingers over the rest of her scalp. *No scars. But I had them just a few seconds ago.*

"Elizabeth? You are there, yes?" The guy with the whisper-man lisp again, right in front, behind that hole in her vision. God, if she hadn't just seen the thing die—*with Eric and Casey and Rima, and* Eric, *oh Eric*—she'd have sworn she pulled that monster through with her. "Come now, no need for a fuss. Let's all be calm, shall we?"

Calm? Oh, that was a good one. "Wh-where . . ." Her mouth tasted awful, like she could scrape mold off her tongue. "Where am I?"

"Oh my, disoriented again"—although, from her tone, the woman sounded more put-out than sympathetic. "Poor dear."

"Doctor, I thought you said she was well enough to withstand this." A second man: older, gruffer, with a note of impatient authority. "You assured me mesmeric interventions would help, not hinder our work. This is the best you can do?"

Mesmeric. She knew that word, an old-fashioned term. *He means hypnosis.*

"Thus far, what you've obtained is nothing but fantastical fabrications: ravings of doubles, body-snatching, *animism*." Gruff sounded disgusted. "What good your work if nothing you unearth is of the slightest merit? I've murders to investigate, and she is the only living link. I need what she knows, what is locked in the stronghold of her mind, Sir, not the hysterical rants of a lunatic."

"Please do recall that she *has* refused or purged herself of her medicines," the first man said, the one who could've doubled for the whisper-man. "Even if the Lunacy Commission gives us license in these extreme times, we are doctors, not barbarians."

Extreme times? Doctors? Lunacy? The words kicked, as if someone had planted a boot in her back and given her a hard shove. She felt the sudden slam of recognition and memory, and then it was as if the machinery of her mind whirred into overdrive. The world firmed, that dark mote at the center of her vision cleared, and everything rushed to a crisp, colorful, painful focus.

Oh shit. She felt her legs trying to fold. *I'm back.*

2

THE GALLERY WAS both the same and very different. Above, the whitewashed iron plates of that strange ceiling stretched not to a dead end but a T junction. Ceiling-mounted gas lamps hissed, and the light from wall sconces, mounted high on dingy, soot-stained walls, was yellow and too bright. The hall itself was long and very stark, with no pictures, bric-a-brac, or floral arrangements, and only a few stuffed birds, like the snowy, still cockatoo poised on a branch made of wire and covered with coarse brown cloth, trapped under a bell jar on a small table to her right. Every door was closed and locked, but she could hear the muffled cries and shouts of the others on this and every floor, a continual background yammer that steamed through iron grilles set low. The smell was right, but much stronger: a choking fug of overflowing toilets, unwashed skin, and old vomit.

They ranged before her as they had when House whisked her here, but with a few differences. While Nurse Graves, rigid as a post and decked out in her navy blue uniform, seemed unchanged, neither she nor Kramer wore panops this time around. A long white doctor's smock hung from Kramer's bony frame instead of a suit coat. Jasper was nowhere to be seen, although Weber, the blunt-faced attendant, held a strong dress clutched in one huge fist and seemed poised for a grab. She caught only a brief glimpse of another ward attendant—younger, with muddy brown hair—in a slant of shadow just behind Weber, and felt her attention sharpen. *That kid . . . I know him.*

She thought the same about a young man to her far right: not much older than a boy, really; tall and lean and a little hungry looking, although his face was square and his neck thick, like he'd once been a linebacker in high school and then decided working out was too much trouble. His skin, pallid and pinched, tented over his cheekbones. A brushy moustache drooped from his upper lip. His hair, a lank mousy brown, was slicked back from a broad forehead and plastered to his scalp with a pomade or oil that gave off a slightly rancid odor, like he might not have washed his hair for several days. He wore some sort of military-looking uniform, navy blue with big buttons and numbers done in tarnished brass on a high collar.

Towering over them all was a much older man. Burly and thick-necked, Gruff was a study in gray: dark gray checked flannel trousers, with a matching vest and jacket and a light gray houndstooth coat. A steel-colored bowler firmly planted atop a thick mass of salt-and-pepper hair made him seem much taller than he already was. But it was his eyes, piercing and bright, that drew her most: so light blue they were nearly as silver as bits of mica.

"Elizabeth." Her eyes ticked back to Kramer. She couldn't shake the feeling that Kramer was, somehow, even *more* different than before. His face was . . . off, a little out-of-kilter and unnatural. She couldn't put her finger on what was wrong. Hand outstretched, Kramer eased toward her. "Come now. You're back with us, Elizabeth."

Why does he keep saying that? And Jasper, where was . . . Still staring in wonder at Kramer, that's when she saw. That's when she understood why his voice was so odd.

When Kramer spoke, only the right half of his face actually moved. She saw now that the entire left side of his face, from forehead to jaw, was waxen and immobile, and there was something wrong with his nose, too. He looked, she thought, as if he'd had a stroke.

Just like Jasper. Her skin fizzed with fresh anxiety. *Another echo.*

"Let's not make a scene," Kramer continued, his lips twisting into a grimace that might have been a smile. "What say you put down that knife and we go to my office for a chat and a nice hot cup of tea?"

Knife? She stared at her right fist. The blade's steel—six inches, wickedly sharp—was smooth and so flawless she could make out the deep blue of her eyes. What had she fallen into the middle of?

"Wh-why do you keep calling me Elizabeth?" Her voice was still rusty, as if the gears powering her mouth just didn't want to mesh. "That's not my name."

"You see? This will not do, Doctor," Gruff said, darkly. "She's even more disordered. She's always come back as herself before."

"Yes, yes, Inspector, and she *is* herself now," Kramer said, without taking his eyes from Emma. "But please do remember, Battle, that the girl's endured a severe trauma."

"Battle?" The name flew from her mouth. Knife still in hand, she took a half step forward. "Battle, it's me, Emma. Don't you recognize—"

And then she actually *heard* herself for the first time. Not only was her voice higher and lighter; she had an accent, too, as if she'd just stepped out of a Jane Austen novel. *Oh my God, oh my God, oh my—*

"Of course I recognize you, Miss Elizabeth." There was no warmth in Battle's coldly analytical stare. "We've spoken several times from the very first, while you were in hospital immediately after your escape. Do you"—Battle cocked his massive head as if inspecting a fascinating new species—"do you remember my man, Constable Doyle?" He hooked a beckoning finger over a shoulder, and the kid in the dark blue uniform, with that face she thought she ought to recognize, took a reluctant step forward. "*You* found him after clawing your way out of that warren of catacombs. He conveyed you to safety, to hospital. Do you recall that?"

"Recall . . . ?" *Murders? Catacombs?* Her eyelids fluttered. *What . . . like tunnels?* The only catacombs she knew about were crypts where they put dead people. She peered into Constable Doyle's light, slate-colored eyes . . . eyes that seemed to want to jitter away from hers. "We've . . . I *know* you? You saved me?"

"Well, no, not really. Like Inspector Battle said, you saved yourself, Miss. I just brung you to hospital is all." Doyle had a touch of a brogue, different from Kramer or Battle, his accent like something that might've come from Sean Connery or Ewan McGregor. Face shiny with sweat, he slid an uncertain glance to Battle, then back. The tiny muscles around his eyes twitched. "Inspector Battle thought it might be good to have a familiar face, yes? You remember me, Miss? Conan Doyle?"

"No." She was starting to hyperventilate; her skull was going hollow again. *Slow down; can't faint.* Gulping a breath, she held it a moment, listening to the rush of blood in her ears, the banging of her heart. "I'm s-sorry," she said, trembling all over, hearing the minute *tick-tick-tick* of her teeth. "But I d-d-don't know what you're . . ." She stopped.

"Elizabeth?" Kramer said.

She only half heard. *Doyle. He said his name is . . .* "You"—she swallowed—"is . . . is your first . . . is your name Arthur?"

"How do you know that?" Battle rapped, at the same moment that Doyle, startled, went a deep shade of plum and spluttered, "Sir . . . Inspector, I did *nothing* familiar; I would *never* presume to—"

"Oh Jesus. Where am I?" Although she thought she now knew; the city, anyway. Her weird and accented voice came out ancient and rough, like flat tires crunching gravel. "What *year* is this?"

She watched as Kramer and Battle exchanged glances, and then Kramer seemed to shrug an assent, because it was Battle who said, "You are in London. It is December 1880. You have been remanded to the care of Dr. Kramer and the staff of the Bethlem Royal Hospital at His Majesty's pleasure until such time as you are sound of mind."

London. And Bethlem Royal Hospital . . . they called it *Bedlam.* She remembered because Jasper had told her so; the article had been on a CD, a compilation of works taken from one of Dickens's magazines. *All the Year Round?* Or maybe it had been *Household Words.* Unless this *Now* had no Dickens, or if it did, maybe he wasn't a writer at all. *Battle said 1880.* Was Dickens still alive then? She didn't think so. God, what if he was dead? Would there even be a Dickens Mir—

Wait just a minute. Her runaway thoughts suddenly bucked as if they'd been tethered to a galloping horse the rider had just wrestled to a halt. *His Majesty.* Had Battle just said there was a . . . a *king?*

She almost blurted, *Where's Victoria?* but said instead, "Why am I in the hospital?" She looked to Kramer again. "I'm not sick. I'm *fine.* You said I got away, that I'm a witness? So why am I in an asylum? I'm not crazy. What the hell are you people talking—"

Then, everything—the words poised on her tongue,

her thoughts that would not stay still—turned to dust. That was the moment she finally realized what was wrong with Kramer's face.

Half of it wasn't his.

3

IF SHE'D BEEN looking more carefully—if she hadn't just popped out of the Dark Passages, lost her friends, nearly died—she might have thought he'd gotten too much Botox or plastic surgery, like Cher, who looked more like a wax mannequin or an alien than anyone real.

Kramer's forehead was absolutely smooth. No worry lines. It didn't wrinkle at all, and his nose didn't move either. His left eyebrow was a thick black gash with no arch, and while Kramer's wiry gray tangle of mustache looked normal on the right, the left half was perfectly smooth and much darker.

Not paralyzed. Not a stroke.

He's wearing a kind of mask, like the Phantom, only painted to look like skin and hair.

Her gaze shot to Graves. Instead of panops, a pair of steel-framed spectacles perched on her knife's-edge of a nose. The nurse's face seemed flesh and blood, but her left eye was fish-belly white, with no tracery of thin red capillaries. A muddy gray iris floated in its center like a dirty mote.

It's artificial. It's glass. Oh my God. Now that she knew what she was looking for, Emma saw that one attendant held his right arm at a stiff, forty-five-degree angle. The fingers didn't move, but they weren't paralyzed. The arm and hand were prostheses. Another man wore an odd leather headpiece to which a pair of tin ears, gray as an elephant's, had been nailed. A nurse was minus a hand, the sleeve of her blouse neatly sewn shut at the wrist. Still another woman's nose had been eaten clean away until there was nothing but two black pits set in a shriveled, weathered gargoyle face marred by strange, fleshy knobs that sprouted from her skin like mushrooms.

What happened here? How could these people be so different from what House had shown her? Then she remembered what the shadow-man had said, right before he faded: that she mustn't hang on too long or let the creeping black that was the whisper-man reach her. *He called it an infection. That must be what he meant: something of the whisper-man, a creature of the Dark Passages, remains bound to the blood.* She had been bleeding, her skin torn and slashed by the birds. Worse, the whisper-man had already used her before, many times over, whisking her away in *blinks* to other timelines, different *Nows*. So had this final exposure to the whisper-man's energy, his blood, been enough to tip the balance?

Or could this be something different? *McDermott was always worried about the characters he didn't finish infecting other book-worlds and Nows.* She'd assumed it meant breaking a *Now* in the same way that the snow had disintegrated around Eric and Casey and the others, but these people . . . Her eyes darted to Graves's artificial one, that nurse's prosthetic hand. Kramer's mask. Was *this* what McDermott meant?

Am I to blame for this?

She had to get out of here. There must be something like the Dickens Mirror here; there *had* to be. *Maybe that's why House showed me this before. The bell jar's the key.* She threw a glance at the dead-eyed, stuffed cockatoo under glass. *Got to get back to the domed chapel, get out onto the roof, and then . . .* Would a slit-mirror appear as it had before? Maybe not. This reality, this *Now*, was very different from what she'd been shown. Still, she had the cynosure; felt the weight of it between her breasts, on Eric's beaded chain with his dog tags. *So not everything's disappeared; but why don't I have skull plates anymore?* Because *this* was where she belonged? This was her true and real *Now*?

"Oh." She inhaled. A different *Now* meant a different version, *another* Emma. Had she then slipped into *that* Emma's body? She remembered that deflated, flat feeling before everything snapped into focus. Yes, that would explain what was happening here. But wasn't there something wrong with that? If this body belonged to a different Emma . . . *Then why don't I have her memories? Where* is *she?*

Here. A wisp of sound drifted past her right ear, light as the decaying mist of a dying dream. *Here.*

"What?" She jerked her head around for a wild look. There was only the dead cockatoo, with its eternal stare, in a shell of glass. *"Where?* Where are you? Who's there?"

"Elizabeth," Kramer began.

The breathy voice, so small, came again: *Here.* Something stirred, like the creepy-crawly scuttle of spider's legs, in the middle of her mind. *And who am I? No, the question is who—*

"Are . . . you." That spidery scuttle had worked its way onto her tongue, and now it clambered, a leg at a time, over the fence of her teeth to move her mouth, form words with this new strange voice: "Wh-who . . . are . . ." *Stop, stop!* Choking, she clapped a hand over her mouth. *Don't let it win. Be quiet, be quiet!* Oh, but the urge to speak, let this thing squatting in the center of her mind have its say, was ferocious, like a burn. *I am me,* she thought back to whatever this was, fiercely grinding this alien presence under the boot of her will, killing it, *killing it. I am Emma, and I don't hear you, I don't know who you—*

"Are you in pain, Elizabeth?" Kramer oozed forward. "Maybe a tonic . . ."

"No!" She whipped the knife down, and Kramer stopped dead in his tracks. But she was grateful for the distraction—for anything that might muffle that spidery little voice. "Just back off and let me think. Don't push me, don't crowd me!"

"Of course." Without turning, Kramer put up a hand, and Weber, who'd been sidling closer, stopped as well. "Let's not get excited."

Oh, easy for you to say. This was a different London, but Jasper—whether he was a Dickens creation or not—might still be her guardian. Did he have a house with a cellar? If so, there might be a door, a way into the Dark Passages. She could push through, go somewhere else, get back to her own life where there must be versions of Rima and Bode and Tony. *But not Eric, and there won't be a Casey.* God, could she bring them back somehow? Might they really exist as something more than words on a page?

Worry about that when I can. Nothing will happen if I don't get out.

"I want to go home," she croaked. "I want to see my guardian. I want Jasper."

"Guardian?" Despite the knife, Kramer sidled just a touch closer. "Elizabeth, we've spoken about this at great length. You have no guardian and no home to which you may return."

"No . . . ?" She felt that sudden flower of hope wilt. "Listen to me, please. I'm fine. All I need is to get out of here. I only want to go . . . to go . . ." She pulled in a short, hard breath at a sudden pop of memory.

"Go where?" Kramer said. "Where would you go, Elizabeth?"

Lizzie. She would find Lizzie and her mother, Meredith. In one of her Lizzie-*blinks*, there had been talk of London and something bad happening that they couldn't reverse. Was this it? Had to be. She and Lizzie were tangled, so the chances were good the McDermotts were here, in this London. Wait, hadn't Lizzie and her mother left for several months? To go where? *But if I can find them, find McDermott, I've got a chance . . .*

"Elizabeth?" Kramer prodded. "Tell us which home you mean."

"My . . . house, of course." If he asked where, she was screwed, but if she had a life in this *Now*, she must live *somewhere*. She hurried on. "Where I live."

"And where is that?" When she didn't reply, Kramer said, "Or don't you remember that there is no longer a home to which you may return?"

Something about the way he said that made a cold knot form where her stomach ought to have been. "I don't know what you're talking about."

"Then let *me* refresh your memory. Do you remember going down . . . what did you call it . . . such a curious phrase . . ." Battle pulled his brows together in a frown. "Down cellar?"

Oh, Jesus. *Okay, be calm; you can talk your way out of this, if you just stay calm.* "Yes, of course I remember," she said, carefully. "I went down cellar to look for a book."

"So you say." Battle's icy gaze stroked a shiver. "But do you recall what you found instead? You discovered a . . . what did you call it? Ah, yes, a *gateway*, correct? A secret *passage* to other realms filled with *beings* that exist between worlds?"

Oh crap. She must have talked about the door, the click, the cold that ate the flame, and something living in the dark. How nutty would all that sound to these people? "I might . . . I might have made a mistake about that," she said.

"Yes? And what mistake might that be?" When she was silent, Battle said, "Or mightn't there have been something else you discovered below stairs, secreted down a hidden passage off the servants' quarters? Something so horrible that your mind completely unhinged? That this is a hysterical fantasy of dual identities you've manufactured because it is preferable to the truth?"

"No," she said, with a sudden, sickening dismay. "I . . . I know what I saw." But did she? The doctors were always so pissed that she wouldn't take her meds, and she *blinked* away so often.

Stop this. You know what you know. Listen to the way you think. It's not like them at all. You know things they don't. You've seen the future.

Kramer said, "No one doubts your sincere belief in the fiction you've written or the characters; the duality of the brain and *variations de la personnalité* that allow you to people your world. Anything is better than remembering what was *really* there: not a door—"

"No." She felt her fist tighten around the knife. This was

like *The Bell Jar*: Esther Greenwood going slowly nuts, déjà vu all over again. "No, there was a door, a *hand*, and it was cold, it was—"

"It was not a door, but a gap, a tomb, an abomination of a reliquary," Battle said. "A pile of rubble, a heap of crumbling mortar and disintegrating brick. Not a phantasmagorical tale out of Poe or Wilkie Collins, but something *real*, with texture and color and a *stink* of decay—"

"Stop. I won't listen to you." This couldn't be happening. She knew about 9/11 and movies, relativity and Hardy's Paradox and Starbucks. "I don't remember anything but my life, my life, my real—"

"And bones," Battle interrupted. "*Bones*, Elizabeth."

"B-bones?" She couldn't pull in enough air. "No, no, I don't know . . . I didn't see—"

"But I did. I've seen the evidence myself in the blackened skeletal remains of the corpses you discovered below stairs. You found the murderer hard at work, a demon masquerading as a man; a monster that spirited you away and would've made you his next victim. There is no house to which you may return because he burned it to the ground in a futile attempt to obliterate any evidence of his crime. In that, at least, he has failed. But make no mistake: whatever feelings you may still have for him, this man is a lunatic. He is depravity and evil incarnate," Battle said, in a voice so heavy with doom, with words so weighty with the inevitable, they felt as remorseless as hammer blows. "And he wears your father's face."

4

THE WORLD STOPPED. It just. Paused. The time was short, only as long as the speed of thought, but it was as if she were falling again, swooning into a great darkness from which she would never escape.

Then the world began to spin once more, and a flood of horror washed through her veins at the same instant that a bright flash, like the death of a lightbulb, popped in the black of her mind, as if the private movie that was her life had decided to start up again.

The image, every sensation, was crisp and brutally clear: broken bits of mortar on chill, packed earth; the funk of mold and something gassy and much fouler, like meat going green with decay; an empty black square from which rotten bricks had tumbled; and a scurrying, *scritch-scratchy* sound of rats' feet over stone. Of *whispers* from shadows, in the dark. And when she lifted her candle and reached in . . . When she reached *in*, she'd touched . . .

Fingers, limp and still. A hand as cold and smooth as glass with nothing beyond the wrist but hard bone stringy with dead flesh and leathery sinew . . .

And, farther back, gleaming in the candle's uncertain light, a face with wide, black, staring sockets . . .

No. Her mind shied away. *No, that can't be right, not when I can remember the others and Eric, Eric, where are you, where—*

"Listen to him, Elizabeth," Kramer said. "Inspector Battle is telling the truth. Your father was a monster. He would've murdered you."

No, no, that wasn't true. Her father was a pathetic asshole

who strangled himself with the ratty laces of tattered All Stars. "No, I know what I saw, what I *felt*." She was panting again as sobs swelled in her chest. "When I reached into the Dark Passages, something grabbed me and . . . and . . ." Her tongue stumbled.

"Yes?" Kramer prompted. Two attendants had sidled closer, but he put out a restraining hand. "What is it?"

The radios. She almost said those words aloud, but she'd sound even crazier spouting nonsense about boxes that talked. Radios would not be invented for, well, a long time. Yet talk of the murders had been on every station. Lily mentioned how that was *all* the radios talked about. Lily had known. So had Bode. Had the others?

The important thing was *she* hadn't known one single solitary thing about the murders. Not. One.

And yet, at different points during this long night, she'd heard radios and words, so broken and distorted she barely understood. What issued from their mechanical throats were always portions of the same story, like the recurring theme of a melody she didn't know, whose words she just couldn't catch.

Police. Investigation. A young girl's discovery of . . .

'Orrible murder. She could hear the Kramer of her *Now* in an exaggerated Cockney: *'orrible murders and ghastly crimes fit for a Victorian tabloid.*

My God. She was shaking so hard, it was a wonder her body didn't break into a million pieces. *This Now . . .* this *is my reality? The rest was a . . . a delusion? A hallucination?*

"Would you like to know how many children your father murdered, Miss Elizabeth?" Battle asked.

No, she didn't need him to tell her, because she knew, exactly: *There will be—*

"Eight bodies," Battle intoned, in his heavy doom-voice. "Eight children. Five boys, three girls. You'd have been the ninth."

The same number I put in my story, the one I wrote for Kramer; the one he accused me of stealing from a dead man. Her heart boomed. Her skull was breaking apart. This was like when she'd perched on the other side of White Space, watching Lizzie crash, her mind so tangled in the little girl's she'd felt Lizzie's terror, known her thoughts. *But that was House . . .*

—no, *this* house, an asylum with its stark walls and many rooms and whispers issuing up from grates and the dark.

That was the whisper-man

—Kramer, with his lisp and snaky hiss—

manipulating me, showing me what to do until I understood enough to use the cyn—

Wait a minute; wait just a goddamned minute. Her free hand crept to her neck. The galaxy pendant, the cynosure, was a dead cinder, a chill ball of lifeless glass on a beaded chain, but the relief that washed over her mind made her want to cry out. *That* was real. Her fingers traced the edges of Eric's dog tags. *Eric* had been real; everything in that valley happened.

"You're trying to trick me," she said, and thought, *Shit, I sound paranoid.* "I know what happened. You can't take that away—"

From the corner of her left eye, Emma caught a sudden flurry of movement and jerked her head around just as Weber passed off that sack of a strong dress to the boy behind him, and charged. As Weber danced forward, she threw the knife, not with the intention of hitting anything, but she needed Weber to look at something else for a split second. He did, batting the knife to one side with his arm, and in that instant, she whirled, snatched up the cockatoo's bell jar in a one-handed grab, and hurled it as hard as she could. There was a dull *bock* as the heavy jar struck Weber above his nose, right between the eyes. Bellowing, Weller staggered back against Kramer and Battle, and all three men crashed to the floor.

"Elizabeth!" Kramer managed to get to one knee. "What are you—"

"Doyle!" Battle shouted, struggling to extricate himself from the bawling, bleeding Weber. "Stop her! Don't let her—"

She didn't stay to hear more. Turning, she vaulted in a bloom of white down the hall and saw, instantly, that there was no iron gate, no inset door, but only another T junction. *Shit.* The layout was different. She dug in and ran as fast as she could. So, which way: right or left?

This is no way out. It was the spidery voice again, and nothing hesitant about it this time around. *They'll trap you the way you've trapped me.*

No, no! Air tore in and out of her lungs. She was Emma Lindsay; she didn't belong here. She had a life elsewhere, elsewhen. *And Eric, I remember Eric, how he felt, his voice, his eyes, how he smelled and tasted, and I remember Casey.* She could hear them coming now, as she had before, the heavy footfalls. They'd be on her soon. *Think, Emma, think; there has to be a way.*

At the T, she doglegged a sharp right, and then she saw it at the end of yet another very long, very stark corridor: an oval flash.

A mirror. *The* Mirror. *Yes.* She forced her legs to go fast, faster. *I'll go there, I'll go through!*

"*Emma!*" It was Kramer, behind her. "Don't! You *can't.* It's not what you think!"

How could he know what I— That made her falter, but for only a moment. *Emma, he called me Emma. He knows I'm telling the truth.* Or maybe he was only humoring her, trying to get her to hesitate just long enough for them to catch up. *No, not going to fall for that.* The way out was right in front of her. All she had to do was run, and then she would be through, falling to some other—

"Don't do it, Emma!" Kramer cried. "That's not—"

"I'm not *listening* to you!" She charged. *Get me out,* she thought to the cynosure, *get me out, take me anywhere but here; just get me out!* Behind, she heard Kramer still shouting, the thud of boots as the others closed, but she had a head start, was nearly there; so close now she saw her reflection rushing to meet her—

But something was wrong. There was no bloom, no heat, no swoon, no purple maw chewing holes through the back of the world. On the beaded chain, the heavy glass orb and Eric's tags only clattered against her chest.

There is no Sign of Sure. Spider, in her web, in the dark heart of her brain, and what was left of this body's rightful owner. Yet what and who that girl had been in this *Now,* Emma couldn't tell. *It's only glass,* Spider rasped. *Those are strips of ordinary tin, only so much rubbish picked from a dustbin. You're a mad girl in a ruined world. Look in the mirror, Little Alice, looooook.*

Dead ahead, there was a girl rushing through the mirror, ready to break free and—

Wait. Heart pounding, she realized what else was wrong, what was *different*, as her face filled the glass and became the world—*this* Now—blotting out all else.

She saw eyes. They were cobalt, with that golden birthmark, but they were all she truly recognized. Oh, there *was* a girl, a wild thing with hair bright as corn and violent as a gorgon's serpents, but she did not have Emma's face.

The girl hurtling headlong to meet her—twin to her twin, image to her reflection, this *Now*'s version of all that she was—was little Lizzie, all grown up.

"*NO, NO, NO!*" she shrieked, and rocketed for the mirror with all she had left.

5

MAYBE A PIECE of her knew the truth or had listened to the seeds of doubt Spider planted, because, at the very last second, she'd thrown up her arms to shield her face.

It was an explosion. The impact was as much sound as it was something physical, a bright detonation of shock and pain that wiped away all thought in a stunning, violent burst. There came a glissando splash as the mirror shattered and rained razor-edged daggers. A second later, there was a heavier crash as the now-empty frame—and it was only blank, unblemished wood—toppled.

The world stuttered. Someone began to wail, the sound wordless and horrible and black. From the coppery taste at the back of her throat, she realized that this wailing someone was she. Staggering, she felt her knees wobble, then buckle, and then she was sinking into a warm, wet tangle of bloodied nightclothes and torn flesh as a Babel of voices swelled: *She's bleeding, she's bleeding; quick, fetch bandages; I'll need my bag . . . someone fetch the surgeon; hold her, hold her; she's a spitfire, sir, an alley cat; hold her fast, don't let her . . .*

"Easy, Miss Elizabeth, easy." There were rough, hard, strong hands on her now, wrapping her up, bracing her shoulders. But the voice was young, that of a boy not quite yet a man, and reached through the fog of her pain to stir memory. "I've got you, Miss . . . Here, here, what's your name—Doyle? Take her hands; soon as we've got her into the strong dress, we'll slip on those gloves."

"No, no!" Gasping, she looked up and then let out a small cry that was half a scream, half a sob. If her mind had been glass, it would have ruptured as the mirror just had. *My God, it's . . .* "Bode," she rasped. "Bode, help me, please, let me go, please don't do this, *don't!*"

"Shhh, shhh, I've got you, you're safe now." His hair was longer but the same muddy brown, and looking into Bode's eyes was like staring into a cloudless sky. "I knew you'd recognize me, Miss, yeah? Your old pal?" This *Now*'s Bode turned a grin that twitched a thin thread of scar stitching its way from the corner of his jaw down his neck and under his ear. "I won't let them hurt you, Miss Elizabeth, but you got to stay still now."

"Bode. Listen to me," she moaned as Doyle, his face flushed and a splash of her blood on his jaw, wrapped his huge hands around her wrists. "Please, I don't need the dress. I'll be quiet, I won't make trouble, but *please* . . ."

"Shhh. You know the rules." Nodding at Doyle, who thrust her right arm into a sleeve of the strong dress, Bode tipped her a wink. "Not that I blame you," he said, as Doyle shoved her left arm to. "Got a good one off. Wouldn't mind taking Weber down a *notch* . . ." He grunted as she bucked, arching her back and thrashing. "Now, Miss *Elizabeth*," he said, expertly rolling her onto one side before straddling and then holding her clamped between his legs as he secured the strong dress with leather straps. She heard the chink of metal chain and the *snick* of hasps. "None of *that*. You'll make it worse for yourself."

"All right, that's enough." It was Kramer, somewhere over her head, out of sight. "I'll finish dressing her wounds. Bode, if you would, make sure the others stay back while I tend to her? And for God's sake, someone find that surgeon."

"N-no," she said, and choked on thick blood. She tried to spit it out but was so weak her tongue only managed to shove a gob of foamy spit past her lips. She could feel it worm down her jaw like a slug. "Puh-please, Bode, d-don't leave . . ."

"I can stay." Bode sounded both sympathetic and, she thought, pretty freaked out. "I don't mind. She knows me, sir. She'll listen to me. Please, sir, I *want* to help her."

"No. Thank you for your assistance, Bode, but if you and the constable would now withdraw?" There was a pause, followed by the fading clop of boots. Through a haze of pain and blood, she saw Kramer suddenly float into her field of vision like a bad dream.

"Well," Kramer said, reaching into an inner pocket of his waistcoat and withdrawing a pair of brassy spectacles, "let's take a look at the damage, shall we?"

Her breath thinned to a wheeze as he unfolded the earpieces. Yet only when she caught a flash of purple and saw him carefully unhinge the third and fourth lenses was she certain. *I was right. He knows . . .*

"Ah," Kramer said, and used the tip of his pinky to push his spectacles up the bridge of his nose. As he did so, she heard an anomalous sound, something that didn't belong: the faint tick of metal . . . against *metal*. "That's better," he said, sinking to the floor and gathering her onto his lap. "All the better to see you with, my dear."

Balanced on Kramer's nose was a pair of panops.

6

"YOU . . . you're wearing . . ." Trussed and chained in the strong dress, she couldn't fight him, and the pain was so intense, she could see it, raw and white and too bright. "You called me Emma. You *know* I'm telling the truth."

The magenta lenses seemed to smolder. "I know *what* you are, yes. Here." He pressed a bottle to her lips. "Drink this."

"No, I don't w-want . . ." A sickly, cloying scent curled into her nose, and she gagged, tried turning away, but Kramer clamped her aching head to his chest with one arm and pinched her nostrils shut until she couldn't hold her breath any longer and opened her mouth. Gagging against the too-sweet syrup flooding her throat, she thrashed and spat out a rust-red spume of a tonic of laudanum and passionflower. "N-no!"

"*Yes.*" Kramer slapped her cheek, twice, hard enough to make her gasp, and then the drug was streaming down her choking throat. "*Drink* it."

She had no choice. He was killing her. This was prison;

this was poison. Emma felt the swoon beginning to overtake her as a remorseless, inexorable tide, and it would have her, it would carry her away, and she was lost, and Eric, the others—

"You . . . you know the truth. I'm n-not Elizabeth. *Puhplease*," she moaned, and the higher, lighter register of her voice—this *stranger's*—frightened her even more. "Let me go. You know I don't *belong* here."

"But you do. In this world, you are the mad daughter of a lunatic genius who is, unfortunately . . ." Kramer held up a hand, turning it back and forth in an echo of McDermott for Meredith: *See? Not a scratch.* "A killer. A murderer. A *host* to a black evil from the Dark Passages . . . just as this body is for you. I wondered when you would return, be drawn back."

Return? Drawn back? She'd been here before? Maybe so. The whisper-man had stolen her in *blinks. And Lizzie said a different London . . .* But the Lizzie she'd known was a little girl. Yet this *Now* was new—and so was Lizzie? Wouldn't Lizzie have remembered being older? Maybe not, if whatever had happened to her mother to cause those odd gaps in her memory had affected Lizzie, too. But what? "Wh-what do you want? Why are you d-doing this?"

"You have knowledge I need. I will help you, Emma, and in return, you will help me," Kramer said in his sibilant, snaky whisper. They were on the floor together, her body pressed to his, and his mouth so close to her ear that she heard the sigh and felt the hot steam of his

—*Breath of My Breath*—
breath.

And she saw it then, reflected back to her from the purpling mad lenses of the panops: her true face, the one she had always worn, seeming to bloom the way the shadow-man had smoked from Casey's body. *Like the characters in that painting of Dickens, bleeding out of thin air into outlines and filling with color.* It was eerie, like looking at a nearly transparent mask trying to seat itself and failing. It was, in fact, very similar to what it had been like when she was a child—ugly and orphaned—and the craniofacial doc had sat her down at a computer to show what new face he might make for her.

Everything echoes. She could feel her mind slipping. *Everything repeats.*

"Yes." Kramer's cradling arms tightened and held her fast. "I know you for who and what you are, Emma; I see you. You ran for the mirror. *That* means you've seen the Dickens Mirror. You've *used* it, and I *will* have what you know. Battle and I are alike, but only in that way. He wants to catch a murderer, but *I* would save this world."

"Save this . . . Wh-what . . . ?" *The Mirror's real; it exists; I have to find it.* But how would she manage that? She was trapped. Her lips were cold as marble, and she heard herself beginning to slur. She could feel her blood, fresh but starting to cool, oozing through the strong dress and dribbling from a ragged gash on her forehead. Kramer's hands were smeary, with rust crescents under his nails.

Blood binds. Spider flexed and then folded her many legs. *You belong here, to this* Now. *You belong to him.*

No, I am Emma; I'm still Emma. She had to hang on to that. *Don't let them take that away. Quiet, Spider, quiet.* She slicked her lips, her tongue curling against sweet poison and salty blood. "What are you t-talking about?" she said to Kramer. "What do you w-want?"

In answer, Kramer raised a hand to his left ear—

And removed his face.

1

IF NOT FOR the drug, the scream might have made it out of her chest.

The mask was painted tin. What remained beneath was a ruin. Kramer's flesh was raw and oozy; the purple bellies of exposed muscle jumped and quivered. His left eyelid was gone. His nose had sheared away or rotted, leaving behind two mangled, vertical black slits like the nasal pits of a viper. Below a purplish ridge of upper gum, the entire left side of Kramer's lower jaw looked to have been carved with a paring knife. Naked bone showed in a dull gleam, from which the pegs of his teeth thrust in an impossibly white row, like the posts of a picket fence.

And he had no tongue. What was left was only a liverish, vestigial stub, like a worm cut in two.

"Take a good look, Emma," Kramer hissed, his naked left eye fixing her with a baleful glare. "You and your kind are blight and infection, but *you* are the key."

"M-my kind? The k-key?" She could barely find her voice. Her mind was slewing, sliding away into the deadening fog—and who would she be when she woke? "To what?"

"To that which you are."

"And what . . ." She swallowed, working to peel the words from her thickening tongue. She was so thirsty. She could feel her brain slowing down, like a clock whose battery's nearly dead. "What's that?"

"Well, let's see, shall we?" And then she felt his fingers, cold and dry, snaking over the collar of her strong dress to slither over her neck. There was a tick of glass against metal as Kramer reeled out her beaded chain.

And all of a sudden, she didn't want to look. She couldn't. Maybe it was a good thing her vision was starting to fuzz, because she was afraid. If everything, *all* that she'd experienced, echoed and doubled on itself, what really hung around her neck? Was she Schrödinger's cat, trapped in a box, neither alive nor dead? Waiting for someone to look; to collapse all probabilities to a single path, a solitary outcome? Were these tags, this complex bit of alien glass, like her skull plates: phantoms caught in between and given substance and finality depending on who looked, with no more *real* reality than the spoon Neo decided wasn't there? Forget that Kramer called her *Emma* or that she thought her real face swirled in the violet whirlpools of the panops. Doctors humored their patients, especially the really sick ones. Hadn't there been a novel and then a movie about this, some island where everyone pretended to be characters in a patient's private drama? For all she knew, only she saw that those lenses were purple and not clear—because what *is* color but perception dependent upon the machinery of the mind to capture light in a very specific way? How *red* is red? Is red *only* red because that's what everyone agrees is true?

Am I Emma only because Kramer thinks so, too?

Or . . .

In *this* London, could *only* she and Kramer see Eric's tags and the cynosure for what they were? To everyone else, were they nothing more than scraps of tin and a worthless, if very pretty, marble?

Alive or dead, alive or dead . . . Round and around. It felt like a prayer. *Please, God, please. I am me; I am real. I felt Eric; we touched, and blood binds. I have to be me.*

Because what else was there? Everything she was depended on what Kramer said next.

"Ah, yes. Excellent." A satisfied sigh. A musical tinkle. "I will tell you what you are now. You are mine, Emma, you are mine, and I want what you know, what you've seen. I want what only you can do." Kramer brushed the hair from her face with a touch as gentle as a lover's, but his voice was a serpent's from somewhere deep and dark and very distant now, because she was sinking fast, going down full fathom five.

"I want it all, Emma," Kramer said. "I want everything."

ACKNOWLEDGMENTS

As always, it takes a village to make a book, and so my deepest thanks go:

To Greg Ferguson, for reading this, being thoroughly creeped out, and *getting* exactly what this book is about without my having to explain.

To Elizabeth Law, for her intelligence, enthusiasm, and general all-around cheerleading—and, yeah, that Champagne was pretty nice, too.

To Jennifer Laughran, for her continued advocacy, hard work, good common sense, and high tolerance for authors who sometimes need a road map for the simplest things.

To Ryan Sullivan, for a nip here, a tuck there, and yet another spectacular copyedit.

To the entire Egmont USA team and Random House sales force, for their dedication and willingness to pound the pavement for books they believe in.

To Sarah Henning, archivist at London's Imperial War Museum, for graciously providing both historical context and a personal tour of the Bethlem Royal Hospital's Dome Chapel and other portions of the old hospital that are extant.

To Colin Gale, archivist at Bethlem Royal Hospital, for answering my many questions regarding treatments, patient care, and the general layout of the old Victorian-era asylum.

To librarians Erin Coppersmith, Rachel Montes, Tracy Maggi, Ann Reinbacher, Karen Hogan, Jackie Rudd, Gena Gebler, and Sue Jaberg, for tirelessly tracking down whatever arcane book or article I need *this* week, and without complaint. Ladies, you kick some serious butt.

To Dean Wesley Smith, for telling me to stretch and try something new with every book.

And, finally, to David, my rock: for his patience; for his faith that, really, I can do this; for eating whatever's lying around if I just . . . I just *can't*, don't bother me, I just *can't*; for encouraging me to take risks; for keeping me and the cats in kibbles; for being so proud of me; and for reminding me, daily, why we ended up together in the first place. Every book owes its life to you.